Kerrelyn Sparks

BE STILL MY VAMPIRE HEART

FAIRMONT BRANCH LIBRARY
4330 Fairmont Pkwy.
Pasadena, TX 77504-3306

AVON BOOKS

An Imprint of HarperCollinsPublishers

This is a work of fiction. Names, characters, places, and incidents are products of the author's imagination or are used fictitiously and are not to be construed as real. Any resemblance to actual events, locales, organizations, or persons, living or dead, is entirely coincidental.

AVON BOOKS
An Imprint of HarperCollins*Publishers*
10 East 53rd Street
New York, New York 10022-5299

Copyright © 2007 by Kerrelyn Sparks
ISBN: 978-0-06-111844-9
ISBN-10: 0-06-111844-3
www.avonromance.com

All rights reserved. No part of this book may be used or reproduced in any manner whatsoever without written permission, except in the case of brief quotations embodied in critical articles and reviews. For information address Avon Books, an Imprint of HarperCollins Publishers.

First Avon Books paperback printing: April 2007

Avon Trademark Reg. U.S. Pat. Off. and in Other Countries, Marca Registrada, Hecho en U.S.A.
HarperCollins® is a registered trademark of HarperCollins Publishers.

Printed in the U.S.A.

10 9 8 7 6

If you purchased this book without a cover, you should be aware that this book is stolen property. It was reported as "unsold and destroyed" to the publisher, and neither the author nor the publisher has received any payment for this "stripped book."

*In memory of the strong women
who taught me to be strong—
Faye Oldham, Twila Sparks,
Sally Rundle, and Margaret Smith.*

Acknowledgments

Writing this book became a long journey of laughter and tears. I wish to remember those who traveled the road with me, for I would have never reached the end without their loving support. My critique partners and best friends: MJ Selle, Sandy Weider, Vicky Dreiling, and Vicky Yelton. My traveling buddies Linda Curtis and Colleen Thompson. My husband, my parents, and my children. Dr. Chapman, Dr. Vela, Gay McDow, and Guylene Lendrum, who helped my daughter return to good health and happiness. My agent, Michelle Grajkowski, who is always there for me, and my editor, Erika Tsang, who always displays kindness and compassion. I also wish to thank my fellow writers of the West Houston, Northwest Houston, Lake Country, and PASIC chapters of RWA for their unfailing support. I was fortunate, whenever times were bad, to be surrounded by love. I am blessed to be able to write about the most powerful and beautiful force around us—love.

Chapter 1

After four hundred and ninety-three years of teleporting from one place to another, Angus MacKay still felt an urge to peek under his kilt to ensure everything had arrived in fine working condition. There were some areas where a man, vampire or not, would hate to find himself shortchanged. He resisted, though, since he wasn't alone. He'd just materialized in Roman Draganesti's office at Romatech Industries, and the former monk was sitting behind his desk, watching him calmly.

Angus swung his claymore off his back. "All right, old friend, who can I kill for ye tonight?"

Roman chuckled. "Always ready for action. Thank God you never change."

Angus winced inwardly. He'd only been kidding. "Ye . . . *do* want me to kill someone?"

"Hopefully not. I think a good scare will be enough."

"Ah." From the corner of his eye, Angus saw the

door open. "You couldna have Connor do the scaring? He's a verra frightful-looking man."

"I heard that." Connor entered the room, carrying a folder.

Grinning, Angus took a seat and lay the sheath containing his favorite claymore across his lap. "So what's the problem?"

"The slayer is at it again. A vampire was murdered last night in Central Park," Roman explained. "A Russian Malcontent."

"Och, that's good." Angus nodded. One less Malcontent to worry about. Those bloody vampires refused to modernize and drink the synthetic blood manufactured at Romatech.

"No, it's bad," Roman countered. "Katya Miniskaya just called and accused us of the murder."

At the sound of her name, Angus's grip tightened around the leather sheath. He kept his face blank. "I'm surprised she's still coven master."

Connor sat in the chair next to Angus. "She's vicious enough for it. I heard some of the Russian men complained about having a female master, and they dinna live through the night."

"Aye, she can be verra vicious." Angus felt Roman's sympathetic gaze on him and looked away. The monk knew too much. Fortunately, any transgressions he'd confessed to his old friend were held in strictest confidence.

"Katya's threatening us," Connor continued. "If anyone else in her coven is slain, she'll declare war on us."

"Bugger," Angus muttered. "So who *is* the slayer?

He may be causing trouble, but he deserves a medal." He looked at his employee.

Connor snorted. "I dinna do it, and neither did my men. Ye pay us to protect Roman, his wife, his home, and his business, and there's only three of us for the job. We doona have time to wander about Central Park."

Angus nodded. As owner of MacKay Security and Investigation, he provided protection for a number of important coven masters like Roman. He'd recently reassigned five of Connor's men. "I'm sorry to leave ye shorthanded, but I need every available man in the field. 'Tis imperative we locate Casimir before he . . ."

Angus didn't want to say the words. Hell, he didn't even want to think them. For three hundred years, they'd believed the world's most evil vampire was dead, only to discover he was still lurking about and still intent on murder and destruction.

"Any luck finding him?" Roman asked.

"Nay. Nothing but false leads." Angus drummed his fingers on the leather sheath in his lap. "So do ye have any idea who the slayer is? Could he be the same one who killed a few Malcontents last summer?"

"We believe so." Roman sat forward, leaning on his elbows. "Connor thinks he's working for the CIA."

Angus blinked. "A *mortal* killing vampires? 'Tis highly unlikely."

"We think it's one of the Stake-Out team." Connor tapped the folder he was carrying. Written in bold letters across the front was *Stake-Out Team*.

There was an awkward pause, since they all knew

the leader of the Stake-Out team was Roman's mortal father-in-law.

Angus cleared his throat. "Ye think Shanna's father is the slayer? No offense to yer wife, Roman, but I wouldna mind scaring the shit out of Sean Whelan."

Roman sighed. "He is a . . . nuisance."

Angus agreed, though he would have used more colorful language. "How many did the slayer kill last summer?"

"Three," Connor answered.

Angus narrowed his eyes. "Why did he stop for a while, then start killing again?"

"Since the beginning of March, two mortals have been killed in Central Park, their throats slashed," Roman explained.

"To cover up bite marks," Angus concluded. It was an old vampire trick. "So the Malcontents started this, and the slayer is exacting revenge."

"Yes," Roman agreed. "After those mortals were murdered, I threatened to run Katya and her coven out of the country. So it's logical for her to assume we're the ones retaliating."

"Aye. No one would ever believe a mortal capable of killing a vampire." Angus frowned. This was lousy timing. He didn't have time to go hunting for some mortal slayer, not when Casimir was growing his army by transforming criminals and murderers into vampires. The evil vampires needed to be stopped before they outnumbered the good Vamps and another war erupted. No doubt that was exactly why the Malcontents were stirring up trouble at this time. They wanted to distract Angus and his employees from their true purpose.

"Hi, guys!" The door swung open, and Gregori strode inside. "What's up?" His grin faded as he studied everyone's faces. "Sheesh, you look like you've been to a funeral. What happened, MacKay? Did you get a run in your fancy knee socks?"

"They're called hose," Angus grumbled.

Gregori snorted. "Oh, that's manly. Wait, I know what happened. You put your kilt on backwards and when you sat down, ouch! Your little sword-shaped kilt pin poked you in the ass."

Angus arched an eyebrow at Gregori, then glanced at Connor. "How can it be that ye havena killed this one?"

Gregori blinked. "Excuse me?"

Roman chuckled as he fumbled in a desk drawer. "Play nice while I'm gone."

"Ye're leaving?" Angus asked.

"I'm going to Shanna's doctor appointment with her." He set a bottle of reddish-amber liquid onto the desk. It boasted a shiny gold label that said *Blissky*. "This is for you, Angus. We start selling it next week."

"Och, good." Angus stood and picked up the bottle. He'd been waiting for Roman to finish his latest Fusion Cuisine drink. "I've sorely missed the taste of good Scotch whisky."

"Enjoy." Roman headed for the door. "I'll be back in an hour or so. Gregori will let me know what you decided."

Angus dragged his eyes away from the bottle of Blissky. Why was Roman's mortal wife going to the doctor at night? "Is there a problem with the bairn?"

"No. Everything's fine." Roman avoided looking at Angus.

Bugger. There *was* a problem. The monk had always been a lousy liar.

"Boy, you should see Shanna. I swear she's *huge*." Gregori spread his arms wide enough to indicate a hippopotamus.

Roman cleared his throat.

Gregori winced. "But she's still as lovely as ever."

Roman smiled faintly. "I'll talk to you later, Gregori. And thank you, Angus, for helping us find this slayer."

Angus smiled back. "Ye know me, I'm always ready for a good hunt." When Roman shut the door, he turned to Connor and Gregori. "All right, you two. What's wrong with the bairn?"

"Nothing." Connor slanted Gregori a warning look.

"Yeah, right." Gregori rolled his eyes, then circled the desk to sit in Roman's chair.

Angus frowned as he opened the bottle of Blissky. He'd get the truth out of Gregori later.

"Back to business." Connor dropped his folder on the desk. "These are the profiles and photos of the Stake-Out team, minus Austin Erickson, who's working for us now."

Angus yanked out the cork and was rewarded with the smell of fine Scotch whisky. "Maybe Austin knows who the slayer is."

Connor winced. "He does. He told me last summer he'd convinced the slayer to stop."

"Bloody hell, he dinna say who it was?"

"Nay." Connor sighed. "I should have pressed him harder. I tried calling him just now, but he and Darcy have gone undercover in Hungary, looking for Casimir."

"Bugger," Angus muttered, then gulped down some

Blissky. The concoction of synthetic blood and fine whisky burned his throat, wove a warm trail to his belly, and left a smoky aftertaste on his tongue. He slammed the bottle down. "Och, that was good."

"It smells good." Gregori reached for the bottle.

Angus grabbed the bottle and sat on the desk.

Connor smiled as he opened the folder. "One of these four people is the slayer."

Gregori picked up the first profile. "Sean Whelan. Boo, hiss. I betcha he's the one."

" 'Tis true that Whelan hates us, especially after his daughter married Roman." Connor retrieved the profile from Gregori. "But Austin acts protective of the slayer, and he wouldna feel that way about a former boss who blacklisted him."

Angus enjoyed another gulp of Blissky. " 'Tis no' Whelan. The man hasna got the balls for it."

Connor handed him the next profile. "This is Garrett Manning."

"Whoa!" Gregori jumped to his feet, pointing at Garrett's photo. "That guy was on the reality show last summer." He gave Connor a stunned look. "You told me Austin was masquerading as a contestant, but you didn't say anything about this guy."

Connor shrugged. "There was no reason to tell you."

"Aye." Angus nodded. "Ye're not important enough to know everything."

Gregori made a face. "Piss off."

Connor chuckled. "I seriously doubt Garrett is the slayer. He has verra little psychic power, and he was busy doing the reality show last summer when the first slayings occurred."

"Well, who else is here?" Gregori turned over Garrett's photo. "Whoa, a babe."

"Aye." Connor nodded. "The last two are female."

"A female mortal killing male vampires?" Angus plunked his bottle on the desk. " 'Tis no' possible."

Gregori snickered. "So much for your theory about needing balls." He made a grab for the bottle of Blissky.

Angus stood, taking his bottle with him.

Connor passed him the next profile. "A female slayer would explain Austin's protectiveness."

"Whoa, baby. She's hot." Gregori grabbed the photo.

Angus studied the profile on Alyssa Barnett. Psychic power: five. She was brand-new to the CIA. No field experience prior to the Stake-Out team. "She's no' the slayer."

"Bummer." Gregori dropped the photo and reached for the next profile. "How about this one? Emma Wallace."

Angus stiffened. "The Wallace?"

"You mean like Braveheart?" Gregori's eyes widened. "Hey, did you guys know him?"

Connor snorted. "The puir man was executed long before we were born." He turned to Angus. " 'Tis a common name these days."

" 'Tis the name of a warrior." Angus snatched the profile from Gregori. Psychic power: seven. Black belt in several styles of martial arts. Trained by MI6 in antiterrorism. His heart began to pound. Could it be true? Could the slayer be a female?

"Sweet." Gregori was practically drooling over her photo.

Angus set down his bottle and yanked the photo

from Gregori's grasping fingers. His heart stammered and lunged up his throat. No wonder Gregori was panting like a hound dog. She had creamy pale skin that contrasted dramatically with her rich brown hair. Her eyes were a golden-brown that glimmered like amber. There was a sharp intelligence in her eyes. A strong will. A fierce passion that marked her as a warrior.

"She's the one," he whispered.

Connor shook his head. "We canna be sure until we catch the slayer in the act."

Angus set her photo down. Her eyes seemed to be following him, calling to him. "We'll catch her. Tonight. Connor, you take the northern half of the park, and I'll take the southern half."

"I'll come." Gregori took a swig from Angus's bottle. "I can spot a good-looking babe a mile off."

"Hey." Angus grabbed his bottle back. He'd been so intent on Miss Wallace's photo, he hadn't seen Gregori nabbing his Blissky. "And what will ye do when a black-belt slayer knocks ye down and whips out her wooden stake?"

"Oh, come on, dude." Gregori straightened his tie. "No woman wants to kill a sharp-dressed man."

"Angus is right." Connor gathered up the profiles and photos and closed the folder. "Ye're no' prepared to fight a slayer. Stay here and tell Roman what we decided to do."

"Damn." Gregori tugged at his shirt cuff. "Not fair."

Angus removed a pewter flask from his sporran and filled it with Blissky. "'Twill be a long night. This will keep me warm."

"I'll fetch my claymore, and we can go." Connor headed for the door.

"Wait." Gregori's mouth twitched. "You two guys are going to Central Park in the middle of the night, wearing skirts?" He laughed. "No one's gonna believe you're looking for a woman."

Angus glanced down at his kilt. "I dinna bring any trousers."

Gregori snorted. "You mean you own some?"

"Doona worry." Connor rested a hand on the doorknob. "Today was St. Paddy's Day. The city is full of men in kilts. No one will think twice about it."

"What will you do if you find her?" Gregori asked.

"Have a wee chat," Connor replied as he left the room.

Angus recalled Emma Wallace's whisky-colored eyes and intoxicating mouth. He'd be sorely tempted to do more than talk. He smiled as he screwed the top on his flask. Let the hunt begin. He slung his claymore onto his back and strode toward the door.

"Okay, if you insist, I'll stay here." Gregori picked up the bottle Angus had left on the desk. "I'll just guard this for you till you get back."

Emma Wallace stomped her feet silently in the grass. The chilly air felt good as long as she was walking, but whenever she crouched behind a tree for very long, her legs grew stiff.

This part of Central Park was dead, even too dead for the Undead. Time to move on. She slung her canvas tote bag over her shoulder and enjoyed the comforting sound of wooden stakes clattering against one another.

She slipped out of her hiding place and skidded down the sharp incline to the brick path below. Her movement startled some birds from a nearby tree. They cawed, beating the air with a fluttering of wings as they flew into the darkness.

Emma waited, blending easily into a tree's shadow with her black pants and jacket. All was quiet once more. Hard to believe that a short walk south would deliver her to noisy avenues where postparade celebrations still raged.

Maybe that was why the park was so quiet. The vampires could be hunting in the streets. After a long day of green beer and whisky, the revelers would never remember what bit them.

Suddenly the brick path beside her was clearer. Brighter. She could make out individual trees and bushes. She moved quietly onto the pathway and looked at the nearly full moon. The clouds had moved away, leaving the orb bright and glowing.

A slight movement caught her attention, and her gaze lowered. To the south, a lone figure stood on top of a huge crag of granite. His back was to her. Wisps of clouds floated past him, stirring his kilt. Moonlight gleamed off his dark red hair.

Mist swirled around him, making him look ethereal. Like the ghost of a Highland warrior. Emma sighed. That's what the world needed more of today—brave warriors, willing to fight evil.

Sometimes she felt vastly outnumbered by the creatures of the night. As far as she knew, she was the only vampire slayer in existence. Not that she blamed anyone for that. Most people didn't know about vampires. But she did blame her weak and ineffectual boss. Sean Whelan was afraid to pit their small team of four against a group of vampires in battle, so he had assigned them to merely watch and investigate.

Watching wasn't enough for Emma. Not since that horrid night six years ago. She refused to dwell on it. She'd found a much better remedy than grieving. The trick to killing vampires was to find one alone in the act of feeding, then take him by surprise with one swift stake through the heart. With every vampire she turned to dust, she was one step closer to finding peace.

She patted her bag of stakes. With a permanent marker, she'd written *Dad* on half of them and *Mum* on the other half. The stakes were working great, and the death count was up to four. It could never be high enough.

She glanced again at the kilted man standing on the boulder of granite. Where had all the brave men gone? Fierce warriors who could stand alone in the face of danger.

The mist drifted away, leaving the man's form outlined in silvery moonlight. Her breath hitched. He was stunning. His broad shoulders filled the dark sweater he wore. His kilt fluttered slightly in the breeze, revealing strong, muscular thighs. Good heavens. He would make a great warrior. Strong and relentless in battle.

Suddenly he leaned over, grabbed the hem of his kilt, and peeked underneath. Then he dropped the kilt and fumbled at something below his waist. Emma winced. Was he playing with himself? He lifted something to his mouth and drank. Moonlight glinted off the metal.

A flask. Super. He was a pervert *and* a drunk. With a sigh, she turned north and walked away.

What a silly waste of her time, fantasizing about a brave Highland warrior. She should have known he was just one of the thousands of kilted, liquor-guzzling men roaming the city after the parade. Besides, in her line of business, she couldn't afford to get sentimental. The enemy was ruthless.

Scrunch. Emma halted and listened. The path curved to the left and out of sight, but she could hear the sound of footsteps shuffling through dead leaves. She lunged to the left and hid behind a tree. The footsteps grew closer.

A lone man came into view. Emma caught her breath. He was wearing a long black trench coat. The vampire she'd killed last night had sported one just like it. Maybe they all shopped at the same store, Vampires "R" Us. She lowered her tote bag to the ground and retrieved one stake.

He came closer. He'd be easier to kill if he was feeding, but there were no victims nearby. Emma slipped the stake into her belt behind her back. She'd lure him in, using herself as bait.

She sauntered onto the path and gave the man an innocent look. "I think I'm lost. Do you know the way out of the park?"

The man halted and smiled. "I was hoping to find someone like you."

Right, someone to feed from. Damned bloodsucker. Emma widened her stance so she wouldn't lose her balance when he attacked. She reached behind her back and curled her hand around the stake. "I'm ready when you are."

"Okay!" The man untied the belt on his trench coat.

It was then that Emma noticed the hairy calves below the hem of his coat. Good heavens. He wasn't wearing any pants.

"Ta-da!" The man whipped open his coat.

Shit! He wasn't wearing any clothes at all. She grimaced. Just her luck to go vampire hunting and find a flasher.

"What do you think?" The man fondled himself. "Pretty impressive, huh?"

"Excuse me a moment." She let go of her stake and removed her cell phone from its holster on her belt. She'd call the local police to pick this guy up before he gave some poor lady a heart attack.

"Oh, is that one of those picture phones?" The flasher grinned. "Great idea! Could you put me on the Internet? Here, let me give you a profile shot." He turned to the side so his erection would stand out.

"Brilliant. Just hold that pose." Emma flipped open her phone. A dark shadow obliterated her view.

She immediately reached behind her back. False alarm. She released the stake. It wasn't a vampire. Even so, her heart raced, for there in front of her was the man in the kilt.

Chapter 2

He was even more stunning close up. Emma slapped herself mentally when she realized she was gawking at him. How could she forget he'd been looking under his kilt just minutes before? Why were men so obsessed with their equipment? She called into evidence exhibit number one—the flasher.

She glanced over her shoulder. He was still there. Still exposed. But the arrival of serious male competition had left him looking a bit . . . deflated.

"Are ye in need of assistance, miss?" The kilted man's soft burr caressed her nerves like a Highland breeze ruffling a hillside of heather. It brought back memories of happier times when her family had been alive and well, living in Scotland.

She frowned. She couldn't afford good memories. Not until the horrid ones had been thoroughly avenged.

"Is this man pestering you?" the Scotsman contin- ued. His eyes were a vibrant green that sparkled with intelligence and something else she couldn't quite place. Curiosity? Perhaps, but something bolder. He seemed to be searching for something.

Emma lifted her chin. "I can handle him myself, thank you."

The flasher snickered. "Yeah, sugar, you want to handle me?"

She winced. Poor choice of words. The display on her cell phone had gone dark, so she lit it up and pressed nine.

The kilted man stepped toward the flasher. "I suggest ye leave this young woman alone."

"She was talking to me first," the flasher snarled. "So buzz off, buddy."

Emma groaned inwardly. Just what she needed. A drunk Scotsman and a flasher arguing over her. She punched number one.

"Och, how rude of me to interrupt. Especially you, a fine, upstanding paragon of good manners and propriety." The Scotsman arched a brow with a skeptical look. "After all, here ye are, prancing about the park with yer wee willie flopping about."

"It's not flopping! It's hard as a rock." The flasher glanced down. "Well, it was until you came along." He started rubbing himself. "Don't worry, sugar. I'll be back in full form before you know it."

"Don't hurry on my account." She snapped her phone shut and changed her mind about calling the police. She wouldn't get any hunting done if she had to stay here to give a statement. She clicked her phone back into its holster on her belt. "I have to go. I forgot to feed the cat." Probably because she didn't have one.

"Wait!" the flasher yelled. "You didn't get my picture."

"I assure you, the image has been permanently scalded into my brain for all time."

The Scotsman chuckled. "Off you go, lad. No one wants to see yer wee willie."

"Wee? You call this—this Mack truck *wee*? I bet it's bigger than yours, buddy."

The Scotsman folded his arms across his broad chest and widened his stance. "That would be a wager ye'd lose."

"Oh yeah? Prove it!"

"Oh, come on, guys." Emma raised her hands to stop them. "I really don't need to see—" She bit her lip and lowered her hands. So what if the gorgeous Scotsman lifted his kilt? He'd already done it once tonight, and who was she to stop him? It was a free country, after all. Her gaze drifted over to his kilt.

"Ye were saying?"

She glanced up at his face. A corner of his mouth quirked. His green eyes sparkled with humor. Oh no! He suspected she was secretly hoping for a peep show. Her cheeks flooded with heat.

"What are you waiting for, Scottie?" The flasher grinned. He'd achieved impressive proportions and was, no doubt, anticipating an equally sizable victory.

Emma figured he usually won by a head.

"The pretty lady can be our judge," the flasher announced.

She stepped back, shaking her head. "I really don't feel qualified." Or particularly honored.

"Don't worry, sugar. I came prepared." The flasher

pulled something round, silver, and shiny from his trench coat pocket. "All you have to do is measure which one of us is longer."

The Scotsman arched a brow. "Ye brought a tape measure?"

"Of course." The flasher huffed. "I keep a daily journal, and I want it to be as accurate as possible." He planted his fists on his hips. "I take this seriously, you know."

"Brilliant," Emma muttered. "Well, guys, it's been . . . real, but I need to go. Feel free to do your own measuring." She turned toward the tree where she'd left her tote bag.

"No!" The flasher shouted.

Her training had taught her how to anticipate an attack. How to interpret the stirring of air behind her back. As soon as the flasher made a grab for her, she jumped out of his reach and assumed her favorite attack pose. Her reaction time had been as swift as ever, but not nearly as quick as the Scotsman. In a mere second, he'd reached behind his head, pulled out a sword, and pointed it at the flasher's neck.

With a gasp, Emma froze. He had a sword? And not just any sword. This sword was *huge*.

The flasher halted, his eyes wide with fear. He gulped and promptly wilted down south.

"I told ye mine was bigger," the Scotsman growled. "Make a move for the lass again, and I'll be shortening yers by a few inches."

"Don't hurt me." The flasher backed away, closing his coat.

The Scotsman advanced, his sword only inches from

the flasher's fluctuating Adam's apple. "I suggest from now on, ye remember to wear yer knickers."

"Sure. Whatever you say, man."

"Leave us."

The flasher scurried away, disappearing around the bend. The Scotsman lifted the sword over his head so he could slide it back into its sheath. The long blade made a soft scraping noise as it slid home.

Emma was distracted momentarily by the bulge of his biceps, but she quickly came to her senses. "What are you doing with a sword?"

" 'Tis called a claymore." He turned to face her. "Doona worry. Ye're safe now."

"I'm supposed to feel safe with a stranger who's packing a humongous weapon?"

He smiled slowly. "I told ye mine was bigger."

What typical male arrogance. "I was referring to your sword. Not your *wee willie*."

He gave her an injured look. "If ye're going to insult my size, I'll have to defend myself by offering ye proof."

"Don't even think about—"

" 'Tis a matter of honor." His mouth twitched. "And I'm a verra honorable man."

"Very drunk is more like it. I can smell the whisky on your breath."

His eyes widened in surprise. "I've had a wee dram or two, but I'm no' drunk." He stepped closer, lowering his voice. "Admit it, lass. Ye were wanting a private showing."

"Ha! Of all the . . . I'm going now. Good night." She strode toward the tree to retrieve her tote bag. Anger

pricked at her. Shame on her. She'd had too much training to get distracted by bulging biceps or a broad chest.
Or gorgeous green eyes.

"I owe ye an apology."

She hitched the bag onto her shoulder, ignoring him.

"I doona generally discuss private parts, at least until I've introduced myself first."

She stifled a grin. Something about this man was too
appealing. Maybe his accent and kilt made her feel
homesick. She'd been in America for only nine months.
She glanced at him, and his soft smile tugged at her
heart. Shit. She needed to go.

She removed the stake from her belt behind her back
and dropped it into the bag. Her nerves tingled, every
strand aware that he was watching her closely. Instinct
told her to leave, but her curiosity was stronger. Who
was this man? And why did he carry a sword? "I assume you came to town for the parade?"

He paused. "I arrived today."

An evasive answer. "To celebrate or for business?"

The corner of his mouth tilted up. "Are ye curious
about me, lass?"

She shrugged. "Professional curiosity. I'm in law en-
forcement, so I have to wonder why you're carrying a
lethal weapon."

His smile grew wider. "Perhaps ye should disarm
me."

Her chin went up. "Make no mistake, I could if I
needed to."

"And how would ye do that?" He pointed at her bag.
"Will ye take on my claymore with yer wee sticks?"

She wasn't about to explain why she was carrying

wooden stakes. So she folded her arms across her chest and changed the subject. "How did you get the sword on a plane? Or through customs?"

He mimicked her move, crossing his arms over his chest. "Why are ye wandering about the park all alone?"

She shrugged one shoulder. "I like to jog. Now it's your turn to answer."

"Dinna anyone tell ye 'tis dangerous to run with a pointed stick?"

"It's my protection. And it's still your turn to answer. Why do you have a sword?"

" 'Tis my protection. It chased that wee man away."

"A loud *boo* would have chased him away."

He grinned. "I believe ye're right."

She bit her lip to keep from smiling back. The blasted man was aggravating and attractive at the same time. And he still hadn't answered her question. "You were about to tell me why you're wandering about Central Park with a sword?"

" 'Tis called a claymore. And I like to keep it handy at all times."

An image flitted through her head of the Scotsman naked in bed with his huge weapon. And the sword. "I fail to see why you need the claymore. You certainly look muscular enough to protect yourself."

"How kind of ye to notice."

Notice? She was doing a lot more than that. Her brain was busy undressing him, and if the rascal's twinkling eyes were any indication, he'd guessed she was enjoying the view. Her gaze ventured south once again, past his blue and green plaid kilt, and this time, she noticed the hilt of a knife peeking from the edge of his sock. Her heart raced faster. The man was packing multiple weapons. Maybe she should frisk him. Maybe she should call the paramedics first. "Do you have a name?"

"Aye."

She raised her eyebrows, waiting for a response, but he merely smiled. Aggravating man. "Let me guess. You're Conan, the Barbarian?"

He laughed. "I'm Angus."

As in prime beefcake? She should have known. "Do you have a last name?"

"Aye." He opened the leather bag hanging from his belt.

She stepped back, wondering if he was packing heat. "What do you have in there?" His sporran looked well-worn, as if he used it every day.

"Doona worry, lass. I'm looking for a business card." He removed the metal flask she'd noticed earlier so he could rummage through the remaining contents of the brown leather pouch.

She folded her arms while she waited. "Whenever you need something, it's on the bottom. I have the same problem with my purse."

He shot her an irritated look. "This is no' a purse. 'Tis a fine, manly tradition amongst the Scots."

Aha. She'd found a weak spot. She gave him a wide-eyed Bambi look. "Looks like a purse to me."

He gritted his teeth. " 'Tis called a sporran."

She bit her lip to keep from laughing. No wonder she found this guy appealing. He made her smile, and it had been a long time since she'd acted happy and playful. Her mission dominated her life, and she had to take it seriously. The enemy was deadly. "So, what do you keep in there? Besides the whisky. Do you have any shortbread or leftover haggis?"

"Verra funny," he grumbled, although his mouth was curling into another smile. "If ye must know, I have a cell phone, a roll of duct tape—"

"Duct tape?"

He arched a brow. "Doona mock a man's duct tape. It comes in verra handy for binding wrists and ankles."

"Why would you bind someone?" She gave him a sympathetic look. "Oh, poor baby. Is it that hard to get a date these days?"

He grinned. "'Tis also good for covering up a saucy mouth." His gaze lowered to her mouth. And stayed. His smile faded.

Her heart stuttered. His gaze moved back to her eyes with an intensity that squeezed the air out of her lungs. And made her nerves tingle. Even her toes were curling under.

There was more than desire in his dark green eyes. There was a sharp intelligence. He wasn't drunk at all, she realized. And he saw a lot more than any man she'd ever encountered before. She suddenly felt as exposed as the flasher.

He stepped closer. "And yer name?"

Name? Good heavens, the way he was looking at her, her pulse was taking off at warp speed, but her brain was barely on life support. More power to the engines, Scottie. "I—I'm Emma." She decided to play it safe and give only her first name. He'd done the same.

" 'Tis a pleasure to meet you." With a slight bow, he offered her a crumpled business card.

Clouds had shrouded the moon once again, and she couldn't make out the small print. "Do you happen to have a torch in your sporran?"

"Nay. I see verra well in the dark." He motioned to the card. "I own a small security company."

"Oh." She slipped the card into a pants pocket, so she could check it later. "You're like a professional bodyguard?"

"Do ye need one? A lass who wanders about the park alone at night should have protection."

"I can take care of myself." She patted her bag of stakes.

He frowned. "Ye have an unusual method for protecting yerself."

"So do you. How do you protect a client when someone's packing a gun? No offense, but your claymore is a bit outdated."

He arched a brow. "I have other skills."

She bet he did. Her throat felt dry.

He stepped toward her. "I could ask the same question. How do ye protect yerself with a wee stick when the attacker could have a gun . . . or a *sword*?"

She swallowed hard. "Are you challenging me?"

"I'd rather not. 'Twould not be a fair fight."

Male arrogance, again. "You're underestimating me."

He tilted his head, studying her. "That may be true. May I see one of yer wee sticks?"

She hesitated. "I suppose." She reached into her tote bag and handed him a stake. If he got any funny ideas, she could kick it out of his hand in a second.

He closed a fist around the stake, examining it closely. "This is a sorry excuse for a stake."

"It is not. I've been very successful—" She winced. The rascal was getting her to admit too much. "I find them very useful."

"How?" He ran a finger along the edge to the tip.

"They're sharp enough to provide protection."

He frowned as he rotated the stake in his hand. "There is something written here."

"It's nothing." She reached for the stake, but he stepped back.

His eyes widened. "It says *Mum*."

Emma winced. He did have good night vision. And now his eyes were focused on her, studying her. She grabbed the stake. His grip tightened. She yanked, but he wouldn't let go.

"Why would ye write yer mother's name on a stake?" he whispered.

"None of your business." She jerked the stake from his hand and dropped it back into her bag.

"Ah, lass." His voice was soft and full of compassion.

Anger flared inside her. How dare he open that wound? No one was allowed to crack her armor. "You have no right—"

"Ye have no right to endanger yerself," he interrupted with a scowl. "Roaming about this park with nothing but a few sticks for protection? 'Tis foolhardy. Surely there are people who love ye dearly. They wouldna approve of ye risking yer life."

"*Don't!*" She pointed a finger at him. "Don't you dare lecture me. You know nothing about me."

"I'd like to know."

"No! No one is going to stop me." She spun on her heel and strode south down the brick pathway. Damn him. Yes, there had been people who loved her dearly, but they were all dead.

"Emma," he called after her. "If ye're here tomorrow, I'll find you."

"Don't count on it," she yelled without looking back. Anger surged through her with each step she took. Damn him! She had every right to avenge her parents.

She should have shown him just how tough she was. She should have disarmed him and bound his wrists with his own freaking duct tape. She slowed her steps, tempted to go back and teach him a lesson.

She glanced over her shoulder. The path was empty. Where had he gone? He didn't seem like the type to slink away in defeat. She swiveled slowly in a circle. No one in sight. No movement among the trees. A cool breeze blew a lock of hair across her face. She shoved it back and listened. Not just with her ears, but with her mind. She stretched psychic feelers out, searching for the thoughts of a nearby brain.

A sudden chill made her shiver. She zipped up her short jacket and flipped the collar up over her ears. An eerie feeling settled in her gut. She hadn't heard any thoughts, but she'd definitely felt a presence. Someone was watching her.

She reached in her bag for a stake. At least she'd only felt one presence out there. Was it Angus? Who was he exactly? As soon as she returned home, she'd check him out.

The park entrance wasn't that far away. She crossed

the stone bridge and strode alongside the Pond. The Scotsman was downright confusing. Gorgeous and sexy, without a doubt. She'd enjoyed talking to him until he'd started scolding her like a two-year-old. What had come over him? The minute he'd taken her stake in his hands, he'd become rude and overbearing. Why would a man with a huge sword be so uptight over a wooden stake?

She halted with a jerk. *God, no.*

Her heart pounded. No, not him. He couldn't be a vampire. Could he? She spun in a circle, searching the surroundings. She even looked at the Pond, as if he were going to rise out of it and fly toward her.

Get a grip! The man was *not* a vampire. She would have known. She would have felt it. And he would have attacked her. Instead he'd lectured her on safety. She'd smelled the whisky on his breath. What vampire would drink anything but blood? And he was drinking from a silver flask. She'd read in reports that silver burned their skin.

Oh, shit. Months ago, when she'd first arrived, she'd read a report about last summer, when the Stake-Out team had spotted a bunch of vampires in Central Park with the boss's daughter. Many of the vampires accompanying Shanna Whelan had been wearing kilts. Scottish vampires. All armed with swords. And just because Angus's flask was silver in color, that didn't mean it was actually silver. It could be stainless steel or pewter.

Oh God. He might actually be a vampire.

Shit! She should have taken him down while she had the chance. Emma strode toward the corner entrance to the park, then ran up the stairs to Fifth Avenue. Good heavens, Angus had seen her stakes. He had to know she was the slayer. He'd probably report her to all the other vampires.

She froze, her arm lifted to hail a cab. Cars zoomed by. Horns blared in the distance. The *clip-clop* of horse hooves approached slowly from an open carriage. All the sounds of the city blurred as the full truth unfolded in her mind.

Angus knew who she was. Her nights of secretly slaying vampires and remaining anonymous were over. The vampires would want revenge. They'd want to kill her. Her quest to avenge her parents had just escalated to a new level.

She was at war.

Chapter 3

The devil take it. He'd screwed up royally.

Angus watched Emma cross the stone bridge, her stride quick and determined. Instead of convincing her to retire, he'd made her even more determined to use her bloody stakes.

Roman and Jean-Luc were right. He was too hot-headed. But damn it all, it pissed him off that such a lovely young lass would place herself in so much danger. He suspected she was avenging more than the innocent mortals killed recently in Central Park. She was avenging her mother. That would explain her passion and determination, but even so, her behavior was suicidal. It was an idiotic, reckless thing to do, and yet there was nothing stupid or careless about Emma Wallace.

She was clever and quick. She possessed enough psychic power to detect his presence, though he'd managed to shield his thoughts and location from her. He'd never had to do that with a mortal before, which only gave further proof of how special she was. He had hoped reasoning with her would be enough, but she was so determined, it was going to be difficult to persuade her. He might have to pin her down just to get her to listen.

The thought of her lying beneath him caused him to swell. Bugger. He glanced down at his sporran, which was now hanging askew. He couldn't go to Roman's townhouse with an erection. They'd tease him about it for the next century.

He watched her jogging up the steps to Fifth Avenue. He moved quietly to the street, far enough away that he could still see her with his superior vision. She was hailing a cab, a worried look marring her pretty face. Good. It was about time she realized she was playing with fire.

He had to do something. If the Malcontents caught her in the act, they would kill her without a second of remorse. They considered mortals nothing more than a food source, a herd of cattle. Vampires were naturally faster and stronger than any mortal could be. The lass was doomed if he didn't stop her.

He watched her slip into the backseat of a taxi with a graceful, controlled movement. So lovely. And amazing. Three kills last summer and one more this spring. She had to be one fierce little fighter. If only he could direct that passion elsewhere . . .

His swollen groin throbbed. Bugger. Over five hundred years old, and here he was, reacting like a randy youth. He didn't know whether to be annoyed or relieved. It had been so long since he'd felt arousal, he'd suspected he was more dead than alive—a theory that had made sense given his circumstance.

With a sigh, he headed toward Roman's townhouse on the Upper East Side. Teleporting would be faster than walking, but he wanted time to think. And time for the bulge under his kilt to settle down.

Why didn't he react this way among his own kind? There were plenty of available Vamp women, including those in his own harem. They were pretty enough, but they were also demanding and vain in a whiny, helpless way. Emma was totally different. Clever, independent, and bold. She had all the qualities he admired most in men. She was even a warrior.

With a small jab of surprise, Angus realized she was just like him. Well, no. She was a great deal younger. And a great deal more alive. And she also had a very lovely female body.

But her pull was more than a physical attraction. She was a warrior like him, battling evil in the wee hours of the night. She shared his need to protect the innocent. Beneath their obvious differences, they were kindred spirits. If he could make her see that, she could be an ally instead of an enemy.

He turned onto Roman's street and approached the townhouse. The windows were dark now that Roman's harem was gone and he was living in White Plains with his mortal wife. Now the only inhabitants were Connor and two Vamp security guards. Ian would be guarding the townhouse, while Dougal watched over Romatech.

Angus always stayed at Roman's townhouse when

he was in New York. The bedrooms were equipped with aluminum shutters to keep the occupants safe during the day. And the daytime guards were completely trustworthy. They worked for MacKay Security and Investigation.

No doubt, Emma Wallace would run a check on his company as soon as she read his business card. She'd probably figure out he was undead. That was all right. He didn't want any secrets between them. He wanted her to learn to trust him.

He planned to investigate her, too. If he knew all about Emma Wallace, he could figure out the best way to win her over. Psychological warfare. Not as straightforward as his usual methods, but the target in this case was unusual. He couldn't simply bash her on the head with a claymore. He'd have to be more subtle. More . . . seductive.

He smiled to himself. Let the battle begin.

He glanced around as he climbed the steps to the townhouse. The street was empty and quiet. This was the perfect opportunity to test the alarm system he'd installed a few months ago. Ever since Roman had teleported straight into the lair of the Russian coven, Angus had worried that the Russians would attempt a similar maneuver.

He checked once more that the street was empty, then teleported into the dark foyer. As soon as his body materialized, an alarm went off—an alarm pitched at a high frequency so only dogs and vampires could detect it.

Immediately the kitchen door swung open, and a figure zoomed toward him with vampire speed. The blur stopped, revealing Ian, his kilt swirling about his knees and his dagger pointed at Angus's throat.

"Och, 'tis you." Ian slid his dagger back into the sheath beneath his hose. "I nearly skewered you."

Angus patted the youthful-looking vampire on the back. "Ye're as quick as ever, lad. 'Tis good to see ye again." He strolled over to the control panel by the door to turn the alarm off. "If ye'd been here by the monitor, ye'd have seen me come up the steps, and ye wouldna have been caught by surprise."

Ian hung his head, looking properly embarrassed for not being at his post. "I was in the kitchen. We have company."

"Who?" Angus strode past the grand staircase to the kitchen, where a sliver of light could be seen beneath the door. He gave the swinging door a push and caught a glimpse of Gregori, sitting at the kitchen table, drinking his bottle of Blissky.

Angus marched into the kitchen. "Why are ye here, interfering with Ian's duties? Ye should still be at Romatech."

Gregori made a face. "Aren't you the friendly one? Roman's expecting me to give him a report on the slayer, but you and Connor never came back. Besides I'm doing you a favor, returning your bottle to you."

Angus grabbed the bottle and held it up to the light. "The bloody thing's half empty."

Gregori grinned. "I get it. The Blissky is bloody. Right. You're trying to be funny." His grin faded as Angus continued to glower at him. "Okay, so I drank a little. But I prefer to think of it as half *full*."

Angus set the bottle down as Ian strode into the room.

Gregori motioned to him. "He had some, too."

Angus arched an eyebrow at Ian.

"Just a wee drop," Ian insisted. "I know I'm on duty."

"Ye're damned right." Angus bit his lip to keep from smiling. Roman's new Fusion drink was going to be very popular. "Can ye call Connor and let him know I'm here?" He motioned with his head for Ian to leave the room.

"Sure." Ian grabbed a cell phone off the kitchen counter and went back into the foyer.

"So, big guy, are you ready to report?" Gregori slouched back in his chair. "Did you find the slayer? Was it one of the hot babes?" He waggled his brows.

Angus glared at the young Vamp. "I might be willing to forgive ye for drinking my Blissky, if ye'll tell me what's wrong with the bairn."

"The *what? Sprechen sie* English, dude."

"The bairn, the wee babe. I want to know what's wrong."

"Oh." Gregori's face turned serious as he leaned forward onto his elbows. "Well, that's kinda personal."

"So are yer balls, laddie, but if ye're wanting to keep them close and personal, ye'll tell me what's going on."

"Sheesh!" Gregori gave him an incredulous look. "Lay off the steroids, man."

"I doona need drugs. I'm naturally a mean bastard."

"Yeah, I noticed." Gregori narrowed his eyes. "You didn't hurt the hot babe, did you?"

Angus smiled. He was beginning to see why Roman

liked this young Vamp. "I'll tell ye what. Ye tell me about the bairn, and I'll tell you about the hot babe."

Gregori nodded slowly. "Deal." He motioned to the chair across from him.

Angus laid his claymore across the center of the table, then sat. "Is the bairn in danger?"

"We don't know. The Vamp doctors say he's healthy."

" 'Tis a boy?"

Gregori smiled. "You should have seen Roman's face when he told me. He was so proud."

"Then what is the problem? And doona lie, lad. I can always tell, and you wouldna want to see me angry."

Gregori rolled his eyes. "Oh, I'm so scared."

Angus stifled a grin. He folded his arms across his chest and narrowed his eyes.

Gregori sighed. "Okay. Shanna mentioned a few months ago that the baby seemed to be sleeping all day and turning somersaults all night. Really freaked Roman out."

Angus rested his elbows on the table in front of his sword. "Roman fears the bairn is a night creature? That's why they're seeing a Vamp doctor? But dinna Roman use live human sperm?"

"Yep. But he erased the donor's DNA and inserted his own."

"So he would be the father. I doona see the problem." Angus glanced to the side when the kitchen door swung open. Connor strode inside, followed by Ian.

"I hope ye had better luck than I." Connor retrieved a bottle of synthetic blood from the fridge and popped it into the microwave. "I scoured the northern half of

Central Park all night and never saw anything but a few couples making love."

"Damn!" Gregori thumped the table with his fist. "I knew I should have gone with you."

The room grew quiet except for the whir of the microwave. The three Scotsmen regarded Gregori silently until he blushed.

He shifted uneasily in his chair. "I guess I need a girlfriend."

"Don't we all," Ian muttered.

The microwave beeped, and Connor removed his bottle of blood. "Before we start moaning over loves lost, I want to know about the slayer. Did ye find her, Angus?"

"*Her?*" Ian repeated.

"Aye, I found her." Angus motioned toward Gregori. "But first, this one is telling me about Roman's bairn."

Gregori gave Connor a sheepish look. "He wouldn't talk about the slayer until I spilled the beans."

Connor grimaced, then took a long swig from his bottle. "Roman wanted to keep it quiet."

Angus gritted his teeth. "And ye doona think I can keep a secret? I ken more secrets than ye can imagine, Connor. And do I need to remind ye that ye work for me?"

"Aye, that I do, but my job is to provide Roman with security, and that's exactly what I'm doing."

"Tell me the problem," Angus insisted.

With a sigh, Connor leaned against the kitchen counter. "After the bairn was conceived, Roman was conducting some tests to see if he could transform himself back into a mortal."

Angus nodded. "The procedure he did on Darcy Newhart. What of it?"

"Roman learned the procedure only works if he has a sample of the Vamp's original mortal DNA," Connor continued. "While studying our DNA, Roman discovered something . . . odd. By then, Shanna was already pregnant from the sperm with Roman's DNA."

"What are ye saying?" Angus demanded.

Connor took another long drink. "Our DNA has changed. A verra slight mutation, but still, 'tis no' the same as when we were mortal."

Angus swallowed hard. "Then Roman's baby . . ."

"Could be like us," Connor finished. "And we're no longer quite human."

A chill skittered down Angus's spine. No longer human? No wonder Roman was nervous. What would the bairn be like? *No longer human.* Bugger.

"Are ye all right?" Connor asked softly.

"Aye." Except that Gregori was drumming his fingers on the table, and Angus found the noise very annoying. *No longer human.* How could he ever convince Emma he was good when he wasn't even human? He balled his fists with a sudden urge to clobber someone. Gregori would do nicely. "Does Shanna know?"

"Aye," Connor replied. "But she insists she doesna care, that she loves Roman and will love the bairn, no matter what."

"She's a rare woman." Angus scowled at Gregori to get him to stop making noise.

It worked. Gregori leaned forward. "Can you believe it? We're all a bunch of *mutants*! Just like the Ninja Turtles."

Angus blinked. "We—we're like . . . *turtles*?"

Gregori burst into laughter.

Ian shook his head, grinning.

Connor snorted. "Nay. We have vampire DNA. No turtles."

"Snap!" Gregori rocked back in his chair, laughing. "I had you worried, huh?"

Angus narrowed his eyes. "Connor, if ye doona kill this fledgling, I will. The lad is begging for it."

Ian covered his mouth to hide a grin. Connor simply crossed his arms and looked bored.

Gregori wiped his eyes. "You can't kill me. I'm the vice president of marketing at Romatech."

Angus lifted a brow. "Ye claim to serve a purpose?"

"Damn straight. I sell Roman's Fusion Cuisine. You know those commercials on the Digital Vampire Network?" Gregori smiled proudly. "I make those."

Angus slipped his *sgian dubh* from its sheath beneath his hose and studied the sharp, lethal knife. "I doona watch the telly much. I'm too busy killing."

Gregori's smile withered. "Sheesh, bro. Get a hobby. Buy yourself a new skirt. Find some joy in life."

Angus smiled grimly. "I find joy in my work, and the bloodier the better." He glanced at Connor. "Do ye want the pleasure, or shall I?"

Connor's mouth twitched.

Gregori jumped to his feet. "You can't hurt me. Roman needs me to sell his stuff."

"And if ye stopped making yer commercials, would Vamps stop drinking Roman's stuff and turn to the competitor?" Angus asked.

With a frown, Gregori loosened his tie. "There is no

competition. Roman is the sole producer of synthetic blood."

"Ah." Angus slid a finger down the single-edged blade of his *sgian dubh*. "Ye see, I've watched enough telly to know what the proper term is for the likes of you. Ye're what we call an expendable crew member."

Gregori's eyes widened. "You're not hurting me. Roman likes me."

Angus tilted his head. "Are ye sure about that, laddie?"

Connor chuckled. "Enough with the jest, Angus. I want to hear about the slayer."

"Verra well." Angus slipped his *sgian dubh* back into its sheath. He smiled at Connor and Ian, who were both grinning. "We can always kill the fledgling later."

"Shit." Gregori glared at the Scotsmen. "You guys have a sick sense of humor." He shoved Angus's claymore to the side and perched on the corner of the table. "I'd like to see you and your ancient sword take on the slayer armed with a bazooka."

Angus nodded. "Ye might have yer wish before all is done."

"So were ye right?" Connor asked. "Is the slayer Emma Wallace?"

"Aye. I found her wandering about with a bag of stakes."

"Did ye destroy her stakes?" Ian asked.

"Nay." Angus stood and swung his claymore onto his back. "I made sure she left the park. She willna be killing anyone tonight."

"And tomorrow night?" Connor stepped toward him. "Did ye talk to her? Convince her to stop for good?"

"I'll see her tomorrow." Angus pushed open the kitchen door. "Tell Roman no' to worry. I'll take care of Emma Wallace." He left, leaving the door swinging behind him.

"Wait." Connor slipped through the door on a swing and joined him the foyer. "What kind of person is she? Will she be easy to persuade?"

"Nay, she feels strongly about her work. She's verra stubborn. And proud."

"Sounds familiar."

Angus arched a brow. "If ye're saying we're somewhat similar, I've already realized that."

Connor lowered his voice. "Do ye want help?"

"*Nay.*" Angus didn't realize how abrupt his response had been until Connor regarded him with raised eyebrows. He cleared his throat. "I'll handle this on my own."

"I thought our side of the story might be easier for her to believe if she heard it from more than one person."

"Nay." Angus gripped the newel post at the base of the grand staircase. Why this sudden possessiveness when it came to Emma Wallace? Was it due to his pride that he refused to consider her more of a challenge than he could handle? Or was it more? "I'll take care of this. Alone."

Connor inclined his head. "As ye wish."

Angus moved to the center of the staircase spiral where he could see the landing on each floor. It would be faster to teleport to the fifth floor than climb all the stairs.

"She's a bonnie lass," Connor whispered behind him.

Angus whipped around to glare at his friend, but Connor just gave him a knowing look. Bugger. Angus switched his gaze back to the fifth-floor landing. "Will Roman mind if I use his office?"

"Nay. Ye plan to do some research on Miss Wallace?"

"Aye. If I can figure out what motivates her to be a slayer, then remove that motivation, then—"

"She would stop slaying," Connor finished the sentence. "A good plan."

"I hope to make her an ally."

Connor stepped toward him, a doubtful look on his face. "That's a far step, from slayer to ally."

"We brought Austin Erickson over to our side."

"But he was never an actual slayer. Miss Wallace has killed our kind four times that we know of. She's a fiercer enemy than Austin ever was."

"Aye, she's a challenge, but make no mistake." Angus lifted his chin. "I willna be defeated."

With a nod, Connor stepped back. "Good night, then."

"Good night." Angus teleported to the fifth floor, then entered Roman's office. While he waited for the computer to boot up, he helped himself to a bottle of synthetic blood from the mini-fridge. Type O, the same blood type as Emma. Some Vamps considered it too bland and common for their tastes, but Angus had always preferred simple meals. He warmed up a glass in the microwave, then removed it, sniffing the fresh, wholesome aroma. Just like Emma. She came from strong stock. Strong enough to sustain a man forever.

He wandered back to the desk, sipping from the

glass. By the time he met her tomorrow night, he'd have all the information he needed.

He could hardly wait for the battle to begin.

Emma dropped her bag of stakes on the kitchen counter, then headed to the fridge to look for breakfast. Or supper. Or whatever you called it after working all night long. Her stomach rumbled with hunger as she opened the refrigerator door.

"Brilliant," she muttered as she stared at one tiny container of low-fat yogurt and a bag of wilted lettuce. She'd forgotten to drop by the store on the way home. It was all that Scotsman's fault. *Angus.* All the way home, she'd wondered about him—was he a vampire or not?

With a sigh, she grabbed the strawberry-flavored yogurt. Was she overreacting? Angus could be just a normal guy. Yeah, right. She ripped the foil top off the yogurt and stuck a spoon in the container. There was nothing normal about Angus. He was clever, handsome, dreamy in every way, but was he alive? She glanced toward her front door. All three deadbolts were locked, and the blinking light indicated the alarm system was on. Still, a vampire could teleport anywhere.

In her tiny SoHo apartment, she was across the kitchen and in her living room in five steps. She left the yogurt on the coffee table and wandered to the window to peer through the blinds. Dawn would be breaking soon, and she would be safe during the day.

The street was empty except for a row of parked cars and a few early risers who had taken out their dogs. The dogs were doing their business around trees while their sleepy masters waited, a cup of coffee in one hand and a plastic doody sack in the other.

Emma closed the blinds and wandered toward her bright red loveseat. Maybe she should get a dog. Then she wouldn't always be alone. It was hard to have any sort of relationship when she had a job she couldn't discuss and secrets she couldn't share. Unfortunately, her slaying activities might no longer be secret. If Angus was a vampire, he'd know exactly what her stakes were for. The next question was—would he spill her secret to other vampires?

She dug his business card from her pocket. It was white, with a clan crest in the upper left-hand corner. The tartan was a blue and green plaid just like the kilt Angus had been wearing. His name was listed under MacKay Security and Investigation, addresses in London and Edinburgh.

MacKay Security and Investigation? That sounded familiar. She opened her laptop on the coffee table, and accessed her files from work. The Stake-Out team logo came on the screen, and she did a search for Angus's company. While she waited, she spooned yogurt into her mouth.

If Angus's company was based in London and Edinburgh, why was he in New York? The search ended. Angus MacKay's company provided security for Romatech Industries.

Emma swallowed hard. This wasn't absolute proof that Angus was a vampire, but it certainly proved he was in league with the enemy. Romatech was owned by the most powerful and rich vampire on the East Coast, Roman Draganesti. Emma's boss, Sean Whelan, had a ton of info on Roman. He was coven master of the East Coast Vampires, inventor and producer of synthetic blood at Romatech, and Sean's son-in-law.

Sean was spending all the Stake-Out team's time and resources in his quest to find and rescue his daughter. Emma disagreed with his primary mission, but didn't argue with the boss. She simply did her job at the office, then went out hunting afterward. Killing vampires should be the primary mission. It was the reason she'd joined the Stake-Out team.

Sean was into collecting information. As far as Emma was concerned, the only info you needed to know was whether the suspect was a vampire. If he was, he needed to die.

She typed in the website address from Angus's business card. The home page for MacKay Security and Investigation came on screen. Beneath the title of the company, in small print, it read "Founded in 1927." At the bottom of the page, it listed the addresses in London and Edinburgh, then warned "Consultation by appointment only." There was an e-mail link.

Emma clicked on it, and the recipient was listed as Home Office. She wrote a short note.

> This message is for Angus MacKay. Just wondering if you're dead or alive.

She debated whether to send it. What if he responded? Her pulse quickened at the thought. She clicked on *Send*. And winced. She shouldn't communicate with the enemy, but then she wasn't sure he was the enemy. His website was no help. It consisted of only one page. Clearly he wasn't offering any information about himself.

She opened her cell phone. With any luck, her old workaholic supervisor at MI6 would still be in the office. He always claimed terrorists didn't take the weekend off, so why should he? She punched in his number. Two rings. Three. She jabbed another spoonful of yogurt in her mouth.

"Robertson here."

She swallowed quickly. "Brian, this is Emma."

"Emma, love. How are you? Are the Yanks treating you well?"

"Yes. Thank you. I . . . I was wondering if you knew anything about a company based in London and Edinburgh. It's called MacKay Security and Investigation."

"I'll take a look. Hang on."

Emma ate more yogurt while she waited. What kind of case was Angus working on? He certainly wasn't attempting to work undercover. A man in a kilt with a claymore tended to stand out. It was a wonder half the women in Manhattan weren't following him around drooling. Or praying for a sudden, brisk wind.

Mum had always insisted that Dad wear black unders when wearing his kilt. Dad would then tease her that he'd forgotten, and Mum would drag him into the bedroom to make sure he was properly dressed. The inspection tended to take an hour or more. Emma smiled to herself. She'd been thirteen years old before she'd figured out what was taking them so long.

"Emma?" Brian's voice interrupted her musings.

"Yes, I'm here."

"MacKay Security and Investigation was founded in 1927 by Angus MacKay the Third. In 1960 the president is listed as Alexander MacKay. Then in 1995 Angus MacKay the Fourth took over."

"I see." So Angus was the son of Alexander and grandson of the founder, Angus the Third. Unless . . . he was all three? "Are there any photos of them?"

"No. They keep a low profile," Brian continued. "Don't advertise. Can't even find them in a phone book."

"That's odd."

"Well, I suppose they've been in business long enough, they have all the clients they need. Here's something interesting . . ."

"What?"

"The company performed some secret missions during World War II. Angus the Third was even knighted."

Emma blinked. "Really? I wonder what he did that the armed forces couldn't do."

"Don't know. And it looks like Angus the Fourth has done a few favors for the queen."

"You're kidding. Like what?" There was a pause while Emma could hear her former supervisor grumbling.

"Crap. It's been erased."

Emma stood and paced across her tiny living room. The more she found out about Angus, the more confused she became. He didn't sound like an enemy. "So his company has done top secret missions for our government and the queen."

"Yes, and—bloody hell. Angus MacKay has a clearance rating of nine. That's as high as my own."

And much higher than Emma's rating had ever been. "That's totally unheard of. The man's a civilian."

"I gather it has something to do with those top secret missions. At any rate, he's well trusted. What do you know about him?"

Other than the fact she wanted to undress him? "Not much." She should be greatly relieved to find out he was trustworthy. Good heavens, even the queen trusted him. But dammit, he provided security for the most powerful vampire on the East Coast. Who could protect Roman Draganesti better than another vampire? Chances were great that Angus was a vampire.

She perched on the loveseat. "Do you have a list of his clients?"

"Let's see. He provides security for several members of Parliament, a few bigwigs at the BBC, and a fashion designer in Paris."

Those clients didn't sound like vampires. Could he actually be human? Shit, she still didn't know for sure. "Thank you, Brian. You've been a great help." She pushed the off button and dropped the phone on the loveseat.

She paced about her small living room. How could Angus be a vampire when the queen trusted him? And what kind of services was he providing that an agent from MI5 or MI6 couldn't do? She winced. A vampire could do things a human agent could never do.

Her laptop made a chiming noise to let her know an e-mail had arrived. She rushed to the loveseat and checked the sender. *Angus MacKay.*

Her heart lurched. She opened the message.

```
Dear Miss Wallace, my office in London
forwarded your note. Please meet me
tomorrow night in Central Park at
eight P.M., in the same vicinity where
we met tonight. I will answer all
your questions then.
```

That was it. Very businesslike. She was . . . almost
disappointed. What had she wanted? More flirtatious
banter? She'd enjoyed talking to him earlier before
he'd turned dictatorial.

She sat there, frowning at his message. Then she
typed

```
I'll be there. I'll be the one wearing
the pants. Don't forget your purse.
```

She pushed *Send*.

She jumped up and paced around the room. What
was she doing, joking with an alleged vampire? Did
vampires even have a sense of humor? Well, Angus
had joked with her in the park.

Her computer chimed. He'd answered? She ran to
the loveseat and opened the mail.

```
I'll leave my sporran at home, if
you'll leave your pants.
```

She gasped. That naughty man! She laughed, then
stopped abruptly. He might not be a man. He might be
the enemy.

She collapsed back against the cushions. What a

stupid thing to do. Flirting with the enemy. Why did he have to be so damned attractive? She needed to get her priorities straight and plan her strategy for the next night. She usually killed vampires by catching them completely off guard. She wouldn't have that advantage with Angus. She would need . . . a trap. And a way to restrain him.

The jangle of her cell phone startled her. Had Angus found her number? "Hello?"

"Emma, Brian here. I just received an odd report from data security, and I thought you should know."

She sat forward. "Yes?"

"Someone accessed the personnel files about ten minutes ago. They had clearance, but they didn't identify themselves, so a flag went up. Before security could break the connection, this person managed to download one file." Brian cleared his throat. "I thought I should warn you."

A chill seeped through Emma's skin. "Whose file was it?"

"Yours."

"I see." Her voice sounded far away. "Thank you." She set the phone down and took a deep breath to steel her nerves. So Angus was checking her out. He would know all about her. Her gaze drifted to the naughty e-mail he'd sent. If he was a vampire, tomorrow night would be his last.

And even a pardon from the queen couldn't save his gorgeous ass.

Chapter 4

At twenty minutes till eight, Emma spread dead leaves over the ground to hide the rope. She was in a wooded area of Central Park, secluded enough that she didn't need to worry about innocent people blundering into her trap, but close to the place where she'd met Angus MacKay the night before. Her black jeans were topped with a bright red sweater to make her easier to find. She stashed her bag of stakes under a nearby rhododendron and wedged four stakes under her belt.

Fifteen minutes till eight. Would he be on time? The minutes stretched out, ticking by at an incredibly slow rate. What would it be like to have an eternity of nights? Or the ability to teleport somewhere in an instant? With their superior abilities, Emma could understand why vampires considered themselves superior. But in her experience, all serial killers considered themselves superior.

That's all vampires were, really. Serial killers with superior abilities that made them harder to kill. The only good thing about them was that they were already dead. She didn't have to capture one and wait for a slow justice system to deliver a satisfactory ending. No delayed gratification here. When she found one, she killed it.

Ten minutes till. She circled the oak tree where the rope was anchored. She needed to keep her muscles warm and her senses alert. She'd have to act quickly. Not think about how handsome he looked in a kilt. Not think about witty, clever conversation. Her mission was two-fold. Discover his status—human or monster. Then kill him if he was the latter.

She cringed at the thought of watching the sparkle die in his lovely green eyes. She'd never talked to a vampire before killing one. The four she had killed had been in the process of attacking and raping a woman while they fed from her. The sight had been so horrid and repulsive, she'd had no trouble delivering justice.

She couldn't imagine Angus doing that to a woman. He'd seemed offended by the flasher. And he'd lectured her on safety. What vampire would act that way? Oh God, she prayed, don't let him be a vampire. Let him be the queen's hero and the grandson of a knighted war hero. Let him be the man of her fantasies—a fierce, honorable warrior who could fight evil by her side.

"Good evening, Miss Wallace."

She whirled toward the deep voice but could barely discern his dark silhouette in the distance. Her heart raced. He looked wonderful. He looked dangerous.

He stepped toward her, and his kilt swirled around his knees. "Thank ye for coming. We need to talk."

"Yes, we do." She put her psychic defenses up. If he was a vampire, he could try to manipulate her mentally. She edged toward the middle of the small clearing. All he needed to do was walk straight toward her, and he'd step into the trap. "I was beginning to think you weren't coming."

"I am a man of my word."

But are you alive? That was the real question. If he was undead, he wouldn't know the meaning of honesty. Or honor.

He sauntered toward her, close enough that she could see him more clearly. His kilt was the same blue and green plaid he'd worn the night before, but tonight's jumper, or sweater as the Yanks called it, was blue. There were no leather straps crossing his chest like last night. He hadn't brought his sword. Her gaze lowered to his socks. He wasn't completely unarmed. His *sgian dubh* was in place beneath his right sock.

He paused, tilting his head to study her. She held her breath. Did he suspect something? With two more steps he'd be in the trap, swinging upside down. She knew good and well a vampire wouldn't stay trapped for long. He'd simply teleport away.

"Ye have stakes in yer belt."

She shrugged one shoulder. "Better safe than sorry."

He frowned. "Ye are safe with me, lass. I would never harm you."

"You have a knife."

He glanced down. "A mere habit. I usually have my claymore, too, but I left it behind so ye'd know I meant ye no harm."

"Are you confessing to being my enemy?"

"Nay. I could be a . . . good friend."

He looked so sincere. What if he really was a champion for the queen? What if he risked his life for his country, asking for no recognition or credit in return? He could be a hero. He could be everything she'd ever dreamed a man could be.

"Miss Wallace?" He stepped toward her.

A surge of panic swept through her. Suddenly she didn't want to know the truth. She wanted to believe that strong, gorgeous men in kilts were heroes, not demons. She held up a hand. "Stop!"

Too late. He stepped right into the center of the noose. It snapped tightly around his ankle. He shot her a look right before the rope jerked him off his feet.

That look had hurt. Shock, anger, betrayal—she'd felt it all in his eyes. Shit! It couldn't be helped. She had to know if he was friend or foe. She whipped a stake from her belt. If he was a vampire, she'd have to act quickly.

She looked up. And her mouth fell open. The stake tumbled from her hand. *Good heavens.*

Angus MacKay was hanging upside down with the hem of his kilt dangling around his neck.

Emma blinked. Good Lord, she'd never been mooned by such a heavenly body. Narrow hips, muscular buttocks, smooth skin kissed with silvery moonlight. The tree branch overhead swayed from his weight, causing his body to bob softly up and down. She matched the rhythm, nodding like a bobble-headed toy to stay focused on his glorious bare bum.

"Miss Wallace? Can ye hear me?"

She jerked herself from the rump-induced hypnosis. How long had he been talking to her? "Excuse me?"

"Or shall I call ye Emma, since apparently ye're better acquainted with me now?"

Heat invaded her face. How long had she stood there, ogling his rear end? And good heavens, what was she doing staring at his backside when she could get the full panoramic experience by simply walking around him?

He twisted, trying to look at her. "Why have ye strung me up like a smoked ham? Surely we could have a wee chat, face to face."

It wasn't his face she was thinking about. "Feel free to talk." She edged slowly around. So far, he hadn't attempted to escape. Did that mean he was human? Hallelujah!

Of course, this meant she owed him a big apology. Emma smiled to herself. She could certainly help him get over this.

He wiggled like a hooked fish. Her breath hitched. Oh yes. She would be very apologetic.

A soft, scraping noise drew her attention. His wiggling must have loosened his knife from its sheath, for it was sliding downward. He doubled over, reaching for his sock. His fingers curled around the hilt.

"No!" She ran toward him. With a flying kick, she knocked the knife from his hand. It flew through the air. She landed, then quickly jumped out of Angus's reach. While he muttered curses, she sprinted to where the knife had fallen.

"Nay!" he shouted behind her.

She dove for the knife, rolled over, and sprang to her

feet, the hilt grasped in her hands. She pointed the sharp, seven-inch blade toward him.

He was gone.

Her heart froze. Quickly she spun about, looking for him. The rope remained dangling from the tree limb, uncut. A crushing sensation squeezed her heart. No hero. No man of her dreams. He'd failed the test and teleported away. He was the enemy.

She'd have to kill him.

She tamped down the growing ache of disappointment within her. She couldn't afford sentimentality. The battle had begun, and he could see better than she. He was stronger, too, but she had his weapon.

She advanced slowly toward the center of the clearing, revolving in a circle to look for him among the trees. The woods were quiet but for the sound of her accelerated breathing. There! Was that him? Yes, she could make out his dark silhouette. The bastard was leaning against a tree with his arms and ankles crossed like it was just another day at the office.

She pointed the knife at him. "Now I know the truth about you."

He adjusted the folds in his kilt. "And I know about you. Some women will do anything to look under a man's kilt. Did ye enjoy the view?"

She scoffed. "That's quite beyond the point. I know you're a vampire."

"I know ye're the slayer." He pushed away from the tree. " 'Tis time for ye to stop."

He meant to kill her, the thought shuddered through her. She widened her stance and prepared for an attack. "Tonight you die by your own weapon."

He shrugged. "I died once. Dinna care for it much."
He stepped toward her.

She raised the knife so the blade was even with his
neck.

He gave her an annoyed look. "Put the knife down
so we can talk. Ye're no match for me in battle."

"Come a bit closer and find out."

He regarded her silently, then nodded as if he'd
reached a decision. "Verra well. I'll give ye a demon-
stration."

She blinked as his body zoomed past her on the
right. She spun to keep him in view.

He halted on the other side of the clearing. "Ye
missed."

Vampires were such an arrogant bunch. But she
could use his over-inflated pride against him. "I didn't
think you'd run like a coward."

His brows shot up. "Ye expect me to stand still while
ye stab me in the heart?"

"I expect you to face me like a man."

"So to prove my manhood, I should act like a lamb
before the slaughter?" He chuckled. "Ye slay me."

Her mouth twitched with amusement. Damn him.
Why couldn't she find a *live* man this charming and
attractive? Apparently all the good men were married . . . or dead.

He zipped by her again, but she was faster this time
and swatted his rump as he passed by. He laughed and
kept dashing about the clearing like a pinball racking
up points.

"All right, I get it. You can move really fast." Maybe
she shouldn't complain. After all, he hadn't attacked

her. Yet. But she was getting dizzy, whirling about to keep him in view. Was that his plan—to totally disorient her before he attacked?

She halted. His body was a blur as it swept past. "Coward! Be still."

Suddenly he grabbed her from behind, pulling her hard against his chest. His hands locked down on top of hers on the knife. She gasped. His breathing was fast and stirred the hair by her temple. His chest moved against her back with each breath he took.

He lowered his head and whispered in her ear. "Is this still enough for you?"

She shivered. "Let me go."

"Not only am I faster than ye, but I'm stronger." He forced her arms to bend. She resisted, her arms shaking with effort, but he soon had the knife up to her neck.

She swallowed hard. Normally, in this situation, she would stomp on the assailant's foot while doing a back jab into his ribs with her elbow. But she couldn't move her arms. He had her hands pinned beneath his.

"Ye see how easy it is, lass," he whispered in her ear.

"I won't let you kill me."

"Sweetheart, I only want to talk to ye." His breath wafted across her neck, causing little hairs to stand up.

"Don't you dare bite me!"

"Emma." His hands dropped. "Ye wound me."

She jumped away, turning to slash him with the knife. He dodged her attack, then yanked the knife from her hands and flung it to the side. It spun through the air with a whirring noise, then the blade embedded itself into a tree with a thud.

She grabbed the second stake from her belt and charged.

He seized her by the wrist and ripped the stake from her hand. "Sweetheart, 'tis difficult to have a wee chat if ye keep trying to kill me."

"There's nothing to talk about." She backed away, breathing heavily and rubbing her wrist.

"Och, did I hurt ye? I dinna mean to."

She snorted. "Like you care. You've been feeding off humans for years. How many people have you killed?"

He threw her stake far into the woods, then faced her, scowling. "I have killed more than I wish to remember, but I only kill in battle."

Like tonight. Her blood chilled. "If you have any honor, you'll give me a fair fight."

"Lass, ye've already decided I'm evil. Why would an evil man have any honor?"

He had her there. She swallowed hard. He hadn't even bothered to deny his evilness. She crouched in a defensive position, watching. Waiting. She ripped the third stake from her belt.

"Bugger," he muttered. He folded his arms across his broad chest, frowning. "Ye're a black belt in Tae Kwon Do?"

"You should know. You read my personnel file."

"Aye. Put away yer stake if ye want a fair fight." He glanced around, then pointed to his left. "We'll fight over there. The ground is softer for yer fall."

She huffed. "I'm not falling. You are."

"We'll see." He turned his back to her as he sauntered over to the area he'd chosen.

Arrogant vampire. She wedged the stake under her belt, then charged. After a few running steps, she leaped into the air and caught him square in the back with a flying kick. "Aagh." It was like hitting a brick wall.

She landed on one foot and scrambled to a defensive pose. Meanwhile he merely stumbled forward one step. Damn him.

He turned with a smile. "An eager lass. I like that."

She snorted. "Typical vampire arrogance. It's your greatest weakness, and you're too arrogant to even know it."

He affected a wounded look. "Sweetheart, be fair. I was an arrogant bastard long before I became a vampire."

She was tempted to ask how old he was, but his personal history didn't matter. He was like all the others. An evil murderer. She assumed her favorite attack posture. "A fair fight. No cheating."

The corners of his mouth tilted up. "On my honor."

She attacked with a quick series of kicks and punches. He blocked each one.

She jumped back and prepared for another round. Damn, he was good. "Where did you train?"

"In Japan. I've been going there for lessons for the last two hundred years."

Her mouth fell open. Good heavens. The things he must have seen. "How old are you?"

"Five hundred and twenty-six years, if ye include my time as a mortal."

She gulped. He was a walking museum. He'd lived through the Renaissance, the Restoration, the Age of

Enlightenment. He'd worn the clothes, walked the muddy streets, seen history unfold before him.

"Och, the stories I could tell ye," he whispered.

She stiffened. He'd read her personnel file. He knew she'd been a history major at the University of St. Andrew in Edinburgh. She'd been totally immersed in the mysteries of the past until that cold night when her parents' murder had snapped her into harsh reality. She'd put away the books and her dreams, and had changed her studies to law, martial arts, and firearms.

"Damn you." She lunged forward, kicking and spinning to kick again.

He blocked each move. She danced back and assumed another pose. He waited. And that's when it struck her. He was only defending himself. Not that she should complain. If he did attack, she'd be sore pressed to stay conscious. Still, he was so arrogant, she couldn't help but goad him. "Why don't you attack, vampire? Haven't you worked up an appetite?"

He planted his hands on his hips, looking annoyed. "I havena fed off a mortal in eighteen years. I take my meals from a bottle."

"Well, isn't that noble of you? I believe that leaves about five hundred years unaccounted for."

"Aye, I fed when I needed to, but I never killed for food." His gaze wandered down her body, then back to her face. "In fact, I left the lassies feeling . . . verra satisfied."

Her skin tingled. She could almost believe him. "It was a false feeling for your victims. You used mind control on them."

"To give them pleasure, aye." He stepped toward her. "A great deal of pleasure."

"Stop right there." She yanked the third stake from her belt. "Are you controlling the queen's mind? Is that why the British government thinks you're some kind of hero?"

"Och, ye've done some research on me. I'm flattered."

"Don't be." She raised the stake.

He sighed. "Sweetheart, can we no' talk without ye threatening me with yer wee stick?"

"Stop calling me *sweetheart* and answer my question. Are you controlling the queen's mind?"

"Nay. I have always been a loyal subject." He shrugged slightly. "Except for the time I was a Jacobite. But I have always served whomever I believed was the rightful king."

Did he actually know Bonnie Prince Charlie? Good heavens, the questions she would love to ask. But he was tempting her on purpose, luring her in, no doubt, to make her easier prey.

"I read that yer parents were murdered," he whispered.

Her hand squeezed tight around the stake. "It's none of your business." She was wrong about him using temptation. That was too gentle a word. This was an outright psychological attack. The bastard.

"And ye lost yer brother. And yer aunt." His gaze was full of sympathy. "I know how it feels to lose loved ones."

Rage boiled within her. Pity from a vampire? He was the same kind of monster as the fiends who had murdered her parents.

"Shut up!" She charged at him. One way or another, she'd take him down and use her stake. She kicked at his groin.

He jumped back into a crouch and spun, knocking her legs out from beneath her. She fell back.

"Bugger." He dove for her with amazing speed. Her rump hit the ground as he landed beside her, reaching a hand behind her head.

"What?" She stared at him, dazed. For some reason, he was lying beside her, cradling her head a few inches above ground.

He leaned over her, so close she could see the reddish glint of whiskers along his jaw. His massive chest pressed against her. What was he doing? Examining her neck?

"Stop!" She swung the stake toward his back.

"Enough!" He yanked the stake from her hand and tossed it into the woods.

She had only one stake left in her belt. She'd have to be careful. Catch him by surprise. For now, she'd act calm, subservient.

He leaned over her again, fiddling with something behind her head. His breath wafted across her face, surprisingly sweet. In fact, his whole body smelled surprisingly good. Clean and masculine. How could that be?

"What are you doing?" she whispered.

Slowly he lowered her head to the ground, but kept his hand on the back of her neck while he rested on his elbow. "I dinna want ye to fall on this." He showed her a sharp rock in his other hand. " 'Twas on the ground where yer head was about to hit." He tossed the rock into the woods.

"You—you were trying to protect me?"

"I apologize for making ye fall, but I was a wee angry after ye tried to kick me below the belt." He frowned at her. "Whatever happened to yer fair fight?"

"You're faster and stronger. I had to do something to even the odds."

"Ye're a fierce fighter." His gaze wandered to her mouth and lingered there. "We're more evenly matched than ye think."

A shiver coursed through her. Had he actually tried to protect her? But there was no such thing as a *nice* vampire. This had to be part of his psychological warfare. "What do you want from me?"

His gaze lowered to her neck.

"If you bite me, I swear I'll kill you."

"Ye have so much rage trapped inside." His gaze drifted downward. He placed a hand lightly on her thigh and dragged it up to her hip. "There are other ways to find release."

Her heart thudded. She was wrong again. He was using more than psychological warfare. He meant to seduce both her mind and her body. And it didn't help that his gentle touch was igniting a trail of sparks along her thigh and hip. She sucked in a shaky breath. Okay. She could play this game, too. And once he was thoroughly distracted, she'd use her one remaining stake.

She placed her palms on his forearms and glided up and over his bulging biceps. Good heavens, no wonder he wielded that heavy sword so easily. "I suppose you're just the man to help me." She slid her hands onto his shoulders and gave him what she hoped was a seductive look.

She gasped. His eyes were red. And glowing. Her fingers dug into his shoulders. Shit, this had to mean he was hungry. She needed to act fast. Remain calm. She forced her fingers to relax and slid her hands down his chest.

"Ye're so beautiful," he whispered, brushing her shoulder-length hair away from her neck.

Oh God, he was preparing her neck. But she was ready. Her hands had reached his waist. She fisted one hand and punched him in the gut while she whipped the final stake from her belt and aimed for his godforsaken heart.

"The devil take it, woman." He yanked the stake from her hand and slammed it into the ground beside her head.

With a gasp, she turned her head to look. Only an inch of the stake showed above ground. She'd be dead if he'd impaled her with it.

He placed a thumb on the rounded end of the stake, and with a growl, he pushed it so far into the ground, it made a hole. He glowered at her, his eyes still red but less luminous. "I was a fool to think ye could like me."

For some strange reason, she actually felt bad about disappointing him. "I had to defend myself. You were going to bite me."

"Nay, I only wanted to kiss you."

She snorted. "Right. A kiss with teeth. You were looking at my neck. And your eyes were red and glowing. You were hungry."

"Ah, lass." He closed his eyes briefly. When he opened them again, they were turning back to their usual forest green. " 'Tis a hunger of another sort."

What did a vampire need besides blood? Her question was answered when he shoved his sporran aside and lay close beside her. She gasped. He was pressed against her in a big way. Very big. Very swollen. Very hard. How could a cold, dead creature be so turned on?

And why did her hands itch to touch him? He had to be playing with her head. "You—you must be controlling my mind."

The corner of his mouth quirked. "Are ye having naughty thoughts?"

"No! I . . ." She didn't know what to say. Or think. She was supposed to be killing vampires, not lying next to one with a hard-on. She glanced over at the rhododendron bush where her bag of stakes was hidden. She'd never reach it in time if he attacked her. "If you try to rape me, I'll hunt you to the—"

"Emma." He sat up with a jerk. "I would never harm you."

"You wouldn't have to. You would take control of my mind to make me willing. That's how you turn a woman into a victim."

"I have no desire to make ye a victim. I admire yer strength and fiery spirit."

Did he really? No. Emma rejected the warm, fuzzy feeling. Nothing was warm and fuzzy when it came to the Undead. "You're trying to confuse me. I won't have you playing games with my head."

His mouth twitched. "Can I play with yer body then?"

"No! I want you to leave me alone."

He nodded, his face growing sad. "Ye're right.

Nothing good could come of this." He hefted himself to his feet.

She felt suddenly cold without him next to her. She sat up slowly and hugged herself for warmth.

He wandered to the tree where his knife was embedded. "I'll leave ye alone if ye agree to one thing." He yanked the knife loose. "Ye'll give up slaying."

"Never." She scrambled to her feet. "Your fellow vampires are murdering people. I have to protect the innocent."

"I know about evil vampires, lass. I've been fighting them for centuries."

"Yeah, right." She scoffed. "Then how come there are so many of them? You haven't been doing a very good job." As if she believed him in the first place.

"They have us outnumbered, that is true." He slid his knife into the sheath beneath his knee sock.

"Then I'm helping to even the score. I know what I'm doing."

"Nay, ye do not." He straightened, scowling at her. "Ye'd never survive a real fight. I lost count of how many times I could have killed ye tonight."

She raised her chin. "You can't make me stop."

"Then I'll need to be more persuasive." The look he gave her made her heart pound. "I'll see ye tomorrow." He picked up the stake she'd dropped by the trap. Then he strode over to the rhododendron and grabbed her bag of stakes. "Face the facts, Miss Wallace. Ye're out of business."

"You can't stop me. I have more stakes at home."

His wide mouth curled up in a smile. "Then perhaps I should drop in for a wee visit. Ye live in SoHo, aye?"

She swallowed hard. Her and her big mouth.

"Be sure to wear something sexy," he whispered, then vanished right before her eyes.

She glanced around to see if he had reappeared behind her. Or somewhere in the woods. No, he was gone. He knew she couldn't hunt without her stakes. *Wear something sexy.* Was he going to appear in her apartment tonight? Maybe she shouldn't go home.

Maybe she should.

Damn him. He was messing with her mind. It was supposed to be so simple. Vampires were evil and deserved to die.

But he had refused to hurt her during the fight. In fact, he'd tried to protect her. Was it all a game to get her into his bed? And then what? Would he drain her dry like the bastards who'd killed her parents?

Slowly she wound up the rope she'd used to trap Angus MacKay. This much was clear. He meant to keep interfering. He meant to seduce her. The safest thing to do was a preemptive strike. Kill him. After all, it was self-defense.

Last night, that decision would have felt good. Now, she felt hesitant. Even sad. Damn him. His psychological warfare was already working.

Chapter 5

On the fifth floor of Roman's townhouse, Angus dropped the sack of stakes on the desk with a noisy clatter. He'd teleported to Roman's Upper East Side home so many times over the years, he no longer needed a sensory beacon. The journey was embedded in his psychic memory. He had merely closed his eyes, concentrated, and he was there. Even so, he lifted his kilt to make sure he'd arrived intact.

Bugger. He was still swollen. What the hell was wrong with him? It was one thing to lust after a mortal, but to desire one who wanted to *kill* him? Roman would have a field day analyzing that. Over the centuries, Angus had come to rely on the former monk for advice and counseling. Roman would probably announce that good ole Angus was suffering from some sort of middle-aged crisis, trying to prove his youth and vigor by seducing a beautiful mortal young enough to be his great, great, great, great granddaughter. Come to think of it, that was probably not enough *greats*.

He was being a fool. All he had to do was talk to her. Convince her to quit slaying. Getting her to like him wasn't on the agenda. She would never like him. Why torture himself by longing for the impossible?

"Och, 'tis you." Ian spoke behind him.

Angus quickly dropped his kilt and turned to greet Ian. "I've just returned."

Ian nodded, his gaze dropping to Angus's lopsided sporran. "I thought I heard some noise up here." His gaze shifted to the sack of stakes on the desk.

Angus removed his pewter flask from his sporran, using the opportunity to straighten the leather bag. "I was just about to refill my flask. Would ye like a wee dram?"

"Aye. Thank ye for offering. Most Vamps would not."

Angus headed toward the mini-bar. "Why wouldn't I?"

Ian snorted. "Roman's ex-harem opened a racy vampire club, and the damned bouncer there says I'm too young to go in."

"Ridiculous." Angus located his bottle of Blissky and unscrewed the top. "Ye're almost as old as I am."

"No one believes it."

Angus glanced at his old friend with the smooth, youthful face. He'd found Ian fatally wounded on the battlefield of Solway Moss in 1542, and he'd transformed him there in the dark, amidst the groans of dying soldiers. What else could he have done? Leave a fifteen-year-old to die? At the time, it had seemed a terrible, tragic waste of youth, and Angus had thought he was doing the young soldier a great favor. But he had trapped Ian for all eternity with the face of a boy.

Angus sighed as he poured himself and Ian a glass. It just went to show him. Interfering with mortals was always messy and tainted with regret. He should never allow himself any sort of feelings for Emma Wallace.

"So, I take it ye found the slayer?" Ian peeked into the sack on the desk. "Are these her stakes?"

"Aye." Angus refilled his flask with Blissky. Bugger. His bottle was almost empty. "She tried to use a few of them on me."

"Really?" Ian's eyes widened. "Are ye all right?"

"Aye, I'm fine." Angus carried the two glasses back to the desk and offered one to Ian. "But I'm having trouble convincing her I'm a nice guy."

Ian laughed. "Why am I no' surprised? Ye do have a fierce look about ye. Maybe I should talk to her." His grin faded. "No one ever thinks I'm scary."

Angus patted him on the back. "They fear ye on the battlefield." He downed his glass and winced. Bloody strong stuff. But it would take the edge off his hunger for blood. And his lust for Emma Wallace.

He upended the bag and dumped some of Emma's stakes on the desk. He picked one up and read the word *Mum*.

Ian grimaced. "Nasty things. They look verra sharp."

"Aye, they can kill us." Angus picked up another stake. *Dad*. Bugger. No wonder she hated vampires so much.

Ian motioned to the computer. "There are some e-mails waiting for ye in the inbox. From Mikhail in Moscow."

"Och, good." Angus circled the desk and sat in front of the computer. He'd downloaded Emma's personnel file the night before. He'd learned a lot of interesting information, most importantly that her parents had been murdered in Moscow six years earlier. He had e-mailed his Russian operative for more information.

Given the time difference, Mikhail would now be in his death-sleep, but he'd e-mailed earlier to report on his findings. He had teleported into the police station in the middle of the night and copied the report on file. He'd attached the report. The first attachment was the report in Russian; the second one, Mikhail's translation of it into English.

Mikhail had done a thorough job. He'd sent a second e-mail an hour later that included a translation of the coroner's report and a copy of the crime scene photo. According to the coroner, both victims had suffered slashed throats and all their blood was missing.

Angus studied the photo. No pools of blood under the victims, so they hadn't bled out where they were found. The police must have assumed the bodies had been moved.

It was a typical vampire cover-up. Cut a throat so the fang marks no longer showed. The police had concluded the mafia was responsible, and that's what they would have told Emma.

Somehow, she knew the truth. The fierce love she'd

felt for her parents had transformed into a fierce hatred of vampires. Like himself. Angus sighed.

"This is strange." Ian sipped from his drink as he rummaged through the pile of stakes. "They're all labeled *Mum* or *Dad*."

"Her parents were murdered by vampires."

"Och, that explains her slaying."

"Aye, but I doona know how she figured it out. The Russians told her the mafia was responsible. Why would she suspect vampires? How would she even know we existed?"

Ian shrugged. "Maybe she witnessed the attack."

Angus shook his head. "They would have never let her survive." He double clicked on her personnel file to open it, then skimmed through it. "She was in Edinburgh when the attack took place."

Ian leaned against the desk. "But she's psychic, no?"

Angus glanced up from the report. "Ye may be on to something." Had she somehow witnessed her parents' murder in her mind? It would certainly explain her rage and need for revenge.

"Did ye convince her to stop?" Ian asked.

"No' yet. She's verra stubborn."

"Well, she *is* Scottish."

Angus smiled. "Aye. She's a fierce fighter, too."

"Gregori says she's hot."

His smile faded. "Gregori will be lucky if he lives another week."

Ian's mouth twitched. "He complained to Roman about you."

Angus shrugged and started typing an e-mail to Mikhail.

Your next assignment: Locate the
vampires who murdered Emma Wallace's
parents.

It might be an impossible request, but Mikhail would
give it his best shot. Angus clicked on *Send*, then noticed Ian was still hovering by the desk. "Anything
else?"

"Aye. Roman wants to see you. Shanna, too. She
says it's been six months since yer last checkup."

Angus shook his head, smiling. Was there anything
Roman wouldn't do for his wife? The man was so be-
sotted, he'd actually opened a dental clinic at Romatech so Shanna could continue her profession in a safe
place. Most Vamps had been a bit wary of having a
mortal poking around their mouths, so Angus had
been the first in line to show his support. Then he'd
quietly suggested all his employees get a checkup.
Anything to help Roman. The monk had saved Angus's life and given him a reason to live. Angus wanted
his old friend to be happy, but he couldn't understand
how marriage to a mortal could ever work.

Mortals were so short-lived. So emotional. Their
wounds were all recent and raw, whereas a Vamp had
the luxury of centuries to cushion the blows.

Emma Wallace was the perfect example. Her whole
life was focused on a passionate quest for revenge.
But her life was so short. She should be enjoying it,
not squandering it away on some creatures that would
still be here a hundred years from now. He really
needed to get through to her. And take away the rest
of her stakes. He located her profile sheet from the

Stake-Out folder and found her address and phone number.

"Hello?" Ian waved a hand to get Angus's attention. "Roman is waiting for you. He's at Romatech with Shanna."

"No' tonight." The fastest way to Emma's apartment would be to call her and use her voice to teleport. But would she be there after his silly remark about wearing something sexy?

"All right," Ian conceded. "I'll tell him ye're joining us tomorrow night for Mass."

"For what?" Angus scowled at having his attention drawn away from the problem at hand. "Mass?"

"Aye. Father Andrew does a Mass for us Sunday nights at eleven. Roman had a room made into a chapel at Romatech. Then Shanna had the bright idea of offering free Fusion Cuisine afterward. We have about thirty Vamps showing up now."

Angus scoffed. "I doona need a priest praying for me. Unlike Roman, I'm verra happy being a vampire."

"So ye have no regrets?"

Angus shrugged. Every life had regrets, and his life had been longer than most. "I've always done what I thought was right at the time." And prayed that others didn't suffer for it. He glanced at Ian's permantly youthful face and winced inwardly. "I have made . . . mistakes."

"Then we'll see ye tomorrow."

Angus sighed. "Tell Roman I'll see him sometime tomorrow. I canna say when. I need to see Emma every night until I can convince her to stop her slaying."

"Connor thinks we should help, that ye shouldna handle this on yer own."

"He's wrong," Angus gritted the words out between clenched teeth while he glared at Ian.

"Right." Ian's innocent blue eyes widened. "Ye're the boss." He backed away toward the door. "Roman's going to want to know why ye canna come tonight."

Angus scowled at Emma's address on the profile sheet. "She has more stakes in her apartment."

"Ye're invading her home? Alone? She'll put up a hell of a fight, for certain. Let me come with you."

"Nay. I can handle her."

"She's murdered four vampires that we know of."

Angus stood. "I said I can handle her."

Ian hesitated, his hand on the doorknob. "Ye're no' immortal, Angus. None of us are."

Angus softened the scowl on his face. "I know. I'll be fine, lad. I'll see you when I get back."

Ian nodded. "All right." He left the room, calling back over his shoulder. "At least ye'll have the element of surprise."

Angus winced. No, he didn't. What a fool he was. And what a clever and feisty lass she was. She would probably have another trap ready for him. Blood rushed to his groin in anticipation. God help him, he was out of his mind.

Katya Miniskaya smiled politely as one of her Russian coven members entered her office. It was Boris, one of the whiners. Alek had informed her two months ago that Boris was complaining about her behind her back. Apparently he was upset that two of his whiny friends had suffered unfortunate, fatal accidents in her office.

She motioned to the chair in front of her desk. "How may I help you?"

His eyes lingered on her lace camisole too long before he sat. "Alek says you're offering a reward to whoever killed those mortals in Central Park."

"I am." She had suspected Boris was responsible. She'd also suspected he was stupid enough to fall for this bait. "Are you saying you killed one of those mortals?"

"Maybe." He lifted his chin with a challenging glare. "Maybe I killed all three. What's the reward?"

Katya stood slowly. She still had on her hunting clothes—a black lace camisole and a clingy skirt sliced up to her right hip. She wore nothing underneath. Dressed like this, she could usually scrounge up dinner in less than five minutes. Mortal men practically lined up to donate blood. She would feed from several, play with one or two if they were pretty enough, then send them away with their memories erased and an erection they couldn't explain.

She perched on the edge of the desk and crossed her legs so her right leg was exposed up to the hip. "What kind of reward would you like?"

He licked his lips. "I was thinking money or a bigger coffin. Or maybe—" His gaze feasted on her body, then lifted to her eyes. "You."

Her grip tightened on the edge of the desk, but she kept her smile even. "Are you admitting to the murders then?"

"Hell yes, I killed the women. Fucked them first, then drained them dry and slit their throats."

"How sporting of you." Katya pushed away from the desk and returned to her chair.

Boris shrugged. "There's plenty more where they came from. It's not like we're going to suffer from a food shortage." He grinned. "So are you giving over?"

She sat. "I am your master, not your whore."

Anger flashed in his eyes, and he stood. "Galina does it. She's upstairs right now, entertaining Miroslav and Burien."

"Then get in line. Galina enjoys boosting morale with her revolving door policy. I'm the one running this coven, and I have real business to attend to."

He snorted. "You're only master because you killed Ivan."

"Something you didn't have the balls to do." Katya opened her top drawer and inserted a dart into a blowpipe. "No, you attack defenseless women and call yourself a man."

He stiffened. "It is no crime to kill mortals. It is our right." His eyes narrowed. "There's no reward, is there? I should have known you were a lying bitch."

"Oh, there *is* a reward." Katya lifted the blowpipe to her mouth, and with a puff of air, she sent the dart flying straight to Boris's neck.

"I—" He stumbled back with a stunned look. He yanked the dart from his neck. "Nightshade?" He crumpled to the floor.

"It works fast, don't you think?" Katya strolled over to his paralyzed body, then placed a foot on his chest.

She pressed down on the stiletto heel. "How do you like your reward?"

Boris's eyes clouded with pain and fear.

"You see, normally I wouldn't object to a mortal dying. I've killed quite a few myself. It's your motivation I object to. You're trying to cause a war between my coven and Draganesti's. You think if a war erupts, I'll be replaced. And you thought I was too stupid to figure that out." She leaned over. "I'm not going anywhere. You, on the other hand—"

The phone rang, interrupting her speech.

"Damn." She glanced at the phone, then at Boris. "Don't go away." Chuckling, she strolled back to the desk to answer the phone. "Hello?"

"Is this Katya Miniskaya, co-master of the Russian-American coven?" The masculine voice had sneered over the word *co-master*.

She tamped down on her anger. A male vampire would never get this kind of disrespect. Only one man had ever recognized her talent and potential. He'd praised her for what others failed to see. She'd set out to seduce him for the sheer challenge, but she'd fallen into her own trap. She'd fallen for him. And the bastard had abandoned her.

She should have killed him.

She shoved the memory aside. She was a coven master now. She didn't need any man, and she wasn't going to let this arrogant creep on the phone jerk her around. "Who are you? What do you want?"

"I am an associate of Casimir." The voice paused.

Katya waited, but he remained silent. Maybe he thought the mere mention of Casimir would scare her to the point she'd be unable to carry on a conversation. She snorted. "So?"

"He is unhappy with you."

"Big deal. I'm not real happy with him, either." Casimir had let everyone think he had died in the Great Vampire War of 1710. He'd left everyone feeling defeated and leaderless.

A form wavered beside the empty chair, then solidified. He was a chunky man with a neck thicker than his head, wispy brown hair, and cold blue eyes that regarded her with bored condescension. His gray suit and leather briefcase looked strictly business, but Katya knew danger when she saw it.

She eased around the back of her desk, making a show of hanging up her phone and sitting down. Her new position put her close to her blowpipe and supply of nightshade darts.

His lips curled into a sneer. "Thank you for seeing me." He snapped his cell phone shut and dropped it into his coat pocket.

Crap. He'd used her voice as a beacon. "Who are you, and what do you want?"

"I am Jedrek Janow, a close friend of Casimir."

She carefully kept her face blank. She'd heard his name mentioned in whispers over the years. He was Casimir's favorite hit man. "How do you do?" She motioned for him to take a seat.

He didn't. The bastard preferred staring down at her. He gently deposited his leather briefcase in the chair.

She lifted her chin. "How come you're awake? Has the sun not risen where you and Casimir are hiding?"

His eyes narrowed. "Casimir's location is none of

your concern. As for me, I teleported from Paris. I cannot stay long."

"What a shame."

"Your arrogance is not becoming." He stepped toward the desk. "Make no mistake. Casimir has allowed you to remain in power. He could remove you at any moment."

Katya tried hard to show no reaction, but she could feel the blood draining from her face. When Casimir removed someone, it was permanent. Was that why Jedrek had come? Did he mean to kill her tonight? "There is no reason to be displeased with me. This coven was poor until I took over. Now we're rich."

"There has never been a female coven master before."

She stood. "You think I'm not tough enough for this job?" She motioned to the floor behind Jedrek. "Say hello to Boris."

Jedrek glanced at Boris without comment, then returned his gaze to her. "You dress like a slut."

"These are my hunting clothes. I'm guaranteed several quarts within five minutes. I like to call it fast food."

"You took over by murdering Ivan Petrovsky."

She shrugged. "An ancient and time-honored method for career advancement."

"Petrovsky was the one who saved Casimir's life at the end of the Great War."

She was screwed. "I didn't know that. Everyone thought Casimir was dead."

"According to my sources, Ivan admitted Casimir was alive before you killed him."

She swallowed hard. One of her coven members was snitching on her. "Galina and I are doing an excellent job as co-masters. Perhaps you would like to meet her?"

"She is a whore."

"But such a good one. The men are very happy."

Jedrek slammed a beefy fist on the desk. "You fool. Casimir doesn't want *happy* followers. Why do you think the enemy calls us the Malcontents?"

Katya planted her hands on the desk and leaned toward him. "My coven follows all the traditions of the True Ones. We feed off mortals. We manipulate them for money. We detest the weak vampires who drink from bottles like babies. And when Casimir is ready to slaughter them, we will be there."

Jedrek snorted. "How can you fight for Casimir when you cannot defend your own coven? How many of your members have been slain in the last year?"

Crap. The little snitch was doing a thorough job. "There were three murders last summer. And one last week. But I have taken care of it."

"How? Did you capture the slayer?" Jedrek glanced back at Boris. "Is this the slayer?"

She was tempted to say yes. "He is . . . involved in the matter. As I said, I have the situation under control."

"Casimir wants proof of your commitment."

"Proof? That's easy enough. Say good-bye to Boris." Katya grabbed the wooden letter opener off her desk, marched over to Boris, and stabbed him through the heart. He turned to a pile of dust on her carpet. "Shall I pack you a to-go box for Casimir?"

Jedrek's arched brow indicated he was not impressed. "Casimir wants the slayer. He has special plans for him." The hit man turned to the chair where he'd deposited his briefcase and removed a small electronic device. He wandered about the room, watching a small screen on the device.

Katya dropped her letter opener on the desk. "What are you doing?"

"Casimir doesn't believe you can properly defend your lair. He heard Draganesti teleported into your home last spring and rescued someone you were holding prisoner."

"Ivan was in charge then. We've had no invasions since then, and I've increased the number of our daytime guards."

Jedrek continued to move about the room, looking at his device. "Did you know Angus MacKay was here in New York?"

Katya swallowed hard.

Jedrek sneered. "I'll take that as a *no*."

"I'm sure he comes often. Draganesti is one of his clients." Not that Angus would ever bother to see her.

"Interesting that he's here at this time, don't you think?"

Did Casimir suspect Angus was involved in the slayings? Well, he had killed more True Ones in the Great War than anyone else, and his company had a nasty way of investigating matters and dispensing their own brand of justice. The last time she'd seen him was last spring at the Gala Opening Ball. He'd acted like he didn't even know her. He'd only looked at her once when he'd slapped her with sarcasm. *And what is yer idea of fun? Were ye planning to kill someone tonight?*

Damn him. She should have killed him a long time ago.

"Aha!" Jedrek ran his fingers along the back of a curtain rod, then plucked off a small metallic object. "Still think you're qualified to lead this coven?" He dropped the listening device on her desk and smashed it with a paperweight.

She winced. How long had her office been bugged? Who was doing it? Draganesti? Or Angus MacKay?

Jedrek unscrewed the receiver to her phone and located another listening device. He glanced at her with a sneer. "Pathetic." He crushed the bug with the paperweight.

She gritted her teeth. Jedrek was going to enjoy telling Casimir about this. "I *can* protect this coven. And I will capture the slayer."

"Good." Jedrek dropped his bug detector into his briefcase and snapped it shut. "I'll expect delivery in a week."

Katya blinked. "Next Sunday?"

"Saturday." Jedrek shrugged. "Like I said, Casimir is unhappy with you. He's just looking for a reason to remove you."

To kill her. Katya clenched her fists. "I suppose he has a replacement picked out?"

"Yes." Jedrek straightened his tie, smiling. "Me."

"That is ridiculous. You're not even Russian. My members won't take orders from a Pole."

"Half Polish, half Russian." Jedrek shrugged. "Casimir doesn't give a damn about our heritage. What he wants, or demands, is loyalty."

"I *am* loyal."

"Prove it." Jedrek checked his watch. "Time for me to go."

"I will prove it." Katya marched toward him. "I'll do more than capture the slayer. I'll give you Angus MacKay."

Jedrek's brows shot up.

Katya smiled. At last she'd gotten a reaction.

Jedrek snorted. "You think you can capture the general of the Vamp army?"

"Wouldn't Casimir love to have him?" And wouldn't she love to watch him suffer. "I'll deliver him and the slayer by next Saturday. And you can stop lusting after my job."

Jedrek sneered. "We'll see about that. You'll never pull this off." He vanished.

Katya took a deep breath. Now she had to capture Angus MacKay. That would be extremely difficult. Was he involved with the slayings? It was very coincidental that he was in New York at the same time, but whether or not he was involved, it no longer mattered. She'd promised both Angus and the slayer, and her life was going to be very short if she didn't deliver them both by Saturday.

Crap! She needed a plan. Katya paced about the office. It would take a whole team of men to capture Angus. And once she had him and the slayer captured, she would have to hold them prisoner without them escaping.

She needed silver. Tons of silver. Thank God the coven was now rich. Months ago, she and Alek had teleported into a few shops in the Diamond District, helped themselves to some loose gems, then teleported to an associate in California who had paid them 1.2 million dollars. They were back, all cozy in Brooklyn, before the police even knew the gems were missing.

She would make a room of silver. That would keep the slayer and Angus unable to teleport to freedom. And she would need lots of nightshade. Her supply was running low.

She paused when another problem occurred to her. How could she turn Angus and the slayer over to Jedrek on Saturday? He wanted her to fail, so he could take over her coven. She couldn't trust him at all. No, she would have to deliver the prisoners herself. Not easy, when she wasn't quite sure where Casimir was. Somewhere in Eastern Europe or Russia, she would bet.

Galina would help. Her neck was on the line, too. Didn't she own some place in the Ukraine?

Katya called Galina and Alek on the phone and demanded they come immediately to the office. Then she grabbed a pen and started making plans. Who could the slayer be? Only a vampire could possibly kill another vampire, and she strongly suspected the slayer was one of Draganesti's coven members. Or perhaps one of Angus MacKay's employees. Or even Angus MacKay himself.

Damn him. He would finally get what he deserved.

She looked up when Alek strode into the office. "We have one week to capture the slayer and Angus MacKay, then deliver them to Casimir."

Alek's mouth dropped open. "One week? When did this happen?"

"I just had a visitor. A Polish man named Jedrek Janow."

"I've heard of him. He's an assassin for Casimir."

Katya sighed. "He'll be . . . removing Galina and me if we don't make the delivery."

"Jesus," Alek whispered.

"I want you to find the slayer. Have our members work in teams of three. One can act like bait to draw the slayer in, while the others stay hidden and ready to attack."

"I'll get right on it." Alek started toward the door, then hesitated. "I—I never said anything, but . . ."

"What?" Katya glared at him. "We don't have much time."

Alek winced. "I saw Vladimir get murdered."

"What?" Katya rushed toward him. "You saw the slayer, and you never said anything?"

"They shot me with silver bullets. I was in so much pain, I didn't know what was happening. And then the girl, she came up from behind. We never saw her coming."

"The *girl*? They? Are you saying there are two of them?"

"Yes. A male and a female, working together. He shot me full of holes while Vladimir was feeding. Then she snuck up behind Vlad and staked him in the back."

Katya grabbed Alek by the shirt and pulled him forward. "You fool. Why didn't you tell me this before?"

"I—I had to get the bullets dug out. The silver was

killing me. I had to go to an emergency clinic and take over the nurses' and doctors' minds. It took the rest of the night."

Katya gritted her teeth and pushed him away. "You could have told me the next night."

He hung his head. "I was ashamed. Vladimir had been a close friend. I should have saved him somehow."

Katya sighed. "So you're certain there are two slayers? A man and a woman?"

Alek nodded, still avoiding her gaze.

She smoothed down his shirt where her grasp had wrinkled it. "You failed to save Vladimir, but you can save me and Galina."

"I will." He gave her a beseeching look. "I'd do anything for you, Katya. I swear."

She'd always suspected his willingness to help was based on more than loyalty. She patted his cheek. "Help me catch the slayers, Alek, and I'll do anything for you."

His eyes glimmered as he looked her over. "They're as good as dead." He rushed out the door, nearly running over Galina.

"Where's he going in such a big hurry?" Galina asked.

"We're rushed for time. Don't you own some sort of fortress in the Ukraine?"

"It's more like an old manor house. Why do you ask?"

"You're leaving tonight. We need a prison cell, completely lined with silver. I'll give you the money."

Galina raised her perfectly plucked eyebrows. "We're going to hold a vampire prisoner?"

"More than one. The slayer, or perhaps two slayers. And Angus MacKay."

Galina's mouth dropped open. "The general of the Vamp army?"

"Yes." And the bastard who had abandoned her years ago. "I wouldn't be surprised if he's one of the slayers." And he was working with a woman? That made Katya's blood boil. She hadn't been good enough for him, but this bitch was? "Casimir wants them. Either they die, or we do."

Galina winced. "Well, that's a no-brainer."

Katya nodded. The night was full of surprises. She hadn't realized Galina had a brain.

Chapter 6

Emma checked the time on her cell phone. Shit.
An hour and twenty minutes had passed since she'd left
Central Park. After Angus MacKay's remark about
visiting her at home, she'd realized she was in dire
need of more ammunition. She'd taken a cab to the
federal office building in Midtown, then rushed to the
Stake-Out team's office on the sixth floor. There she'd
helped herself to several items from the armory—a
pair of silver handcuffs, some silver chains, silver bullets for her Glock, and a crate full of stakes since she
had only a handful left in her apartment.

Unfortunately, the security guards on the first floor
hadn't liked her waltzing off with so much equipment
and no requisition forms. She'd been forced to spend
fifteen minutes filling out bloody paperwork. And then
she'd had trouble finding another cab. They didn't hang
around office buildings on a Saturday night.

Now she was almost home with her stash of goodies.

She glanced at the meter on the taxi dashboard and pulled out some bills to pay the driver. She could only hope Angus MacKay hadn't beaten her to the apartment.

The driver pulled to a stop in front of her building in SoHo. The street was dark, except for little circles of light surrounding the street lamps. A few people were out, walking dogs or chatting happily with neighbors. She paid the driver and climbed from the backseat. The silver stuff had all been stuffed into a grocery sack. She set the sack on the roof of the taxi, then reached in for the crate of stakes.

As she straightened, something prickled the back of her neck and caused her to hunch her shoulders. She was being watched. Even with her psychic powers relaxed, she could feel a presence.

She glanced at the third floor of her apartment building. All the windows were covered with closed blinds. Her apartment was the third window from the left. Was that a gap between two slats? She narrowed her eyes.

The blinds flipped open. She gasped.

Angus was there!

"Hey, lady!" the cabbie yelled. "You gonna stand there all night? Shut the door."

Emma tossed the crate back into the cab, grabbed the sack off the roof, and climbed back into the cab. "Drive."

"What?" The cabbie gave her an annoyed look. "Where to?"

"Just drive. Now!"

He stomped on the accelerator.

Emma twisted to look out the back window. The

blinds had been pulled up in her apartment, and the dark silhouette of a man filled her window. She could feel his eyes on her, watching. She could feel his presence, hovering around her.

She faced front. Shit, she hated running away. But there was no way she was going to fight a vampire unprepared. And it wasn't like she could ask him to please step out for ten minutes while she set a trap to kill his ass.

His gorgeous ass. The memory of him hanging upside down sneaked into her head.

The taxi reached the end of the street. "Where to, lady?"

"Ah, turn right." Emma pounded a fist on her knee in frustration. She hated to retreat, even when it was the best choice. *Think, think.* She needed a place where she could prepare for battle in secret. Then, when she was ready, she'd invite him over.

Of course! Austin's apartment. It was close by in Greenwich Village. And it was bigger than her place. A much better place for battling a vampire.

She gave the cabbie the address. She had become good friends with Austin Erickson while he was on the Stake-Out team. After Sean had blacklisted him from any decent work, Austin had taken a construction job in Malaysia. It had to be paying really well, since he'd kept his apartment in Manhattan.

Emma had volunteered to keep an eye on it. Thank goodness. It afforded her the perfect place to set her trap. Maybe she would lure Angus into the bedroom. The bed was decorated with cast-iron spindles. It was perfect for the silver handcuffs.

And Angus—surely he would follow her into the bedroom. His attraction to her was no secret. She recalled the feel of his erection pressed against her thigh. The touch of his hand as he caressed her hip. His boast about leaving women *verra satisfied*.

She was tempted to see if that was true. He did claim to be a man of his word.

No! He wasn't a man. With a groan, Emma leaned back against the seat. A part of the battle was within herself.

The devil take it, she was getting away. Angus had been disappointed when Emma didn't answer the phone. He'd been forced to use her answering machine as a directional beacon.

Since his arrival a few minutes earlier, he'd taken the liberty of examining her tiny apartment. Nothing interesting but a handful of stakes on her coffee table with a permanent marker nearby. He could imagine her watching the telly while she labeled each stake with *Mum* or *Dad*.

He wondered if she was simply going somewhere to wait for sunrise. He'd be forced to leave before dawn. Still, he wanted to talk to her tonight. He needed to convince her once and for all to give up slaying.

He gazed out the window. Her cab had reached the end of the block. He could teleport to the corner in a second, but an elderly woman was standing there with her dog, waiting to cross the street. If he suddenly appeared beside her, she might keel over and die of fright. Or break a hip. Mortals, especially old ones, seemed so fragile. Angus spotted a dark area next to a flight of stairs leading into the corner building. He focused and teleported into the shadowed area. He felt under his sporran to make sure he was intact, then stepped from the shadow.

The cab turned right. The lady hobbled across the street, unaware of his presence. Her dog spotted him, though, and pranced about, yapping. He glared at the little terrier. *Silence.* With a whimper, the dog sidled up to the old woman.

Angus groaned inwardly. He'd always loved animals as a mortal, so it irked him when they acted terrified of him. *Not quite human.* Roman's discovery still nettled him. No wonder animals reacted poorly around him. They could sense what he hadn't realized all these years.

He watched Emma's cab driving away in the distance. It slowed to make a left turn. He zoomed after it at vampire speed and continued to follow. Whenever the cab stopped, he remained hidden. If Emma saw him, she'd lead him on a wild-goose chase all over Manhattan.

Luckily she didn't go far. The cab halted in front of an apartment building in Greenwich Village. He waited behind a delivery van while she unloaded a bag and a crate from the backseat onto the sidewalk. More stakes? He'd seen an empty crate like that at her apartment.

She paid the driver, then dug a key ring from her pants pocket. A key? She had a boyfriend. The conclusion slunk into his thoughts like a poisonous snake. He gritted his teeth as she unlocked the entrance door and carried her belongings into the foyer. A damned boyfriend. A mortal lover. Whoever he was, he wasn't good enough for her. Did he even know what she was doing at night? There was no way *he* could protect her. Angus was the only one for that job.

He clenched his fists, knowing good and well that the snake coiled in his belly had a name. *Jealousy.* He marched across the street, scowling at the glass door Emma had just entered. It would be locked now, but that wouldn't keep him out. He'd simply teleport—

Brakes squealed, and a horn blared. He spun to his left just as a taxi screeched to a halt a few inches in front of him. The devil take it! He'd nearly been run over. Not that a few broken bones would kill him, but it would have hurt like hell. The taxi driver yelled a few obscenities at him. Angus nodded in agreement. He *was* a damned fool. He'd let an alleged boyfriend get him so upset, he'd walked right in front of a moving car.

He stepped onto the sidewalk to let the taxi pass. He needed to get a grip. Emma could be staying with a girlfriend. Why would he automatically assume she had a boyfriend? Well, maybe because she was beautiful, clever, courageous, virtuous, and everything else a man could ever want.

He strode to the glass entrance door and peered inside. She'd already taken the elevator, but if he scrunched to the left, he could make out the floor lights above the elevator door. She had stopped on the fourth floor. He glanced around to see if it was safe to teleport inside.

Bugger. The cab that had nearly run him over had stopped in front of the apartment building. Two young blond women stumbled from the backseat, giggling. The taller one handed the driver some money and planted a loud smacking kiss on his cheek. This caused the shorter blonde to burst into more giggles. She waited on the sidewalk, wavering on her shiny silver stilettos that matched her sparkly silver halter top and handbag. Her shorts were pink, and across her rump, written in silver glitter, was the word *Juicy*.

Angus shuddered. He couldn't teleport into the building with these women as witnesses. He pressed into the shadows, hoping they wouldn't see him.

"Come on, Lindsey," the juicy blonde whined. "We can't stop partying now. Let's go to The Hiccup and Hook Up."

The taller blonde, Lindsey, tripped onto the sidewalk and wobbled toward them in high wedge-heeled sandals that matched her turquoise purse and T-shirt. Brown letters crossed her chest, saying CUTE IS OKAY, BUT RICH IS BETTER. She planted her fists on the strip of bare skin above her brown mini-skirt. "I am never going back to that club. The guys there are a bunch of losers! I swear all the hot guys have left town."

"I know, right?" Juicy flipped her long hair over her shoulder. "I think they all left the country."

"Yeah, I think they all went to like . . . Pittsburgh," Lindsey concluded.

Angus sighed. How long were these ladies going to stand around, talking about nothing? He realized there were hot-pink streaks in Juicy's hair. Could that cause brain damage? Hard to tell with these two. Maybe he should go ahead and teleport inside. They were so drunk, they'd never notice.

"Ooooh. Look, Tina." Lindsey careened toward her friend. "There's a hot guy behind you."

Tina, the princess formerly known as Juicy, whirled around, lost her balance, and crashed into Lindsey. They both giggled.

Angus groaned inwardly.

"Ooooh, he's yummy." Tina wove toward him.

"I saw him first." Lindsey pushed her friend, and Tina crashed into a potted plant next to the door.

"Ouch." Tina rubbed the wrong hip while she gave Angus a helpless, injured look.

"Aren't you the guy we almost ran over?" Lindsey squinted at him. "We stopped so fast, I thought I was gonna hurl."

"You wish," Tina muttered. "You only drank like ten thousand calories tonight."

Lindsey leaned toward Angus, making his eyes water from the fumes on her breath. "I love your skirt. Is it Versace?"

"'Tis called a kilt. I have a tailor in Edinburgh."

"Ooooh, you must be Irish." Tina lurched toward him. "I just love your accent."

"Actually, I'm Scottish." He tried to back up, but was already pressed against the building's brick wall.

Lindsey ran a long pink fingernail down his arm. "Would you like to come upstairs for some coffee?"

"Yeah, some Irish coffee." Tina snickered.

"You look a little hot in this sweater." Lindsay traced a knitted cable with her polished fingernail. "We could help you get more comfortable."

"It'll be fun." Tina pulled a key from her silver spangled purse and unlocked the entrance door.

Angus cleared his throat. "I do need to see someone inside this building, if ye doona mind letting me in."

"Oh, darling. We'll let you in." Lindsey gripped his arm to drag him into the foyer.

Tina punched the elevator button. "I get him first."

"Do not." Lindsey released Angus to get in front of Tina's face. "I saw him first."

Angus wandered over to the mailboxes while the two blondes argued over him. Luckily, each box was listed by number and the last name of the occupant. He examined the boxes for the fourth floor. One name looked familiar.

"I know!" Tina announced. "Let's do him together!"

They burst into giggles. The elevator door opened.

"Come on!" Lindsey called. "Irish boy! Let's go."

He frowned at them. "Would ye really let a strange man into yer apartment? I could turn out to be some kind of . . . monster."

The girls' eyes widened and they stared at him, then at each other. Then they erupted with laughter.

"Yeah, right." Tina held the elevator doors open. "I'm so scared, I think I wet my panties."

"Mine are already wet." Lindsey slunk toward him, trying to give him a sexy look through her lashes. Unfortunately, her wilted mascara stuck one of her eyes shut, and she ended up twitching and blinking to get her eye open.

"Would ye happen to know this person?" Angus pointed at the mailbox for apartment 421. "The name is Erickson."

Lindsey wrinkled her nose. "Yeah, I know him." She turned to Tina. "Remember the guy in 421? He was like . . . so rude."

"I know, right?" Tina leaned against the elevator

door. "I asked him to help me open a jar of pickles, and he said I was already pickled."

"I haven't seen him in months," Lindsey said. "But he was really cute. I swear all the hot ones have left town."

"Is his name Austin?" Angus asked.

"You're looking for Austin?" Lindsey's mouth fell open. "Oh my God, you're gay."

Angus stiffened. "Nay, I—"

"Shit! We should have known." Tina pointed at him. "I mean, look, he's wearing a purse."

" 'Tis no' a purse." Angus gritted his teeth. " 'Tis called a sporran, and 'tis a fine, manly tradition—"

"Whatever." Lindsey waved a hand in dismissal. "Why were you trying to pick us up when you're gay?"

"Yeah." Tina sneered at him. "You're just a poser."

"Yeah, he's a poser." Lindsey marched toward the elevator. "I bet he's not even Irish."

Angus heaved a sigh of relief when the elevator doors swooshed shut. Thank God he drank out of bottles and no longer had to deal with the modern, mortal world in order to survive. Courting women like Lindsey and Tina could drive a vampire to leap into the sunlight. Thank God Emma was different. She was special, clever, and lovely. And most probably, staying in Austin Erickson's apartment.

The elevator stopped at the fourth floor. Bugger. Lindsey and Tina would be floundering around that hallway for five minutes. He'd have to wait. Or maybe he should just go home. If Emma realized he knew where she was, she'd leave again. No, it was better to leave her alone. He'd teleport back to Roman's town-house and send her an e-mail, asking to see her tomorrow night. He closed his eyes, thinking of her shiny, dark hair and amber eyes, the graceful curve of her cheek and neck. *Good night, Emma. Sleep well.*

Emma dropped the crate on Austin's sofa, then took the sack of silver goodies into his bedroom. She studied the room. Yes, this would work nicely. She'd put some fresh sheets on the bed, and after sunrise, she'd go back to her apartment for her laptop and some clothes. Some sexy clothes.

She headed back through the living room to the kitchen, where she found a knife to pry open the crate.

Good night, Emma. Sleep well.

With a gasp, she fumbled the knife on the counter-top. *Angus.* She grasped the knife in her fist and whirled around. The room was empty. Of course it was. The voice hadn't been close by. It had been inside her head.

She poured psychic energy into a wall of defense. How dare he enter her mind like that? She knew it was him. The voice had kept all the qualities of Angus's voice. The deep, masculine tone, the soft lilt of his accent.

How had he managed the connection across town? Unless . . .

She dashed to the living room window and peeked through the blinds at the street below. A few pedestrians were out, but no men in kilts. She closed the blinds. Had he somehow discovered her whereabouts? She ran to the front door, flipped the locks, and looked outside.

Two blond women were teetering down the hallway, jabbering and laughing. The taller one wore brown and turquoise; the shorter one, pink and silver. They stopped a few doors down. The taller one struggled to get her key into the lock.

Emma stepped into the hall to peer around the women. She hid the knife behind her back to keep from alarming them. The hallway was empty.

The taller blonde dropped her key on the floor. "Shit!" She leaned over to pick it up and tumbled onto her face.

The shorter one giggled. "God, Lindsey, you're so smashed."

Lindsey stood and smoothed down her brown mini-skirt. "I am not smashed. I'm totally hammered."

With a shake of her head, Emma headed back into Austin's apartment.

"Let me try." The shorter blonde pushed Lindsey aside to unlock their door.

Lindsey careened into the opposite wall, then spotted Emma. "What are *you* doing? Isn't that Austin's apartment?"

"Yes. He's out of town, so I'm house-sitting for him. We're good friends." Emma started to close the door.

"Wait!" Lindsey lurched toward her. "You can't be his girlfriend. We know about Austin."

Emma hesitated.

"We know Austin's secret," the shorter one announced in a singsong voice.

They knew he'd been a spy for the CIA? "What exactly do you know?"

"We know he might as well come out of the closet."
Lindsey snickered. "Right, Tina?"

"I know, right?" Tina gave Emma a doubtful look.
"You can't be much of a friend if you didn't know he's
gay."

Emma's mouth dropped open. Why on earth would
Austin tell these women he was gay? Unless . . . "Did
either of you make a pass at him?"

Lindsey snorted. "Well, duh! The guy's totally hot."

"I tried a jillion times to get him to come inside."
Tina flipped her pink-streaked hair over her shoulder.
"He always had some kind of excuse, like his iron
was on."

Lindsey scoffed. "That is so rude."

Emma knew Austin wasn't gay. The guy had snapped
a hundred photos of a girl he was lusting for. "I'm
afraid you're mistaken about him."

"'Fraid not!" Lindsey yelled. "We have proof. We
met his boyfriend."

"Yeah, he was a total poser," Tina boasted. "He's not
even Irish."

"Yeah," Lindsey added. "His fake accent and little
skirt couldn't fool us."

Emma caught her breath. "There was a man downstairs with an accent, wearing a skirt? Was he tall with
incredibly broad shoulders, a gorgeous face with green
eyes, and long auburn hair?"

"Sheesh, don't get all worked up." Tina rolled her
eyes. "The guy won't be interested in you. He even had
a purse."

"Yeah." Lindsey nodded. "Like that's a clue."

Emma squeezed the knife in her fist. "He was downstairs in the lobby? Just now?"

"Yeah, we just saw him." Tina scratched at her pink highlights. "He kept talking about Austin."

"And he wouldn't come upstairs with us," Lindsey mumbled. "Anyone who refuses us has got to be gay."

"I know, right?" Tina nodded seriously. "'Cause we're so totally hot."

Emma took a deep breath. Angus had been downstairs. He knew where she was. "Good night, ladies." She shut the door and bolted the locks. Shit. A hell of a lot of good these locks would do. Angus could teleport inside whenever he wanted to.

Why hadn't he? Why was he leaving her alone? She strode to the sofa and pried open the crate of stakes. Damn that Angus MacKay! He could invade the apartment or her mind whenever he damned well pleased.

And if that wasn't bad enough, there was a part of her that actually *liked* the fact that he'd gone to the trouble to track her down. He was interested in her, not the blond bimbos in the hall who'd tried to pick him up. Did this mean he never took advantage of mortal women for a little nibble? Did he only take his meals from a bottle like he said? Good heavens, she was starting to believe him.

Just the fact that she was flattered by his attention was a major disaster. He was sneaking into her confidence. He was trying to burrow into her heart. Dammit, no one was allowed there.

The only way to get rid of him was to kill him. And if part of her objected to that, then it just made her decision more imperative. He had to go. He had to die before he weaseled his way into her heart.

Quickly she stashed stakes around the apartment so she could access them easily. She made up the bed and placed the silver handcuffs and chains under her pillow. She stripped down to her bra and panties and lounged on the bed, waiting. Whether he came tonight or tomorrow night, it didn't matter.

She was ready for him, and he would die.

Chapter 7

Emma woke with a start and glanced at the bedside
clock. It was almost noon. Sometime, close to dawn,
she'd fallen asleep. And Angus hadn't come.

She threw her clothes on and jogged to her apartment in SoHo. She ate a quick breakfast, took a quick
shower, then packed some clothes to take back to
Austin's place. Unfortunately, she didn't have much in
the realm of sexy. Her clothes tended to be practical
and comfortable, clothes she could fight in. She'd
never played the seductress before. Where did you
hide a stake if you were wearing nothing but lacy underwear?

She ended up tossing all her lingerie into the suitcase. She could figure out the sexy outfit later. She
wheeled her suitcase into the tiny living room.

Half a dozen stakes remained on the coffee table.
Angus had left them alone. She settled on the loveseat
in front of her laptop. Since it was Sunday, she didn't

expect many e-mails. Actually, she never had many. It was hard to maintain friendships when so much of her life was secret. She clicked on the inbox and saw one message that had been sent at four-forty-three A.M. From Angus MacKay.

Her heart took a little leap, but she quickly squelched it. Of course she found the man exciting. She was planning to kill him tonight. She took a deep breath. *Correction.* She was planning to seduce him, then kill him.

She'd never done anything so blatant before, but she felt sure Angus would do his part. He'd gotten an erection just lying next to her in the park. He was probably well experienced when it came to sex. Centuries of leaving the ladies *verra satisfied.* Not that she would ever know. She wasn't going to let it get out of hand.

She opened his message.

```
Dear Emma, I was sorry to miss you. I
was tempted to take your laptop since
it might be filled with interesting
information, and obtaining informa-
tion is what I do. I declined, though,
in hopes that you will realize I am
trustworthy.
```

Emma snorted. A trustworthy vampire?

```
I know where you are. I will meet you
at Austin Erickson's apartment Sunday
night at eight. I will not harm you.
I simply want to talk.
```

What on earth was there to talk about? Obviously, he wanted her to stop slaying. He claimed to be worried about her safety, but she suspected he was more worried about the safety of his vampire buddies. How far was he prepared to go to stop her? If she refused to stop, would he try to kill her? She almost wished he would. It would justify her plan to kill him.

And yet he claimed he meant her no harm. He'd clearly refrained from hurting her in the park. He'd refrained from attacking her last night in Austin's apartment. He claimed to drink blood from a bottle, and she'd seen him drink from a flask.

Emma closed her eyes and rubbed them. This was wishful thinking. She was attracted to him. She enjoyed talking to him, looking at him. She liked indulging in a fantasy of the brave, heroic warrior. And if he wore a kilt, so much the better.

But that's all it was. A fantasy. The reality was he'd existed for centuries by preying on innocent mortals. It was about time the tables were turned, and an innocent mortal preyed on him.

She leaned forward and typed him a message.

I'll be ready. Wear something sexy.

She held her breath and pushed *Send*.

There, it was done. She glanced at the computer clock. Three P.M. In little more than five hours, Angus MacKay would be dead.

He had worn something sexy.

Emma had been in the bathroom, applying a darker

shade of lipstick than she normally wore, when she heard him call out to her from the living room. She fluffed up her hair, wished herself good luck in the mirror, and rushed into the bedroom. A quick glance at the bedside clock confirmed it was eight P.M. He was right on time.

She'd left the bedroom door slightly ajar, and she peered into the living room. Her mouth dropped open. No kilt, no sporran. He was wearing black jeans, a tight black T-shirt, and a black duster—all sexy. His long auburn hair was tied back with a black leather cord. Her heart squeezed in her chest. Oh God, why couldn't he be human? Over five hundred years old. They just didn't make men like this anymore.

She swung the door open, and he turned to look at her. His gaze lowered, taking in her short silk bathrobe. When his eyes returned to hers, she could see the heat sizzling to life. So far, so good.

"I'm running a bit behind. I still need to get dressed." She raised her arms to prop them against the door and doorjamb. His expression remained the same. She glanced down. Shoot. She'd practiced this maneuver a dozen times in front of the mirror. Her robe was belted loosely so when she raised her arms, it was supposed to come undone and accidentally cause her robe to fall open. But no, the robe had remained closed.

"Ye look fine to me." He motioned to the leather sofa. "Have a seat and we'll talk."

She forced a smile. What a mess. The trap was in the bedroom. "I—I need to get dressed. I'm practically naked."

The corner of his mouth lifted. "I doona object."

He gestured toward the couch once more. "I'll be a gentleman."

She gritted her teeth. What was she supposed to do now? Yell at him, *You're my love slave, get in the bedroom now!* "I'm uh, really thirsty. Could you bring me a bottle of water from the fridge?"

She didn't wait to see how he would react to that. She turned and strode into the bedroom. She stopped in front of the bed and gripped the cast-iron railing of the bed's footboard. Shit. She was a lousy seductress. It just seemed wrong, somehow. Dishonest. She'd been trained, though, in her counter-terrorism classes, to expect one's hands to get dirty when fighting evil. The problem was, she hadn't seen any real proof that Angus was evil other than his status as a vampire.

She'd caught the other vampires in the act of raping and feeding. Angus had done nothing but ask to talk to her. Was his status as a vampire enough to warrant his execution? A few days ago she would have said yes. Now she wasn't sure.

"Ye wanted this?" he asked softly.

She whirled around to face him. His eyes widened.

She glanced down. Brilliant. Now her robe decided to fall open. Her lacy black panties and bra didn't conceal much. "Thank you." She stepped forward with her arm extended.

He placed the water bottle in her hand, then gazed around the room.

He suspected something, she could tell. She unscrewed the top of the bottle and took a quick gulp. "I'd offer you something to drink, too—" She winced. "Actually, no, I wouldn't."

His mouth twitched. "That's all right. I drank quite a bit before coming."

"Is it true then? You drink all your meals from a bottle?"

"Aye." His gaze drifted south and lingered. "I no longer have to seduce a woman for food. I only make love when I truly wish to." His eyes met hers, and the heat was unmistakable.

She ignored the tingling sensation sweeping over her skin. "And you no longer use mind control to get what you want?"

"I try not to."

She took another gulp of water. "I don't believe you. You invaded my mind last night."

"I did?" He looked doubtful. "I doona remember that."

"You did." She lifted her chin. "I cannot allow such a threat to continue."

"I threatened you? What did I say?"

"You . . . you wished me good night."

His mouth curled up. "Och, how insulting of me."

"That's not the point. You entered my mind without my permission."

"I dinna try to. Believe me, ye would know if I tried. Ye'd feel a blast of cold air tunneling between yer eyes. Did ye feel that last night?"

"No. But why should I believe you?"

He frowned. "Verra well. I'll show you."

A swoosh of frigid air blew toward her with enough power to knock her back a step into the footboard. She immediately strengthened her wall of defense, but still, she could feel his presence, swirling about her, seeking entrance, powerful yet restrained. A terrible suspicion crept into her thoughts. If he unleashed his full power, she might not have enough strength to withstand it. "That's enough!"

The swirling stopped. The cold dissipated.

He tilted his head, studying her. "Did ye feel that last night before I wished ye good night?"

She inhaled deeply and let it out. "No, I didn't." There was no mistaking a true psychic assault from him.

"There's only one explanation. I wasna broadcasting my thoughts, but ye picked them up. Ye're a powerful receiver."

She already knew that. She'd caught her father's last minutes in Moscow, even though she was in Edinburgh. The memory hit her like a punch to the gut. She'd seen her mother murdered through her father's eyes. Heard her father's last words before dying. *Avenge us.*

Angus stepped toward her. "Are ye all right?"

"I—no." She turned her back to him so he couldn't see the pain in her eyes. She skirted the bed and set the water bottle on the bedside table. Her father's dying words kept echoing in her head. She had to do this. She had to kill Angus MacKay.

"I should leave ye alone."

She glanced up to see Angus watching her with a confused look. He could probably tell she was upset about something. "I'd like to talk, if you don't mind." She sat on the bed, close to her pillow, and turned to face him. Her robe fell open as she rested one bent leg on the bed in front of her.

His jaw shifted. Heat blazed in his eyes as he approached her. "Are ye trying to get me in yer bed, Miss Wallace?"

Her pulse quickened. "I thought we could talk, maybe get better acquainted."

He paused beside the bed, frowning. "Ye hate vampires with a passion. They murdered yer parents, and ye've been seeking revenge ever since."

"I call it justice." She closed her eyes and rubbed her brow. Shit. She should have known he'd see through this.

"If it helps, I can tell ye that I'm having my operative in Moscow investigate the matter."

She lowered her hand. "You are? You'd do that for me?"

"I want to know who's responsible."

She stood. "Thank you. I have tried and tried to find out, using my resources in MI6, but they don't know about vampires, so there was no information."

"I'll do what I can to help ye find the culprits. I'm hoping once ye've had justice, ye can stop the slaying."

She blinked. Stop slaying?

He tilted his head, studying her. "Can ye stop, Emma?"

She sat on the bed. How could she stop when vampires were killing night after night? Didn't the other innocent victims deserve as much justice as her parents?

Angus sat beside her. "Ye have to stop. 'Tis suicidal to keep attacking an enemy who is stronger and faster than ye are."

"I've done all right so far."

"Ye canna catch them by surprise any longer. They'll

start hunting for ye in groups. Ye canna survive if several attack ye at once."

She clutched the comforter in her fist. "What if you never find the ones who murdered my parents? You think I should just give up?"

He gave her a stern look. "Aye. Ye must."

Rage simmered inside her. "And I should just let those monsters feed off people? Rape women? Murder the innocent?"

"Leave vampire justice to Vamps like me. I'm much more capable than you."

"You think you're so much tougher than me?" Emma slammed her hands against his shoulders and knocked him back onto the bed. She jumped on him, straddling his lap.

"Emma, what are ye doing?" He started to sit up, but she shoved him down, pinning his shoulders onto the bed.

His mouth curled. "Ye like to be on top? Ye only needed to say so."

She ignored him as she reached under her pillow for the silver handcuffs. They were sideways on the bed, so she couldn't lock his hands over the headboard like she had hoped. No matter.

"Is that silver?" he muttered.

She snapped a handcuff around his wrist. She grabbed his other arm to bring his hands together. Just as she clicked on the second handcuff, she heard him inhale with a hissing breath. A burning smell wrinkled her nose, and she glanced at the first wrist she'd imprisoned. The silver was sizzling against his bare skin, cooking the raw flesh into ugly red welts.

"Oh, I'm sorry." She tugged the sleeve of his duster underneath the handcuff to insulate his wrist. His other wrist was safe, the silver wrapped around his sleeve.

"Thank ye."

She detected anger and pain in his sharp green eyes, although his voice remained soft and calm. In fact, he seemed very calm for a man who was being restrained. Maybe the silver was sapping his strength like kryptonite.

"I'm no' verra experienced with such games, but shouldna ye be wearing a black leather corset and high-heeled boots? And ye forgot yer whip."

"This is not kinky sex, and you know it."

The corner of his mouth tilted. "It should be. Will ye no' honor a dying man's last wish?"

She snorted and whipped the silver chain from under her pillow.

He smiled slowly. "Yer idea of foreplay is killing me."

Unbelievable. She was getting ready to kill him, and he was amused? She crouched on the floor where his feet were dangling off the bed and wrapped the silver chain around his ankles. With his legs restrained, she stood, her legs straddling his knees. "Still think you're tougher than me?"

With a blur of speed, he sat up, looped his handcuffed wrists around the back of her neck, and pulled her forward. He fell back onto the bed, taking her with him.

Her nose bumped into his hard chest. "Oof." She breathed in the scent of cotton and soap. He smelled good and felt warm.

"Now this is more like it." His hands cradled the

back of her head. " 'Twould be grand if ye could work yer way down about ten inches."

She jerked her head up, but was stopped by his hands. She could only rest her chin on his chest while she glared at him. "Let go of me."

"Uncuff me."

"No."

His mouth twitched. "Unzip me?"

"No!"

"Emma." His expression grew serious. "If ye really want to kill me, aim for the heart. Put yer ear to my chest so ye can hear it."

She scowled at him. "You can't have a heartbeat. You're dead."

"Listen and find out."

"No." She caught his arms and pulled them over her head. He didn't struggle. She grabbed the stake from under her pillow and straddled his lap.

"Emma."

"Don't talk to me." She shoved his duster aside so only the thin cotton T-shirt covered his heart. Was it really beating under there? Did it matter? He was a vampire. He'd existed for centuries by feeding off women, controlling them, and using them.

She lifted the stake, ready to plunge downward.

She hesitated, expecting him to do something. Yell at her. Make a grab for the stake. Cover his heart. Invade her mind. Something. He just lay there, watching her with such sadness in his eyes.

She flexed her fingers around the stake. "I have to do this. You're evil."

He frowned. "I have lived a verra long time, lass,

and there's one thing I have learned. We are all capable of evil."

She squeezed the stake in her fist. This wasn't evil. It was justice. She focused on the spot above his heart. Her eyes burned. "Are you just going to lie there?"

"Are ye really going to kill me?"

She lifted her eyes to meet his. There was no hatred in them. Only sadness and compassion. "You should hate me."

"How can I? I know too well the pain of grieving. I have outlived every mortal I ever loved."

She lowered her arm and dropped the stake on the bed. "I can't do it. You—you're too human."

He winced. "That's debatable."

She leaned forward and laid her ear against his chest. The rise and fall of his chest was oddly soothing. The pounding of her own heart slowly subsided, and she relaxed against him.

"Ah, Emma." His hands gently stroked her hair. "Can ye hear me?"

The steady beat of his heart thrummed in her ear. "How can this be? I thought you were dead. Or un-dead."

"My heart beats at night. Blood flows through me so I'm able to think and talk and . . . function."

She lifted her head and realized with a small shock that his eyes had turned red. She scrambled off him. "Don't get any ideas just because I let you live."

"I could have stopped ye at any time."

"But you didn't."

"I would have, but I wanted to see if ye would go through with it."

She closed her robe and tied the belt. "And now you're going to gloat because I failed."

"Nay, lass." His eyes glimmered with emotion. "I'm verra happy that ye passed."

She stiffened. "You were testing me?"

He sat up. "I wouldna want to be attracted to a murderer."

"I'm not a murderer. You are."

His eyes narrowed. "I have killed in the past for self-defense, but never for revenge. Unlike you."

He considered himself morally superior? Anger snapped inside her. She stood and slapped him.

"The devil take it, woman. Ye're trying my patience."

"You're trying mine. How dare you judge me? You're the one who's existed for centuries by exploiting people. I should have killed you when I had the chance."

His jaw clenched. "Ye never had a chance." He stretched his hands apart, and with a snap, the chain on the handcuffs broke.

With a small gasp, Emma stepped back. Humiliation seeped into her and increased her anger. Damn him. He could have escaped all along.

He kicked off his shoes, and the chain slipped to the floor. He stood to the side of the chain and lifted his cuffed wrists. "The key?"

She motioned to the key on the bedside table and walked away. Damn him. Arrogant bloodsucker. She strode into the living room, then stood by a window, peering out onto the street.

"Emma." His voice was soft behind her.

"Please go."

He stopped beside her at the window. "I doona want ye feeling like a failure. Personally, I was verra happy ye dinna kill me."

She glanced at his wrists and noted the handcuffs were completely gone. He was wearing his shoes once again. "You could have escaped at any time."

"And missed having ye sit on my lap in yer sexy knickers? Nay, I couldna have left, even with my life in the balance."

Did he really find her that attractive, or was he just humoring her? Probably the latter. She looked out the window. "I want you to stop seeing me."

With a sigh, he leaned against the wall. "And here I was, thinking ye might have grown to like me a wee bit."

She folded her arms across her chest. "I like you enough to make an exception for you and not kill you. But I can't let that stop me from slaying other vampires."

"Lass, how many times do I have to tell ye, ye canna do any more slaying."

"You can't tell me what to do. I expect you to respect my decision and let me live my own life."

His eyes blazed with anger. "Ye willna live a week!"

"It's none of your damned business!"

"Ye're the most stubborn woman I have ever known."

"I'll take that as a compliment since I'm sure you've known thousands."

His eyes narrowed. "You doona know what ye're up

against." He glanced out the window. "Do ye see that building there?"

He was pointing at the tallest building across the street. Emma gasped when his arms suddenly surrounded her. "What are you—"

Everything went black, and she felt a swirling sensation around her. Her feet stumbled onto cold concrete, and she grabbed at his coat to steady herself.

"What?" She looked around. She was no longer in Austin's apartment.

"Look below." Angus stepped to the side.

She peered over the waist-high brick wall. The street was far below, at least fifteen stories. They were on the roof of the building Angus had pointed to. "You teleported us?" she whispered.

His arms enveloped her from behind. Slowly they rose into the air. Their feet cleared the wall.

"This is levitation," he whispered in her ear. "All I have to do is drop you over the wall."

"Stop it."

"Stop yer slaying."

She closed her eyes. "You just want to protect your own kind."

"Those murdering bastards are no' my kind." They dropped back onto the cement roof. "I'm trying to save yer life."

She pushed away from him. "By dropping me off a roof?"

He glowered at her. "By showing ye how damned easy it is to kill you!" He marched away, muttering curses under his breath.

Emma stared at him. She'd always assumed his

agenda was to save other vampires from her stakes, but now she wondered. Did he really care about her? She flinched when he pummeled a fist into the metal door that led to the stairwell. Even in the dark, she could see the dent he'd left behind.

"I'm sorry I frightened ye." He paced across the roof. "I just doona know how to get through to you."

"Why do you care what happens to me? Haven't you've seen thousands of mortals come and go?"

He stopped and looked at her. "I've never met a woman like you. Ye're different. Ye're . . . like me." He shrugged with an embarrassed look. "Well, ye're a hell of a lot better looking than me."

Emma made a face. "You think I'm like a vampire?"

"Nay, ye're a warrior. Brave and relentless. Ye spend yer nights fighting evil."

"Like . . . you?" Her fantasy man. Except she'd always expected him to be alive 24/7. A chilly breeze ruffled her silk bathrobe and she shivered.

"Och, ye're cold." He strode toward her. "Shall I take ye back?"

"How do you do it?" She glanced over the waist-high wall to Austin's apartment building. "Do you simply look at a place and then go there?"

"Aye, or I can hear a voice and go. If it's a place I've been before, I can remember the way without a beacon."

"So, in just a few seconds, you could be in London or Paris?"

"Aye. Would ye like to see?"

She blinked. "Now? I'm not exactly dressed."

"Then I know exactly where to take ye." His arms enveloped her. "Will ye go out with me, Miss Wallace?"

"What? I—" She grabbed on to him. "This isn't a date."

He smiled slowly. "I believe it is."

Everything went black.

Chapter 8

Angus materialized in a familiar place—the Parisian office of Jean-Luc Echarpe. Emma stumbled, and he steadied her. An alarm went off, one that Angus had installed himself, that she couldn't hear. Jean-Luc heard it, though, for he jumped from his desk with a dagger pointed at them.

"*Merde*." He lowered the dagger. "You should warn me when you're coming."

The door burst open and Robby MacKay dashed in, his claymore drawn. "Och, 'tis you." He hit a button by the door to turn off the alarm.

"*Bonsoir, mademoiselle*." Jean-Luc's gaze shifted to Emma. He looked her over curiously.

Angus kept an arm wrapped around her and gave his old friend a warning glare.

Jean-Luc responded with a slow smile. "*Bravo, mon ami*."

"Jean-Luc, Robby, this is Emma Wallace," Angus

announced, keeping her close to his side. "Emma, this is Jean-Luc Echarpe."

"The famous fashion designer?" Her eyes widened. "Then we are in Paris?"

"Aye." Angus motioned toward the kilted Scotsman. "This is Robby, who works for me and guards Jean-Luc. He's something like a grandson."

"We forget how many *greats* should be in front." Robby bowed. "A pleasure to meet you, miss." He gave Angus a questioning look.

No doubt, they were wondering why he was teleporting about with a mortal woman. He was usually all business. "I . . . thought I'd take Miss Wallace on a picnic. Could ye find us a basket of food, Robby?"

Robby's mouth dropped open. "You? On a picnic?"

Jean-Luc chuckled. "Ask Alberto. He'll know what to do."

"Verra well." Robby left the room with a stunned expression.

Angus winced inwardly. They acted like he'd never courted a woman before. Well, it had been a century or two. And it wasn't like he was courting Emma for romantic purposes. He merely wanted to gain her friendship and trust so they could work together against their common foe.

Then why did he still have his arm around her, claiming possession? He released her. "Miss Wallace needs . . . something to wear."

"Indeed?" Jean-Luc's eyes twinkled with mirth. "I hadn't noticed."

Emma glared at Angus and whispered, "I knew this would be embarrassing."

"Come." Jean-Luc led the way from his office. "The storeroom is downstairs. I'm sure we can find something suitable for a . . . picnic." He glanced back at Angus with a grin.

He was going to get teased about this for a hundred years, Angus realized. Showing up in the wee hours of the morning with a barefoot, half-naked mortal woman.

Jean-Luc showed them the official showroom where a handful of his latest creations were on display. Then he took them to a large room where rack after rack of clothes were stored.

"Oh my God," Emma whispered as she studied a price tag. "I can't afford this."

"Doona worry. I can."

Her eyes widened. "I can't accept a gift from you. It's against regulations."

Jean-Luc snorted. "Come, you two. That is no way to start a night of romance."

"This isn't a date," Emma insisted.

The Frenchman smiled. "How about this—I will loan you anything you want for the night, and Angus can return it later." He slanted Angus a teasing look. "As long as it is not torn."

Angus scoffed. "I'm no' going to tear her clothes."

"A pity," Jean-Luc muttered, then motioned to the racks. "Help yourself, *mademoiselle*."

"That's very kind of you." Emma wandered off.

Jean-Luc drew closer to Angus. "You old dog. I never knew you had such good taste."

Angus folded his arms across his chest. "This is business."

Jean-Luc snorted. "I wasn't born yesterday."

"I mean it. I'm gaining her confidence so she'll stop slaying."

Jean-Luc's mouth dropped open. "She's slaying vampires?"

Angus nodded. "Doona be fooled by her sweet face and beautiful body. She's a fierce and clever warrior."

Jean-Luc regarded Angus in silence.

Angus arched a brow. "What?"

Jean-Luc shrugged. "Nothing." He turned away, then muttered, "First Roman, and now you."

"There is nothing happening between us."

"Right." Jean-Luc patted him on the back. "I wish you two the best."

Angus snorted and walked away. Jean-Luc was making too much of this. He located Emma three racks down. She was studying some black dress pants.

Pants? Why did she always cover up her lovely legs? Something in a golden-amber color caught his attention and he grabbed it off the rack. "I like this. It reminds me of your eyes."

She gave it a dubious look. "It's a dress. A gorgeous dress, but I don't wear dresses."

"Sweetheart, this is no' a karate tournament ye're going to. 'Tis a picnic."

"A picnic in Paris, wearing designer clothes?" She shook her head. "It's all a bit hard to believe." She stepped closer. "Are those other guys vampires, too?"

"They're my friends, Emma. Are ye planning to kill them?"

"No, I'll behave." She swatted his arm. "Besides, where would I hide stakes in my underwear?"

He smiled. "I could pat ye down just to be safe."

"That doesn't sound very safe."

He chuckled and handed her the dress. "Will ye try it?"

Ten minutes later, she was looking grand in the golden dress with a pair of sparkly golden sandals.

Robby had their basket of food ready. He grinned, but wisely kept his mouth shut.

Jean-Luc liked to live more dangerously. "Enjoy your date," he called after them as they headed for the front door.

Angus shot him a glare that promised retaliation in the near future. Jean-Luc merely laughed.

They emerged from Jean-Luc's studio onto the Champs-Elysées. The street was lit up and noisy, even at four in the morning. The Arc de Triomphe gleamed in the distance.

Emma grinned. "This is great! Sure beats sitting on a plane for eight hours."

"Aye." Angus pointed at lights in the distance. "That looks like a good spot."

"The Eiffel Tower?"

"Aye." He wrapped an arm around her. "Hold on."

Blackness swirled around them for a few seconds, then melted away. They were standing on the top level of the Eiffel Tower, looking down at the City of Lights.

Emma peered over the railing. "This is cool." She hugged herself. "But a bit chilly."

"Here." Angus offered her his coat. While she put it on, he flipped open the tartan blanket Robby had placed on top of the basket.

Emma sat and rummaged through the basket. "Wow, real food." She removed bread, cheese, and grapes. A bottle of wine. "I hope there's something in here for you."

He found a bottle. "This is for me." He popped the cork. Foam bubbled out, so he held the bottle to the side.

"It looks like champagne." Emma handed him a glass.

" 'Tis called *Bubbly Blood*, a mixture of champagne and synthetic blood." He filled the glass. "Would ye like some?"

"No way." She watched him curiously as he drank. "I've seen the commercials for Fusion Cuisine on DVN, but I thought it was a joke 'cause I've seen vampires feeding off humans."

"Those are the Malcontents who refuse to drink from bottles. They enjoy torturing mortals." Angus opened her bottle of wine. "They're our sworn enemies. We've been fighting them for centuries."

"Then Shanna Whelan's claim is correct? There are two factions of vampires?"

"Aye." He filled her glass with wine. "Ye see, Emma, we share a common enemy, the Malcontents. And our goal is the same, too—protecting the innocent." He handed her the glass. "We should be . . . good friends."

She accepted the glass. "I'll have to think about it."

"I understand." He leaned back against the grill-work. "Ye were just trying to kill me an hour ago."

She nibbled on some cheese. "I'm struggling with

this idea of good vampires. I suppose Jean-Luc and Robby are like you?"

"Aye. Robby is a descendant of mine. I found him dying on the field at Culloden." Angus closed his eyes briefly. "I lost so many of my family that day."

"I can't imagine witnessing something so horrific." Emma shuddered.

"Ye witnessed yer parents' murder, did ye no'?"

She flinched. "I don't want to talk about it." She sipped some wine. "Tell me about yourself. When were you born?"

"In 1480."

"And you have descendants? So you . . . were married?"

"Aye. Three children." Angus quickly changed the subject. "I was mortally wounded at Flodden Field in 1513. Roman found me that night. I was barely alive. I thought I was dreaming when I heard this voice asking me if I was willing to continue the fight against evil. I thought it was an angel. I said yes." He smiled. "And not just because I wanted into heaven. I was pissed about dying so young. I really wanted to do more."

"Were you upset when you realized you were a vampire?"

He shrugged. "I was a bit surprised. I dinna know such creatures existed. But I never felt bad about it like Roman. I realized early on that death hadna changed me. I was still the same, only much better."

She threw a grape at him. "Vampire arrogance."

He smiled. " 'Tis only the truth. We can do things a mortal could never do."

"You can't go out in the sun."

"But we can live for centuries."

She pulled off a hunk of bread. "Tell me about the past—places you went, people you met."

Angus launched into some of his favorite stories about meeting Mary, Queen of Scots, and hiding Bonnie Prince Charlie. Emma was full of questions, and he enjoyed seeing how comfortable she now was in his presence. She was able to laugh with him and tease him.

After an hour, he corked his half-empty bottle of Bubbly Blood and set it in the basket. "I'm afraid dawn will come soon, and we need to go."

"All right." She gathered up the remnants of her meal and returned them to the basket. "I . . . hate to admit it, but I really enjoyed this."

"You mean our date?"

She shot him an irritated look. "This is not a date."

He chuckled. "I'm satisfied as long as ye know I'm no' yer enemy. Ye can trust me." He'd enjoyed it, too. More than any evening he could remember.

She stood and brushed bread crumbs off his coat.

He jumped up and folded the blanket.

"I made a mistake." She folded her arms, frowning. "I got carried away, listening to all your stories about the past."

He placed the blanket in the basket. "There was nothing wrong with that."

She shook her head. "I should have gathered more information about the Malcontents. I should have found out where you're holding Shanna Whelan."

"Holding her? She's a happily married woman."

"My boss thinks she's been brainwashed. His first priority is to rescue her."

Angus snorted. "She's perfectly happy where she is. Is it that hard to believe a mortal woman can love a vampire?"

Emma's eyes widened.

Angus swallowed hard. Deep inside, a need was growing. An impossible desire. He wanted what Roman had. The love of a mortal woman.

Emma picked up the basket. "How do we get down from here?"

"Ye let me hold you." He stepped closer. "And ye hold on to me."

She smiled nervously. "Or we could always take the stairs."

He wrapped his arms around her. "It will only take a moment."

She looked sad as she looped an arm around his neck.

Blackness enveloped them for a mere second, then they were standing on the ground in front of the Eiffel Tower.

Emma released him. "Thank you, Angus."

He stepped back. "Ye're welcome."

They strolled silently down the gravel path in the small park. Angus frowned. The atmosphere of friendship they'd shared during the picnic had melted away. The air between them seemed strained and sad. As if something was missing. As if friendship wasn't enough. He glanced at her, wondering if she felt it, too.

A noise came from behind some bushes. Angus halted. Emma stopped beside him with a questioning look. She'd probably not heard it yet. He raised a finger to his lips and eased forward. She stayed beside him.

More noises emanated from the bush. A grunting noise. A female gasp. A French Malcontent, possibly, attacking an innocent woman. Angus leaned over to retrieve a knife from under his sock. He motioned to Emma to stay behind him.

With an annoyed look, she shook her head.

Stubborn woman. But he admired her bravery. She set down the picnic basket and retrieved the wine bottle. Holding it upside down in her fist, she went to the left. He headed around the right side of the bushes.

He jumped out. "Release her and back away!"

Emma leaped into position.

Angus winced. They'd interrupted a couple making love. Emma was standing at their feet, rather his feet, since the woman's feet were wrapped around the man's bare rump. Angus was by their heads, his dagger pointed at the man.

With a gasp, the man scrambled off the woman. He grabbed his discarded pants to cover up his crotch. He yelled something in French about a *voleur*, then yanked his wallet from his pants and tossed it at Angus's feet.

Angus ignored the wallet, for he'd noticed something awful. The woman had pantyhose wrapped around her reddened neck. "I should gullet you! Ye're strangling this puir woman."

The man motioned to the woman on the ground, who was busily covering herself up with the man's shirt. They both babbled in French so fast, Angus had trouble understanding.

But the evidence was clear. "Ye're strangling her!" Angus stepped toward the man, his knife aimed at the man's face.

"Good heavens," Emma whispered.

"Don't hurt us, please," the woman gasped in accented English as she unwound the hose from her neck.

"Hurt you?" Angus gave her a baffled look. "I'm trying to save yer life. This bastard was choking you."

"I asked him to!" The woman glared at Angus, then at Emma.

"We should go." Emma motioned for Angus to follow her.

"Nay! I canna leave a defenseless woman with a strangler."

The man and woman cursed profusely.

"Angus!" Emma grabbed his arm and pulled. "Come on."

"But—" He glanced back at the French couple, who were still hurling curses at them. "Is it safe to leave her?"

"Yes." Emma retrieved the basket and hurried down the gravel path, tugging him along with her. "He isn't going to kill her. At least, I hope he won't."

"But he was choking her."

"She asked him to." Emma let go of his arm and fiddled with the basket. "They do it for . . . an erotic thrill. The choking causes heightened responses during sex. She'll have a bigger orgasm, I suppose. Not that I would know, but that's what I've read about it."

He halted. "She asked him to hurt her?"

"Yes."

Angus was stunned. He stared at Emma in disbelief, then strode down the path.

Emma followed him. "Are you all right?"

He shook his head and quickened his stride.

"The woman will be all right. It really was consensual."

With a growl, Angus tossed his knife. It embedded with a *thunk* into a tree. "I doona understand." He marched toward the tree. "I have lived too long. I no longer understand this world."

"I know it's a bit weird, but people do strange things—"

"Nay!" He ripped the knife from the tree. "A man should never harm a woman. Not even if she begs him to. There is no honor in hurting a woman!"

"Well, I—"

"I canna believe it." He leaned over and stuffed his knife into the sheath around his calf. "If a man loves a woman, how can he bear to harm her?" He jerked his jeans down over the sheath, then straightened. "How could he do that to her?"

Emma shrugged. "She asked him to."

"Why? What kind of man would pleasure his woman by hurting her?" Angus paced across the path. " 'Tis a man's duty, nay, his privilege, to give his woman all the pleasure she can bear. She should be panting and writhing with pleasure."

Emma remained silent, staring at him. Did she not believe him?

He walked toward her. "A real man would take all night if need be to make sure his woman was fully sated. She should be screaming that she canna endure any more."

Emma's eyes widened.

"It should be a man's greatest pleasure to see his woman shuddering in the throes of passion."

She took a deep breath and shifted her weight from one foot to another.

He paced back and forth. "Only when she is begging for him, should a man see to his own needs. And he should never, ever harm her." He stopped in front of her. "Am I totally wrong in this?"

"No," she squeaked.

His eyes narrowed as he studied her face. "Och, lass, ye shouldna look at me like that."

"I'm not looking." She turned away. Her cheeks flushed with pulsing blood. Her heart was racing, he could hear it.

"Emma."

"I think we'd better get back home." She looked at him, her eyes glimmering with desire.

He stepped closer. "Yer heart is pounding."

"Your eyes are turning red."

"Ye'll have to face the facts, Emma. This is a date." He touched her cheek.

The picnic basket she was holding tumbled to the ground. With a low growl, he pulled her into his arms and lowered his mouth to hers.

He wrenched every ounce of pleasure from the kiss. He tasted Emma's lips, skimmed them with his tongue, and nibbled them till every curve and texture were embedded in his memory for all time. He held her tightly so he'd know exactly where her breasts pressed against him. He smoothed his hands down her back to learn the exact curve of her spine, the delicious way it sloped inward and then flared out again at her hips.

He nibbled down her neck. Her pulse throbbed just beneath her tender skin, filling his senses with the fragrance of blood and desire. Her breath puffed against his cheek in tiny, feminine gasps. Her sweet body melted against him. The scents, the sounds, and the sensations clouded his brain till he could no longer think, only feel joy, passion, and a hunger that demanded more and more.

With a groan, he returned to her mouth and demanded entrance. She opened without hesitation, and that moment of surrender sent a surge of heat to his groin. He'd been struggling with arousal since she'd first straddled his lap that evening. And now, with her soft and compliant in his arms, and her tongue touching his own, he began to ache with need.

He planted his hands over her sweetly rounded arse and ground her hard against his erection. She broke the kiss with a gasp. The look of alarm in her eyes should have warned him, but he was too hazy with lust to take heed.

"I want to make love to ye, Emma."

Chapter 9

"No." She pushed against his shoulders. Make love? With the Undead? Although she had to admit there was nothing dead about the erection pressing against her. And there was nothing truly objectionable about Angus. God help her, if he were human, she'd have stripped him naked by now. But dammit, he wasn't. He was a vampire.

She stepped back. "I—I can't."

"I'm no' yer enemy." His eyes still glowed red. "Do ye no' trust me now?"

"I do, I think." She rubbed her brow. "But we're just barely friends. It's a big jump to being . . . lovers."

"Friends doona kiss like that."

"We got carried away, that's all. It—it was just a kiss."

He frowned. "One hell of a kiss. Shall I give ye a reminder?"

"No." She whirled around and picked up the basket.

"Like you said, dawn is approaching. And we need to take this food back, and the dress I'm wearing, and get back to New York." She was talking too fast, anything to keep from thinking about what she'd done.

"Emma."

She took a deep breath and faced him. The glow in his eyes had faded to a dull pink. Thank God. "Are you ready to go?"

"I want to know how ye're feeling."

She forced a laugh. "Well, that's not very manly, is it? What man wants to talk about feelings?"

"I know ye have feelings. Ye loved yer parents greatly, and ye feel passionate about yer work."

"Please." She lifted a hand. "I don't know what to feel. Or think. I can't even believe I did that. I shouldn't have."

He regarded her sadly. "Lass, we've been headed down this road from the beginning."

"No, we're too different. We can't possibly . . ."

"I've always done what I felt in my heart was right, yet I have my share of regrets." His mouth tilted in a crooked smile. "You would not be one of them."

Her heart ached in her chest. Oh God, he was everything she'd ever wanted in a man. Except for the part about being undead. Or immortal. How could she possibly get around that?

"Have I at least convinced ye to give up slaying? Do ye believe that I care for yer safety?"

"I—I have to think about it." She raised a hand when he started to object. "I know you care. And I'll be more careful. I'll be more discerning now that I know some of you are noble and kind."

He nodded. "That is, at least, some progress. And ye should know that I will always seek to protect you. I will always be here for you."

Her eyes burned with unwanted tears. She hadn't heard words like that in years. Not since the last of her family had died. "I have to be honest with you. If I discover the bastards who murdered my parents, I will go after them."

"And I'll be there beside you." He extended a hand. "Deal?"

"Deal." She shook his hand.

He pulled her into his arms and kissed her brow. "Let's go."

She grabbed on to him as everything went black.

Bugger. He was falling for her fast. During his four hundred and ninety-three years as a vampire, his kisses had rarely been for pleasure. There had always been a dinner to gain or something to prove. Kissing Emma had not been spurred by lust for blood or prestige. It was Emma herself who had pulled him in.

And what a kiss. You would think a man his age would have hundreds such moments to recall. But instead of becoming commonplace, such moments had become more rare.

When he dropped Emma off at Austin's apartment, she insisted he leave her be. He still worried that she nursed regrets. Hell, he had some doubts himself. Not about his feelings. He knew he cared deeply for Emma. He just didn't know if it was fair to woo her when he was undead. How could such a relationship work?

After making her promise not to go out hunting

alone, he teleported to Roman's townhouse. The alarm went off the second he materialized in the foyer.

Connor rushed in from the parlor, his claymore drawn, while at the same time, Ian dashed in from the kitchen.

"Och, 'tis you." Ian turned and headed back into the kitchen. "Ye should learn to call first."

Angus watched Connor sheathing his sword. "Why are ye here? Ye should be guarding Roman and Shanna."

Connor gave him an exasperated look. "They're here. Ye dinna show up for Mass, so we all came here to see you."

"Mass?" Angus winced. "I . . . forgot. I was busy."

"So we heard." Connor's mouth twitched. "Jean-Luc called about an hour ago with an interesting story."

"Bugger." Angus frowned. Now the teasing would begin. "I have some work to do upstairs."

"Angus, I can hear you," Roman shouted from the parlor. "Come on in."

Connor chuckled as Angus trudged toward the open double doors of the parlor. Three maroon couches surrounded three sides of a square coffee table. The fourth side was taken up with a huge wide-screen television that was turned off.

"Here's Angus," Connor announced as he entered the parlor. He strolled to the couch on the right where Gregori sat.

"What?" Gregori stared at Angus, dumbfounded. "What happened to his skirt?"

Connor cuffed Gregori on the head before sitting down.

"Ouch. See what I put up with, Father?" Gregori muttered to the elderly man on the middle couch.

"I shall pray for you," the priest answered, smiling. He stood and greeted Angus.

"Father Andrew." Angus bowed his head to the priest he recognized from Roman's wedding. "How are you?"

"My life has become much more interesting since the night I took Roman's confession."

Angus nodded, then noticed Shanna struggling to get up from the couch on the left. She was huge. As he watched Roman assist his pregnant wife to her feet, a memory flashed from long ago. Joy and pride on the birth of his three children. Worry and guilt over the labor his wife had endured. And then pain and betrayal when he'd tried to return to them after the Battle of Flodden Field. He'd felt sure his wife would understand his new undead status.

She had not. She'd forbidden him to ever see his children again. In anger, he'd disobeyed and watched them grow over the years. And watched them die.

If he pursued Emma, wouldn't he be asking for that same pain and despair all over again? He would have to watch her die. If they had mortal children, using Roman's scientific technique, he would have to witness their deaths, too.

"Are you all right?" Roman asked quietly as he gave Angus a quick hug.

Angus noted the sharpening of Roman's eyes. Bugger. Roman could always see right through him. "Could we talk later?"

"Of course." Roman stepped aside for his wife.

"Angus, it's so good to see you." Shanna kissed his cheek.

"Ye're looking grand, lass."

She laughed. "More like *mucho grande*."

"She's about to pop," Gregori muttered, then winced when Connor elbowed him in the ribs.

"I feel like bursting." Shanna rubbed her enormous belly. "The baby's already dropped."

"We've decided to induce labor this Friday night." Roman guided her back to the couch. "That way, we can be sure the Vamp doctors will be awake and ready."

"Ye have more than one doctor?" Angus asked as he rounded the middle couch to take a seat next to the priest.

"Two, just to be safe. I'm not taking any chances." Roman helped Shanna sit.

"You worry too much." She settled on the couch. "This baby is perfectly fine."

Roman sat beside her, frowning. "I've prepared a delivery room at Romatech. Just in case."

In case the bairn wasn't human? Angus could understand Roman's reluctance to have Shanna deliver in a mortal hospital.

Shanna shook her head. "I'm telling you, this baby is perfectly normal. It kicks me during the day as much as night."

"I agree," Father Andrew said. "I've been praying, and I have a very good feeling about this child."

"Thank you. Gregori's mother said the same thing." Shanna took Roman's hand and smiled at him. "And you know Radinka is never wrong."

Father Andrew turned toward Angus. "Roman has been telling me some fascinating things about you."

"All lies, for certain."

The priest smiled. "Then you weren't knighted for heroism during World War II?"

Angus shrugged. "That was over sixty years ago."

"Aye, and he's been a coward ever since," Connor added with twinkling eyes.

Angus gave his old Scottish friend an annoyed look while everyone laughed.

Ian marched into the room with a tray full of drinks. He set the tray on the coffee table and handed a glass of ice water to Shanna, then a glass of wine to the priest. All the Vamps helped themselves to an empty glass.

Connor grabbed the bottle of Blissky and poured himself a drink. "Grand stuff, Roman." He passed the bottle to Gregori.

Gregori filled his glass to the brim, then passed the bottle to Angus.

"I'm glad you like it." Roman accepted the bottle next, then passed it on to Ian.

Connor stood, raising his glass in the air. "To Shanna, Roman, and the bairn. May ye be healthy and happy."

Everyone murmured in agreement and drank.

"What have you been up to, Angus?" Shanna asked. "We heard you went on a picnic."

The male Vamps snickered.

Angus glared at them. "It was business. I've been trying to talk sense into the vampire slayer."

Connor snorted. "Talk sense to a female? That's doomed from the beginning."

Shanna huffed. "Excuse me."

"Begging yer pardon." Connor raised a hand in peace. "Unfortunately, this particular female works for yer father, and I'm certain he's poisoned her mind against us."

"Probably so." Shanna nodded, then turned to Angus. "Would you like me to talk to her? She might listen to another mortal."

"I'm doing fine," Angus grumbled. "I can handle it."

"There's no reason for ye to do it alone," Connor said.

Angus shot him an irritated look. "I'm doing well. We made a great deal of progress tonight."

Gregori snorted with laughter. "Yeah, we heard. She was barefoot and half—ouch." He glared at Connor, who'd elbowed him in the ribs.

"Did ye convince her to stop slaying?" Connor asked.

Angus shrugged. "Somewhat. She trusts me now." He glanced down to make sure his long coat covered up the bulge in his pants. His erection had gone down quite a bit, but the jeans were still uncomfortably tight. He should have worn his kilt.

"There's something different about you." Roman studied Angus. "I know. You're not carrying your claymore. That's highly unusual."

Angus shrugged. "I could hardly convince her I mean no harm if I was armed."

"Well, I think it's sweet," Shanna announced. "A picnic in Paris in the spring. Very romantic. I'm proud of you."

Angus gulped down some Blissky, too aware of the amused glances from the male Vamps in the room.

"Are you injured?" Father Andrew gestured to Angus's wrist, which was still red and raw with welts.

"I had an encounter with a pair of silver handcuffs," Angus grumbled. "Nothing I couldn't handle."

Gregori sat forward, his eyes twinkling. "She handcuffed you? Boy, she's hot."

Angus glowered at him.

Connor frowned. "That doesna sound like progress to me."

"I think you should let me talk to her," Shanna insisted.

"No." Roman shook his head. "If you arrange a meeting with Miss Wallace, she might let your father know, and he would try to kidnap you."

Shanna sighed.

"Roman's right," Angus said. "Emma told me that rescuing you is your father's top priority. She's starting to trust me, but that trust is verra new. She only learned tonight about the difference between Vamps and Malcontents, and she's still struggling with the idea that some of us can be decent folk."

"You know what, guys?" Gregori set his drink on the table. "This is a marketing problem."

Angus scoffed. "I'm no' selling anything."

"But you are," Gregori insisted. "You're trying to sell the idea that good Vamps really do exist. The problem is, we don't have a product name to differentiate ourselves from the bad vampires."

"But we *are* vampires," Angus countered. "And I doona claim to be good."

"But you have a good heart," Father Andrew said.

"There is a world of difference between you and a Malcontent."

"I think Gregori's on to something." Shanna sipped her ice water. "The Malcontents have a name, the True Ones. Why don't you guys have a name, too?"

"Hmm." Gregori lounged back against the sofa cushions. "A name." He contemplated the ceiling with narrowed eyes. "How about Nonbiters? Bottle Guzzlers? Friendly Fangsters? Ouch! That was my foot." He glared at Connor.

"I know." Connor glared back. "Ye made the mistake of calling me friendly."

While everyone laughed, Roman stood and motioned to Angus to join him. Angus rose and strode to the door.

"I've got it!" Shanna announced. "Fang-free and proud to be me!"

Roman chuckled as he motioned to the room across the foyer. Angus sauntered into the library, a room with bookshelves on three sides of the room and a large curtained window on the wall adjoining the street.

Roman shut the double doors, then took a seat in one of the leather wingback chairs by the window. Angus strolled about the room. He could feel his friend waiting but hardly knew how to begin. He'd always been better with a sword than with words. In fact, his words tended to cut just as sharply. He wandered along the bookshelves, looking at books without really seeing them.

Finally he stopped. "I . . . I had a mortal wife and children."

"I remember that," Roman said quietly.

"My wife . . . rejected me and remarried, since to her way of thinking, I was already dead."

"That must have hurt."

"It did." Angus paced about the room. "But in time, I realized she was right. A marriage between a mortal and a vampire canna work."

Roman remained silent.

"Even after my wife's betrayal, it pained me to see her grow old and die. And seeing my children die was more than any man should bear."

Roman's mouth thinned. "You feel compelled to tell me this now? When my son is about to be born?"

"I doona wish ye any ill will, Roman. Ye're like a brother to me. I just doona want ye to endure the pain that I did."

Roman sighed. "I knew when I married Shanna that I could lose her. But Angus, she has brought me great joy. Should I turn my back on all that happiness for fear of what could happen down the road?"

"Ye're a braver man than I." Angus continued to pace. "Shanna is a loving soul, understanding of our condition. Yet still, she doesna want to become one of us."

"I'm glad she chose to remain mortal. We couldn't be having a child now, if she were undead. And once the baby is born, she can be there for him during the day. As much as I would love to have Shanna with me for all eternity, I must put the needs of my child first."

Angus frowned. "I heard about our DNA mutation, that we're no longer quite human."

"And you're concerned about the baby? We all are, but there's nothing to be done now. It's in God's hands."

A half-vampire baby? Angus resumed his pacing. "Shanna is no' upset over this?"

Roman smiled. "She's the least upset of any of us. She's very happy and excited."

"Ye're a fortunate man. No' many women would be as understanding as she." Angus raised a hand to look at a book, then spotted the red welts on his wrist. The injury would heal during his daily death-sleep, but the worry in his heart would remain. "Most women wouldna be able to love a vampire."

There was a long pause when he could feel Roman watching him. *Bugger.* He'd probably said too much.

Roman cleared his throat. "You're convinced a relationship between a mortal and a vampire cannot work?"

Angus nodded, avoiding Roman's eyes.

"Why do I get the feeling you're not referring to Shanna and me?"

The devil take it. Angus turned his back to Roman and pretended to be studying book titles. Footsteps approached.

Roman leaned a shoulder against the bookshelf. "The slayer?"

Angus took a deep breath and nodded. "The relationship is a wee . . . volatile."

Roman smiled. "I wouldn't expect anything less from you."

"I dinna expect to feel this way." Angus paced away. "What is wrong with me that I keep falling for the enemy?"

Roman folded his arms across his chest. "If you're referring to Katya, she purposely seduced you."

"Nay, I pursued her."

"She let you think that, Angus. You wanted to re-form her, but all along, she's was trying to change you, trying to make you one of her evil cohorts."

"I failed her."

"No. She never intended to change, Angus. She used you."

Was that true? Angus resumed his pacing about the room. If Roman was right, then he'd been a fool to ever involve himself with Katya. And now was he being a fool again? "The devil take it. I keep repeating the same mistake, falling for the woman most likely to destroy me."

"Not necessarily. Katya has an evil heart. I don't know the slayer, but I doubt she's evil."

"Nay, Emma's brave and good. She's been risking her life to protect the innocent."

"How does she feel about you?"

Angus swallowed hard. "She hates vampires with a passion, but she—I think she could like me."

"I'm sure she can if she spends more time with you."

"I kissed her."

Roman's eyes widened. "She didn't object?"

"That's what has me confused." Angus strode to the window and sat. "She kissed me back like she was en-joying it, but now she wants to stay away from me and act like it dinna happen."

Roman frowned. "She's conflicted."

"So am I." Angus rested his head in his hands. "I

should leave her alone. But I don't dare leave her un-protected. If the Malcontents catch her, they'll kill her for certain. I swear that would kill me."

"Then you must continue to protect her," Roman concluded.

Angus nodded. "I *will* protect her. But I'll keep my distance. No more kissing. I willna risk a situation that could break my heart. Or break hers."

Roman frowned. "Very well."

"Ye doona approve?"

Roman shrugged. "It's not my decision. I just hope you're not throwing away something wonderful."

Angus shook his head. "Even if she could care for me, how could it possibly work?"

"Some things you have to risk on faith." Roman gave him a pointed look. "Believe me, old friend, some things are worth the risk."

In her office in Brooklyn, Katya read the lengthy e-mail from Galina one more time. Galina had teleported to Paris on Saturday night, then to the Ukraine on Sunday. She'd traveled with two vampire lovers, Burien and Miroslav, and the three of them had taken control of the minds of the nearby villagers they were feeding on. The village men were put to work, repairing Galina's manor house and preparing the prison cell for the vampire slayers and Angus MacKay.

Katya clenched her fists. It was about time Angus MacKay had been made to suffer.

A knock sounded on the door. Alek strode inside, carrying a brown bag. "Phineas came through for us."

He set the bag on Katya's desk. "He found the drugs you needed."

Katya peeked inside the bag. Excellent. She'd be able to make two dozen new doses of nightshade. "Thank you, Alek. How is the hunt for the slayers coming?"

Alek winced. "There was no sign of them tonight. I don't know how we can catch them if they've stopped hunting for us."

"Then make them start hunting again. Make them so angry, they have to come after you."

Alek gave her a blank look.

"It's simple, my dear." Katya patted his cheek. "All you have to do is kill some mortals."

Chapter 10

Emma dragged herself to work Monday evening. After her *date* with Angus, she'd been unable to sleep well. Each time she dozed off, her mind and body betrayed her and replayed that glorious kiss. Then she'd wake up and refuse to think about it.

Instead, she considered the new idea of good Vamps versus the Malcontents. She'd heard Austin say that Shanna Whelan insisted there were two different kinds of vampires, but Emma had dismissed that as brainwashing. Any woman married to a vampire would want to think he was good.

Emma also knew that Austin had befriended one of the female vampires during the taping of the reality show. He must have gone through the same learning process she was going through now. And there was no way Austin had been brainwashed. He had the strongest psychic power ever registered at the CIA.

She wasn't sure what exactly had happened to Austin. She only knew that he and Sean had argued, then Austin quit and Sean blacklisted him from any government job. Ever since then, Sean was suspicious of all of them and more paranoid than ever.

When Emma strode into the conference room for the usual seven P.M. meeting, her two fellow team members were already there.

Alyssa frowned at her. "Are you all right?"

With a sigh, she realized she'd done a poor job of covering the dark circles under her eyes. She sat in a chair next to Alyssa. "I haven't been sleeping well."

"Too much partying, huh?" Garrett slurped coffee from a cup that boasted *Too Hot to Handle*.

While pretty-boy Garrett launched into another chapter of his romantic conquests, Emma tuned him out. She didn't believe half of it, and besides, the last thing she wanted to think about was romance.

Who in their right mind would kiss a vampire? She was lucky she didn't end up with a pierced tongue. And even crazier than that—she'd enjoyed it! Good heavens, what a kiss. Her face burned, just thinking about it.

"Emma," Alyssa whispered. "Are you sure you're not ill? You look awfully flushed."

"I'm . . . super." She sat up straighter when her boss strode into the room and slammed the door behind him.

Sean Whelan, their team leader, looked even angrier than usual. He marched to the head of the table and set down his laptop. "It's been ten months since my daughter was kidnapped by those vicious demons. Ten months! They've probably drained her dry by now and turned her into one of them."

Not if they drank synthetic blood from bottles like Angus. Emma had been told just the night before that Shanna was happy, but she knew Sean would never believe it. Her friendship with Angus was going to put her in an awkward position at work. This must have been what had happened to Austin. She'd try e-mailing him to see what else he had learned.

"Garrett, I want you to continue watching the Russians," Sean ordered. He turned to Alyssa. "How is your research going on Romatech?"

"Very well," Alyssa answered. "I've learned the names of the vampire employees by running their license plates. I'm unable to go inside, of course, due to their security measures, but last week I successfully hacked into their mainframe."

"Excellent!" Sean leaned forward. "Did you learn anything about Shanna? I need to know where she's living."

Alyssa winced. "There was nothing personal in the files about Draganesti or your daughter. But I did find a list of cities and towns where they're shipping the Vampire Fusion Cuisine. Obviously, those must be locations where vampires exist. I'd like to go investigate."

Emma frowned. Those vampires were all drinking their meals from bottles. They belonged to the good camp, and yet they were the ones ending up on Sean Whelan's database of vampires to be eliminated.

Sean sighed. "All right. But I still want someone watching Romatech. My daughter's been seen there several times. I'm hoping someone can manage to follow her to her new home." Sean glanced at Emma. "Can you take over while Alyssa's out of town?"

"Yes." Although Emma was no longer sure she wanted to find Shanna. What if the woman was truly happy? But how could a marriage work out between a mortal and a vampire?

"Damned bloodsuckers," Sean muttered as he searched through a file on his laptop.

As she had many times before, Emma wondered if her boss had been bitten. She'd suspected several times that he must have been the victim of a vampire attack. His hatred was so intense.

She'd considered telling him a few times about her slaying activities. In theory, she knew he would understand. But she also knew how obsessed he was with finding his daughter. He'd be furious that she hadn't interrogated the vampires before killing them. But how could she? The only way she managed to kill them was to take them by surprise.

With a sigh, she realized the point was now moot. It looked like she was going to have to retire from slaying for a while. If what Angus said was true, and the Malcontents were going to hunt in groups, then she needed to take a break.

"Here it is." Sean turned his laptop screen to face them. "I was watching Draganesti's house Friday night and spotted someone new. Anyone recognize this guy?"

The blood drained from Emma's face as she watched the surveillance video. There on the sidewalk, approaching Roman Draganesti's house, was Angus MacKay. That was the first night she'd met him, when she'd thought he was a gorgeous and mysterious human. If only he were.

"Another Scotsman in a kilt," Alyssa murmured. "Aren't there several living in Draganesti's house?"

"I wouldn't call it *living*, but yes." Sean pointed at the claymore on Angus's back. "This one is different. He's heavily armed, as you can see."

"He looks like one of the Scottish guys we saw in Central Park," Garrett said. "You know, that night when the Russians vampires were there. I saw a bunch of guys in kilts, but they all look the same to me."

Emma shook her head. How could anyone ever forget meeting Angus MacKay? She watched him on the computer screen as he climbed the steps to Draganesti's townhouse. He paused at the top, looked around, then vanished.

"Whoa," Garrett whispered. "He's definitely a vampire."

Emma sighed. Yes, he was, and if she was smart, she'd stay far away from him. He was much too tempting.

"Well, Wallace? What do you say?"

Emma jumped when she realized Sean was watching her. "Pardon?"

"You watch the vampire *Nightly News* every night," Sean said. "Ever seen this Scotsman before?"

She carefully kept her face blank. "I've never seen him on the news." That much was true.

Sean crossed his arms. "You've never seen him at all?"

"No." Heat crept into her cheeks. What was she doing? Lying to protect Angus? No, she calmed herself. She was simply protecting herself and her own secret slaying activities. She couldn't talk about Angus without explaining her own business in the park.

Sean closed his laptop. "I'm out of patience with these stake-outs. We need to actually *do* something." He headed to the door. "Go to your assignments for now. I'll let you know what I decide."

Within ten minutes the men were gone. Alyssa was busy at her computer, hacking into Romatech's files. Emma settled at her desk and turned on the television that was rigged to receive the Digital Vampire Network.

At eight, the *Nightly News* began with Stone Cauffyn droning on in his monotonous voice. Emma watched it each night while she scanned police reports, looking for possible vampire criminal activity.

She tried focusing on the police reports, but the words blurred before her weary eyes. What was Angus doing tonight? She'd checked her e-mail numerous times, but there'd been no message from him. Was he having second thoughts? Maybe he'd come to his senses and realized, like her, that a relationship between them was doomed. And that hurt.

She turned up the volume on the telly. A commercial was on, selling some sort of exercise DVD, starring the famous Parisian fashion model Simone. It sounded silly to Emma, but one part caught her attention—a warning that the superior lifestyle of the nonbiting Vamp could lead to gum weakness or even fang loss, therefore making exercise a necessity.

The nonbiting Vamp? Here it was—more evidence that Angus was telling the truth, and so-called Vamps no longer fed off humans. Why would DVN lie about it when they believed their audience was made up entirely of the Undead? As far as Emma knew, she was the only human watching DVN, and the vampires didn't know it. So whatever she saw on DVN was probably true.

Two factions—the Vamps and the Malcontents. Why would Angus object to her killing Malcontents, other than his concern for her safety? He had said something about leaving vampire justice to him. Did that mean he killed Malcontents? If he did, why not let her help him? They could be a team.

What was she thinking? She was already on a team. She closed her aching eyes. This was all too confusing. Her loyalties were getting all screwed up.

She refocused on the police reports. There on page two was the news she dreaded the most. A body had been found this morning in Central Park. A woman's body with her throat slashed.

"Shit!" Emma sprung to her feet.

"What's wrong?" Alyssa asked.

"Nothing. I spilled coffee." Emma strode into the kitchen area where she could fume in private. Damn! Another vampire murder. She couldn't just ignore this. Either Angus MacKay was going to help her, or she was going solo. She was not going to let more innocent people die.

She hurried to her laptop to write him an e-mail, but something on the telly caught her attention. Corky Courrant had started her gossip show called *Live with the Undead*. Half of the screen was taken up with a picture of Roman Draganesti.

Emma turned up the volume.

"Remember, you heard it here first!" Corky screeched in her strident voice. "It's the most miraculous news ever! Roman Draganesti is about to become the first vampire in history to be a father!"

Emma gasped.

"What?" Alyssa came running over.

"Yes!" Corky laughed. "Hard to believe, isn't it? But just look at this exclusive video we obtained last night. Roman and his mortal wife have started going to Mass on Sunday night, and my cameraman caught them as they were arriving."

Emma punched the record button on the television's VCR. If there was news about Shanna, her boss would want to see it.

A video flashed onto the screen, fuzzy at first, then sharpening on a building in the distance. Emma recognized it as Romatech Industries. The cameraman was obviously far away, but he managed to zoom in on the front door as a black car pulled up to the entrance. A youthful-looking, kilted Scotsman climbed out of the driver's seat and opened the car's back door. Roman Draganesti stepped out, and next to him was Shanna Whelan. A huge, very pregnant Shanna Whelan.

Emma's heart leaped. Good heavens! How could such a thing happen? Surely a vampire couldn't father a baby?

"Oh my God," Alyssa whispered.

The video stopped, and Corky reappeared on the screen, grinning. "I know what you're thinking! You're thinking Draganesti couldn't be the father. But he's a scientific genius, the inventor of synthetic blood and Vampire Fusion Cuisine. So, I for one am thoroughly convinced." She waved the camera closer, then whispered, "He *is* the father."

Emma pressed a hand to her chest. Good God, what was Shanna thinking? Was she having a half-human, half-vampire baby?

With shaky fingers, Emma stopped the recording.

"Oh my God," Alyssa repeated. "Sean is going to go ballistic."

"We have to tell him," Emma said.

Alyssa scoffed. "Don't look at me. He said I could go out of town, and I am out of here." She rushed to her desk and gathered papers. "He's going to go berserk."

Emma had to agree. How on earth would she break the news?

Never trust anyone or anything. Sean Whelan had learned that the hard way. And when you added vampires with their mind-controlling capabilities into the mix, then anyone could be turned against you. Anyone.

After his daughter's betrayal, Sean had hoped to recapture her by staking out Roman Draganesti's townhouse on the Upper East Side. He'd left a surveillance van parked across the street for the first few weeks, but the damned vampires had caught on. His tires had been slashed, and his surveillance equipment stolen. He'd tried a variety of cars and SUVs, but parking was such a bitch, he couldn't always find a place close enough.

So, eight months ago, he'd rented a small room cattycorner across the street. It was damned expensive, but Homeland Security had gladly footed the bill when he'd explained he was observing a terrorist cell.

He strode into the tiny room and with a swipe of his

arm, he cleared a space on the small table for his laptop. Empty take-out containers tumbled onto the floor, and he reminded himself for the jillionth time to take out the trash. Later.

For now, he was anxious to see what the video camera had recorded the night before in his absence. The camera squatted on top of a tripod by the window, its lens carefully positioned to peek between two slats of the blinds. Sean peered out the window. Draganesti's house was usually quiet this early in the evening, and tonight appeared no different.

He removed the camera's memory card and quickly downloaded Sunday night's recording. Then he inserted a fresh memory card into the camera and pushed record. Back at the table, he settled into a rickety chair and started watching the video from Sunday night. Boring. He pushed fast forward and poured himself a cup of coffee from his thermos. This was so damned boring, and it was getting him nowhere. Shanna could be dead by now.

His cell phone rang, and he flipped it open. "Whelan, here."

"This is Garrett. There's a . . . problem here in Brooklyn, sir."

With a sigh, Sean rose to his feet and looked out the window. Still no activity outside Draganesti's house. "What kind of problem?"

"Our bugs inside the Russian coven were destroyed."

"Dammit." Sean paced across the room. "Is the van all right, and our surveillance equipment?"

"I'm in the van now. Everything's fine, but all I get is static from the Russian house."

Sean muttered another curse. "You need to get back in. Plant some more bugs."

"That's kinda hard when the place is crawling with mafia thugs during the day."

"Is that my problem?" Sean snarled. "When did they discover the bugs? Did you get any recordings at all for the weekend?"

"Yes, I've been listening to them. The bugs went dead on Saturday night, right after Katya received a visitor. Some guy from Poland."

"Did you get his name?"

"Yeah. He introduced himself, said he was a friend of some guy named Casimir who was unhappy with Katya for killing Ivan Petrovsky. Then he said she needed to find the slayer or she was toast."

Sean walked back to his chair. "Slayer? What slayer?"

"I don't know. It seems that some vampire dude's been killing off some of the Russian vampires."

"That's good."

"Yeah." Garrett laughed. "I wish they'd all kill each other off. Anyway, it looks like this Janow dude will kill Katya if she doesn't deliver the slayer."

Sean froze. "What? Did you say—" His throat constricted. He couldn't say the name. "Who—who did you say he was?"

"Jedrek Janow. Some Polish dude."

The phone tumbled from Sean's hand and clattered on the floor. He collapsed into the chair. Sweat popped out onto Sean's brow, and a stabbing pain pierced his gut. The bastard was back. The one who had wreaked revenge on Sean after he'd killed a vampire in Russia.

The bastard hadn't attacked Sean. No, he was too cruel and sick for that.

Sean doubled over as the pain wrenched his gut. He covered his face to shut out the memory. Poor Darlene. How could he forgive himself? He'd controlled his wife's mind for so many years. Just to help her, of course. To help her adjust to living overseas, so she could be happy. It had been for her own good, but it had left her brain so easy to manipulate, to control.

Jedrek Janow had discovered her weakness. He'd called her to him, and like a robot, she had complied. Then Jedrek had delivered her back, naked and so drained of blood, she'd barely been alive. Thank God she'd recovered and had no memory of that hideous night.

But Sean remembered. He remembered every damned day.

Slowly he became aware that Garrett's voice was yelling on the phone. With a shaky hand, he picked up the phone. "Yes?"

"Sean, are you okay?"

"I—no." He glanced at the video still going in fast forward on his laptop. A black four-door sedan stopped in front of Draganesti's house. "Just a minute." He slowed the recording down.

Two kilted Scotsmen emerged from the front seat of the car. They peered around the neighborhood, then opened the back doors. On the street side, Roman Draganesti climbed out.

"Bastard," Sean growled.

"Who, me?" Garrett asked. "Hey, I'm sorry about the bugs, but—"

"Quiet." Sean leaned forward to watch the second person emerge from the car onto the street. Whoever it was, he appeared to be getting assistance from a Scotsman. A blond head appeared.

Shanna! Sean caught his breath. "She—she was here! Sunday night."

"Who? Shanna?" Garrett asked.

Sean's mouth fell open as his daughter stepped away from the car. He blinked several times. It couldn't be true. She walked toward the steps to the townhouse. He quickly rewound the tape. It had to be a mistake. Maybe she'd just gained a lot of weight. He replayed the section where she was getting out of the car, then froze on the image of his daughter. His very pregnant daughter.

"That bastard." This was it. Draganesti had gone too far.

"Sean, what's going on?"

"Get over here." Sean jumped to his feet. "No, go to the office first. Arm yourself. I want weapons, silver bullets, handcuffs, and a battering ram."

"Are you serious?"

"Yes, and bring the girls with you. I want you all here in thirty minutes." Sean strode to the window and looked through the blinds at Draganesti's house. "We're going in."

Chapter 11

"I don't think this is a good idea," Emma murmured from her crouched position behind an old dented Chevy with a mismatched passenger door.

"Don't be a wuss." Sean checked his pistol one more time, then stuffed it into his belt behind his back. He peeked over the Chevy's rusted trunk. "Coast is clear. Go, Garrett!"

Garrett dashed across the street, carrying the battering ram, and stopped, partially hidden behind the black Lexus four-door sedan parked in front of Draganesti's townhouse.

"Those bastards will pay for what they did to my daughter," Sean growled.

Emma groaned inwardly. This was a classic case of good news, bad news. The good news was she didn't have to tell Sean about his daughter's pregnancy because he already knew. The bad news was Sean was determined to break into Draganesti's house at night.

She considered urging her boss to invade during the day when the vampires were dead to the world, but she held her tongue. What if Angus was sleeping there during the day and Sean staked him?

"Do you have any evidence that your daughter is still in there?" Emma winced when Garrett tripped on the first stair leading up to Draganesti's front door. Any vampire with superior hearing would have heard Garrett's stumble and muttered curse.

"It doesn't matter," Sean insisted. "Those damned Scotsmen inside will know where she is."

Emma sighed. What if Angus was in there? What if he greeted her by name? She watched as Garrett approached the front door. "They have a camera there. They'll see him."

"Stop whining. It's bad enough Alyssa already left town. Now I'm stuck with just you." Sean motioned her to follow, then darted across the street. He stopped behind a tan SUV parked in front of the black Lexus.

Emma joined him. "They probably have us outnumbered."

Sean glanced over his shoulder at her. "I detect a lack of enthusiasm on your part."

"I'm fine. All revved up." Should she confess that she knew Angus before it was too late?

"You have the silver?"

"Yes, handcuffs and chains in my backpack." Only two handcuffs since Angus had broken the third, but Emma doubted this mission would succeed to the point they even needed the silver.

Sean reached behind his back for his revolver. "I'm going to enjoy shooting them full of holes."

A loud bang echoed as Garrett swung the battering ram into the front door.

Emma gasped. A body had suddenly appeared on the front steps behind Garrett. A youthful-looking vampire in a red and navy plaid kilt. He clobbered Garrett with the hilt of his sword, and their teammate crumpled onto the porch. The battering ram fell by the door.

"Dammit!" Sean dashed across the back end of the SUV. Emma followed, but screeched to a halt when the blunt end of a claymore crashed down on Sean's head. Another Scotsman had been waiting on the other side of the SUV for them to pass by. Sean's unconscious body fell to the sidewalk in front of her, and the Scotsman flipped his claymore so the sharp end now pointed at her.

She stepped back. An arm seized her from behind and yanked her back against a hard body.

"Umph." Her head snapped back against a man's shoulder.

A deep voice whispered softly in her ear. "Do we need to knock ye out, too, Emma?"

"Angus." His voice tickled the hairs on her neck and sent gooseflesh down her arms. She didn't know whether to melt against him or elbow him in the ribs.

"Ah, lass." His chin nestled against her temple. "What are ye doing here?"

"What will you do with them?" Emma noted the youthful-looking vampire binding Garrett's wrists and ankles with duct tape. "Please don't hurt them."

"Bugger," Angus growled. He took Emma by the shoulders and turned her to face him. "How many times must I say that we doona wish to harm ye?"

She searched his deep green eyes and could detect only frustration. "You knocked them out."

"Self-protection," muttered the Scotsman who was wrapping duct tape around Sean's ankles. "Why were ye attacking us?"

"Sean just found out about his daughter's pregnancy. Surely you can understand how upset that made him."

The Scotsman straightened and gave Angus a questioning look.

"Call Shanna," Angus ordered. "See if she wants to talk to him."

The Scotsman nodded. Stepping away, he pulled a cell phone from his sporran.

"Who is he?" Emma whispered.

"Connor Buchanan." Angus gestured toward Garrett. "The young-looking one is Ian MacPhie. They know who ye are."

Angus reached behind her back and confiscated her weapon. "Shame on ye, Emma." He dropped her pistol into his sporran. "I thought we were friends."

Heat rushed to her face, and she shoved the memory of his kiss away. "When I'm working with the Stake-Out team, I'm the enemy."

She instantly regretted her words. The tinge of pain in his eyes meant she had hurt him. His large hand curled around her arm, just above the elbow, and she swallowed hard. What was he going to do with her?

Connor walked toward them, dropping his cell phone in his sporran. "Shanna wants to see her father. She can be at Romatech in five minutes. Dougal's already there."

"Teleport Whelan there while he's still unconscious,"

Angus ordered. "Keep him bound, and doona take yer eyes off him."

Connor nodded. "I can handle him." He leaned over and swooshed Sean's limp body onto his shoulder with an ease that made Emma's mouth drop open. Were female vampires that strong, too? Connor vanished, taking Sean Whelan with him.

Emma blinked at the blank space. "How does he know where he's going?"

"Connor teleports to Romatech every night." Angus ushered her onto the sidewalk. "The journey is embedded in his psychic memory."

Emma allowed Angus to escort her toward the townhouse. What else could she do? If she ran away, he'd catch up with her in a second. But the scariest part of this wasn't him. It was a growing desire inside her to surrender completely. "What will you do with Garrett?"

Ian was examining Garrett's wallet and pulled out his driver's license. "I could just take him home."

Angus nodded. "Fair enough. If I remember correctly, this one has verra little psychic power. Erase his memory of us."

"Will do." Ian scooped up Garrett's body and strode toward the black sedan.

"Why erase his memory?" Emma winced as she watched Garrett getting tossed like a sack of potatoes into the backseat of the Lexus. "Sean will just retrain him."

"And that will keep him busy for a while." Angus released her and climbed the stairs to the front door. "We have bigger problems than the CIA to deal with right now."

"Like what?" She glanced back to see Ian driving off with Garrett.

Angus picked up the battering ram and examined it. "I suppose we could use this, though teleporting is much easier." He punched some numbers on the keypad by the front door, then opened it. He set the battering ram inside, then turned toward Emma with a questioning look.

She wondered what to do. She could walk away and hope to never see him again. That would be safe . . . and painful. Or she could venture inside and be alone with Angus MacKay.

A sad, resigned look settled on his face. "I understand if ye wish to leave. 'Tis for the best, most likely."

Since when had she done what was best for her? Ever since her parents' murders, she'd taken one risk after another. But somehow, Angus MacKay didn't seem like a risk. At least not a physical one. With him, it was her heart that was in danger.

She went up one step. Then another.

His sad expression took on a look of wonder. She felt it, too, as if she and Angus were alone in the world with a mysterious force drawing them together.

Her heart pounded in her ears. What was she doing? The heat between them would be too hard to resist. She'd end up in his arms again. Did she really want that? She paused at the doorway, giving him a wary look.

He arched a brow. "Is this another date?"

With a lift of her chin, she entered the townhouse. "I'm only here for the information I can learn." She winced when the door banged shut behind her. She turned in time to see him flipping the locks. "I reserve the right to leave whenever I wish."

"Of course ye do." A corner of his mouth tilted up. "Would ye like something to eat or drink? I'm feeling a bit peckish myself."

The minute Sean Whelan regained consciousness, he focused on self-control. No movement whatsoever to indicate he was awake. He kept his eyes shut, his body relaxed, his head slumped forward, but his senses alert. He appeared to be tied to a chair, a hard wooden one, he guessed by the slats pressing into the small of his back. The slight whir of air conditioning proved he was indoors. Footsteps paced behind him, steps made on a hard floor. Heavy steps, most probably made by one of those damned Scottish vampires.

Sean didn't dare send out psychic probes to read his captor's mind. A vampire would feel it and know his victim was awake. Sean listened to the pacing till he had a feel for the rhythm. Then he waited for the pacer to reach his farthest point to the left, a time when the pacer would have his back turned. Then Sean strained at the bindings on his wrists. No luck. Too tight. His ankles, too. He leaned forward as if his unconscious body was about to tumble on the floor, but ropes across his chest restrained him. The Scottish bastard had tied him to the chair.

The footsteps came closer and stopped just to his left. Sean could feel those demonic eyes studying him. He struggled to breathe normally, but his heart raced. What kind of torture did the bastards plan for him?

God help him, if they tried to transform him, he would find a way to kill himself first.

"I know ye're awake."

Sean flinched at the deep voice so close to his ear. And his neck.

"I can hear yer heart pounding. I can smell yer blood rushing through you."

Sean turned his head toward the voice and opened his eyes. "Go to hell."

The Scotsman straightened and narrowed his blue eyes. "I will, most likely. But ye'll be there long before I will."

A door flung open, and Sean's breath hitched at the sight of his pregnant daughter. "Shanna!" He strained at his bindings.

"Dad." She rushed toward him.

The Scotsman stopped her. "No' too close."

She frowned at him, then at Sean. "Why not? What can he do? You have him all tied up."

The Scotsman crossed his arms. "And that is how he will stay."

Sean rocked forward, trying to get onto his feet. "You see how they treat us, Shanna?" He wiggled his chair toward her. "What have they done to you? I swear I'll kill them all."

The Scotsman dashed around him in a blur. Two hands clamped down on his shoulders from behind. He couldn't budge.

"Doona threaten us, mortal." The Scotsman leaned forward. "Ye wouldna want to see me angry."

Sean glanced to the side just in time to see the Scotsman bare his teeth. With a hiss, his fangs shot out.

Sean recoiled.

"Connor!" Shanna glared at the Scotsman. "Behave."

The Scotsman's fangs slowly receded into his gums. He gave Sean a warning look, then released him.

Shanna shook her head. "Really, Connor. How can I convince my dad you're the good guys when you act like that?"

Connor stepped back, folding his arms across his broad chest. "My apologies." He slanted a look toward Sean that was anything but apologetic.

"Shanna." Sean turned to his daughter. "I need to talk to you in private."

"No' happening," Connor growled.

"Do you think I would harm my own child?" Sean shouted, then looked at Shanna. "Don't you see what they're doing? They never leave you alone, do they? They never let you make a decision. They're controlling you."

"It was my decision to see you." Shanna crossed the small room to a table against the wall. She pulled out a chair and sat.

Sean glanced at the mirror that spanned the entire wall above the table. He and Shanna showed up in it, but the Scotsman wasn't reflected. "We're being watched?"

Shanna glanced at the mirror behind her. "Yes. My husband and another guard are on the other side."

Sean looked to his left to see if the Scotsman was still there. He was. It was unnerving how he didn't show up in the mirror. "This is an interrogation room."

Shanna laughed. "No. You're at Romatech. This room is used for marketing research." She motioned to the mirror behind her. "That's the observation room."

"You're always watched, aren't you? You're a prisoner." Sean wondered for the millionth time if he'd made a huge mistake by not telling Shanna what the vampires had done to her mother. But he couldn't stand for anyone to know how Darlene had been punished for his mistakes. And he'd worried that Shanna would tell her mother the truth.

"Dad, you have to believe me. I married Roman because I wanted to. I love him, and he loves me."

"He's a demon!" Sean shouted. "Look what he's done to you. How could he get you pregnant? Did he pimp you out to other men?"

"*What?*" Shanna scrambled to her feet.

Behind him, Connor growled.

Shanna marched toward him, a hand placed protectively on top of her huge belly. "My husband is the father of this child. How dare you accuse me or him—"

"That's impossible," Sean hissed. "He's dead. He can't father a child. Goddammit, Shanna, he's duped you. He's controlled your mind and used you like a prostitute!"

The door swung open with a bang, and Roman Draganesti stepped inside. His dark eyes blazed with anger. "No one speaks to my wife like that, not even her father."

"You can't be this baby's father," Sean insisted.

Roman strode toward him, his jaw clenched. "Your disbelief does not give you the right to insult your daughter."

Shanna touched his arm. "I can handle this."

Roman stopped. His face softened when he regarded Shanna. Sean could only hope that meant the vampire didn't abuse her.

His daughter and the demon gazed at each other for a while, then Roman bowed his head. "I will be watching. Be careful. I don't want you upset right now."

Shanna smiled at him. "I'll be fine."

Roman turned to glare at Sean. "I'm only leaving so you can see that Shanna is the one in charge here. I would do anything for her."

"Then go die," Sean muttered.

The Scotsman cuffed him on the back of the head.

"Connor." Shanna shot him a disapproving look.

"My apologies," Connor growled. "I have verra little patience with morons."

Roman chuckled and planted a kiss on Shanna's brow.

Sean flinched, recalling how his wife had been controlled and molested. He glared at Roman's back as he left the room.

"You should get used to him," Shanna said quietly. "He's going to be my husband for a very long time."

Sean stiffened. "He's going to transform you?"

"And risk killing his own child? Don't be silly."

"How—?"

"How can this child be his?" Shanna patted her belly. "Roman is a brilliant scientist. He used live human sperm with his own DNA—"

"What?" Sean strained at the duct tape around his wrists. "That bastard's performing experiments on you. Shanna, you have to get out of here."

The Scotsman grabbed his shoulders to keep him still.

Shanna stepped closer. "I wanted this baby. I have a wonderful, loving, brilliant husband, and we're going to have a baby. Why can't you be happy for me?"

"Because you married a monster! And you're about to give birth to—" Sean gasped when the full import washed over him. A half-breed baby? A child monster? "Oh God, Shanna. What have you done?"

Her eyes narrowed. "I'm bringing a child into this world who will be blessed with two loving parents. That's more than Roman experienced. It's more than I had, too."

Sean gritted his teeth. "I knew it. You're doing this to get back at me. You were always the rebellious one."

"You mean the one you sent away because you couldn't control me." Shanna's face flushed with anger. "Give me some credit for once in your life. If you couldn't control my mind, what makes you think my husband can?"

Sean blinked. A horrible feeling swept over him. "You—you want this? They're not controlling you?"

"No, they're not."

Anger seized him so hard, he trembled. "Then you are a traitor to mankind."

Shanna sighed. She glanced back at the mirror with an exasperated look. "He's hopeless."

"A stubborn fool." The Scotsman's fingers dug into Sean's shoulders.

Sean glared at Connor. "Get your filthy hands off me."

Connor tightened his grip, and Sean steeled his face to show no pain.

"Connor." Shanna motioned for him to release Sean, and he did. "Dad, I chose to talk to you tonight, because I wanted to assure you that I'm all right."

Sean snorted. About to give birth to a demon baby, and she called that *all right*?

"I also wanted to tell you what's going on. My husband and his followers are not the monsters you think they are. They take their meals from a bottle."

Sean snorted again. "Are you saying your husband has never bitten you?"

She hesitated.

"Aha!" Sean leaned forward. "How often does that bastard feed off you?"

"Never," Shanna insisted. "Roman invented synthetic blood so he and other Vamps like him would never have to harm another mortal again."

"Vampires kill mortals all the time."

"The Malcontents do," she continued. "They're an evil bunch who enjoy hurting mortals. They are our enemy."

"All vampires are evil."

"No!" Shanna planted her fists on her hips. "You have to stop persecuting the good Vamps. They're trying to protect mortals."

"Aye," Connor added. "Ye should let us take care of the Malcontents."

Sean shook his head. "Vampires killing other vampires? I'll never believe it."

"Why not?" Shanna asked. "Haven't you heard of humans killing other humans? Think about it. You know Ivan Petrovsky was killed by other vampires. It happens."

"Ye need to leave us alone." Connor circled the chair to stand in front of Sean. "The Malcontents are raising an army. If we doona defeat them, humanity will suffer greatly for it."

Sean swallowed hard. "You're just trying to trick me, to scare me off." Was this all a pack of lies? He had to know. There was no way he could invade a vampire mind, but there was a human here. He gathered up his psychic power and targeted his daughter with a full assault.

She stumbled back, taken by surprise.

Connor steadied her. "Are ye all right, lass?"

Glaring at her father, Shanna shoved all his power back with so much force, he rocked back in his chair. Shit. She was incredibly strong.

"Are you convinced now?" she asked quietly. "No one can control me."

"Traitor," he whispered.

She turned away. "Take him away, Connor."

"Aye. I'm sorry, lass." Connor circled behind Sean.

He gasped when the Scotsman picked him up, chair and all. "What are you doing?"

"Taking ye on a wee trip," Connor answered.

Shanna regarded him sadly. "By the way, your grandson will be born Friday night."

"He's not my grand—" Sean's voice broke off when everything went black.

Chapter 12

Angus knew he should say something comforting to assure Emma she was perfectly safe, but he didn't. He couldn't. It irked him that she'd participated in Sean Whelan's attack. And that simmering anger made him want to torment her. Or kiss her senseless.

Better to keep his distance. He strode toward the kitchen. "Ye're sure ye want nothing to drink? We have stuff like soft drinks and juice in the fridge."

"You do? Why?" She kept watching him with that wary look, as if he might swoop down on her neck any second now. It was a beautiful neck with pale, tender skin, but that didn't mean he wanted to punch holes in it. Kissing, though, would be very . . .

He shook his head, struggling to keep up with the conversation. Oh, aye, her surprise over mortal drinks. "The mortals who guard the house during the day get thirsty."

"You have human guards during the day?"

"Aye. They're verra good. And trustworthy. They work for me." He paused with a hand on the swinging door. "Anything to drink?"

She hesitated. "Some . . . water, thank you."

A safe choice. She'd be able to taste if anything odd was added. Bugger. Had he lost her trust so easily? "Make yerself at home," he muttered, then couldn't help but add, "If ye try to escape, an alarm will sound."

He strode into the kitchen to avoid the worried look on her face. The devil take it. He was already pissed. Why was he goading her and making it worse?

He grabbed a bottle of Type O blood from the fridge and popped it into the microwave. Maybe her distrust was a blessing. He could use it to keep a distance between them.

He fixed her a glass of ice water and removed his bottled blood from the microwave. The foyer was empty, but he spotted her in the library. She was wandering along the bookshelves, examining the books. It had been only last night that he'd stood in this same room, confiding in Roman and declaring his intent to protect Emma from a distance.

And yet here she was—alone in the house with him. He approached quietly. "Yer water."

She spun toward him. "I—I didn't hear you come in."

He held the glass out to her, and she reluctantly took it. Bugger. "Do ye think I'm poisoning you?"

She blinked. "What?"

"Ye act like I can no longer be trusted. I thought we'd gotten past that."

"We have." She gulped down some water.

"Then why do ye keep looking at me strangely?"

"I'm not. I'm just not sure this . . . friendship is a good idea. It's causing me trouble at work."

"Really? Ye seemed happy enough to attack us alongside Whelan."

She sighed and walked into the foyer. "I tried to talk him out of it, but the man won't listen to reason. He's not going to believe anything I've learned from you. And I'm in an awful position. He had a photo of you tonight, and I had to lie that I don't know you."

"Ye lied for me?" Angus's heart expanded.

She glared at him. "Don't look so happy about it. This whole thing has me in such an awkward situation."

"I'm sorry." Angus smiled. "I'm just happy I havena lost yer trust."

She rotated the glass in her hands. "I'm upset about another murder in Central Park. I know you don't want me to go hunting—"

"Nay, I do no'."

She gave him an exasperated look. "But you said the Malcontents are your enemy, too. Why don't you help me slay them? Wouldn't that be the *friendly* thing to do?"

Ah, so that was the problem. He gave her a reassuring smile. "We *are* friends." He motioned to the parlor. "Let's have a wee chat."

"Fine." She strode into the parlor. "Nice room." She circled to the right around the three maroon couches. "Big telly. I suppose you watch a lot of DVN."

He waited by the door, sipping from his bottle. "No' much, really. I usually work all night."

She set her ice water on the coffee table. "Don't you

get vacations? You know, a week off every fifty years or so?"

"Verra funny." He headed toward the couch to the left. "I give my employees a few weeks every year."

"What about you?" She removed her backpack and dropped it on the couch to the right.

He ignored her question, since he couldn't remember his last vacation. "What's in yer backpack?"

"The usual party favors. Wooden stakes, silver handcuffs, whips and chains." She settled on the couch next to the backpack. "You'll be proud of me. I even brought duct tape."

"Ye're a fast learner." He sat across from her on the left couch. "I'll be keeping yer backpack."

"What? Are you trying to get me fired?"

Angus leaned forward to set his bottle on the coffee table. "Ye can tell yer boss that I took it forcibly from you."

She rose to her feet, glaring at him. He immediately stood.

"I need my weapons to go hunting. And I thought, since you're my *friend*, that you would come with me. After all, you claim to be worried about my safety."

"I am, but you doona know the full story." He motioned to the couch. "I'll tell you."

"Fine." She sat.

He took his seat. "The Malcontents believe the slayer is one of Roman's coven. They assume only a vampire could manage to kill another vampire."

"Vampire arrogance," Emma muttered.

"They have promised to declare war on Roman's coven if another Malcontent is slain."

She frowned. "So you want me to stop in order to save the lives of Roman's coven?"

"To keep a war from breaking out."

She jumped to her feet. "Damn you. You want to save vampires, but you're willing to let innocent humans die?"

He stood. " 'Tis no' like that. Believe me, when a war breaks out, vampires and humans both die. The carnage is great. You doona want to see it."

She clenched her fists. "So we do nothing? You just let the Malcontents kill humans whenever they like because you're afraid of a bloody war?"

"Nay, I have a plan."

She folded her arms, glowering at him.

He stepped toward her. "Emma, trust me."

With a huff, she sat. "This had better be good."

He sat on the center couch. "The Malcontents will only declare war if we *kill* one of their coven. We can still police the park and keep them from murdering innocents."

"So we catch them in the act and then . . . slap their wrists and let them go?"

"Actually, I thought we'd scare the hell out of them."

Her mouth twitched. "That's not too bad."

"I'm glad ye approve." He picked up his bottle and took a long drink.

"So how long have you been fighting the Malcontents?"

He sighed. "As long as I can remember. Their leader, Casimir, is the one who transformed Roman. He tried to force Roman to do evil things, but Roman escaped and began transforming Vamps like me. Eventually we had an army, and we marched on the Malcontents."

She stood. "You went to war with them?"

With a silent groan, he stood. Why couldn't she sit still longer than two minutes? "Aye. 'Twas the Great Vampire War of 1710. I was the general on our side."

Her mouth gaped. "Wicked. You killed a bunch of Malcontents?"

"Aye, I did." He removed his sporran since her gun inside was weighing heavily against his groin.

She gave him a curious look. "Why are you standing?"

He winced inwardly. "Because ye are."

"You're mimicking me?"

"Nay. 'Tis a . . . silly habit. I lived through several centuries where a man had to stand whenever a lady did."

She let out a short laugh. "You mean you're an old-fashioned gentleman?"

He scowled at her. "Ye mean ye never noticed?"

"A vampire gentleman?" She grinned. "That sounds like an oxymoron."

"I'm perfectly capable of being rude," he growled.

"I can believe that." She moved to the middle couch and flopped down.

With a sigh of relief, he sat.

"So I guess you started your company back in 1927? You're Angus the Third and Fourth and Alexander, too?"

"Aye." He bowed his head. "Angus Alexander MacKay, at yer service."

"Such a gentleman." Her mouth tilted up. "Did you ever let Angus the Third or Alexander go on vacation?"

"Now ye're just mocking me."

She grinned. "Which one of you was knighted?"

"I forget."

"Oh, right. I've heard that memory goes with age."

He arched a brow at her. "My memory is fine."

"Then you remember why you were knighted?"

"Aye."

She waited, then gave him an exasperated look. She scooted down the couch to be closer. "Why don't you tell me?"

" 'Tis a government secret."

"I can keep a secret. I haven't told anyone about you."

"Ye're trying to keep yer job."

She made a face at him. "Come on. I won't tell."

"Ye'll swear by the official Angus oath?"

"What's that?"

"I doona know." He smiled. "I just made it up."

She laughed. "I'll swear, as long as there's no biting involved."

"No biting." His gaze meandered down her body. She was sitting very close to him now. "I will never harm you."

Her smile faded. She glanced away. "I don't want to hurt you, either."

He swallowed hard. He didn't know if this friendship was good or bad. He enjoyed talking to her, but his hands itched to hold her. Just being in the same room with her was becoming torture.

She cleared her throat. "So why were you knighted?"

"Some Royal Air Force lads were shot down over occupied France. The Germans claimed they were all dead, but we suspected some had survived and were being held in secret and tortured."

She touched his arm. "How terrible."

"My mission was to teleport from a plane into enemy territory, locate the lads, and teleport them to safety. I erased their memories afterward."

She rose to her feet. "That's brilliant!"

He stood.

"Oh, sorry." She laughed, then resumed her seat. "How many people in the British government know about you?"

He sat beside her. "Three. The queen, the head of MI6, and the prime minister. When they leave their office, I erase their memory of me."

"How interesting." Emma rose slightly.

Angus was halfway up when he realized it was a false alarm. She was simply repositioning herself by tucking a foot beneath her. He sat back down.

Her mouth twitched. "What sort of favors did you do for the queen?"

"One of her dogs got lost in Hyde Park, and I found it for her."

"That's it?"

He gave her an irritated look. "Ye doona realize how important her dogs are to her."

Emma smiled as she reached for her glass of ice water on the coffee table. She took a sip, then winced. "Oh, sorry." She swiped at the wet ring on the table.

She stood, looking around the room. "Don't you have any coasters?"

He stood also. "Doona worry about it."

She noticed he was standing and snickered. "Such a gentleman."

" 'Tis no' funny. I've never seen such a jumpy lass. I swear ye're part rabbit."

Grinning, she set her glass down. Her amber eyes twinkled with mirth. "You make a good rabbit yourself." She sat halfway down, then popped back up.

Angus jerked back to a standing position while she giggled. The devil take it, she was playing with him.

She sat. "Consider this your aerobic exercise for the day."

He sat. "Are ye done?"

"No." She jumped to her feet.

"Enough!" He grabbed her about the waist and pulled her down. She landed, laughing, on his lap.

He chuckled. His hands glided up her back.

Her laughter faded with a long sigh. "I'm sorry. I shouldn't have teased you." She looked at him with that wary expression and tried to move off his lap.

He held her in place. "Ye're doing it again."

Her face went blank. "Doing what?"

"Looking at me like I'm some kind of frightening monster."

"No, I'm not. It's . . . nothing." A blush washed over her cheeks, a beautiful blood-pink blush.

Bugger. Nothing turned him on faster than a woman's blush, especially when the blush was caused by him. He could smell the blood filling her cheeks like a maddening perfume. His groin instantly responded. "Are ye afraid I'll kiss ye again? That I'll lose control?"

Her blush deepened. "No." Her eyes glinted with fear once again.

The truth hit him hard. She was afraid *she* would lose control.

Her gaze met his for an electric second, then she turned away. "We shouldn't."

"Nay, we shouldna." He pulled her closer. It was wrong. It would lead to nothing but heartache and despair. But still, he wanted her. He had to have her.

"Emma," he whispered, just before lowering his mouth to hers.

Chapter 13

Emma was immediately pulled into the kiss. Not only did he ignite her physically, but he overwhelmed her emotionally. He was the honorable sexy hero of her dreams, and she responded with such a strong yearning, her heart ached.

If only he could be alive. He tugged her bottom lip into his mouth and suckled. She moaned as the tug shimmered down to her belly, then lower. His erection pressed against her hip. Good heavens, wasn't this alive enough for her?

But why couldn't he be human like her? He trailed kisses across her cheek. His husky groan tickled her ear before he nibbled more kisses down her neck. His hand covered her breast and gently squeezed. She gasped in response. Wasn't this human enough? Maybe he was technically dead during the day, but oh, imagine the nights she could have with this man.

But you know it can't last. Dammit, was she going

to argue with herself all night? Why couldn't she just enjoy this? She no longer feared he was going to bite her, so what was the problem? *You're afraid you're falling in love.*

No, she could never allow herself to love him. But she couldn't stop her body from responding. The minute he circled her nipple with his thumb, it hardened.

"Oh, the hell with it," she muttered.

"Hmm?" He pulled back to look at her.

His eyes were glowing hotly. Instead of frightening her, they excited her.

She skimmed her hands around the back of his neck and threaded her fingers into his long, soft hair. "Kiss me."

This time, there was no inner argument. She held him close and kissed him with a hunger that matched his own. Their mouths opened. His tongue invaded. She welcomed it, suckling his tongue and stroking it with her own.

He pulled her close so their chests were pressed against each other. His hands slipped under her shirt and up her back. The touch of his fingers against her bare skin was whisper-soft, yet shocked her with its raw power. She explored his mouth and tasted a metallic flavor. Blood.

She drew back. She swallowed and tasted once again the blood from his last meal. Shouldn't she be horrified?

He gave her a quizzical look while his hands examined the back of her bra. "Where are the bloody hooks? Ye puir lass, were ye born into this contraption?"

A small laugh escaped her, and with it, her heart cracked open and all her yearning broke free. This man wasn't horrifying, he was beautiful. Tears sprang to her eyes.

"It opens in the front." She pressed a hand to her chest. "Here. Over my heart."

He studied her face. The red heat in his eyes faded to a warm glow that glimmered around his green irises.

Christmas eyes. If only she could believe in miracles, that there could be a future between them. "This can never work."

He took her hand that guarded her heart and kissed each finger. "I've been told that all things are possible with love."

Was he saying he loved her? Or was he merely seducing her? A tear rolled down her cheek. God help her, the way she felt, seduction was very possible.

"Shh." He wiped her tear with his thumb, then kissed her damp cheek. "I will never harm you. Ye have the official Angus oath."

Smiling, she traced his strong jaw with her fingertips. "We don't know what that is."

He unbuttoned her shirt down the front. "We'll figure it out as we go."

"And what is the punishment for breaking the official Angus oath?"

With a groan, he slid her off his lap and onto the couch. "Having ye sit on my erection was punishment enough."

He pushed her back onto a soft chenille pillow and stretched out beside her. "I can hear yer heart pounding, yer blood rushing." He pressed the palm of her hand against the thin cotton covering his chest. "Can ye feel my heart racing?"

"Yes." She could, though her thoughts were dwelling more on the erection he'd just mentioned. *Oh, Angus, where's the beef?*

He opened her shirt, then unhooked her bra and peeled each side back. Her nipples hardened while his gaze turned glowing hot once more. "Pink," he whispered, and touched a hardened tip with his finger.

She gasped as a small shudder tingled from her breasts down to her belly.

"Blue," he whispered, and traced the veins under her pale skin. He scooted down the couch a bit so his mouth was even with her breasts.

She bemoaned the fact that his erection was now out of her reach, but quickly forgot that problem when his tongue circled her nipple. With a moan, she arched toward him.

"Delicious," he whispered, and drew her nipple into his mouth.

"Oh." She wove her fingers into his hair.

He suckled one breast while his hand teased the other, rolling the nipple between his thumb and forefinger. She tugged at the strip of leather that held back his hair till it unraveled. His long, auburn hair fell forward, tickling her breasts as he made love to her.

His hand glided down her belly, setting her nerves to quivering. He stopped with his hand resting on the zipper of her black trousers.

He glanced at her, his hair wild and his eyes red. "May I give ye pleasure?"

Still a gentleman. Emma smiled. But his voice sounded gruff and his appearance was that of an untamed barbarian. She grabbed handfuls of his hair and pulled his head close to hers. "Make me scream."

His eyes gleamed hotter. "Ye will. Many times ere the night is over."

She almost came then. She squeezed her thighs together, relishing the sweet ache that thrummed deep within her. With a moan, she closed her eyes.

"Sweetheart, doona start without me." In a flash, he had her pants unzipped and pulled down to her ankles.

She kicked off her shoes and her trousers. He skimmed his fingers up her legs.

"I can smell yer scent," he whispered as he drew little circles on the inside of her thigh. "It tugs at my heart like the sweetest of perfumes." He leaned over to kiss her thigh.

Emma's skin tingled. Her heart raced. Moisture pooled between her legs.

He skimmed his hand beneath her red lace panties and gently explored the curls. "Yer first scream will come by my hand. The second one from my mouth."

She gulped.

He dipped a finger between the folds.

She gasped and shuddered.

"Ye're as wet and fresh as the morning dew." He smiled. "So ready for pleasure. I could phone this one in."

"Don't you dare." She raised her hips to press herself against him.

"Patience, sweetheart." He rolled her panties down her legs.

"Patience? Some of us don't have an eternity." She kicked her panties off and watched the red scrap of lace fly across the room.

"I'm still limited. When the sun . . ." He paused, tilting his head as he studied her.

"Something . . . wrong?"

He touched the bare, delicate skin next to her narrow strip of curls. "I have never seen this . . . style before."

"Oh. It's a bikini wax." Was she his first modern woman? She liked that thought. And she liked the idea of showing him how a modern woman approached sex. She raised one leg to rest her calf along the top of the sofa cushion. Then she lifted her other leg over his head and let it rest on his shoulder.

His eyes widened at the sight she'd put on display. His jaw tensed. Suddenly he shifted his gaze to the ceiling.

Had she offended him by her boldness? "Do you think I'm too—"

"Too beautiful." He squeezed his eyes shut. "I doona want to lose control."

"Oh." That sounded like a challenge. How she would love to drive him over the edge. Or maybe not. What did a vampire do if he lost control?

He took a deep breath and opened his eyes. The red color had mellowed to a warm glow. He kissed her leg hooked around his shoulder. "A man could spend a lifetime learning every shape and curve of yer body and count his life blessed."

She sighed. If he kept that up, she'd climax without him even touching her.

He skimmed his hand down her thigh toward her

center. She watched his hand approach closer and closer. It was no surprise, yet still, she jolted when he finally touched her.

"Yer folds are slick and swollen. Engorged with blood."

She shuddered as his fingertips outlined each fold. He circled her clitoris, then tweaked it with his thumb and forefinger. She cried out.

"Even this"—he played with the nubbin—"it has swollen with blood and turned red like the most beautiful of blushes."

Tension spiked, and she writhed under his hand. "Angus."

"I need to kiss you." He lowered her leg from his shoulder and stretched out beside her on the couch.

"Yes." She wrapped her arms around his neck. He kissed her thoroughly, then invaded her mouth at the same time he inserted a finger inside her. With a groan, her back arched.

He stroked the roof of her mouth with his tongue in rhythm to the stroking of his finger. Tension coiled inside her. He broke the kiss when her breathing grew too labored and turned his attention to her breasts.

He drew her nipple into his mouth and gave it a tug just as he pressed against her engorged nubbin. She cried out again. The tension rose abruptly, and she panted for air. He rubbed her faster and faster.

"Oh God." She raised her hips to press against him.

"Oh bugger." He looked up suddenly. "What rotten timing."

"Wha . . . ?" The room swirled around her. She screamed when all the tension shattered.

"What the hell was that?" a man's voice boomed from the foyer.

Emma gasped, even while her body continued to throb with the most glorious shock waves. No, it couldn't be. Not him.

"Was that Emma who screamed?" the voice screeched.

Good heavens, it *was* him. Her boss, Sean Whelan, was in the foyer.

Angus placed a finger against her lips. As if she needed a reminder to be quiet?

"Release me, dammit!" Sean yelled. "One of your bloody vampires is torturing Emma."

A softer voice replied, "I canna release ye from yer restraints until ye calm down."

"Calm down?" Sean roared. "I'll show you calm, you bastard, when I put a stake through your heart."

He continued to shout while Emma gave Angus a frantic look. Bad enough for her to be caught half naked by his vampire friends, but by her boss? This was a disaster! What on earth could she say? She was trying out a new interrogation technique?

Angus enveloped her in his arms and whispered in her ear, "Trust me."

Everything went black.

She was just becoming aware of her body again and Angus's arms around her, when they both dropped a few feet and tumbled onto the floor with a muffled thud.

"Oof." She struggled to breathe. Where was she?

"Sorry about the rough landing." Angus released her and rose to his feet. "It happens if ye teleport not standing up."

She sat up and glanced around the dark room. Moonlight filtered through three narrow windows, giving just enough illumination to make out the shapes of furniture, like dark squatting shadows surrounding her. Where was she? She scrambled to her feet, but the room spun around.

"Careful." Angus grabbed her to keep her from falling.

Good heavens, she was standing in a strange room, half naked. She hoped no one else was here. Dammit, she couldn't see. It looked like Angus was peering under his kilt. "What are you doing?"

He dropped his kilt. "Nothing. A silly habit."

Huh? She tamped down on a rising surge of panic. She could handle this. She'd been in sticky situations before. Of course, she'd always faced danger with her pants on before. She gritted her teeth. "Where are we?"

"Fifth floor of the townhouse. Roman's office."

"*What?* Roman's here?" She spun around, expecting his royal vampire highness to pop out from the shadows.

"He no longer lives here. I'm using these rooms now. Ye're perfectly safe."

"Safe? I don't think so. I'm feeling a bit . . . breezy, if you know what I mean." Her voice rose higher. "I'm half naked."

He gave her shoulders a squeeze. "But 'tis the good half."

"Not helping." She pulled away from him. "I'm half naked, and my clothes are on the ground floor."

"Doona fash. I'll fetch them for you."

She began to pace. "I'm half naked, my clothes are

downstairs, and my *boss* is down there! If he sees me, or sees my clothes, I'll never work again."

"Relax. I'll take care of it."

"How? How can you possibly explain my underwear lying on the floor down there like a bright red beacon? It might as well have blinking neon lights." She continued to pace about in the dark. "I'm so screwed."

"No' entirely. But I'm still hopeful."

"What? I'm half naked, my underwear's downstairs with my boss—ouch!" She collided with a piece of furniture. "And I can't see!"

"Emma, ye're starting to panic."

"I'm in pain!" She jumped up and down, rubbing her sore toes. "And I'm half naked, and I can't see. I bet you can see just fine, can't you, you bloody super Vamp."

"Emma." He grabbed her by the shoulders, led her to a long shadow, and sat her down. "Stay right here, take deep breaths, and I'll be right back with yer clothes." He disappeared.

Now she was *alone*, half naked, in pain, and couldn't see. She closed her eyes, took a big breath, and focused on regaining control. She was a professional, dammit. She'd faced the enemy many times and come through. She'd slain four vampires. She was woman. She was invincible.

She opened her eyes and let her sight adjust to the darkness. She was sitting on some sort of couch that felt like velvet. Across from her was a large rectangular piece of furniture. A desk. Something glowed faintly on top. A computer monitor, facing away from her. To her left were the windows.

She hooked her bra together and buttoned her shirt.

She circled the couch and headed slowly across the room. The carpet was thick beneath her bare feet. From the light of one window, she made out a bar. She reached a wall and found a doorknob. Two doorknobs. She opened the double doors. More darkness. She felt along the wall and clicked on a light switch.

The room was empty, thank goodness. A large bed dominated the room, covered with a tan suede comforter. Very masculine. Was this where Angus slept during the day? Or rather, lay there dead as a doornail. The enormity of her situation punched her in the chest.

She'd been making love to a vampire.

"Oh God." She turned away from the bed.

The light from the bedroom made it possible to see the office. The furnishings looked like valuable antiques. The couch where she'd sat was more like an old-fashioned chaise with one curved arm. A maroon chenille throw lay draped over the raised end. She wrapped it around her waist like a skirt.

She spotted a door and peered outside. The coast was clear. She stepped out and found herself on the top landing of the stairs.

"I'm not leaving here till I know she's safe!" Sean's booming voice echoed up the stairwell.

A man replied with a softer, calmer voice, but she couldn't make out the words. It seemed fairly certain, though, that Sean had to be in the foyer. That was good, if it meant he'd not been allowed into the living room where her clothes were lying about. But it was also bad, because there was no way she could get down the stairs without him seeing her. Maybe Angus could teleport her out. But that still didn't solve the problem

with her clothes. With a silent groan, she padded back
to the office.

A chiming noise came from the computer. E-mail.

Emma glanced back. She was alone. Of course, a
vampire could teleport here in a second. She would
have to be fast.

She rounded the desk and saw that a new message
had arrived. The message was from Mikhail. The
subject—E. Wallace's parents.

Her heart stuttered. Her parents? She clicked the
message open.

```
Still investigating the murders of
E. Wallace's parents. Attaching a list
of all known Malcontents in Moscow
during that summer.
```

Emma's heart raced as she opened the attachment. A
list of eighteen names appeared. She recognized only
one name—Ivan Petrovsky, and he was already dead.
Of the remaining seventeen, two had to be her parents'
murderers.

Seventeen vampires. Could she kill that many? Did
she have any choice?

She clicked on *Print* and straightened.

"Did ye find something useful?" Angus asked softly.

Chapter 14

The fleeting look of guilt on Emma's face did little to soothe the pain twisting in Angus's gut. How could she? How could she writhe under his touch, scream with pleasure, then spy on him at the first chance?

As the whir of the printer started, Emma raised her chin defiantly. "This is information about my parents. You said you would share it with me."

"Did a message arrive from my operative in Moscow?"

"If you're referring to Mikhail, yes."

"Then apparently ye're more up to date than I am."

"Why shouldn't I be? They're *my* parents."

"And that was *my* e-mail on *my* computer." He dropped her clothes and backpack on the red velvet chaise. "I hope ye have yer cell phone here somewhere." It certainly hadn't been on her body. He'd explored every inch of that.

"It's in my backpack. Why?" She removed the paper from the printer.

He tamped down on the anger growing inside him. "Sean Whelan will be calling ye any second now. He's downstairs and refuses to leave until he knows ye're all right. He thinks I'm holding ye prisoner and torturing you."

"Oh." A light blush dusted her cheeks. The afghan around her waist loosened, and she dropped the paper on the desk to adjust her makeshift skirt. "What did you tell him?"

Angus gritted his teeth. She was so damned lovely when she blushed. "I lied. I told him I'd taken ye home."

A jangling sound came from her backpack. She dashed around the desk to the chaise and unzipped her backpack. The phone continued its annoying musical phrase.

"Shit," she muttered as she rummaged through the backpack. The afghan slipped just as she located her phone.

He caught the afghan around her hips.

"Thanks," she breathed, then opened her phone. "Hello?"

Angus yanked the afghan off. Her mouth opened with indignation.

"Oh, hello, Sean," she spoke into the phone while giving Angus an annoyed look.

He stepped back, dropped the afghan on the desk, and picked up the paper she'd printed.

"I'm fine." She glowered at Angus. "Perfectly dandy."

He leaned against the desk, examining the list of names Mikhail had sent. They were all Malcontents who had been in Moscow the summer Emma's parents had been murdered. Angus wondered if he'd over-reacted to her snooping. It was natural for her to be curious about her parents. How could she have resisted such a message?

He could hear Sean Whelan's strident voice on the other end of Emma's phone.

"No, he didn't harm me." She smoothed down the tail ends of her shirt as if to make sure all her private parts were covered. When she glanced up, Angus winked at her. She made a face and turned her back to him.

He cocked his head, admiring the sweet curve where her upper thighs met her rounded arse. A man didn't need to be undead to want to sink his teeth into that glorious flesh.

"He took me home, using teleportation," Emma continued to talk to Sean. "No, I'm fine. I felt a little woozy, but that's all. And they took Garrett home, too. What happened to you?"

Angus winced as he heard Sean's tirade on evil experiments, his victimized daughter, and the demon baby she would deliver in a few days.

Emma glanced back at Angus with a worried look. "I don't know what to say, Sean. We can only hope for the best."

She leaned over to examine the clothes Angus had deposited on the chaise. He tilted his head more to the side. What a view.

"There's nothing more you can do right now." She

leaned over more. "I'm sure they'll let you go. They let me go."

Angus tilted more. Good God, he could see heaven.

"All right. Good-bye." She closed her phone and dropped it in the backpack. "Sean says the Scotsman is escorting him to his car. But there's another problem. I can't find my underwear." She glanced back, then straightened with a jerk.

Angus straightened.

Her cheeks blushed. She tugged at her shirttails. "Your eyes are red again."

"I saw a vision."

"You saw my ass. Where's my underwear?"

"I saw a vision of beauty. I saw our future."

A pained look crossed her face. "We have no future. You know that."

He stepped toward her. "I know I promised to make ye scream several times, and I'm a man of my word."

"I—I release you from that promise."

" 'Tis no' what ye want."

"We don't always get what we want." She snatched her pants up and began putting them on.

"What were ye going to do with this list? Were ye planning to kill all seventeen?"

She turned her back to him to zip up her pants. "If you want to help me, I'd appreciate it."

"And if I doona help ye?"

She glanced at him, frowning. "I have to do it. My father's last words to me were *Avenge us*."

"Then ye did witness the murders. That's how ye knew about vampires."

She sat on the chaise. "A part of me died that night with them."

"Lass, revenge is no' going to bring yer parents back."

"It's not revenge! It's justice."

He picked up the list of names. "I know most of these men. They're the worst assassins in the vampire world." She was trying to kill her grief with violence. He recognized the signs. He'd done it himself after his wife's rejection.

Emma stuffed her feet into her shoes. "I've come too far to give up now. Everything I have done and learned for the past six years has led me to this moment."

"Then it has all led you to me."

Her eyes widened. "I don't believe in fate. We make our own choices in life."

"And you have chosen to trust me. Please, Emma, doona go after these men. You doona need to slay every dragon in the world to prove yer love. Yer parents know ye love them."

She looked away, clenching her fists.

"Let me find the two who are responsible."

She met his eyes. "And then?"

"I'll help you find the justice ye need. In the meantime, I'll transfer two of my employees here and have them watch over Central Park."

"I thought you and I were going to police the park."

She actually looked disappointed. Would she miss him? "We will until my employees arrive. I canna stay here indefinitely. I have to find Casimir. He's growing an evil army, and if there's another war, many will die."

He pushed away from the desk and strode toward her. "Imagine an army of over five hundred Malcontents, all feeding off mortals every night, then killing them because they know too much. 'Twill be a massacre."

Her face paled. "Is that what happened with the first war?"

"Aye. The battle raged on for three nights. A dozen villages in Hungary were destroyed. A few mortals escaped, and their tales spawned some of the legends ye still hear today."

"Stories of evil vampires?"

"Aye." He sat on the chaise beside her. "That was long before synthetic blood. Both sides had to feed off humans. Both sides were killing. Although we tried never to kill mortals, we probably appeared as evil as the enemy."

"If there's another war, will you be the general?"

"Aye."

She winced. "I hate to think of you in so much danger."

"Hopefully, it willna come to that."

"Do you want me to tell Sean about this? I could tell him that we talked before you took me home."

"From what I've seen of yer boss, I doubt he'll believe any of this."

She sighed. "He hates vampires with a passion. I don't know why."

"Ye have cause to hate, too, but ye believe me."

Smiling, she touched his cheek. "I like you too much."

He took her hand and kissed the palm. There was no

such thing as too much. He wanted it all. "Where shall I teleport you—yer apartment or Austin Erickson's?"

"I've been meaning to ask you. How do you know about Austin?"

"He works for me."

Her mouth dropped open. "I thought he was constructing something in Malaysia."

"He and his wife, Darcy, are in Eastern Europe, helping with the search for Casimir."

Emma's eyes widened. "Austin married the vampire director of a reality show?"

"She's no longer a Vamp."

"She's no longer *dead*?"

"No longer undead. 'Tis a long story, but Roman was able to change her back."

"You're kidding! There's a cure?" Emma gave him an incredulous look. "Why don't more of you change back?"

He gritted his teeth. "Maybe some of us like being the way we are."

"Oh." She winced. "I didn't mean to offend you."

He arched a brow. "Being undead comes with some valuable talents. Being mortal does, too. I have quite a few mortals working for me. Ye have the advantage of daylight."

"So Austin is still fighting vampires."

"The bad ones, aye." Angus tilted his head. "Ye could work for me. I'd hire ye in a second."

Her mouth dropped open again. "You would hire me after I tried to kill you?"

"Somehow I was under the impression, while ye

were climaxing in my arms, that ye'd gotten over yer ill feelings."

Her cheeks tinted pink. "It is true that I no longer harbor any ill will toward you."

"Yer kindness is overwhelming. But ye seemed downright happy when ye were shuddering and screaming in—"

"All right!" She held up a hand. "But that's a very good reason why I shouldn't work for you. People would suspect that we were a bit . . . involved, and that's never—"

"A bit *involved*?" He motioned toward the bedroom. "If Connor hadn't returned with yer boss, we'd be in there right now, tupping like rabbits."

She scoffed. "That's not true." She glanced at the bedroom. "I would have—I might have said no."

"When?" He moved closer. "Would ye have said no after I had kissed every inch of yer beautiful body? Or would ye have waited till I made ye scream for a second or third time?"

She pressed her hands to her reddened cheeks. "Please. I—I can't . . ."

"What?" He held her by the shoulders.

She closed her eyes and whispered, "I can't love you."

The words slammed into him like a thunderbolt. He released her and moved back. His heart squeezed in his chest. The devil take it, he wanted her love. When the hell had that happened? She looked so miserable. Bugger. "I'm sorry. I'll take ye home."

She nodded, refusing to look at him.

He handed her the backpack. "Which apartment?"

"Mine."

"I've teleported there before. I remember the way." He stood next to her, his arms opening. "I have to hold you."

"I understand." She stood stiffly as he embraced her.

"Ye need to hold on." Once she'd placed her hands on his shoulders, he closed his eyes and concentrated. When their bodies wavered, her fingers tensed and she clung to him.

In a few seconds, they arrived in her small living room. As soon as she was solid, she released him.

She dropped her backpack on the loveseat. "When will your men be able to guard Central Park?"

"In a night or two. Most of them are working under-cover right now in Eastern Europe, so there's a problem with the time difference and locating them. And I'll have to do some shuffling around to make sure my clients are still protected."

"Then tomorrow you and I will patrol the park?"

"Aye. But ye must understand, Emma, we canna kill the Malcontents at this time. It would only serve to push the vampire world into a war we doona want."

She nodded. "All right. As long as the humans are protected. I'll meet you at the stone bridge by the Pond at nine o'clock?"

"I'll be there." He extended his hand. "Allies?" He wanted to say *lovers*, but this would have to do for now.

She shook his hand briefly, then let go. "Allies."

Chapter 15

He was going to be late. Emma checked her watch once again. Two minutes till nine, and he was nowhere in sight. Granted her eyesight wasn't nearly as good as his in the dark, moonlit surroundings of Central Park. She could always reach out to him psychically, but she really didn't want him inside her head. He was already too much in her heart.

She leaned her elbows on the bridge's stone wall and surveyed the area around the Pond. No men in kilts. He could be wearing trousers, though. The rascal looked equally gorgeous in both. Her gaze zeroed in on a young man in the distance, wearing jeans and a sweatshirt. No, not Angus. There was no mistaking his broad shoulders and long auburn hair.

There was simply no one like him.

Her heart grew heavy. Why couldn't he be human? Fifty years from now, he would have forgotten all about her. She'd be one of many humans who had come and gone, swept away like the dead leaves of autumn. God help her, she wanted to be different. She wanted to be special to him. She wanted to be loved.

Her heart sank lower. Why couldn't she be attracted to a normal guy? Ha! Who on earth would be attracted to a normal guy when Angus was around? His old-fashioned sense of honor and gentlemanly behavior touched her heart. He was the hero of a young girl's fantasies. Strong, brave, dependable, intelligent. But he was also a grown woman's fantasy—sexy, aggressive, and a little bit dangerous. How could she resist such a man?

"Good evening."

She turned with a gasp. "I didn't see you coming."

"Ye were deep in thought."

Thinking about him. Thank God she could block her mind from him. Even so, she realized the warmth invading her cheeks betrayed her innermost thoughts. Angus looked gorgeous as usual. He was wearing the blue and green plaid kilt. His hunter-green socks matched his sweater. The hilt of a knife showed above his right sock. The leather straps crossing his chest could only mean his claymore was on his back.

She cleared her throat. "You came prepared."

"As did you."

"Yes." She hitched her bag of stakes higher on her shoulder. "Thank you for coming."

He smiled slowly.

Too gorgeous. A feeling of awkwardness nettled her.

"Shall we?" He extended his hand.

Did he expect her to hold his hand? Or was he merely motioning for her to start walking? Too awkward. She headed north, leaving the bridge behind. He strolled beside her. Close beside her. For a big man, he moved very quietly. She adjusted her bag to hear the comforting rattle of stakes break the silence.

Why was he being so quiet? She tried to think of something normal to talk about. "So, do you always wear the same plaid?"

"'Tis the MacKay tartan. Ye doona like my kilts?"

"Oh, I do. I just wondered if you had more than one." She winced. Brilliant. Why not insult the man? "I mean, more than one style."

He smiled. "I have actually acquired quite a few clothes over the centuries."

Several centuries of fashion stuffed into one closet? It was mind-boggling. "You mean you still have wigs and waistcoats and lacy shirts?"

"Aye. Stashed away somewhere in my castle."

Her mouth dropped open. His *castle*? Good heavens, how could anyone have a normal conversation with Angus MacKay? He was . . . fascinating.

His hand brushed against hers as they walked.

She thought about moving a bit to the right, out of his reach, but she didn't. It would be too obvious and more . . . awkward. "You'll be able to hear an attack anywhere in the park?"

"Aye. Just to be safe, I asked Connor to patrol the northern half."

"That's good. We'll have backup, if we need it."

"Aye." His hand lingered close to hers.

Her heart beat faster. "It seems odd that we just met last Friday night."

"Aye." He entwined his fingers with hers.

Her heart swelled with longing. "This is only our fifth night together."

"When ye've lived as long as I have, ye realize how relative time is. I've endured centuries that passed in the blink of an eye as if I were barely breathing." He stopped and faced her. "Or I can experience an entire lifetime in the span of a few nights. All the hope and passion that makes life worth living, 'tis suddenly surrounding me like a gift from God."

"Oh, Angus." Then she *was* different. She *was* special.

"We canna deny what is happening to us, Emma."

She released his hand. "I don't deny it. But we also can't deny that there's no chance for us."

"Emma—"

"No." She held up a hand. "I don't want to be one of a long line of human girlfriends. I—I feel special to you right now, just as I am. And I need to leave it that way. I want to be able to say good-bye when you go with my heart still full. Not drained and desolate. Can you understand?"

"Nay. For one thing, ye're assuming a sad ending."

"How could it possibly be anything else but sad? We're from two different worlds."

He frowned. "We're more alike than ye think. And there has never been a long line of mortal girlfriends."

"You fed off human women for centuries. You told me you left them all very satisfied. That sounds like a long line of lovers to me."

"That was survival. That was me giving back to faceless women I canna remember, so I wouldna feel guilty for stealing their blood. Ye *are* different,

Emma. I doona need ye in order to survive. But surviving is no' the same as living. Or the same as feeling human again. I am alive when I'm with you. Ye feed my soul."

She stared at him, unblinking. Good heavens, what could she say to this? *Take me, I'm yours?*

He turned his head to the side. "I heard a scream."

She listened carefully, but heard nothing.

"This way." He motioned for her to follow.

She jogged alongside him, going north. "I don't hear anything."

"They'll have control of their victim by now. There will be no more screams." After several minutes, he halted. "We're close now," he whispered. "Yer stakes are making noise."

She removed the bag from her shoulder and wrapped the stakes tightly together. "Better?" She cradled them against her chest.

He nodded and placed a finger to his lips. She followed him quietly as he left the brick pathway and headed through a grove of trees. The moonlight barely pierced through the canopy of budding leaves overhead. The air grew more chill. Angus became a large shadow that she trailed closely. A breeze ruffled the leaves and brought the sound of a male voice.

"Hey, man, leave some for me."

Emma's skin prickled with gooseflesh. Angus was moving very slowly now. She glanced around nervously, hoping all the dark shapes around them were only trees.

"Shit, what are you doing?" the same voice complained loudly. "That's no way to treat a woman. I wouldn't treat a ho like that."

"Quiet, you fool," another voice hissed.

"Hey, feeding is one thing, but you're killing her. That just ain't right."

Angus drew Emma alongside him so she could see the clearing in front of them. Moonlight gleamed off a huge granite boulder, tinting the clearing with ghostly shades of gray. A male vampire, dressed in black, had a woman pinned to the ground. She looked silvery pale in the moonlight. Her eyes were black and glassy. The only color was the red blood oozing from twin punctures on her neck.

A second vampire, a black man dressed in torn blue jeans and a gray hooded sweatshirt, paced nervously close by. "Shit, man. I hate this."

The first vampire sank his fangs into the woman's neck once again. Emma flinched. The woman would never survive a second bite. Angus held her arm to keep her from moving forward.

"Cut it out, bro!" The black vampire jumped about, trying to get the other vampire's attention. "You're sucking her dry. She's gonna die!"

In a flash, Angus zoomed into the clearing, drawing his claymore. He pricked the first vampire in the neck. "Release her."

Emma flipped her bag open and retrieved a stake.

"What the hell?" The black vampire moved away.

Emma jumped into the clearing and blocked his escape. She pointed her stake at his heart. "Stay right where you are."

"Shit." The black vampire stared at her, then at Angus. "Who the hell are you?"

The first vampire rose slowly to his feet. Blood

dripped from his distended fangs. He backed away, but Angus followed him, his sword aimed at the evil vampire's heart.

"This park is under my protection," Angus growled. "Ye will do no more killing here."

"I remember you," the evil vampire spoke with a Russian accent. "You were at the ball last year at Romatech. You crushed Ivan's watch. You're Angus MacKay."

"So now you're following orders from Katya?" Angus asked softly. "Did she ask you to kill for her?"

"I would do anything for her."

"Then tell her this, *Alek*." When the vampire flinched, Angus continued, "Aye, I know who ye are. Ye were an errand boy for Ivan Petrovsky, and now ye're doing Katya's dirty work."

Emma glanced at the injured woman. How long were these guys going to chat while she lay there bleeding to death? "I'll call an ambulance."

Alek gasped when he looked at her. "You! You're the one I saw before. You killed Vladimir."

Emma swallowed hard. This was the vampire who had gotten away last summer. The only one who knew who she was.

"I was right." Alek glared at her. "The slayer is a mortal woman." He glanced at Angus. "But you're helping her, aren't you?"

"Angus." Emma gave him a pleading look. If this vampire lived, he would tell all the Malcontents that she and Angus were working together.

He charged at Alek, but just before his sword could make contact, Alek vanished.

"Nay!" Angus's sword impaled a tree. "The devil take it." He ripped his sword loose.

"Damn," the black vampire muttered. "Who are you guys? The vampire po-po?"

Angus strode toward the black vampire, scowling. "Doona move."

The vampire raised his hands in surrender. "You da man. I don't mess with no brother with a three-foot blade."

While Angus pointed his claymore at the black vampire's heart, Emma rushed to the injured woman. "She's dying. We have to help her."

"I've called Connor mentally. He should be here—" Angus stopped when Connor appeared beside him.

Connor quickly surveyed the scene. His eyes flashed with anger when he saw the injured woman. He glowered at the black vampire. "Ye bastard, I should throttle you."

"I didn't do it!" the black vampire shouted. "I know, I know, I always tell the po-po I didn't do it, but this time I really mean it. I didn't get a drop out of her. I'm still starving." He glanced at Emma with a speculative look.

She glared back. "Don't even think about it."

"Connor, can ye take the woman to Romatech?" Angus asked. "Roman can save her. Then ye can remove her memory and take her home."

"Will do." Connor gathered the woman in his arms, then vanished.

"Where's everybody going?" the black vampire asked.

"Who are you?" Angus stepped toward him.

He backed up. "I'll be a damned shish kebab if you come any closer with that super-sized switchblade. I've already died once this week, and I don't want to go through that again."

"Ye were transformed this last week?"

"Yeah. That psycho Russian dude did it to me. I was minding my own business, and business was good, if you know what I mean. I had a fine reputation. I had it going on. Then that son of a bitch Alek came along—"

"You were selling drugs?" Emma moved toward him.

"Now, ain't that just the way?" The black vampire frowned at her. "Just because I'm a brother, you assume I'm trafficking."

"Were you?" she asked.

He shrugged. "A man's gotta make a living. Look, girlfriend, I ain't got nothing against you, but I'm starvin', and you're smelling really sweet."

"Touch her and ye die," Angus growled.

"Whoa, bro." He lifted both hands in surrender. "I didn't realize you were, uh, interested in those of a female persuasion, what with that skirt you're wearing and—"

"Enough." Angus slid his claymore back into its sheath. "Drink this." He opened his sporran and removed his flask.

"Nice purse," the black vampire muttered. "I know a guy who can get you a designer one real cheap."

Angus gritted his teeth. "'Tis no' a purse!"

"Whatever you say, man." The black vampire accepted the flask. "This ain't no poison, is it? You know, that's why those bastards killed me. They're making some kind of vampire poison."

" 'Tis safe. Drink," Angus ordered.

"Vampire poison?" Emma asked.

"Nightshade," Angus muttered.

"Yeah, that's what they called it." The vampire sniffed at the contents of the flask. "Whoa! This smells good. What is this shit?"

"Blissky. A mixture of synthetic blood and Scotch whisky."

Ah. Now Emma understood why she'd smelled whisky on Angus's breath that first night. She waited for the black vampire to finish his drink.

And waited. She glanced at Angus.

His mouth twitched. "Apparently, our guest is verra hungry."

"Oo-wee!" The black vampire wiped his mouth. "That's some good shit." He upended the flask again, but it was empty. "You got any more of this?"

"We have dozens of bottles at home," Angus answered. "And we can get more whenever we like."

"No shit? You know, those damned Russians don't have anything to eat at their house. They go out every freaking night to attack people. I told them they should be attacking the local blood bank, you know, and storing up some snacks at their crib, but would they listen to me? No."

"You doona wish to harm people?"

"Hell, no. I ain't no killer." He winked at Emma. "I'm more of a lover, you understand."

"You're not exactly a law-abiding citizen," Emma reminded him.

"I gotta make a living. I—I have people depending on me."

"What is yer name?" Angus asked.

"Phineas McKinney."

"McKinney?"

Phineas shrugged. "The brothers used to call me Master Phin." He raised his chin defiantly. "Now I wish to be called Dr. Phang."

Angus arched a brow.

Emma dropped her stake back into her bag. "Why would the Russians transform you?"

Phineas frowned and shuffled his feet. "They wanted easy access to some drugs. Their queen bitch is making that poison."

"You mean Katya?" Emma asked.

"Yeah, her royal highness bee-yotch." Phineas waved a hand in the air. "She had her evil minion kill me, then she acts like she's done me some big favor. Made me sleep on the floor in her basement like some kind of dog. And when I tried to go back to my family, she— she threatened to kill them all."

"I'm so sorry," Emma whispered.

"We've stayed here long enough." Angus retrieved his cell phone from his sporran. "Alek could return with a dozen Malcontents. We'll teleport to the townhouse."

Phineas winced. "I ain't very good at that teleporting."

"I'll take you." Angus punched in a number on his phone. "Ian? Ye wanted advance warning. This is it. I'm coming in with two." He dropped his phone back into his sporran, then wrapped one arm around Emma and pulled her close. Then he motioned for Phineas to approach.

Phineas gave him a wary look.

" 'Tis either us or the Malcontents," Angus told him. "Do ye want to spend an eternity attacking the innocent just to survive?"

Phineas took a hesitant step forward. "But I don't even know you, man."

"I'm Angus MacKay." He grasped Phineas around the shoulders. "Ye've made the right decision."

Phineas snorted. "Maybe I'm just coming for the Blissky."

Everything went black, but only for a few seconds. Emma's feet landed solidly in the foyer of Roman's townhouse.

Ian was standing by the staircase, his weapon drawn. His gaze passed over her, clearly not seeing her as a threat, then focused on Phineas. "Who are you?" He marched toward Phineas, raising his sword.

"Shit!" Phineas ducked behind Angus. "What's with you guys and the swords?"

" 'Tis all right, Ian," Angus said. "I brought him here on purpose."

Ian nodded. "I had to make sure he hadn't coerced ye somehow." He slid his claymore back into its sheath.

Phineas peeked around Angus. "You know, you guys wouldn't have to act so macho all the time if you weren't wearing those skirts. It's called compensation, you know."

Ian grimaced. "Are ye certain I canna skewer him?"

"Nay." Angus patted Phineas on the back. "He's going to stay here for a while."

Ian gave him a dubious look. "Who are ye, exactly?"

Phineas lifted his chin. "I'm Dr. Phang."

"Oh." Ian's eyes widened. "Ye're here for Shanna then?"

"Shanna who?"

"Shanna Draganesti," Ian said. "She's having a baby."

"I didn't do it!" Phineas stepped back, raising his hands. "I don't even know a Shanna."

Emma laughed.

"Ye're no' the father," Angus growled.

"That's what I always say." Phineas planted his hands on his hips. "But does anyone ever believe me? No."

"We believe you." Angus turned to Ian. "He's no' a real doctor. His title is somewhat . . . honorary in nature."

"That's right." Phineas nodded. "That's me, I'm honorary."

"And he's working for me now," Angus announced.

Phineas blinked. "I am?"

"He is?" Ian looked skeptical.

Emma smiled. Tonight had given her an excellent opportunity to watch Angus in action. She liked what she saw. He was a noble and kindhearted man.

He folded his arms over his chest, studying Phineas. "Can ye fight, lad?"

"What do you think? I'm from the Bronx."

"Ye must follow our rules," Angus continued. "And the main rule is ye can never harm a mortal again. No biting. Ye'll take yer meals from a bottle. Can ye do that?"

"Hell, yeah." Phineas looked at Ian. "Hey, you got any more of that Blissky around here? I'm still hungry."

"No more Blissky tonight," Angus ordered. "Ian, bring him a warm bottle of Type O."

"Sure." Ian strode to the kitchen.

Phineas wandered around the foyer. "You all stay here?"

"I'm just visiting," Angus explained. "Connor, Ian, and Dougal live here. Ye can live here, too."

"No shit?" Phineas's eyes lit up. He peeked into the library. "Cool."

"I expect ye to work for me."

"In exchange for room and board. I get it." Phineas peered into the living room. "Whoa, what a mother of wide-screen TVs. Do you get the Knicks?"

"Ye'll be working under Connor, and ye'll be paid twice a month."

Phineas spun around to stare at Angus. "Paid? Like real paychecks?"

"Aye."

Phineas's mouth dropped open. "No one's ever offered me a real job before."

Angus regarded him sternly. "Doona make me regret it."

"No, no. I'll be cool. I—I need a job. I have family that depends on me. I can send them some money, right?"

"Of course. But ye canna tell them what ye have become, or what kind of work ye're doing. Believe me, they willna understand."

"I kinda figured that." Phineas's eyes glistened with tears. "I have a little brother and sister. They're staying with my aunt, but she's got diabetes real bad, so she can't work. They all depend on me, and I—I've been real worried about them."

"You have no parents?" Emma asked.

Phineas shook his head. "My mom died of AIDS,

and my dad ran off when I was little. I've been worried sick about my family. They don't know what happened to me, and those damned Russians wouldn't let me go."

Angus nodded. "Ian can drive ye home for a wee visit." He removed a wad of bills from his sporran. "This is an advance on yer first paycheck. Leave it with yer family, for I canna guarantee how often ye can go back to see them."

"That's cool, brother." Phineas accepted the cash.

Ian came back with a bottle of blood which he passed to Phineas. "I'm Ian MacPhie. I still doona know yer real name."

"Phineas McKinney." He took a swig from the bottle.

Ian blinked. "McKinney?"

Angus smiled. "Apparently he's Scottish."

Ian studied him with narrowed eyes. "I've known a few McKinneys over the years, but they never looked like him."

Angus shrugged. "He's one of us now. After ye drive him home for a wee visit, ye need to start his training."

"What training?" Phineas gulped down more blood.

"Martial arts and fencing," Angus replied.

"Oh hell, brother, I already know how to fence things."

Ian laughed. "We mean sword fighting."

Phineas's mouth dropped open. "You mean I get one of those gargantuan mother switchblades?"

"A claymore, aye." Ian grabbed Phineas by the arm and led him to the front door. "Ye'll be a warrior just like us."

"Cool." Phineas glanced back at Angus before leaving. "But I ain't wearing no skirt!"

Emma laughed as the door shut. "You're a sweet man, Angus MacKay."

He snorted. "I dinna help him entirely out of kindness. The Malcontents outnumber us, and Roman is opposed to transforming more honorable vampires. It puts us in a bind."

"I see." Emma nodded, then smiled. "But I still think you're sweet." He'd seen a goodness in Phineas that many would have overlooked.

Angus stepped closer to her. "So ye find me attractive, do ye?"

"Yes. And I trust you." What a huge change in just a few days. Only Angus could have managed that.

He held her by the shoulders. "Then trust me on this. Ye're in grave danger. I want ye to spend the night with me."

Chapter 16

Somehow Emma didn't feel that a night alone with Angus MacKay would be entirely danger-free. But it would definitely be exciting. "It's not as bad as you think."

Angus frowned at her. "Alek knows ye're the slayer. No doubt he's told Katya by now, and they're looking to murder you."

"Maybe, but they don't know my name or where I live. Until they figure that out, I'm relatively safe."

"Relatively is no' good enough. They know ye're mortal and easy to kill. They know I'm helping you."

"All the more reason for us to separate."

"Nay." He gently squeezed her shoulders. "I willna leave ye unprotected."

She fought the urge to melt into his arms. "It's not that I don't appreciate your concern. You're very kind—"

"Kind, my arse. 'Tis more a case of pride and stubbornness. I'm determined to keep ye safe, lass, and I willna be thwarted. I'm a man of my word."

An honorable, medieval knight in shining armor. He was so irresistible, she could almost forget about his undead status. Almost, but not quite. She touched his cheek. "I know you're an honorable man, but I don't think I should be alone with you."

"You're not alone," a strange voice muttered.

With a gasp, Emma spun around. Two men were standing by the staircase. Very handsome men. One was wearing a kilt. She recognized him as Robby from Paris. The other man was wearing an expensive suit and a knowing smirk. They must have teleported in.

"The answering machine was on." Robby dropped his cell phone into his sporran. "We heard ye needed help, Angus."

"Indeed." The suited one smiled slowly as his gaze swept over Emma. "I can see your hands are full."

She blushed. Was there no privacy at all in the vampire world? At least tonight she was fully dressed. She strengthened her mental firewall to block all attempts at telepathy.

"Thank ye for coming." Angus strode toward the front door and punched a button on the security panel. Then he approached the visitors and patted Robby on the back. "Thank ye for coming, but are ye leaving Jean-Luc unguarded?"

Robby shrugged. "He insisted he dinna need a nurse-maid, and ye needed me more." He bowed to Emma. "How do ye do, Miss Wallace?"

"I'm fine, thank you." Emma adjusted the strap to her bag on her shoulder. The stakes rattled.

Robby blinked.

The one in a suit smiled. "*La signorina* likes to live dangerously."

Emma recognized his voice as the first one who had spoken. His Italian accent was faint, but still there.

Angus motioned toward him. "This is Jack from Venice."

He rolled his eyes. "Angus is always trying to anglicize me. I am Giacomo *di Venezia*."

With a snort, Angus glanced at Emma. "If he tells ye his family name is Casanova, doona believe it."

"Ah." Giacomo placed a hand over his heart. "You wound me, old friend." He bowed to Emma. "Consider me at your service, *signorina*."

Who were these guys? Rob Roy and Casanova? Emma couldn't believe how much her life had changed in just a few nights. It was enough to drive her to drinking Blissky *sans* blood.

"Any news about the search for Casimir?" Angus asked.

"The latest rumors indicate he's somewhere in Eastern Europe," Robby answered.

"We can rule out Poland," Giacomo added. "I was just there with Zoltan and his men. We found a village that experienced a number of unexplained, sudden deaths a month ago. We believe he was there, but has moved south."

"Then we're catching up with him. Good." Angus nodded. "Meanwhile, I have an assignment for you here."

"Can we eat first? I've been working for over eight hours now, and I'm starving." Giacomo's dark eyes glimmered as he gazed at Emma.

She glared back.

Angus shook his head. "Doona tease her, Jack. She has stakes, and she's no' afraid to use them."

He chuckled. "I hear Roman's new drink is excellent."

"Aye, Blissky. This way." Angus led the two men into the kitchen while he explained about the murders in Central Park.

Emma stood alone in the foyer for a few seconds, then decided she might as well go into the kitchen, too. She pushed open the swinging door.

"Ye'll be keeping the park safe every night." Angus stood at the kitchen counter pouring Blissky into glasses.

While Robby and Giacomo asked questions, Emma surveyed the kitchen. Refrigerator, microwave, pristine stovetop. Obviously, no one did any real cooking here. Her gaze wandered toward the table and did a double-take when she spotted red lace. Her mouth fell open.

Her underwear?

She glanced back at the trio of vampire men. They were busy with their Blissky, drinking and praising it in all its gory glory. She edged toward the table, then making sure she blocked their view, she plopped her bag of stakes on top of her panties.

"Emma?"

She whirled around at the sound of Angus's voice. "Yes?"

"Would ye like something to drink? We have some soft drinks, and I still remember how to make a cup of tea."

"Cola's fine. Something diet, please." She circled the

table to sit facing them, then rested her hands on top of her bag. Slowly she dragged it toward her.

When Angus turned his back to open the refrigerator, she slid the bag to the edge of the table. The red panties fell into her lap. A piece of paper fluttered to the floor. She leaned to the side to see where it landed.

"So you've managed to kill four Malcontents?" Giacomo approached the table.

She slapped a hand over the red underwear in her lap. "Yes, I have."

"Amazing." The Italian Vamp sat across from her and set his drink on the table. "A mortal killing vampires. You must be fearless."

"Emma is verra cool under pressure." Angus filled a glass with ice.

Oh, right. Very cool. She only went berserk the night before when she discovered herself in a strange place with no underwear.

"Well, she *is* a Wallace," Robby observed.

She doubted her famous ancestor had ever tried to hide red underwear. She set her bag in her lap, then slipped the panties inside. She reached down to retrieve the paper that had landed by her chair.

"Did you drop something?" Giacomo asked.

"No." She grabbed the paper and then straightened, slipping it also into her bag. "Just a mosquito bite on my leg. Itches like crazy."

"Bloodsuckers." Giacomo smiled slowly. "Don't you just hate them?"

Did he really expect a response to that? She frowned at him. "I hear some of them carry disease."

He laughed. "I like her, Angus."

"Ye'll like her from a distance," Angus muttered as he set a diet cola in front of Emma.

With a grin, Giacomo raised his glass. "To *amore.*" He drained his glass dry.

"Miss Wallace, may I ask how ye slayed the Malcontents?" Robby strode toward her. "Did ye use a sword or one of yer stakes?"

"Stake." Emma gulped down some cola.

"May I see yer stakes?"

She coughed, then cleared her throat. "I—I'd rather not."

Angus snorted. "Ye were never too shy to show them to me. I had to destroy a few that came too close for comfort."

Giacomo laughed. "She tried to kill you?" He leaned forward to peek at her bag. "They must be terrifying."

"Nay. I'll show you." In a flash, Angus grabbed the bag from Emma's lap. He opened it, looked inside, and blinked. He dipped his head for a closer look.

Giacomo stood, smiling. "What is it? Have you discovered her secret weapon?"

"Nay, a souvenir." Angus stuck his hand into the bag. Emma winced.

"Here ye go." Angus slapped two stakes onto the table. "Souvenirs from the slayer." He returned Emma's bag to her lap.

She sighed with relief. She should have known he would be a gentleman.

Robby and Giacomo each picked up a stake to examine it.

Robby shook his head. "Too small. I prefer my claymore." He dropped the stake into his sporran.

"And I'll rely on my dagger." Giacomo slipped his souvenir into a jacket pocket. "We should be on our way." He bowed to Emma. "A pleasure to meet you, *signorina*."

"Likewise." Emma stood, clasping her bag to her chest. "Thank you both for protecting the park." She waited for both men to leave the room, then sat down with a relieved sigh.

Angus retrieved his glass of Blissky from the counter and took a long drink. "How did yer knickers get into yer bag?"

She gave him an aggravated look. "They were prominently displayed on the kitchen table for the entire world to see. I had to hide them somewhere. That reminds me—" She removed the paper from her bag. "There was a note on the table, too."

Angus strode toward her, his hand outstretched. "That's probably for me."

She glowered at him. "*My* knickers, *my* note." She unfolded the paper.

He waggled his fingers in a *gimme* gesture. " 'Tis *my* note. And I claim yer knickers as spoils of war."

She snorted. She was too irritated to give him the note, even though it was clearly addressed to him. "Don't tell me you collect women's underwear."

"Only yers, love." He leaned over the table. "And only if I've had the pleasure of removing it myself."

Did he realize he'd just called her *love*? Or was it simply a common word to him like it was to many British? Although she couldn't recall him using the word before.

He snatched the paper from her hands.

"Hey!" She stood, slamming her bag on the table.

The rascal had probably said the L-word just to distract her. And worse, it had worked. She was getting in way too deep. She should just take her underwear and leave.

But her curiosity got the better of her. She sidled up beside him to read the note.

Angus,

Phil found these unders in the living room and asked which of us he should congratulate.
We need to talk.

Connor

Brilliant. Emma groaned. Connor knew about them. "Who is Phil?"

"One of the daytime guards." Angus wadded up the paper and tossed it into the litter bin. " 'Twill be easier for me to protect ye if ye live here."

Move in with a vampire? Was he crazy? "I appreciate your concern, Angus, but I don't expect you to protect me. I got myself into this mess, so it's my problem."

"I willna be brushed aside." He tilted his head, studying her. "Yer pulse is racing."

Thanks for the reminder. She squeezed her hands into fists, then slowly relaxed them. "Living here is out of the question. If Sean sees me, he'll fire me and blacklist me from any other job I would ever want."

"Then ye can work for me. Whatever yer salary is, I'll double it."

Her mouth dropped open, then snapped shut. "That's not the point."

"Actually, it is. Ye could help us find Casimir, and that's a damned sight more important than any work ye're doing for Sean Whelan. What is he accomplishing? He's wasting everyone's time, hunting for his daughter when she's perfectly safe and happy." His eyes narrowed. "Yer heart is pounding. I can hear it."

She gritted her teeth. "I don't need the play-by-play commentary on my bodily functions."

"I only mention it because ye're struggling with yerself, and 'tis no' necessary."

She crossed her arms. "You think I should just give in to you. Live with you, work for you, and do everything your way."

" 'Twould be easier, aye."

Caveman! It was too much like total surrender, and she couldn't do it. "I have my own life to live."

"But yer mission is to protect mortals and kill evil vampires. In the end, yer mission is the same as mine." He took her gently by the shoulders. "Ye doona see how alike we are?"

"No. What I see is you would be the boss and I would be the employee. You're the immortal vampire, and I'm the lowly mortal. You're faster and stronger than me. Good heavens, you even own a castle, while I have a little rundown cottage."

"Ye want a bigger house?"

"No! I want to . . . feel more equal. There's an imbalance of power between us that I cannot—"

"Ye think I would take advantage of you? I have sworn to protect you."

"It's too fast." She pulled away. "A week ago, I hated all vampires and I was slaying them. I've only recently come to trust you and . . . like you. I can't . . . live with you."

"Are ye ashamed of me?"

"No! Not at all." She was so attracted to his strength and power, but at the same time, she knew she would be completely overwhelmed by him. "I have to protect myself."

"From what?" he shouted. "I have sworn never to harm you."

She closed her eyes briefly. "I know you mean that, but it doesn't change the fact that we're from two different worlds. There's no future for us."

"To hell with the future. We're alive now."

"And you'll still be alive a hundred years from now."

His jaw shifted as he ground his teeth. "Ye reject me because of what I am?"

Good God, she hated to hurt him. "You're the most wonderful man I've ever met. But I need to protect myself."

He wandered to the counter and finished his drink. He kept his back to her, his hands fisted on the countertop. "This changes nothing. I have sworn to protect you, and I will. Where do ye wish to go?"

A heaviness dragged her heart down. It was better this way. Better to end it now before she was completely lost. "If the Malcontents figure out my name, they'll go to my apartment, so I think Austin's place will be safer. If you could teleport me there, I'll be fine on my own."

"I'll stay till shortly before dawn." He turned to face her. "Doona worry. I'll stay in the living room, watching the telly. Ye'll never know I'm there."

* * *

He must be pouting, Emma decided. He'd been so quiet. But he'd done everything she'd asked. He'd teleported her to her apartment so she could pack more clothes. Then he'd brought her to Austin's apartment. He'd even insisted on paying for the Chinese food she'd had delivered.

He sat quietly on the couch. She turned on the telly and found some old sitcom reruns. He didn't object. She sat on the other end of the couch. The remote control rested on the cushion between them, unclaimed by either of them. She slanted a look his way every now and then. He wasn't laughing at the funny parts. His jaw was set, his brow furrowed. He was so still, you would think he was dead. She groaned inwardly. Not quite true. She could sense the energy in him, straining to explode.

By four-thirty A.M., she was yawning. She covered her mouth when a big yawn overwhelmed her.

"Ye doona need to stay awake," he said softly. "I'll be leaving soon."

She rose slowly and stretched. "I guess I'll take a hot bath and go to bed."

"All right." He picked up the remote and turned on the Weather Channel.

"I'm sorry we don't get DVN here."

"This is fine." He turned down the volume to a whisper. Apparently, with his super hearing, he could still hear. "I have employees around the world. I like to know what kind of weather they're facing."

"I guess you need to know the exact time of sunrise, too."

He gave her an irritated look. "Good night."

Definitely pouting. She wandered toward the bedroom.

"Love."

She halted at the door. Had she heard that? It was so soft, she wasn't sure he'd actually spoken. Maybe it had only sounded in her mind. She glanced back.

He was still staring at the telly.

"Good night." She closed the bedroom door.

In the bathroom, she filled the tub with hot water and bubble bath. She was down to her underwear when she recalled the red panties in her tote bag. When Angus left, would he confiscate her underwear as spoils of war? He'd been the one to pull down her panties, but she'd kicked them free. She'd been an eager and willing participant. Even incomplete, it had been the best sex of her life. Was she being a fool to reject him?

She unhooked her black bra and flung it at the door. Dammit, why couldn't she fall for a normal guy who breathed 24/7? She pushed her black lace underwear to the floor. Was falling for Angus a betrayal of the memory of her parents? Or would her parents tell her to follow her heart and embrace love where she found it? They had loved each other so much. Wouldn't they want that kind of love for her?

She stepped into the tub and settled among the white fluffy foam. The smell of jasmine soothed her frazzled nerves. She lay back with a long sigh.

"Mum, Dad," she whispered. "I'm so confused." If only she could hear them. In the first few weeks after their death, she had thought she'd heard her father's voice a few times. A whisper on the wind or a thought that suddenly appeared in her mind. But that was years ago. Now she was all alone.

She closed her eyes and breathed deeply, easing the tension from her body and opening her mind to any advice, whether from her natural father or the Heavenly One, any help would be welcome.

Her breasts tingled when a few bubbles popped. She smiled as the flowery fragrance wafted up to her nose. A clump of bubbles that was clinging to her neck sluiced down her throat, caressing her skin. It felt almost like real fingers.

Mmm, good bubble bath. She dragged a puffy cloud of foam up to her breasts and covered them. The bubbles clung to her skin, tingling her and gently teasing her nipples. Wow, scrubbing bubbles.

I'm glad ye like it.

She gasped at the sound of Angus's voice. How? She sat up and peered around the shower curtain. "Where are you?"

Still on the couch.

His voice was in her head. *He* was in her head. Good heavens, she'd opened her mind.

Nay, doona shut me out. Ye look so beautiful in my mind. All pink and flushed from the heat of the water.

Her breath hitched when she felt a hand cup her breast. She looked down and saw nothing except bubbles sliding down her torso and her nipple growing hard. "How are you doing this?"

His thumb teased the hardened tip. At least, she thought it was his thumb. She jolted when something lapped at her other nipple. His tongue?

"What are you—" She fell back with a gasp when

she felt him suckling her. The sensations were incredibly strong, yet he wasn't there. She covered her breast with her hand, but the suckling continued. God, he was good. "What are you doing?" She didn't expect an answer. How could he talk with his mouth full?

'Tis called vampire sex.

"Then why am I feeling it?" Her eyes crossed when he tugged at both nipples. Obviously he could talk with his mind while his mouth was busy elsewhere. "I'm not a vampire."

But I am. And I want to pleasure you.

She sank lower in the water, but it made no difference. Even immersed under water, the sensations continued. God, it was wonderful. *He* was wonderful. Oh no! Could he read her mind? "I haven't given you permission."

But ye will. Ye want to scream like ye did last night. His hands massaged her breasts. Another hand skimmed down her belly and delved into her curls.

She moaned, then blinked. "Wait a minute. How many hands do you have?"

As many as I can imagine. He cupped her between the legs. Meanwhile, his hands continued to toy with her breasts.

She felt something hot and moist on her neck. His mouth. His tongue rasped a trail up to her ear.

Are ye ready for me? His voice was soft inside her head.

Her knees sagged open. "You're seducing me."

I'm loving you. He planted a soft kiss on her brow. *Close yer eyes and enjoy.*

Oh yes. Her eyes drifted shut.

She suddenly felt hands all over her, outlining the contours of her arms and legs, her stomach and back. She groaned when fingers massaged her shoulders. His tongue teased her nipples. His hand moved between her legs. His fingers caressed. She cried out when he located her clitoris.

She gripped the sides of the tub. This was one hell of a good use for psychic energy. She jolted when she felt his mouth on her. Unbelievable, considering she was sitting in a tub of water. But then, it was all in his head and hers.

I promised ye that yer second scream would come from my mouth.

"Oh God." It felt so real. She could feel every lick, every dip of his tongue between her folds, every little nudge and nip at her clitoris. She planted her feet against the tub and raised her hips, wanting more. More. The tension stretched thin, ready to snap.

Come with me, love. He squeezed her bottom with his hands. His tongue went wild.

She screamed. Her feet slipped, and she thrashed about, spilling water on the floor. She cupped herself and felt the delicious throbbing against her hand. She curled up, squeezing her thighs together, willing the shudders to go on and on. And they did. She even heard Angus groan, a husky sound that reverberated in her head and intensified the throbbing pulses.

Slowly her breathing returned to normal. She sat up and noted the lake of bubbly water on the bathroom floor. That had been one hell of a bath. She stood on wobbly legs and stepped carefully out.

The question now was what next? She quickly

erected a mental shield to block Angus. She didn't want him listening in on her thought processes. Not that her brain was exactly functioning. Every other thought seemed to be *wow-wee!* She donned a bathrobe and removed her hair clip. What should she do? Act like nothing had happened? But it had, *wow-wee!* Should she open the bedroom door and invite him in for the real thing? *Wow-wee.* She fluffed her hair and glanced in the bathroom mirror. What to do?

She exited the bathroom and approached the bedroom door. Slowly she opened it. He was still on the couch, but the telly was turned off.

He turned to look at her. His eyes were tinted red. "I have to go. 'Tis almost dawn."

"Oh." Now that was brilliant. Couldn't she think of anything to say?

He motioned to her cell phone on the coffee table. "I took your number in case I need to reach you."

"Okay."

"I'll send one of my daytime guards to watch over you. The Malcontents are affiliated with the Russian mob, so ye could be in danger during the day."

"Oh."

He glanced at his lap, frowning. "I have to take my kilt to the cleaners." He stood and picked up his sporran from the couch.

Emma's eyes widened. She recalled the long groan that had echoed in her head. "Angus."

"Good night . . . love." He vanished.

Chapter 17

Angus arrived in the fifth-floor office of Roman's townhouse and quickly turned off the alarm. He dropped his sporran on the desk and punched the intercom button. "Ian, that was me coming in."

"About time," Ian answered. "'Tis almost dawn. Connor wants to see you."

Angus glanced down at the state of his kilt and winced. "Give me two minutes." He dashed into the bedroom, kicked off his shoes, and pulled off his sweater and kilt. He glared at the stained kilt as he pulled on a pair of jeans. You would think he was sixteen instead of five hundred and twenty-six years old, the way he'd lost control. But he couldn't recall a woman who excited him the way Emma did. Or frustrated him.

It was downright infuriating that she wanted to reject him. His wife had done that centuries ago, but Emma should know better. She was too clever and modern to fall for old superstitious fears. Hell, she was too brave to fall for any fears at all. She was a warrior like him. She was perfect for him. And he wasn't giving up without a fight. Invading her mind tonight had been an act of desperation. But the devil take it, if she was going to reject him, she needed to know exactly what she was giving up.

There was a knock at the office door. "Come in." He strode into the office in his stocking feet, wearing jeans and a white undershirt.

Connor entered. "We need to talk."

"Everything fine at Romatech?"

"Aye." Connor shut the door. "The birthing room is finished in case Shanna's bairn has . . . special needs."

A half-vampire baby boy. Angus sighed. "Anything else?"

"The Vamp doctors are arriving tomorrow night, and the delivery is scheduled for Friday night."

"Good." Angus circled the desk and sat.

Connor walked toward him. "I'm glad ye called in more security. We could use them with the doctors coming in, but Jack tells me ye have him and Robby guarding Central Park?"

"Aye, to keep the Malcontents from murdering more mortals." Angus checked his e-mail.

Connor remained quiet for a while. "We appear to have a new friend, Dr. Phang?"

Angus smiled as he deleted some junk mail. "His name is Phineas McKinney. How's he fitting in?"

"He seems eager to please. Ian says he did well in his first fencing lesson."

"Good." No message from Mikhail. Angus turned off the computer. "Has the day shift arrived?"

"Phil's here. Howard should arrive any minute now."

"Tell Phil I want him to guard Miss Wallace today." Angus wrote the address of Austin's apartment on a slip of paper.

Connor stepped closer to accept the piece of paper. "Is she in danger?"

"She was with me when I found Phineas. The Russian, Alek, was there, and he recognized her as the slayer."

"Bugger," Connor muttered. "Ye realize Katya is going to believe we were behind the slayings all along, that we've been helping Miss Wallace?"

"It canna be helped."

Connor scowled. "Ye should have sent her away the minute ye discovered who she is."

"Doona lecture me, Connor."

He paced away, balling his hands into fists. "Is this the real reason Jack and Robby are guarding the park? To keep Miss Wallace from going there?"

"It is the best way to keep her from slaying."

Connor turned to face him. "I gather ye've been using all sorts of persuasive techniques on her."

Angus narrowed his eyes. "Ye're going too far, old friend."

Connor marched toward him. "I fear ye have gone too far. Nothing good can come from this."

Angus slapped a hand on the desk and stood. "Did ye have to leave her knickers in the kitchen where everyone could see them? Why no' leave them here in the office?"

"Ye're thinking of her first."

"So?"

Connor gave him a sad look. "In yer line of business, that kind of thinking can get ye killed."

"I have sworn to protect her. I willna abandon her now." Angus strode toward the bar and grabbed a bottle of Type O from the fridge. He popped it into the microwave. "Ye want some?"

"Nay."

"Then we are done." Angus poured the synthetic blood into a glass. "Good night."

Connor didn't leave. "I realize ye're the boss, but ye've been like a brother to me, like a father to Ian."

Angus sipped from his glass. He'd been friends with Connor for too many years to stay angry for long. He felt the familiar twinge of guilt whenever Ian's name was mentioned, along with the first tug of sleepiness. The sun must be close to the horizon. "I always appreciate yer honesty, Connor." He looked at his old friend. "Do ye think it was wrong of me to transform Ian so young?"

Connor took a deep breath. "Ian would have died if ye hadna changed him. I think he's happy. As happy as any of us can be." He wandered to the door and paused with a hand on the doorknob. "Do ye love her?"

Angus set his glass down. "Aye, I do."

"Then we will do our best to keep her safe." He glanced at Angus with a sad expression. "To keep ye both safe."

Emma woke about two in the afternoon. After a quick shower, she dressed for the day. With a frown, she surveyed the soggy mountain of towels she'd used to soak up the lake on the bathroom floor. It appeared that today, her dangerous, action-packed life would include a trip to the Laundromat. She bagged up the towels and dragged them to the front door.

She heard voices in the hall, so she peered through the peephole. There was a young man standing by her door. He was tall and muscular, dressed in khaki pants and a navy Polo shirt. Two blond women were talking to him. Good heavens, it was the two bimbos who'd thought Austin was gay. Lindsey and Tina. They were practically accosting the poor man in the hall. There was a thud as he backed up against the door.

Emma jerked the door open. The young man nearly fell in, but regained his balance.

"Poor baby." The taller blonde, Lindsey, grabbed his arm to steady him. "Let me help you."

"I'm fine." He tried to move away, but Lindsey dug her long pink fingernails into his arm.

Tina had pink streaks in her hair, presumably to match her pink mini-skirt and skimpy halter top. She squinted up at Emma. "You must be the celebrity that Phil is guarding."

"Phil?" Emma looked at the young man. Splendid. He was the one who had found her red underwear and given it to Connor.

Lindsey stroked his chest with her fingernails. "It's so awesome that you're a bodyguard. I bet you have like super stamina."

"I know, right?" Tina fluffed up her hair.

Phil gave Emma a hounded look. "Angus sent me to guard you today."

"All day long." Lindsey, dressed in tiny brown shorts and a turquoise cami, snuggled up close to Phil.

"When do you get off work? Tina and I live just two doors down."

The shorter one wrinkled her nose while she regarded Emma. "I thought only rich and famous people needed bodyguards. Are you hiding here from the paparazzi?"

Emma shrugged one shoulder. "Something like that."

"Wow." Lindsey let go of Phil and stepped closer to Emma. "I bet you're like . . . filthy rich."

"And famous," Tina added. "Do I know you?"

Emma exchanged a confused look with Phil. "I don't think so. I don't know *you*."

Lindsey leaned close to her friend. "Did you hear the way she talks? She sounds kinda funny."

"I know, right?" Tina whispered back. "I don't think English is her native language."

Emma's mouth dropped open. Phil grimaced, shaking his head.

"I bet she's a foreign movie star," Lindsey whispered.

Tina gasped. "No! She's a foreign princess!"

"Excuse me," Emma said. "I'm right here. I can hear you."

The two blondes jumped.

Tina began speaking in a loud voice, enunciating her words very carefully. "Hello. My name is Tina. I am pleased to meet you." She curtsied.

"My name is Lindsey." The taller one made a wobbly curtsy. "Welcome to America."

"Thank you." Emma gave Phil a dubious look.

He stepped closer. "Would you mind if I guarded you inside?"

"No, that's fine. Come in." She opened the door wider, and he slipped inside.

"Good-bye, Phil," Lindsey called after him. "Remember to come see us after work."

"Good-bye, your royal highness." Tina curtsied again.

"Bye." Emma shut the door and flipped the locks.

"Thank you." Phil leaned against the wall and heaved a sigh of relief. "Those women have been pestering me for hours."

"You poor thing." Emma strode into the kitchen, smiling. She retrieved two bottles of water from the fridge and offered him one. "So what's a mortal guy like you doing working for vampires?"

He unscrewed the top off his bottle. "I'm working for the good Vamps, Miss Wallace. I'm honored that they trust me."

She sat at the breakfast table and motioned for him to join her. "How long have you worked for Angus?"

"Six years." Phil sat across from her. "I heard you killed four Malcontents, and now they want to kill you."

She shrugged one shoulder. "They don't know who I am, so I don't think I'm in as much danger as Angus believes. You really don't need to stick around if you don't want to."

"I always follow orders." He drank some water.

"Even with Lindsey and Tina waiting for you?"

He grimaced. "I'd rather face twenty Malcontents than those two dingbats from hell."

Emma laughed. "They are rather scary."

Phil nodded. "I'm supposed to stay by your side until you're safe at work this evening."

"Then you get to help me lug that down to the Laundromat." She pointed at the bulging garbage sack by the door.

Phil spent the rest of the day helping her do the laundry and grocery shopping. Emma shared a pizza with him at the local deli before they took the subway to Midtown. She wanted to ask a ton of questions about Angus and the vampire world, but Phil refused to discuss business in public.

He escorted her to the federal building where she worked. At the door, he handed her a card. "I wrote the number to Roman's townhouse on the back. Call us if you're in trouble."

"Thank you." She examined the card. It looked like the one Angus had given her. On the back, Phil had scribbled a phone number.

"If you call during the day, either Howard or I will answer," Phil continued. "If you call at night, you'll most likely get Ian."

"All right." Emma shook his hand. "It was nice to meet you, Phil. Thanks for helping with the laundry."

"Good night." He waited until she was safely in the building before he left.

The Stake-Out team's seven P.M. meeting dragged on for an hour as Sean tried to come up with a legitimate reason to shut down Romatech Industries. The fact that the company saved millions of human lives each year with their synthetic blood was lost on Sean. After seeing his daughter there, he'd become obsessed with destroying the place.

"Maybe we can get them on a health code violation," Garrett suggested. "Or tax evasion."

Sean pointed a finger at Emma. "Check on that."

"Yes, sir." She made a note on her legal pad. Maybe Angus was right, and Sean was wasting everyone's time. But if she brought up the subject of Casimir and the prospect of a global vampire war, Sean would wonder where she'd gotten her information. Instead of listening to her, he'd blacklist her like he had Austin.

"All right, dismissed," Sean finally announced. "Off to your assignments." He hurried from the office.

Emma assumed he was headed for his stake-out apartment across the street from Roman's townhouse. Alyssa was still gone, trying to locate covens in nearby towns. Alone in the office, Emma set to work on her assignment. The health department and IRS would be closed for the day, so she prepared some inquiries into Romatech Industries and faxed them to the correct offices. She would have to wait till tomorrow for a response.

She wandered about the office. Tension was building inside her. No doubt she was nervous about spending more time alone with Angus. She gazed out the window at the night sky and wondered what he was doing. Would he come to her apartment again? Would she be able to resist him?

She returned to her desk and checked the police reports from the night before. A few murders, quite a few assault cases, but not a single event in Central Park. Robby and Giacomo were doing a great job. But there had been the incident with Alek and the woman he'd attacked. Emma considered calling the number Phil had given her, just to see what had happened to the poor woman. She was reaching for her cell phone when it jangled.

"Hello?"

"Emma, is it safe for ye to talk?"

Her heart stuttered at the sound of Angus's voice. "Yes, I'm alone here. I was just wondering about the woman we found in the park last night. Is she all right?"

"Aye. She was fine when Connor left her at her flat."

"Oh, good."

"I talked to Phil earlier," Angus continued, "and he says the day was uneventful. Ye were no' followed or watched. We can assume the Malcontents havena figured out yer identity yet."

"I agree."

"Ye should be safe as long as ye stay hidden in Austin's apartment. Doona, under any circumstances, go to Central Park. The Malcontents will be there, looking for you."

"I understand."

"Jack and Robby are there again tonight, keeping it safe." Angus paused. "I was tempted to have them watch ye instead."

"No, no. I'll be fine. Please don't leave the park unguarded." Emma couldn't stand the thought of more innocent people dying.

"All right. Shanna's doctors have arrived, and I'm getting them settled in the townhouse before taking them to Romatech. I can meet ye at Austin's apartment in about an hour."

"Okay." Flashes of last night's bathtub scene rushed through her mind. No wonder she was feeling tense.

"I'm sending Phineas and Gregori to escort ye home.

Phineas hasna finished his training, but he can fight well, and I know ye're one hell of a fighter."

"I'll be fine. I'll see you soon." She hung up, realizing how much she liked his worrying over her. It was unnecessary since she could take care of herself, but still, she liked it. Too much. And soon she would be alone with him all night long. How far would she go? Would she take a vampire as her lover?

Shortly afterward, she received a call from first-floor security. Phineas McKinney was waiting for her. She locked up the office. Hopefully, Sean wouldn't mind her leaving work early. If he complained, she was tempted to quit. She could always have her old job back at MI6. Besides, if she lived in London, she might be closer to Angus. She groaned. Why was she making plans for their future? They had no future.

She exited the elevator and halted when she saw Phineas. His hair had been cut. He'd shaved and was wearing clothes identical to the ones Phil had worn earlier. Apparently khaki pants and a navy Polo shirt was the MacKay uniform for those not wearing kilts. Phineas even sported a navy windbreaker with the words MACKAY SECURITY AND INVESTIGATION embossed in small letters on the upper left-hand side.

"Wow, Phineas, I hardly recognized you." She circled him while he grinned and puffed out his chest. "You look so official."

"I am." He flashed his ID badge. "Cool, huh? I'm even going to get a permit to carry a piece." He lowered his voice to a whisper. "With silver bullets."

Emma smiled. "I'm glad you like your new job."

"My mission for the night is to escort you safely home."

He saluted the security officer as they left the building.

A black Lexus was waiting by the curb, and Phineas opened the back door for her. She climbed in and was greeted by the driver.

"Hi, I'm Gregori." He twisted in the front seat to face her. With a smile, he extended a hand.

"How do you do?" Emma shook his hand while Phineas climbed into the front passenger seat. She did a double-take on Gregori. Somehow, he looked very familiar.

Gregori grinned. "So you're the hot babe that has Angus all worked up."

"Excuse me?" Emma blinked when recognition struck her. "I know who you are. You were the host on the DVN reality show."

"Yep, that was me." Gregori adjusted his tie. "But to-night, I'm your chauffeur. Where to, sweetie?"

Emma smiled as she gave him the address. "Do you work for Angus?"

He snorted as he pulled out into traffic. "No way. I'm the vice president of marketing over at Romatech. Have you seen the commercials for Roman's Fusion Cuisine? I make those."

"Oh, I see."

"I was headed to SoHo to check on some property we're having made into a Vamp restaurant when Angus asked me to give you and Phineas a ride."

"I see." Emma nodded. A Vamp restaurant? Surely the menu would be a bit limited? But then it was certainly much better than attacking humans.

"Don't worry about your safety," Gregori continued. "I've been taking some karate and fencing lessons. I got sick and tired of Connor acting like I was some kind of wimp."

"I had my first fencing lesson last night," Phineas said. "It was cool." He tuned the radio to some hip-hop music.

Gregori started drumming on the steering wheel in time with the music while Phineas wiggled in his seat.

These were vampires? Emma watched in disbelief. They just seemed so . . . normal.

Gregori drove by Austin's apartment and surveyed the street in dismay. "I'll never find a place to park." He circled the block.

Emma leaned forward. "There's no need for you to stay if you have business elsewhere. Phineas and I will be fine."

Gregori double-parked, then glanced back at her, frowning. "I'd better stick around until Angus comes. You two go in, and I'll join you as soon as I park this beast."

Emma and Phineas climbed out onto the sidewalk. She looked around, but there was no one watching them. They hurried into the apartment building while Gregori drove slowly away.

In Austin's apartment, Phineas made a big show of examining each room carefully. He checked all the kitchen cabinets and the refrigerator. Emma bit her lip to keep from laughing. Did he think someone was hiding in the fridge or perhaps the cutlery drawer?

"Kitchen is secure," he announced, then jumped into the living room, assuming a karate pose. "Cool, huh? I learned this last night."

"Lovely." Emma entered the secure kitchen to warm

up some Chinese food left over from the night before.

Phineas checked under the sofa cushions, then proceeded into the bedroom. Five minutes later, he emerged and pronounced the entire apartment was safe.

"What a relief. Thank you." Emma set her plate of Chinese food on the coffee table in front of the couch.

"I'm going to check the hall." Phineas opened the door. "Lock up after me."

"Okay." Emma flipped the locks, then returned to the couch. She settled down with her Chinese food and turned on the telly. A cop show was winding down, and the perpetrators were getting dragged off to jail. She glanced at the VCR to check the time. Angus would be here soon.

The television show was suddenly interrupted by a late-breaking bulletin from a local news station. Three murdered bodies just discovered in Hudson River Park. Emma sat forward.

The newscaster announced they were cutting to the reporter on the scene by Pier 66. Emma set her plate of food aside as the picture shifted to the park. A crowd of curious onlookers surrounded the female reporter. Lights from parked police cars flashed red and yellow in the night sky.

"The bodies were discovered just moments ago," the reporter shouted into her microphone. "We've heard that their throats were all slashed, but we're waiting for confirmation on that. What is interesting, though, is that all three bodies appear to have been moved. They were discovered nearby on the heliport pad. We can only assume that whoever committed this heinous crime wanted the bodies to be found quickly."

Emma jumped to her feet. It was the Malcontents. She was sure of it. They'd simply moved to another park. *Three* murders? Shit!

She had to know more. She needed to check the victims herself. Even with slashed throats, she could often detect the bite marks. Of course, she knew to look for them. And the bodies would also be completely drained.

Dammit! Why couldn't those bloody bastards take a pint and go on their way? But no, they had to kill their victims. They enjoyed killing.

She searched her purse for the card Phil had given her, then called the number.

"Hello?"

"Is this Ian?"

"Aye. Miss Wallace? Are ye in danger?"

"No. But I wanted to tell you that the Malcontents are killing again. Three bodies were just found at the heliport in Hudson River Park. I'm taking Phineas with me to check it out."

"What? Wait! Angus will want to come with you."

"He can meet us there. I'll be perfectly safe. There are a ton of police there."

"'Tis no' a good idea—"

"I'll be fine," Emma interrupted. "Just tell Angus where we are." She hung up, then dashed to the front door. She heard voices outside and peeked through the peephole. Oh no! Tina and Lindsey were outside, and they were dragging Phineas toward their apartment. He didn't appear to be struggling.

Emma flipped the locks and opened the door. "Phineas!"

The blondes giggled.

"We have your bodyguard!" Tina announced.

"Dr. Phang." Lindsey tugged him down the hall. "He's so cute."

Phineas grinned. "Hot damn! I love this job."

"Phineas," Emma shouted. "I need you!"

"Not as badly as we do." Lindsey pulled him inside their apartment.

"Phineas." Emma marched toward them. "This is important."

"Just five minutes." Phineas gave her a pleading look. "That's all I need." He glanced at the two blondes. "Make that ten."

"Bye." Tina shut the door in Emma's face.

"Phineas!" Emma hit the door with her fist, but only heard giggling on the other side.

Fuming, she strode back to her apartment. She paced about the living room. How long would it take Angus to get here? And since when did she wait on men to protect her? She was a black belt, dammit. She'd killed four Malcontents single-handedly. And there were a bunch of cops on the scene. A reporter was there and a ton of bystanders. Nothing would happen to her.

She grabbed her tote bag of stakes and locked the door behind her. She was not going to cower in her apartment in fear. She would be perfectly safe.

In fact, she almost wished she would see Alek. The bastard needed to die.

The two Vamp doctors had arrived at Roman's townhouse, and as honored guests they both expected some personal attention from the CEO of MacKay Security and Investigation. Angus assured them they would be safe during their stay and introduced them to Connor and his security team. As soon as the doctors were happy with their guest rooms, they wanted a tour of Romatech and the birthing room Roman had prepared for his wife. They were both very excited and honored to be the first doctors to deliver a half-vampire baby, but already they were arguing about procedure. Angus was beginning to think Roman had made a big mistake by sending for two doctors instead of one.

Dr. Schweitzer from Switzerland was very pleased with the birthing room, but Dr. Lee from Houston demanded more equipment be on hand just in case. Roman was busily making a list of everything Dr. Lee wanted when Angus's cell phone rang.

He excused himself and stepped into the hall as he retrieved the phone from his sporran. "Aye?"

"Angus." Ian sounded agitated. "Miss Wallace just called. She and Phineas are going to the heliport at Hudson River Park."

"What?"

"She thinks the Malcontents have murdered some mortals there."

"The devil take it," Angus muttered. He'd told her not to go out. "Is Gregori with her?"

"I doona know. She called just now," Ian continued quickly. "If ye hurry, ye might be able to stop her."

"I'm on my way." Angus snapped his phone shut.

Connor cracked the door to the birthing room and peeked out. "Is there a problem?"

"Could be. If ye doona hear from me within thirty

minutes, send Robby and Giacomo to Hudson River Park."

"What's going on—"

Connor's words faded as Angus vanished. In a few seconds, he was in Austin's apartment.

"Emma?" He zoomed into the bedroom, checked the bathroom, then ran back into the living room. Bugger. He was too late.

But they might still be in the building. He unlocked the door, ran into the hall, and crashed into Phineas. He grabbed him by the shoulders. "Thank God ye're still here."

Phineas was shaking. "Oh my God, man, I think I killed her."

"*What?*"

Phineas's face crumpled. "I didn't mean to. She was just so hot. And I lost control. I'm not used to being like this—"

Angus shook him. "What did ye do?"

Tears ran down Phineas's face. "I know it's the number one rule, but I lost control."

A chill skittered through Angus. "Ye bit her?"

"I didn't mean to! God, I'm afraid I killed her."

Angus slammed him against the wall. "Ye killed Emma?"

Phineas blinked. "No, man. I think I killed Tina."

Chapter 18

Angus stared at his new employee as relief washed through him. Phineas hadn't bitten Emma. She wasn't dead. At least, not yet. "Where is Emma? She should be with you."

A door nearby opened. "Woo-hoo, Dr. Phang!" A blonde dressed in a lacy black teddy leaned against the doorframe. "When do I get my turn?"

Angus recognized her as one of the silly mortal women he'd met a few nights ago. Either Lindsey or Tina, he couldn't remember which.

Her eyes widened. "Oh, I remember you. You're the gay Irish guy. If you're still looking for Austin, you're out of luck. There's some kind of foreign princess hiding out in his place."

"Get back inside and shut the door," Angus ordered.

The blonde huffed. "You are so rude. And you're like totally wasting your time with Dr. Phang. He's a ladies' man. In fact, he was so good with Tina, she's still unconscious."

"Inside!" Angus shouted.

"Creep!" She slammed the door.

It was all becoming clear to Angus. His new employee had been busy tupping Tina when Emma decided to leave. Angus grabbed him by the shirt and pushed him against the wall. "Ye left yer post."

"I—" Phineas winced. "It was just for a few minutes. Emma was okay with it." He glanced at Austin's apartment. "Ask her. She'll tell you. Everything's cool. Except for Tina. She's looking kinda bad."

Angus stepped closer and gritted his teeth. His fist twisted Phineas's shirt. "*Ye left yer post.* I've seen soldiers killed for that."

Phineas gulped. "I'm sorry, man. It won't happen again."

"What's up?" Gregori sauntered down the hall toward them.

Angus released Phineas and turned toward Gregori. "Where the hell have ye been? Have ye seen Emma?"

"No, she's with—" Gregori gave Phineas a worried look. "I was parking the car. What happened?"

"Emma is gone." Angus bit out the words.

"What?" Phineas glanced at Austin's apartment. "She was just here a few minutes ago. How'd she get away?"

Angus seized him by the neck. "She got away because ye left yer post!"

"Whoa!" Gregori grabbed Angus's arm. "Easy, Mongo. Relax! We'll find her."

Angus released Phineas and took a deep breath. "I'll deal with this later. I have to find her. She's headed to Hudson River Park."

"Great! You know where she's going." Gregori gave him an encouraging smile. "It'll be fine. I'll drive you."

"Nay. I'll call her and teleport." Angus reached in his sporran for his cell phone. "Gregori, I need ye to clean up the mess Phineas made." He glared at his rookie employee.

Phineas winced and rubbed his throat. "I'm really sorry, man. Tina was just so hot. I didn't mean to hurt her."

Gregori frowned at Phineas. "You hurt her? Where is she?"

"In here." Phineas shoved open the door to Tina's apartment.

Lindsey squealed and jumped back. Phineas led Gregori inside while Angus remained in the hall, calling Emma on his cell phone.

"Hello?"

"Emma!" Relief flooded him so strongly, he stumbled back a step. "Keep talking. I'll teleport to you."

"Not now," she whispered. "I'm in a taxi."

"Ye think I care?"

"I care. I don't want to be in a wreck. I'll call you as soon as I get to the park. Give me your number."

He did. "The devil take it, Emma. I told ye to stay hidden."

"I'll be fine. I'll call you soon." She hung up.

Stubborn woman. Muttering a curse, he punched in Robby's number.

"Aye?"

"Robby, I want ye and Jack to go to Hudson River Park, to the area around the heliport."

"What's going on?" Robby asked. "Connor called and said something was wrong, but he dinna know what."

"The Malcontents may have murdered some mortals. Emma's on her way there." Angus gritted his teeth. "Alone."

"We're on our way." Robby rang off.

Cursing some more, Angus strode into Tina's apartment. Lindsey was hovering by a doorway, trembling.

"Excuse me." He slipped past her.

She jumped back with a squeal. "There's blood on her neck!"

Tina was sprawled on the bed. Phineas was tugging a sheet up to her chin.

"Good news," Gregori said. "She's alive."

"Aye." Angus frowned at the twin punctures on her neck. "I can still hear her heart beating."

"You can?" Phineas gazed at Tina, confused.

Angus gave his rookie an irritated look. "Ye have a lot to learn, lad." He turned to Gregori. "Teleport her to Romatech for a transfusion, then bring her back."

"I'm on it," Gregori assured him. "Were you able to reach Emma?"

"Aye—" Angus stopped talking when Lindsey leaped into the room, waving a foot-long, plaster Celtic cross in front of her.

"Begone, you demons!" She aimed the cross at each of them. "Go back to hell where you belong!"

Angus sighed. "And when ye're done," he continued to talk to Gregori, "be sure to erase their memory."

"What?" Lindsey shook her cross like it might be

broken. "Why didn't it work? Aren't you guys like vampires or something?"

Gregori motioned for Phineas to pick Tina up. "Let's get going."

"Where are you taking her?" Lindsey dropped the cross and fell to her knees. "Oh my God. You're going to change her into a vampire, too. She'll be young and hot forever." Her face brightened, and she jumped to her feet. "Sign me up!"

Angus shook his head as he left the room. "The vampire world could never survive you two."

The police had cordoned off the entrance to the heliport, so Emma asked the cabbie to drop her off nearby. She wove through the noisy crowd, headed for the nearest police officer. She fished in her tote bag for her ID badge. Her hand grazed her cell phone, and she considered calling Angus, but there were too many people jammed together for him to teleport there safely or unnoticed. She located her ID and showed it to those who remained stubbornly in her way.

"Excuse me. Homeland Security." That usually got people out of the way.

She finally made it to the crime scene tape and a police officer. She flashed her badge and shouted to be heard over the noise. "I need to see the bodies!"

"You'll have to talk to the captain first." The officer pointed at a man in a trench coat about a hundred yards away, next to an ambulance. Two medics were loading a gurney with a body bag.

Emma ducked under the tape and strode toward the

captain. She'd gotten about ten yards when another officer yelled at her to stop.

She raised her badge. "Homeland Security."

After another fifty yards, she passed by a police car. She narrowed her eyes against the glare of its flashing lights.

A uniformed officer stepped away from the car to block her path. "This is a crime scene."

She lifted her badge. "Homeland—" She gasped when he seized her upper arms.

"This will be a very bad crime scene."

A Russian accent. She'd caught it too late. Stunned, she gazed into Alek's face. The flashing red and yellow lights made his smile look evil.

"Do you like my costume? The officer no longer needs it." He tilted his head toward the car.

It was difficult to see with the strobe lights flashing in her eyes, but Emma spotted a man in the front seat, his head twisted at a bizarre angle. Without warning, she rammed her knee into Alek's groin.

He stumbled back. She aimed a series of punches at his chest, then spun and kicked him in the face.

Alek fell, blood gushing from his nose.

"Oh my God!" Someone in the crowd shouted. "She's attacking a police officer!"

"Halt!" Several voices shouted.

Emma turned to see two officers running toward her. Her badge—where was it? She'd dropped it when she was punching Alek.

"Looking for this?" Alek jumped to his feet, her ID in his hand. His smile was tinted with blood. He licked the blood from around his mouth, then zoomed away, taking her badge with him.

"Halt, or I'll shoot!" an officer yelled.

Emma dove into the crowd and worked her way in the direction Alek had headed. Pier 66. She dug her cell phone out and called Angus.

"About time!" he thundered. "Where are you? Are ye all right?"

"Yes, I'm fine. Let me find a good place." Behind the crowd, she spotted a local news van. She ducked behind it. "Okay, you can come now. The Malcontents are definitely behind these murders. I saw Alek here. In fact, he tried to capture me, but—" She stopped when Angus appeared beside her.

He caught her by the shoulders. "Are ye all right?"

"Yes. I gave Alek a bloody nose, and he ran away."

Angus laughed and pulled her into an embrace. "That's my girl." He leaned back to give her a stern look. "Doona ever frighten me like that again."

"I can take care of myself." She smiled. "But I'm glad you're here."

"Is Alek still in the vicinity?"

"He ran toward Pier 66." Emma dropped her cell phone into her bag and retrieved a handful of stakes. "We need to take care of him. He's killed at least four tonight, including a police officer." She jammed the stakes into her belt.

"Nay. I want ye to stay here. Or better yet, go back home."

"I'm not leaving you." She looped her tote bag around her neck and one shoulder. "If we don't finish off Alek tonight, he'll keep killing."

Angus frowned at her. "Verra well. But first we call backup." He punched in a number. "Robby, we're going after Alek. Pier 66. Hurry." He dropped his phone into his sporran. "Ready?"

Angus led her toward the pier, using cars and Dumpsters for cover. They hurried along the back wall of a warehouse.

A woman screamed.

Emma cursed silently. How many people did Alek plan on killing tonight?

Angus peered around the corner. "There's a small building on the river's edge. The scream came from behind it."

Emma took a quick look. It was a place that rented Jet Skis. She removed a stake from her belt. "Let's go."

They ran along the side of the warehouse, hugging the shadows, then divided to approach the target. Emma took the southern route and peeked around the corner. A rectangular pier jutted out over the river. There, in the dim moonlight, she could see a woman pinned beneath a man dressed in a police uniform. Alek. The woman lay still on the wooden planks while he rested on top of her and nuzzled her neck.

Angus zoomed toward them and pointed his claymore at Alek's neck. "Release her."

Emma eased onto the pier, looking carefully about. No one else in sight.

"Release her!" Angus shouted.

"Must I?" Alek asked calmly. He levitated off the body.

Angus glanced at the woman, then stepped back. "Emma, get out of here, quick!"

The woman started laughing.

Emma backed up, reluctant to leave Angus on his own. The woman rose to her feet, unharmed. Her fashionably slashed jeans rested low on her hips. Under her black leather jacket, her red halter top barely covered her breasts. She flipped her long, dark hair over her shoulder and gave Angus a look filled with hate.

This was personal, Emma realized. She turned and gasped when a line of shadowy figures levitated around the pier. Six vampires. They'd been hiding underneath, and now they landed lightly on the wooden railing.

She flexed her fingers around her stake, widened her stance, and bent her knees. A total of eight vampires against her and Angus. If they could just hold out until Robby and Giacomo arrived.

A vampire leaped through the air, his sword drawn. Angus charged, knocked the sword aside with his claymore, spun, and skewered the vampire through the heart. With a scream, the vampire burst into a cloud of dust that drifted down onto the pier.

Two vampires dashed toward Emma. She side-stepped the first one, then turned to kick him in the back. That propelled him forward and made him crash into the building. Continuing her turn, she spun to face the second assailant and met him with her stake in his chest. He turned to dust.

The first vampire recovered quickly and charged. He kicked the stake from her hand. She ignored the pain and pressed forward with a series of punches. He was too quick at dodging for her to land a solid hit. Suddenly she was grabbed from behind. She kicked backward to break the vampire's grasp, then grabbed another stake from her belt. When he seized her again, she rammed the stake into his ribs. Howling, he released her. She swiveled and plunged the stake into his heart. Dust again.

The first vampire seized her from behind. She glanced at Angus just in time to see him skewer another vampire. Four down. They were doing well. Another vampire charged at her, and she leaned back on her captor to kick the assailant in the head. He stumbled back.

The first vampire pressed a dagger to her throat. "I should kill you, bitch."

She grabbed his arm to pull the knife away. She heard Angus shout, then the vampire's arm turned to dust, and his knife clattered to the ground. She turned to see Angus behind her, his claymore coated with the dust of the first vampire.

"Thanks." She bent down to retrieve the fallen dagger. There were two male vampires left—Alek and another one. The woman was standing nearby, hatred glimmering in her dark eyes. She raised a wooden blowpipe to her mouth.

"Watch out!" Emma shouted.

Angus raised his claymore, then stiffened. A shocked look crossed his face. "Emma, run," he whispered.

She stepped back, reluctant to leave. She gasped when Angus's claymore slipped from his hand. "Angus!"

He collapsed onto the pier. A dart protruded from his back.

The two male vampires zoomed toward Emma. She

slashed at the first one with her dagger, but he dodged. Alek seized her from behind. The first one kicked the knife from her hand, then punched her in the stomach. She sagged against Alek for only a moment before she kicked and struggled. The first one retrieved the knife and handed it to Alek.

The woman strode toward Angus, speaking with a Russian accent. "I should have killed you years ago." With a booted foot, she shoved him onto his back

Emma winced at the thought of the dart getting pushed farther in.

The woman leaned over Angus. "You can hear me, can't you? The nightshade paralyzes you, but you can still see and hear." She placed her foot on his cheek and pressed his head toward Emma. "See that? We have captured your mortal whore." She kicked him in the ribs with the pointed toe of her boot.

"Stop it!" Emma struggled, but both male vampires held her tight. She grew still when she noticed Angus's face. He was watching her, his eyes filled with pain. Oh God, what had she done? She'd led them into a trap.

The woman gave Emma a disgusted look, then grasped Angus's chin with her long red fingernails and forced his face back to her. "Don't look at her. You could have owned the world with me. But when I asked you to kill one puny little mortal, you refused. And here you are, killing your own kind for what? A *worthless mortal bitch?*"

"Katya, enough!" Alek yelled. "Torture him later. We need to transport these two before it's too late."

"All right, all right." Katya leaned over to grab Angus's arm, and they both vanished.

"No!" Emma screamed. She kicked at her captors.

Alek pulled her tight against him and pressed the knife to her neck. "We've never been there before, Uri. You need to call."

Uri punched in a number on his phone. *"Allo?"*

"Stop!"

Emma glanced up and spotted Robby and Giacomo on the roof, moving toward them with swords in their hands.

"Release her!" Robby yelled.

"Come any closer, and I'm slitting her throat." Alek turned toward Uri, dragging Emma with him. "Grab on to us. Let's go!"

Uri grabbed Emma's arm and spoke into his phone, *"Paris, nous arrivons."*

Emma glanced up at the stricken faces of Robby and Giacomo. "Paris!" she shouted just before everything went black.

Chapter 19

Emma was just becoming aware of her surroundings when she felt a knife prick her neck. She winced, but refused to give Alek the pleasure of hearing her cry out in pain.

"You have a loud mouth," he hissed in her ear.

"Is the mortal giving you trouble?" Katya asked.

"No." Alek yanked on Emma's hair and tilted her head to expose her neck. "I just wanted a little taste." He leaned down and licked the drop of blood from her neck.

Her stomach twinged. Still, Alek's initial reaction gave her hope. He was pissed that she'd yelled out *Paris*, so most likely, she'd steered Robby and Giacomo in the right direction. She also noted that Alek and Uri neglected to tell Katya what she'd done. They were probably afraid of incurring the queen bitch's wrath.

Emma quickly surveyed the scene. They appeared to

be in an old wine cellar. Candlelight flickered from rusty iron sconces along stone walls. Wooden racks cradled row after row of dusty wine bottles. The air was chilly and smelled of ancient mold. Angus lay in a neglected heap on the hard stone floor.

"Zhis woman is zhe infamous slayer?" a man asked in a French accent. He approached Emma with a mincing gait, studying her with eyes that looked like black slits in his puffy white face. "Amazing. She has killed four of your friends, *non*?"

"Six," Emma corrected him. "I've killed six of her little minions, and it was pathetically easy."

Katya slapped her.

The French vampire giggled. "Meow, hiss!" He curled his chubby white fingers to resemble claws. "I just adore a good catfight." He gazed at Emma fondly. "But she is special, zhis one, *non*? May I take a whip to her?"

"If we have time." Katya patted him on the arm. "Brouchard, we need to secure the prisoners before the sun rises."

"Ah, yes. But of course." Brouchard rubbed his plump white hands together. "Zhis is so exciting! It is not often that I have such honored guests." He laughed and waved his hand in the air. "Many visit my cellar, but very few leave."

He stepped closer to Emma. "Shall I tell you my darkest secret, how I lure my victims to their doom?"

"No."

He sneered. His pointed canine teeth looked yellow against his pasty white skin. "You are a fiery one, *n'est-ce pas*? I wager your blood runs hot." He leaned forward to sniff.

"Easy, Brouchard." Katya placed a hand on his shoulder. "I need her alive."

"Ah, yes." Brouchard stepped back. He flipped a lacy handkerchief from the pocket of his velvet dinner jacket and dabbed at his mouth. "She is a little present for Casimir. He will find her quite tasty."

Emma swallowed hard. She glanced at Angus. His eyes were following everyone's movements.

Brouchard strolled to a round table, topped with a pristine white tablecloth. Elegant china was set for two. "You see, my dear, when I invite zhe lovely young men and ladies to dinner, zhey come gladly to see my famous wine collection. Zhey never realize till it is too late zhat *zhey* are my dinner."

Creepy little serial killer. Emma kept her face blank to hide her disgust.

"I am a gentleman." Brouchard sauntered down a row of racks, running his pasty fingers over the wine bottles. "I always allow my guests to choose the wine. Once zhey have enjoyed zheir fill, I take . . . my fill." He patted his plump belly and giggled. "I have a big appetite for life, *non?*"

"Enough, Brouchard." Katya yawned. "The sun is rising."

"Yes, yes. I have coffins zhis way." Brouchard scurried past several rows of bottles. "And zhere is a storeroom where we can lock up zhe prisoners."

Alek pulled Emma along with him. Uri hefted Angus over his shoulder and followed them.

"Here are zhe coffins." Brouchard waved a hand toward a line of eight coffins. "Zhey are very nice, *non?* But you do not need so many now. Only zhree of you came." He looked at Emma and giggled. "Naughty girl. Are you sure I cannot whip her?"

"Later," Katya said. "Where's the storeroom?"

"Here." Brouchard shoved a tapestry on the wall to the side and revealed an old wooden door. He unlocked it with a skeleton key, and it opened with a loud creak. "Spooky inside, *non?*"

He laughed as he removed a candle from a nearby sconce. "I will show you zhe room." He strolled inside. "It is perfect, *n'est-ce pas?* Zhere is no way out."

Uri walked in and dumped Angus on the floor.

Brouchard snickered. "He is a big one." He nudged Angus's kilt up with his foot. "A pity you can only stay one night."

"Leave him alone, you pervert," Emma muttered as Alek hauled her into the room.

"Shut up." Alek yanked her arms back. "I need some rope to tie her."

"But of course." Brouchard exited the room, but Emma could still hear him. "You will tell Casimir I was very helpful, yes?"

"Of course," Katya assured him. "You do have a mortal guard for the daytime, don't you?"

"Ah, yes. Hubert." The way Brouchard pronounced his guard's name, it sounded like *Oo-bear*. He minced back into the storeroom and handed Alek some drapery cords. "Will zhese do?"

"Yes." Alek tied Emma's wrists together behind her back.

"Take her tote bag," Katya reminded him.

Emma cursed silently as Alek cut her bag off with his knife. There went her cell phone and stakes.

Brouchard giggled. "You have made her angry." He patted her on the cheek. "You must behave during zhe day, *chérie*. Do not make my dear Hubert angry. He can be very cruel."

Emma pulled away from Brouchard's chubby hand. "Then maybe you should whip him."

Brouchard yawned. "Oh, but I have. No doubt, it is why zhe poor brute is so foul-tempered. Poor Hubert."

Alek shoved Emma onto the floor next to Angus. "If you try to escape, Hubert will kill you both."

"Come, *mes amis*." Brouchard strolled from the room. "We must have our beauty sleep."

Alek closed the door. Without Brouchard's candle, the room was very dark. Emma remembered seeing some old chairs and tables pushed against the walls, but nothing useful for escape. She listened to the sounds in the next room. Once the vampires were dead for the day, she would only have Hubert to deal with.

"Emma," Angus whispered. When she gasped, he continued, "Speak softly so they willna hear."

She wiggled closer to him. "Has the poison worn off?"

"No' quite. I canna move my arms or legs. Emma, I will fall into my death-sleep soon. If ye can escape, ye must."

She started to protest, since she didn't want to leave him. But he was right. Her best chance for escape was during the day, and she could always bring back help for Angus. "All right. I think we're in Paris."

"Aye. Go to Jean-Luc Echarpe's studio on the Champs-Elysées. The daytime guards there work for me. They can help you."

"Okay." She was still tied up, though. "Is your dagger still in your sock?"

"Aye. Take it." His speech became more slurred. "My sporran. I need the flask. Hide it . . . underneath me."

"Underneath you?"

"In case they take my . . ."

"Sporran?" She waited, but he didn't reply. She laid her head on his chest and heard nothing. He was gone.

A mournful feeling invaded her heart, and she suddenly felt like crying. Everyone she'd ever cared about had died. How could she stand to lose one more? "I'm so sorry. This is my fault."

She took a deep breath to steady her nerves. She needed her wits about her. Angus was counting on her. She rotated about so her head was next to his feet. Then she wiggled around till she felt her fingers make contact with the hilt of the *sgian dubh* hidden under his sock. She managed to pull it out, then sat up to saw through the cords binding her wrists. It was a slow and awkward process, but she kept at it.

So far, no sound from the other room. The storeroom seemed a bit lighter. She spotted a few slivers of light at the top of the far wall. Perhaps a small window that had been boarded up? She would need to make sure none of the sunlight fell on Angus.

She could barely make out his profile in the dim light. He'd told her the truth from the beginning. There were good vampires and bad ones, and Sean's activities with the Stake-Out team were nothing but a nuisance, getting in the way of the good Vamps who wanted to protect mankind. If she ever survived this, she was quitting her job.

Aha! The cords finally broke free. She slipped the knife into her belt, then dragged Angus's body to the darkest corner of the room. Heavy footsteps sounded in the wine cellar, and a shadow dimmed the light under the door. Hubert was there, listening. She needed to act quickly. She opened Angus's sporran and dug around. Thank goodness he carried a purse. She smiled to herself, imagining his reaction to the word *purse*.

She located the metal flask, then wedged it underneath his back. Normally that would be very uncomfortable, but poor Angus was dead to the world right now. She pulled out his cell phone and opened it. Whom to call? Connor was first in his directory, so she called him.

She glanced toward the door. Hubert might hear her talking, so she should text message instead. Unfortunately, the connection to Connor never went through. Shit. She wasn't getting a signal down in this hole.

She slipped the phone into her pocket and carried a chair over to the far wall. It looked like a fragile antique, so she hoped it would carry her weight. She climbed onto the cushioned brocade seat and reached for the window. Too high.

She found a wooden table about the size of a card table, light enough that she could carry it. She set it carefully beneath the window, then climbed on top. Now she could reach the slats nailed horizontally across the small window. She curled her hands around two slats and yanked. They held firm. She lifted herself up and peered through the gap.

There was a dingy narrow street. Sunlight dappled

in puddles of rainwater that gathered in the broken pavement. Footsteps approached.

Emma glanced back. No sign of Hubert. The footsteps drew closer. There was one gait, heavy and determined, and a smaller one, quick and light with a pattering sound. A dog, perhaps.

"Psst!" Emma hissed. "*A moi!*" She flinched when a wet, black nose suddenly nuzzled her hand. Okay, so she had the dog's attention. Now if she could just contact the owner. The dog pranced about excitedly. A white poodle with a pink bow on its puffy head.

"*A moi! Aidez-nous,*" Emma whispered as loud as she dared.

The poodle barked, loud and shrill. The dog's owner shouted and yanked on its leash. They hurried away.

The door behind her slammed open.

She dropped onto the table and turned. Light spilled into the storeroom from the wine cellar, along with the smell of sausage and eggs. In the doorway, a bulky black shadow loomed.

"Brouchard said you would be trouble." Hubert entered the room. His accent was as thick as his neck and arms.

He charged, bellowing like a bull. Emma remained on the table. She landed a good kick to his chest, but it only slowed him down. He grabbed one of her ankles and yanked. She fell onto her rear, but used the momentum to roll back, then forward. She kicked Hubert hard in the gut. He stumbled back. She jumped to the floor, whipped the knife from her belt, and lunged forward. The knife slid in with horrifying ease. He cried out, then collapsed backward onto the floor.

Emma stood over him, the bloody knife in her hand, and her stomach churning. Shit. She was used to killing vampires. They didn't bleed like this. They simply turned to dust.

Hubert writhed on the floor, moaning.

"Hang on. I'll get an ambulance." She'd find her way to Angus's security men on the Champs-Elysées. But first there were four vampires in the next room who needed to be staked. Angus's knife would work just fine. She strode toward the door.

A board slammed into her face. She fell back onto her rear as lightning jolts of pain zigzagged across her face. Her eyes saw double for a second, then focused on one man standing in the doorway. He was small and thin.

"You made a fatal error, *chérie*. *I* am Hubert. And I am prepared for the likes of you."

She scrambled to her feet, but he swung the board at her head once again. She collapsed to the side. Her head throbbed. The knife tumbled from her hand.

With a groan, she turned her head to see him. His figure wavered as pain shot through her.

He withdrew a syringe from his coat pocket. "I should kill you for what you did to my dear Rolfe." A stream of liquid squirted from the needle.

Emma willed her body to stand up and fight, but her brain was too battered to get the orders out. She felt the floor beside her. Her fingers touched the hilt of the knife.

"But my master wants you alive. So I will only make you sleep." He stepped toward her.

She struck at his shins with her feet, and he stumbled back.

"Bitch!" He leaped on top of her and stabbed the syringe into her neck. Instantly his face grew hazy.

He leaned forward, sneering at her. "You should not have made me angry. Now I will have to play with you while you sleep."

With a great surge of effort, she plunged the knife into his back.

He shrieked and twisted, trying to reach the knife. He fell beside her, his body contorting.

Her eyelids drooped. She almost welcomed the drugged sleep, for it numbed the throbbing pain.

Hubert grew still beside her. A sense of doom spread through her as the drug dragged her into oblivion. She'd failed Angus once again.

Angus awoke with the surge of energy that jolted his body every evening at sunset. With his first deep breath, he was accosted by the hideous smell of foul, congealed blood, which meant one thing: death. His heart constricted. No, not Emma!

He scrambled to his feet while his eyes adjusted to the dark room. His metal flask was on the floor. And there were three bodies. The devil take it, what had happened? He rushed to the first body. It was a huge man with a knife wound to the chest. He'd bled out on the cold stone floor. The smell of spoiled blood turned Angus's stomach.

He staggered to the next pair of bodies. A slim man lay dead with the *sgian dubh* in his back. The blood within him had congealed to a slimy goop, unfit for consumption. Beside him was Emma. Her heart was beating, slow and steady. Angus's relief was cut short

by one look at her face. The bastards! Her face was a
mass of bruises and lumps. Poor lass. She must have
fought for her life while he'd rested nearby totally
oblivious. He cursed his inability to protect her during
the day.

He heard sounds from the wine cellar. The enemy
was stirring. If only he had enough energy to grab
Emma and teleport out, but he was too weak from
hunger.

"Puir lass, I'm so sorry," he whispered, touching her
face. The smell of her sweet blood triggered an instant
response. Hunger flooded in. He grabbed his knife and
stumbled back to his flask on the floor. He unscrewed
the top with shaking fingers. Pain lanced his gums
where his fangs strained to surge out. A vampire's hunger was always worst when he first awoke.

He gulped down Blissky. Slowly his hunger was
quenched. His fangs retreated and relaxed. God, how
he hated being a slave to this hunger. It was why he always carried an extra supply of synthetic blood in his
flask. As the last drop slid down his throat, he reveled
in the renewed strength that coursed through his body.
He was powerful once again. He would save Emma.

The door swung open. Brouchard sauntered in, carrying a candlestick. "*Bonsoir, mes amis!* Hubert, I want
you to fetch us some tasty mortals for breakfast." He
halted with a gasp. "Hubert! What are you doing, lying
with zhat woman?"

Angus zoomed toward Brouchard and plunged his
dagger into the chubby vampire's heart. Brouchard
squealed, then turned to dust.

Uri and Alek ran in, both armed with swords. Angus

was outnumbered, but he knew he'd be stronger. He'd already fed, and they had not. He dodged Alek's attack, then fended off Uri.

Katya entered, carrying her blowpipe. "You fools. There is only one way to subdue him." She lifted her pipe to her mouth.

At the last minute, Angus spun, grabbed Uri, and turned him to face the oncoming dart. Uri stiffened and fell, the dart embedded in his chest.

Katya's eyes flashed with anger. "Alek, kill the woman."

"Of course." Alek dashed toward Emma, his sword raised.

"Nay!" Angus shouted.

Katya lifted a hand to stop Alek. "I will spare her, Angus, if you surrender to me."

Angus hesitated. He needed to buy more time so he and Emma could escape. He released his knife. It clattered to the stone floor.

With a sneer, Katya kicked his knife aside. "I always knew you were a fool. You could have had me, but you chose that lowly . . . *bug.* I will enjoy watching you suffer."

Angus gritted his teeth. "I'm certain ye will. 'Tis in your nature to be cruel and vicious."

She scoffed. "There was a time when you said I was beautiful and full of potential."

He eyed her sadly. "I wanted ye to be good, Katya. I wanted ye to use yer powers for good. 'Tis no' too late."

"And you think *she* is good?" Katya glared at Emma on the floor. "That bitch is a murderer. She deserves to

die. And if I give her to Casimir, he will spare my life."
She gave Angus a seductive look. "You wouldn't want
me to die, would you? We had such good times together."

"Ye're already dead to me."

She took in a hissing breath and pulled a dart from
her pocket. "I will make you pay, Angus MacKay. You
will wish you were never born." She jammed the dart
into his chest.

He crumpled to the ground. His body refused to
move. Despair seeped into his bones. He'd bought Emma
some more time, but now he was unable to defend her.

Alek and Katya took turns going out to feed. Then
Katya removed his sporran. He closed his eyes so he
wouldn't have to see her triumphant smirk. Alek hauled
him out of the cellar and dumped him in the alley. Angus cursed silently. Here he was, alone and free to go,
but he couldn't move. Soon Alek returned, carrying
Emma. He set her down and frisked her.

"A cell phone." Alek removed the phone from Emma's pocket and handed it to Katya.

"Ironic, don't you think?" She punched a button on
his phone. "I can use your whore's phone to take you to
your doom." She leaned down to grab his arm. "Galina? We're coming."

Katya vanished, taking Angus with her. He felt a
floating sensation, then a hard floor beneath him. He
opened his eyes to look around. They were in an old
stone building, sparsely furnished. Alek appeared next
to him, carrying Emma.

"How do you like my place?" a red-haired female
asked.

Angus recognized her from the last vampire ball. She'd been there with Ivan Petrovsky. This had to be Galina, the former harem girl who had helped Katya murder Ivan so they could be co-masters of the Russian coven.

"It's perfect." Katya looked around. "Do you have the room ready for our guests?"

Galina laughed. "Oh yes. They're going to love it!" She waved at a bulky blond man. "Burien, will you and Miroslav carry our guest?"

The two male vampires hefted Angus up and followed Galina outside.

"Where's Uri?" Galina asked.

"Detained," Katya muttered. "He'll join us later."

Angus looked around the best he could. The night sky was clear, the stars bright. It was later in the night here than in Paris, so they had traveled east. They might be in eastern Russia since Katya came from there. He recalled reading a report on Galina. She'd come from the Ukraine, so that was another possibility.

They were definitely in the countryside. The nearby hills were forested. An old stone wall encircled the property. A wooden barn nearby was falling down. He spotted Alek, carrying Emma.

They proceeded down some stone steps. A storm cellar? A root cellar? He heard a heavy door creak open.

"Put her on the cot there," Galina ordered.

He heard bedsprings squeak. He was dumped on the floor.

"There's one light," Galina said. With a small click, the room was lit by a lone lightbulb dangling from the ceiling.

Angus blinked. The whole room seemed to shimmer with sparkly lights.

Galina laughed. "Pretty, isn't it?"

"Expensive," Katya muttered.

"The plates on the ceiling are pure silver," Galina boasted. "And the walls, window, and door are covered with silver necklaces. It's almost like the old chain mail that knights wore."

"As long as it keeps them from escaping." Alek prowled around the room, examining the walls.

"Oh, it works," Galina assured them. "I had Miroslav try teleporting through the walls, and he couldn't. He bounced right off and ended up with severe burns. And Burien tried to send telepathic messages to me, but nothing could come through."

"Excellent." Katya sounded pleased. "Now all we need to do is locate Casimir and offer him our little gifts."

They filed from the room and slammed the door shut. A bolt slid across. Angus closed his eyes. As soon as the nightshade wore off, he would see to their escape. But a room lined with silver would be difficult. Thank God Emma was mortal. Silver wouldn't burn her. Nor would it stop her from using her psychic abilities.

An hour or so passed, then he heard movement on the cot.

"Emma?" he managed to croak.

She groaned.

He cleared his throat. "Emma?" That sounded better.

"God, my head hurts." The cot creaked. "Are you all right?"

"Canna move. Nightshade."

"Oh, bummer." The cot squeaked again. "Shit, they took the phone." Footsteps came toward him. She knelt beside him.

He saw her face splotched with purple and black bruises. "Bugger."

She touched her face and winced. "Lovely, huh?"

"Ye're always lovely. But I feel badly that ye were fighting for yer life, and I wasna able to help you."

"I feel badly for getting us into this mess." She looked him over. "They took your sporran." She gave him a sly look. "I mean your purse."

He growled.

"Any idea where we are?"

"I'm guessing either western Russia or the Ukraine. I canna teleport or send psychic messages through the silver."

"Silver?" She glanced around, then up at the ceiling. "Good heavens, it's everywhere."

"I wish I could touch you," he whispered. "It grieves me to see ye in pain."

Her gaze lowered back to his face. With a small smile, she touched his cheek. "What happened while I was knocked out?"

"I killed Brouchard."

"Oh." Her eyes widened. "Wicked. Congratulations."

"Uri and Alek attacked. Katya missed with her blow-pipe and hit Uri."

Emma grinned, then winced at the pain. "Ouch. I guess the royal bitch managed to hit you eventually."

"Aye."

Emma gave him a worried look. "I get the feeling there's something personal between you and her."

Angus closed his eyes briefly. "It was a mistake. And a long time ago."

"She hates you now."

"She hates you, too."

Emma smiled. "Well, I did kill six of her men."

" 'Tis more than that. She . . . suspects that I care very deeply about you."

Emma's smile faded. "She could be wrong."

"Nay. She's always had good instincts."

Emma's eyes glistened with tears as she touched his face. "I'm so sorry. They would have never captured us if I'd stayed put like you asked."

"But they would have kept killing every night until we came. The showdown was inevitable."

She leaned closer. "I'll get us out of here. Somehow."

"We'll do it together."

She searched his eyes, and he thought his heart would break. Her gaze lowered to his mouth. She touched her lips against his, then sat up.

His mouth quirked. "I'm completely helpless. Are ye sure ye wouldna like to have yer way with me?"

She snorted. "You're such a he-man." She rose to her feet and moved from his view.

"Oh, gross!" Her voice came from a far corner. "Our bathroom consists of a wooden tub, a bucket of water, and a chamber pot."

"I used a chamber pot for centuries. Ye'll get used to it."

"I guess," she muttered. "I really need to go."

"Then go." He heard a series of curses and scrambling noises.

"They call this toilet paper? I could file my nails with this stuff!" Finally she announced she was done. He heard a splash of water as she rinsed her hands.

She paced around the room. "Next time we're staying at the Hilton."

Something hit the floor.

"What was that?" Angus asked.

"I turned the cot onto its side." She grabbed him under the shoulders and dragged him. He tried to move his legs to help, but they were still dead weight.

She propped him up against the cot in a sitting position. "There. Isn't that better?"

"Yes." He could see more of the room now. A screen hid the primitive bathroom in the corner. Other than the cot, the only furniture was a small round table and two chairs. High up on the eastern wall, there was a small window.

The bolt on the door scraped.

Emma grabbed a chair and plastered herself against the wall next to the door.

The door creaked open. No one came in. A woman's voice on a walkie-talkie spoke in Russian.

"Put the chair down," Alek's voice ordered. "We know what you are doing. We have cameras in the room."

Emma lowered the chair and gazed around the room.

The Russian vampire Burien stepped inside and pointed a machine gun at her. She raised her hands.

Alek marched into the room with a tray in his hands.

"We saw you were awake. We thought you might be hungry." He set the tray on the table.

"Ye make a good servant," Angus muttered.

"Indeed," Emma agreed with a sweet smile. "Be a dear and empty the chamber pot for me?"

Alek glared at them both. "We are watching your every move. And very soon, we expect it to be quite entertaining." Chuckling, he left the room.

Burien followed him. The door slammed shut, causing all the silver on it to glimmer. The bolt slid home.

Emma brought the chair back to the table. "What a creep. After I eat, I'll find all the cameras and destroy them." She touched the stuff in the bowl and tasted it from her fingertip. "Porridge. Not bad, actually, and I'm starving."

Angus sighed. His flask was gone. His heart twisted. Poor Emma. Katya had come up with the perfect way to torture them both. No wonder she wanted to watch.

"I hate to eat alone." Emma sat at the table, frowning. "Those jerks didn't bring you any food at all."

Then her eyes met his and her spoon dropped with a clatter on the table. At last she was realizing the true nature of their imprisonment.

"Aye," Angus told her. "As far as they're concerned, they have left me a source of food."

Chapter 20

Sean Whelan hesitated on the sidewalk in front of Roman Draganesti's townhouse. He suspected they were holding Emma Wallace prisoner inside.

When Emma hadn't shown up for the Wednesday meeting, he'd been mildly concerned. She could be running late or feeling poorly. But she wasn't answering her home phone or cell phone.

Ground-floor security reported she'd left the building early the night before with a man from MacKay Security and Investigation, the company that provided security for Roman Draganesti and Jean-Luc Echarpe. Since those two were powerful coven masters, Sean figured the company's owner, Angus MacKay, was also a vampire. In fact, he suspected Angus MacKay was the newly arrived Scotsman living at Draganesti's townhouse.

Dammit, Sean had known something was wrong the other night when he thought he'd heard Emma scream.

These vampire men were despicable. First they kidnapped and seduced his daughter. Now they were after Emma.

The front door opened. Sean stiffened. The bastards inside had seen him. His revolver was tucked into his belt behind his back, fully loaded with silver bullets.

The vampire named Connor stood in the doorway, wearing his usual red and green plaid kilt. "Did ye have a question, Whelan, or were ye planning to glare at us all night?"

Sean strode to the base of the stairs. "I have a question, scumbag. Are you holding Emma Wallace against her will?"

The Scotsman arched a brow.

"'Cause if you are," Sean continued, "I'll have fifty FBI agents here in ten minutes to tear this place apart."

"We know Emma Wallace is missing." A pained look crossed Connor's face briefly. "One of ours is missing, too."

Sean frowned. "Are you saying they ran off together?"

Connor's eyes glimmered with anger. "Nay, they were kidnapped, and they're in grave danger. We're doing our best to find them." He started to close the door.

"Wait!" Sean climbed a stair. "Do you know who kidnapped them?"

Connor paused, then opened the door wider. "'Twas Katya Miniskaya and some of her Russian Malcontents."

"Why would they want your . . . friend?"

Connor gave him an irritated look. "If ye had listened to yer daughter, ye would know there are two factions amongst us."

"Yeah, right," Sean interrupted him. "I've heard it before. But why did they take Emma?"

Connor snorted. "It is amazing how little ye know. Emma Wallace is the slayer. She's killed at least four Malcontents since last summer. No doubt Katya is seeking revenge."

"Emma is a slayer?" Sean couldn't believe it. Why would she keep that a secret? Hell, he would have given her a medal.

Connor gritted his teeth. "She's the cause of this trouble. Angus was trying to protect her. Now Katya has them both."

"Angus MacKay?"

"Aye. He's been watching her, trying to keep her safe."

"What can we do?" Sean winced when he realized he'd used the word *we*.

Connor studied him, then nodded once. "All right. I see no harm in an exchange of information."

"Okay," Sean agreed readily since he didn't have any. "You go first."

Connor gave him a suspicious look, then crossed his arms. "They were taken to Paris. We notified the coven there, and they found the place where Angus and Emma were held prisoner. There were signs of a great struggle. Several dead bodies, both vampire and mortal. A Russian named Uri was captured. He'll be interrogated as soon as he can speak."

"And Emma?"

"Her tote bag was found. So was Angus's sporran

and knife. We believe they were teleported some place, perhaps in Russia since Katya comes from there. We're searching for them now." Connor tilted his head. "What information do ye have?"

Sean smiled. "None. But thanks for sharing."

"Pompous arse," Connor muttered. "Have ye no' been conducting a surveillance of the Russian coven? Surely ye heard something. Katya must have been planning this for days."

"Our bugs were discovered a few days ago and destroyed by some nasty guy from Poland. He told Katya that Casimir was angry with her for killing Ivan Petrovsky. He demanded she catch the slayer by Saturday." Sean blinked. "Shit. He meant Emma."

"Ye knew more than ye realized, Whelan. Ye need to plant yer bugs again. Someone in the Russian coven may know where Katya is hiding."

"We can't get in. There are too many mafia thugs watching the place during the day."

Connor tilted his head, thinking. "I know a way in. If we help ye plant the bugs, will ye share any information ye learn?"

Sean hesitated. The idea of allying himself with vampires was sickening.

Connor glowered at him. "We are the best equipped to find Miss Wallace. Would ye sacrifice her because of yer hatred?"

The vampire was right, but it still left a sour taste in Sean's mouth. "We'll cooperate. Just this once."

"Wait here." Connor went into the house, then returned with a piece of paper. "This is my number. As soon as ye have yer surveillance van in position, call me."

Forty minutes later, Sean and Garrett were in their white van, parked down the street from the Russian vampires' house in Brooklyn. Sean made the call.

"Keep talking," Connor ordered.

"What? Hello? Are you there?" Sean glanced at Garrett. "He doesn't answer."

Two figures appeared in the van.

"Shit!" Garrett jumped back and fell off his chair.

Connor let go of the one who had traveled with him. He was a young black man in torn jeans and a gray, hooded sweatshirt.

"This is Phineas McKinney," Connor said. "He knows what to do. Right, Phineas?"

"Right." Phineas rubbed his palms nervously on his jeans. "I hope I can help find Miss Wallace and Angus. I feel really bad about goofing up."

"Goofing up?" Sean asked.

"A long story. Do ye have the bugs?" Connor asked.

"Yes." Sean handed them to Phineas and gave him some last-minute directions.

"I got it." Phineas stuffed the bugs in his sweatshirt pocket and glanced at Connor. "I won't let you down, man."

Connor smiled slightly. "I know, lad. Ye'll do fine."

Phineas exited the back of the van and strolled toward the Russians' house. He opened the front door and sauntered inside.

"Jesus Louise," Garrett muttered. "How can he just walk in like that?"

"They transformed him about a week ago," Connor explained. "They think he lives there."

"But he works for you, now?" Sean asked.

"Aye. He's a good lad. He couldna take to their evil ways."

Sean snorted. "You think the Russians are the only evil ones around here?"

Connor glared at him. "In the mortal world, there are good and evil people. Why should it be any different in the vampire world?"

Because you're all evil. Sean swallowed the words. Though for the sake of his daughter, he hoped her husband wasn't abusing her. And it was odd the way Connor and Phineas seemed to care about Angus MacKay's safety. Was there friendship and loyalty in the vampire world?

The van remained quiet while they waited. A few minutes later, the first surveillance screen flickered, then came on.

"We're live," Garrett announced. "Looks like Katya's office."

The second and third screen came on with different views of her office.

"Testing, testing," Phineas murmured, his face in a camera. He suddenly turned toward the office door. "Oh, Stan the man. Hey, bro. What's up?"

A male entered the sites of cameras two and three. "What are you doing here? Where have you been?" he asked with a Russian accent.

Phineas shrugged. "I needed a sabbatical, man. A little rest and relaxation with my old ladies. You know how it is." He adjusted his jeans. "A man has needs that cannot be denied."

The Russian snorted. "You should have brought them here."

"Oh yeah, you're right. Next time I will. I know this sweet little blonde named Tina. Man, is she hot!"

The Russian wandered toward the desk. "What are you doing in Katya's office?"

"I thought since I was gone a few days, I should tell the queen bitch that I'm back, but she's not here. Hell, nobody seems to be here. Where did everybody go?"

The Russian crossed his arms, frowning. "They left the country, but they didn't invite me."

"Well, that sucks." Phineas looked indignant. "They didn't invite me, either."

The Russian sighed. "I think they all went to Galina's place. She left early to prepare it for their visit."

"Who's Galina? Is she hot?"

The Russian smiled. "Very hot. You don't know her? She's the most beautiful—oh, right. She left before you came here."

"Damn. I hope she comes back."

The Russian nodded. "I do, too. I asked if I could go with her, but she took Burien and Miroslav."

"Those two morons? She's got lousy taste. Where do you think she went?"

The Russian shrugged. "Probably to the Ukraine."

Phineas laughed. "Never heard of it. Well, I'm off. Got some hos waiting for me, you understand." He strolled out of view.

"Can you bring me one?" The Russian followed him.

The office was empty. Five minutes later, Phineas left the house and sauntered down the sidewalk. He tapped on the back door of the van and climbed inside.

"Ye did verra well, lad." Connor patted him on the back.

Phineas sat up straighter. "Hell, yeah. Whenever you need an undercover brother, just call me, Dr. Phang."

"Dr. Phang?" Sean asked.

Garrett snickered.

"We'll concentrate our search on the Ukraine." Connor grabbed Phineas's arm. "We must go."

"Wait!" Sean raised a hand. "If you find out anything, you'll let me know?"

Connor nodded. "We'll do our best to save them both." He and Phineas disappeared.

"They're so weird," Garrett mumbled. "I mean, they really seem to care."

Vampires who cared? Sean wondered. Could Shanna be right? And what about her baby? She was supposed to have it soon. What kind of creature would it be?

Emma gave up on eating her oatmeal. She'd lost her appetite. She stood and surveyed the small room, but avoided looking at Angus. "I'll try to find those cameras."

She spotted one high up on the windowsill of the eastern wall. Too high to reach, so she shoved the table underneath.

"Emma."

She ventured a quick look at Angus. "Yes?"

"Ye're perfectly safe for now. I still canna move. And I found the flask ye left me, so I'm full."

Safe for now. How long could he retain his gentlemanly demeanor before primal survival instincts took over? Would he attack her like the ones who had attacked her parents? She hated the thought of being dinner. Still, she didn't blame Angus. He couldn't help it. He was what he was.

"We'll get through this . . . somehow." She glanced up at the camera. "But I really don't want an audience."

She climbed up on the table and reached between the silver chains to grab the camera. "I bet these chains burned the vampire who put this here."

"Most likely it was mortals who hung all the silver and placed the cameras. The Malcontents have probably taken control of the nearby village, using the mortals for food and labor."

Emma pivoted on the table and examined the sparkling room. "It must have cost a fortune."

" 'Tis easy to steal when ye can teleport."

Emma slanted him a wry look. "And you know this how . . . ?"

He grinned. "My sneaking about is legitimate work for my company."

"Right." She sat and slid to her feet. "With all your powers, you were never tempted to do anything naughty."

His smile faded as his gaze grew more intense. "I have been tempted greatly of late."

Her cheeks grew warm. Time to change the subject. "I know a good place for this camera." She sauntered behind the screen and dropped it into the chamber pot.

She strolled along the northern wall of their cell, searching for another camera. "How old were you when you were transformed?"

"Thirty-three."

She grabbed a silver chain and tugged hard. It held firm. "And you said you were married?"

"Aye. I tried going home after Roman changed me, but my wife couldna accept me. She was afraid of the creature I had become."

Emma glanced at him. "I'm so sorry."

"Are you? I believe ye intend to reject me for the same reason."

Wincing, she turned back to the wall. Time to change the subject again. She spotted a tiny camera over the door. "Were you able to watch your children and grandchildren grow up?" She dragged a chair over to the door.

"I kept an eye on my descendants, trying to protect them, but I could never be there during the day." A pained look haunted his face. "I lost so many at Culloden. And those who survived suffered greatly from the oppression to follow. Many left for America, and I lost track of them."

He closed his eyes briefly. "Nay, the truth is I was weary of watching them suffer. I dinna have the heart to keep up with them any longer."

"I'm so sorry. At least you still have Robby."

"Aye, he'll inherit the company and my castle if I perish."

"Nothing's going to happen to you. We're going to be fine." She stepped up on the chair and ripped the camera off the wall. "You're lucky you still have family."

"Do ye have no one, Emma?"

"A few cousins in Texas, but I hardly know them." She jumped down from the chair and headed toward their primitive bathroom. "My father worked for North Sea Petroleum." She dropped the second camera into the chamber pot. "He was stationed in Houston when he met my mum. My brother and I were born there, so we both had dual citizenship."

She gave him a wry look as she came around the screen. "But I bet you already know all about me from checking out my profile at MI6."

He smiled. "I like hearing it from you. How long did ye live in Texas?"

She scanned the west wall as she talked. "We moved back to England when I was seven. My brother was ten. My dad always liked working abroad, and sometimes he would take Mum with him. My brother and I would stay with Aunt Effie in Scotland."

"And yer aunt had psychic powers, too?"

"Yes. She was my dad's sister. They both had it. She's the one who taught me how to contact Dad over a long distance." No cameras on the west wall. Emma moved to the north wall. "She died four years ago. She left me her cottage by Linlithgow."

"And yer brother?"

Emma sighed. "He died in a motorcycle accident when he was sixteen."

"And then ye saw the deaths of yer parents in yer mind."

She turned to glare at him. "Are you trying to cheer me up? 'Cause you're doing a lousy job of it."

"I'm sorry. I know what it's like to mourn." He extended a hand to her. "Ye're no longer alone."

"You can move?" She walked toward him.

"I have feeling back in my arms, but no' my legs."

He reached for her hand and tugged. "I have a few things to say."

She sat beside him. "Yes?"

"See if any of the chains can be torn from the wall. If ye can remove enough of them, I may be able to teleport us out."

"Okay." She started to stand, but he tugged her back down.

"I canna send psychic messages through the silver, but ye can. Doona do it at night, though, for the Malcontents will hear ye and find a way to stop you. Ye'll need to send yer messages during the day while they sleep."

"But the good vampires will be sleeping, too. Who will hear me during the day?"

"I'm hoping ye can reach Austin. He's somewhere in Eastern Europe."

"Okay, I'll try." She started once again to get up, but he held tight to her hand.

"One more thing. Austin's wife was a vampire, but Roman was able to change her back."

Emma nodded. "You mentioned that before. But I gathered you weren't interested in having the procedure done on you."

"Nay, it wouldna work on me. Roman can only do it if he has a sample of the mortal's original DNA, and mine is long lost. He would need a blood sample taken before ye were transformed."

She blinked. "You think I might get transformed?"

"I think we should be prepared for the possibility. If Casimir transforms you, wait till ye can escape, then go to Roman so he can change ye back."

"It won't get that bad. We'll escape before Casimir arrives."

Angus squeezed her hand. "Emma, I have pledged to protect ye from harm, but we're outnumbered. Casimir and his followers are vicious, and I'm no' invincible."

"Nothing will happen to you. I won't let it."

He smiled sadly. "I love yer fierce spirit, lass, but we must be prepared. Let me do this, so I'll have the peace of knowing that ye can be made mortal again if the need arises."

She frowned. "What do you want to do?"

"We need a small sample of yer blood, and ye need to keep it hidden on you. Not me. If I'm killed, everything on me will turn to dust." He raised her arm and pushed back her sleeve. "We should do it now, while I'm no' too hungry. That way, I willna lose control."

"You're going to bite me?"

"Would ye prefer using the spoon on the table? We have nothing sharp here."

She took a deep breath. "Okay, what the heck. Bite me." She gritted her teeth and turned her head.

He snorted. "Emma, I have promised to never harm you. I'm a man of my word."

She turned back to him. "Then how . . . ?"

"Trust me." He brought her arm up to his mouth and licked the soft underside of her forearm.

Her arm tingled. Pleasantly. Very pleasantly. "How?"

"It needna hurt, lass. Only the evil vampires make it painful, for they enjoy inciting terror more than giving pleasure." He licked her again.

The tingling grew and shimmered up her arm. "Wow," she breathed. "Wicked."

Let me in. His mind spoke to hers.

She relaxed her psychic barrier. *Why?*

To heighten the pleasure. For both of us. He licked her again. Her whole body tingled.

He placed his mouth over her arm and suckled. She felt her blood rushing through her body as it was drawn down her arm to his lips. Gooseflesh prickled her arms and legs. Her toes curled under. Her hands fisted.

Each time he sucked, the pull inside her grew stronger and deeper. It pulled at her chest, then her stomach, then at the core between her legs.

He groaned. *Ye feel so good.*

Something pricked her arm and entered her. She jolted when it mirrored a probing sensation between her legs.

He lifted his head. Blood welled from two small puncture wounds. He grabbed the sheet off the cot. Two tiny droplets of blood ran down her arm toward her wrist.

He wiped them with a corner of the sheet. *There. That should be enough.*

"I'm still bleeding." More blood trickled from the wounds. Oddly enough, it didn't hurt at all. Her skin had become so sensitive that the trickle of blood felt like the tickling caress of a lover.

I can stop it. He placed his mouth over the wounds and sucked.

"Ah!" Emma squeezed her thighs together. It felt like he was between her legs. With each suck, she felt the tension rising.

Ye taste so good. I knew ye would. He swirled his

tongue around the wounds, and her body jolted with spasms.

She collapsed, her head falling onto his thighs.

He let go of her arm and ripped off the corner of the sheet. "Here." He tucked the bloodstained cloth into her pants pocket.

She struggled to catch her breath. "What the hell was that?" She looked at him and was met with red, glowing eyes.

His mouth quirked. The tip of one his fangs showed. "Was it good for you, too?"

She smiled. "Careful, big guy. We don't have any dry cleaners nearby."

Chapter 21

When Emma awoke, it was daytime. She lay on the cot for a moment, wondering how she'd gotten there. Her last memory was her lying on the floor, her head in Angus's lap while he stroked her hair and entertained her with tales from his past. He'd talked into the wee hours of the morning, and she must have fallen asleep. He'd straightened the cot and put her to bed.

She sat up and stretched. Sunlight was pouring through the little window in the eastern wall. It left a rectangular block of light on the western wall. She jumped to her feet, suddenly worried there was too much sun in the room. She spotted Angus, lying on the stone floor beneath the table.

"Angus." She ran to him and crouched beneath the table. His face was lifeless, his body still. She touched his cheek and was surprised by how warm it felt. Too much sun? Those damned vampires should have given him a coffin. But of course, they didn't care if he burned. Katya wanted him to suffer.

She hurried to the primitive bathroom. The cameras sat facedown in the chamber pot, and the urine was reddish, tinted with blood. Was that from Angus? She grimaced. This was more than she wanted to know about the vampire world. The wooden tub also had water in it. He must have cleaned up before his death-sleep.

By the time she used the pot, it was almost full. Hopefully, someone would come to empty it. And that would give her a good opportunity for escape.

She moved the screen to the table, curling it around the table to protect Angus from the sun. She retrieved the pillow from the cot and placed it under his head— not that he could feel the difference, but it looked more comfy.

She began reaching out telepathically. *Austin, can you hear me? This is Emma. We need your help.*

She repeated the message over and over as she methodically examined each wall, testing each silver strand for strength. Every now and then, she found one she could break loose, but never a group together. She doubted Angus could teleport through a six-inch square.

She estimated it was about noon when she heard the bolt scrape. She grabbed a chair and flattened herself against the wall next to the door.

It slowly creaked open. She waited for someone to enter, so she could clobber him. A tray of food was pushed into the room. It scraped along the floor, pushed by a garden hoe. The door started to close.

"Wait!" Emma dropped the chair and jumped in front of the door. "I need to talk to you. The chamber pot needs emptying."

A woman stood at the bottom of the stone steps, holding the garden hoe. The man next to her pointed a hunting rifle at Emma.

She raised her hands. "We'll pay you if you let us go." She motioned toward Angus with her head. "He's a very rich man."

The man and woman gazed at her blankly. Emma translated into Russian, but they didn't seem to understand. She noticed the puncture wounds on their necks. The Malcontents had them on a tight leash. She tried a psychic assault, hoping to break the vampires' control.

The man and woman gasped, then quickly shut the door.

"Wait!" Emma yelled. She heard their footsteps running up the stairs. "What about the chamber pot?

"Shit." She grabbed the tray and settled on the cot. Cold ham and fried potatoes. A jug of water.

Her gaze wandered to the table. She could see Angus's long legs jutting out past the screen. How hungry would he be when he woke up?

She redoubled her efforts to contact Austin. And she kept trying to find a weak spot in the walls. After a few hours, she grew sleepy, so she used the bucket of cold water to take a quick shower. It woke her up, and she kept working.

It was late afternoon when she heard a response.

Emma, I hear you!

Austin. She ran to the window as if expecting to see him peer inside. *Where are you?*

Budapest, Hungary. I heard you and Angus were captured. Any idea where you are?

We think in the Ukraine. Emma sighed. *But we're not sure.*

Can you describe the place?

She recited all the information Angus had told her. Countryside, forested hills, old stone house, rotting wooden barn. There was a pause. *Austin?*

I'm here. Darcy and I will start driving east toward the Ukraine border. Keep in touch. I'll be able to tell if we're getting closer.

An hour later, Austin was sure they were getting closer.

The bolt scraped, and the door swung open. Two men with hunting rifles marched in. Emma held up her hands. The woman she'd seen before came in with a bucket of water. She took it to the bathroom area and picked up the chamber pot.

"Thank God," Emma muttered. She couldn't tell if the woman noticed the cameras inside. Her face remained blank.

Emma tried her Russian on the two men. "The vampires are controlling you."

They stared at her, expressionless.

"Katya is evil!" Emma announced.

One of the guards smiled, his eyes glassy. "Katya."

"Galina," the other one whispered, smiling.

"Slave dogs," Emma muttered, eyeing the punctures on their necks.

A teenage girl came in with a tray of food that she deposited on the cot. Emma frowned at the wounds on her neck. Those damned vampires should leave the children alone. The woman returned with a fresh chamber pot. Then she and the girl hauled the tub of water toward the door.

"How would you all like a free vacation to the resort of your choice? I'm talking first-class hotels with real bathrooms. You know, indoor plumbing? Towels?" Emma was met with blank looks.

The females carried the tub up the stairs, then returned with it empty. They set it back in the bathroom.

"Do you realize those vampires are making you do all the work?" Emma asked. She glared at the men. "And you just stand there and let the ladies do the work?"

The teenage girl retrieved Emma's lunch tray, and they all filed from the room. They shut the door and shot the bolt.

"Nice talking to you!" Emma shouted. With a sigh, she sat on the cot and ate her dinner.

The room grew darker.

Hurry, Austin! The sun is setting.

That's good, he answered. *I can contact our Vamp buddies, and we'll have more people searching for you.*

Angus told me not to talk to you after sunset. Our captors will hear me.

I understand. We're almost to the border. You sound much closer. We'll see you soon.

"I hope so," Emma whispered as the last of the sunlight disappeared. The lone lightbulb on the ceiling shone.

A sudden movement caught her attention. Angus's legs had twitched. She heard a deep breath from behind the screen.

She swallowed hard. Her vampire roommate was awake.

With his first breath, a powerful hunger seized Angus. He was always hungry upon first awakening, but this was worse than usual. He was used to having at least three bottles of synthetic blood during the course of each night. Last night, the contents of his flask and the small amount he'd taken from Emma added up to half his usual intake. He could have taken more from Emma, he'd been sorely tempted to, but he'd wanted her alert and strong during the day so she could try to escape.

She was still here; he could smell her. Her blood rushed through her veins, calling to him, offering him the gift of life. His senses remembered the sweet taste of her. Pain speared his gums when his fangs strained to release. Raw need slammed into his gut, and his brain screamed to take her. His body shook. With a moan, he rolled into a fetal position. *No, no!* He would not become a raging monster.

"Angus, are you all right?"

"Stay back." Luckily the screen she'd placed around the table kept him hidden. He didn't want her to see him so weak. And he didn't want to see her. One look at her and . . .

He cried out when his fangs shot forth. The devil take it. He was losing this battle. His stomach seized with a cramp. He had to bite. Something. Anything. He pushed up the sleeve of his knit jumper and sank his fangs into his arm. There was a jolt of pain, then instant relief. He drew blood into his mouth, and the hunger eased a little. Just enough for him to see and think clearly again.

He could see through the gap between the floor and the bottom edge of the screen. He could see Emma's feet as she paced about the room. Her scent wafted toward him, sweet and fresh. He pulled more blood from his arm. Cannibalizing himself would buy him some time, but it would also make him weak. He could survive tonight, but tomorrow? His primal instincts would take over, and he'd be as vicious as any Malcontent. He would tear into Emma with the ferocity of a monster. His hunger would be so great, he would most likely kill her.

With the edge off his hunger, he was able to retract his fangs. With a groan, he sat up. His head grazed the underside of the tabletop.

"Angus." Emma's footsteps stopped in front of the screen. "Are you all right?"

She smelled so good. "Stay back. Across the room."

"I can tell you're suffering. Maybe I should give you a little . . . like yesterday?"

"Nay. I wouldna be able to stop. And I doona want ye weak." Most likely she would be fighting for her life in the next few days. The best chance he could give her was to keep her strong.

Her footsteps moved back. "I have good news. I made contact with Austin. He and Darcy were in Hungary, and they're coming to the Ukraine. He could tell he was getting closer to us."

"That's good." And now that it was dark, there would be friendly Vamps searching for them, too. They could move much faster than mortals. Still, the Ukraine was a big country.

He pulled his jumper over his head, so his arms would be bare and easy to bite. Hunger still gnawed at his stomach and clouded his thinking. It would be a long night.

Last night, after Emma had fallen asleep, he'd ripped a wooden slat from a chair back and taken the spoon from the table. He'd spent the rest of the night scraping the spoon along the slat's edge. He'd hidden them under his kilt while he slept.

They were still on the floor under the table. He examined the piece of wood. He'd succeeded in narrowing one end, but it still wasn't pointed enough to make a good stake. He grabbed the spoon and went back to work, scraping and whittling.

"What are you doing?" Emma asked from across the room.

"Making you a weapon."

"How?"

He didn't answer. It took all his energy to keep control of his hunger and keep whittling.

After a while, she spoke again. "I tried to pull the silver off the walls, but I couldn't find an opening big enough for you to teleport us out. I'm sorry."

He made a noise of acknowledgment. He wouldn't have the energy to teleport, anyway. His only hope rested in the Vamps finding them before sunrise.

It was Friday night, he realized. Shanna would be having her baby. And it was exactly one week since he'd met Emma. It seemed like a lifetime.

He kept whittling. The wood slowly took the shape of a stake. When hunger overcame him, he sank his fangs into his arm.

Sometime after midnight, he heard the creaking of the cot. "Ye should sleep. Ye need to be awake during the day to make contact with Austin."

"I know." She yawned. "I just kept hoping the good guys would appear. Do you think Katya's found Casimir yet?"

"I doona know. I'm certain she's trying, but I canna hear them through the silver."

Soon after, he heard her soft, even breathing and knew she was asleep. Her pulse slowed to a steady, hypnotic beat. He crawled out from under the table and looked at her. She was beautiful. So brave and pure of heart. He returned her pillow, gently lifting her head to slide it underneath. His hand lingered on her neck. Her pulse called to him, and he backed away.

He stripped and stepped into the wooden tub. He used half the water from the bucket to wash. The mixture of cold water and cool night air was uncomfortable enough to take his mind off the hunger and pain. For a little while.

He put his kilt and T-shirt back on. He returned the screen to the bathroom area. The glaring light from the ceiling lightbulb bothered him, seemed to make his head ache more, so he set a chair under the lightbulb, climbed up, and gave it a quick twist. The light went out, and the room became soothingly dark. He returned the chair to the table, then sat and waited. The stake lay finished on the table in front of him. Emma lay on the cot like a gourmet feast, his for the taking. There were only a few hours before sunrise. He could only hope his friends would come soon.

* * *

Emma had fallen asleep to the soft, rhythmic sound of metal scraping wood. When another similar sound interrupted her sleep, she ignored it and snuggled deeper under the blanket. She turned her head and realized vaguely that her pillow was back. Angus was looking out for her while she slept.

The scraping sound repeated. Poor guy. Still making stakes. It had to be almost dawn. She could hear the birds outside chirping and feel that calm stillness before the day began. She should wish Angus good night before he slipped into his death-sleep. She opened her eyes and noted the lighter gray light around the window. Angus would be settling down underneath the table. She glanced toward the table.

It wasn't there. Neither was the screen. It had been put back in the corner bathroom.

Where was Angus? She sat up and heard a creak behind her. She turned and gasped.

Angus had pushed the table against the western wall and was climbing up. She glanced back at the window and jumped to her feet. When the sun rose, it would pour through the window directly onto him.

"What are you doing?" She ran toward him. Was the fool trying to kill himself? She halted when the truth slammed into her. *He was.*

He looked at her sadly. "I dinna want ye to see this."

"I can't believe you're doing this. Come down before you get burned."

"I swore to protect you, Emma. And yer worst threat right now comes from me."

"Bullshit." She yanked at his kilt. "Shame on you. I can't believe you would give up this easily."

"Ye think I do this lightly?" His eyes blazed with anger. "Look at me!" He showed her his arms.

She gasped at the sight of so many wounds.

He leaned over to make closer eye contact. "That could have been you."

Tears blurred her eyes. How much had he suffered to keep from biting her? "I'm sorry."

"You doona understand the terrible power of this hunger." He straightened. "Even now, I can barely keep myself from tearing into yer throat."

She winced. "I know it's bad, but we can't give up. You'll fall asleep soon, then it won't bother you anymore."

He glanced at the window and set his jaw. "This is the best way."

Stubborn man! He was pissing her off. "Stop being a damned hero and come down." She grabbed his leg and pulled.

He stumbled and caught himself by placing a hand on the wall behind him. A terrible hissing sound came from the silver burning his flesh. He pulled his hand away, grimacing.

"Oh God, I'm sorry." Emma tried to help steady him. "Please come down."

" 'Tis better this way. Let me go."

"No! I refuse to lose you." Her tears threatened to overflow. "I've lost everyone. I'm not losing you."

His eyes glimmered with moisture. "If I wake at sunset, I will attack you. I'd rather die than cause yer death."

"It won't happen!" She grabbed his kilt in her fist.

"When the sun rises, I'll make contact with Austin. I'll lead him here. We'll be rescued. We'll be okay, Angus. *Please*."

He closed his eyes. She could see the struggle he was enduring in his furrowed brow and clenched teeth. He swayed on his feet. She glanced back at the window and saw the rosy tint of the sky. The sun was on the horizon. Soon it would shine through the window and land on Angus.

"Don't leave me," she whispered. A tear rolled down her cheek.

He opened his eyes. "I pray ye're no' mistaken."

"I'm not. Austin will find us today. I swear he will."

Angus bent down and eased off the table. His legs gave out, and he collapsed onto the floor. "Death-sleep," he whispered.

She leaned over him. "It's all right. I'll move you to a safer place."

"Not much time." He motioned to the table. "Stake."

She found the stake. It was crude, but it would work. Even in pain, Angus had managed to give her a way to protect herself. "I'll be honored to use this on the Malcontents. Thank you."

"If Austin doesna . . . make it in time, use it . . . on me."

The stake fell from her hand. Her heart froze. "No."

"If I wake, the hunger will take me. Ye must stop me."

"No!" She scooted back.

Tears glimmered in his green eyes. "I swore never to hurt you."

"You *are* hurting me! I can't do it. I care too much about you."

A tear slipped down his cheek, tinted red with blood. "If ye care, doona allow me to hurt you. I couldna live with myself."

"Angus." She moved closer and wiped the tear from his cheek.

He smiled slightly. "Ye were wanting to kill me for days."

She sniffed and wiped a tear from her face. "Not anymore."

"I'll be in my death-sleep," he whispered. "I willna feel . . . a thing." His eyes closed.

"Angus." She leaned over him, her hands on his cheeks. He wasn't breathing. He was gone. Her heart constricted with pain. She couldn't bear to lose him. "I love you."

She laid her head on his chest and let the tears flow. How could she ever harm Angus? In just a week, he'd taught her so much. That good, honorable men like him stayed the same after death. That she'd existed for too long with only hatred and revenge in her heart. Love was a much nobler cause to live for. Love didn't follow its own selfish agenda; it was willing to make sacrifices for others. How strange that it took an undead man to show her how to live.

Sun poured through the window, and she hustled to pull Angus's body to a darker side of the room. She placed the screen around him.

She began calling out to Austin telepathically. No answer. She washed up. The human slave dogs brought her breakfast. She tried communicating with them, but they wouldn't respond.

By noon, she was frantic.

Emma, I'm here, Austin called.

Oh, thank God! Where have you been?

Asleep, sorry. We were up till dawn, searching for you. I figured you were safe during the day, so we took a nap.

You need to find us by this evening. Emma glanced at the stake on the floor where she'd left it. She didn't want to think about it.

We set up headquarters in Kiev, Austin explained. *There were ten of us last night. We spread out in a circle and checked a two-hundred-mile radius. During the day, it's just me and Darcy, but I have a plan to help us narrow the search parameter.*

Sounds good. Emma paced about the cell. *What can I do?*

Just keep in touch. We're going to start traveling one direction. Eventually I'll be able to tell if we're getting closer or farther away. If I'm getting cold, I'll turn another direction and see if that works.

The rest of the afternoon passed while they played psychic Marco Polo. Austin discovered south was the wrong direction, then headed west. That direction worked.

You must be close to the Carpathian Mountains, Austin observed. *There are four passes through the mountains. I'll start with the one to the south.*

By suppertime, Austin had determined they were on the wrong pass. He had to backtrack to get to the next one.

Hurry! Emma nervously watched the window as Austin tried the second mountain pass. The sun was lowering in the sky.

I think this is it! Austin sounded cheerful. *As soon as the Vamps wake up, I'll call them here, and we can spread out and find you.*

Emma glanced at the screen where Angus's body was hidden. *That will be too late. I need you now.*

There was a pause. *Emma, we'll try our best, but I can't make any promises.*

I understand. As the room dimmed, Emma realized the lightbulb was no longer working. The room would be dark when Angus awoke. She walked behind the screen and crouched beside him. He looked so peaceful and harmless.

She touched his cheek. "I know you don't want to live with the guilt of hurting me." She took in a deep, shaky breath. "But I can't do it. I can't kill you." Tears welled in her eyes. "Even if it means my own death."

Chapter 22

With her decision made, Emma prepared herself.
She stood in the tub, soaped up, then poured cold water
on her head from the bucket. She washed her undies
and hung them over the screen to dry. Then she pulled
the thin mattress off the cot and dragged it behind the
screen. She positioned it beside Angus.

Dressed only in her shirt, she sat on the mattress
and waited for the last of the sunlight to fade. She ran
her fingers through her wet hair to ease out the tangles.
The room grew darker. A quiet stillness filled the air.
She imagined the sun on the western horizon sinking
lower and lower, and her spirit sank with it. Was she
making a terrible mistake? What if Angus lost com-
plete control and attacked her like the monster who
had attacked her mother?

A wave of panic seized her. She ran to fetch the
stake, then returned to the mattress. She placed it on the

floor within her reach. Just in case she ended up struggling with a mindless creature intent on killing her.

Surely not. Surely Angus would be as gentle as possible.

She jumped when his body jolted. His chest expanded with a deep breath. She placed her palm over his heart and felt the strong pounding through the thin cotton T-shirt. How amazing that his heart could suddenly leap to life with the setting of the sun.

He grabbed her wrist, locking his fist around it. She flinched. He'd moved so fast. She'd barely detected the blur of motion before he'd seized her. His eyes opened. The green irises glowed, focusing on her with the look of a predatory animal.

"Angus?" Did he even know it was her?

He pushed her down. A growl rumbled deep in his throat as he leaned over her.

"Angus!"

He blinked. The ferocious look on his face melted into an expression of sheer horror. "Emma." He released her and sat up. His body shook with a great tremor. He cried out as his fangs erupted.

Oh God, they looked so sharp. Emma squeezed her eyes shut.

He cried out again, a sound so full of pain that Emma knew he was as terrified as she was. She opened her eyes and reached out to him.

"Nay!" He rolled onto his side, facing away from her, and sank his teeth into his arm. His body trembled.

She wrapped her arms around him and hugged him from the back. Slowly his body ceased shuddering.

"I—I was afraid I would kill you," he whispered.

She nestled her cheek in the dip between his shoulder blades. "I hate to see you mutilate yourself."

"Better me than you." He turned to face her. His fangs had retracted. "I only bought a little time. I'm so verra hungry."

The need in his eyes was so strong, she couldn't deny him. "It's all right." She touched his cheek. "I love you, Angus MacKay."

A look of wonder crossed his face, then he frowned. "How can ye? I nearly attacked ye like a monster."

"But you didn't. Even in the worst throes of pain and hunger, you protected me. You're the most beautiful man I've ever known."

"Emma." He propped himself on an elbow. He skimmed a hand down her face and gazed into her eyes. "I love ye, too. So verra much." His arm shook, and he collapsed onto his back. "Bugger. I'm so weak."

Emma smiled. He might feel weak, but his declaration of love filled her with a sense of power and contentment. She sat up and gave him a seductive look. "I believe I have just what you need." She brushed her hair back to expose her neck.

His gaze drifted to her throat. "Ye smell verra good."

"I *am* good." She unbuttoned her shirt. "I'm everything you need." She peeled her shirt back to reveal her breasts.

His gaze shifted lower. "Oh, aye," he whispered.

She pulled off her shirt and dropped it. It fell on top of the stake. She glanced back at him. He was watching her, his eyes glowing red.

He moved suddenly, pushing her down on the mattress and leaning over her. She smiled at his amazing resurgence of energy. He might be weak, but he was definitely motivated.

He nuzzled her neck and whispered in her ear, "I want ye, Emma. I want to taste you. I want to be inside you."

"Yes." She smoothed her hands down his back and grabbed the bottom edge of his T-shirt. She tugged it up. "I want to feel your skin against mine."

He pulled his shirt over his head. "Just a minute." He sat beside her to remove his shoes and socks. Then finally, off came the kilt.

The room was dark, but his skin was pale enough to give Emma a good glimpse. Her heart stuttered. Beautiful man. Muscular, lean, and graceful.

He lay beside her and gathered her in his arms. She shivered at the feel of her bare breasts grazing his skin.

He licked her neck. *I love you, Emma.* He licked again. The artery beneath her skin began to throb.

"Angus." She kneaded her fingers against his bare back. His skin was smooth. She loved the way his muscles bunched. He tickled her neck with his tongue, and tingles radiated down her arms and torso.

I'm so hungry. His mind sounded desperate. With the mental connection, she could sense his struggle to retain control.

Take what you need. She turned her head to better expose her neck. *I trust you.*

His body shook. His cry was muffled against her shoulder. She flinched when she felt the scrape of a fang.

His tongue swirled around the sensitized area of her neck. The tingles shimmered down her body in an erotic wave. Her nipples hardened. Her womanly core ached with emptiness and begged to be filled.

Love me, Angus. She tangled her fingers into his long hair.

He cupped her breast and teased the nipple with his thumb. She felt a slight prick on her neck at the same time that he gave her nipple a little tug.

"Ah!" She jolted. Good heavens. His fangs were inside her. It felt strangely erotic, as if he were probing her between the legs. She felt moisture pooling below, and hot blood gathering at her neck. Each time he sucked on her, blood coursed through her like a long, delicious throb. She needed him inside her.

I need you. She dug her fingers into his back.

He smoothed a hand down to her curls, then cupped her. *Ye're so wet.* He inserted a finger inside her. *So hot.*

Her inner muscles squeezed his finger. *I need . . . I need . . .*

Stay with me. He inserted two fingers inside her and located her clitoris with his thumb. Each time he sucked on her neck, he pressed up with his fingers and down with his thumb. He kept feeding and stroking. She writhed with pleasure.

She cried out when the climax hit. It shot through her, then eased into a series of delicious pulses.

She felt both sated and drained. She wasn't sure how much blood he had taken. She didn't really care. She felt so damned good, just floating along in a sea of sweet aftershocks. She noticed somewhat hazily that he'd withdrawn from her neck. He was still leaning over her, but now his arms were strong and steady. His face was flushed.

He retracted his fangs, and a drop of blood fell from one and landed on her chest. He bent down to lick it, then ran his tongue over her nipples. Her body shuddered.

She sighed with contentment at the feel of his erection pressed against her hip. She glanced down to see it. It was engorged, pink with blood she'd given him. He eased between her legs. She jolted when he thrust deep into her. Wow. No hesitation. It was a powerful declaration of possession. And God help her, she loved it.

He filled her. *Emma.* He lowered his head to her breasts and drew a nipple into his mouth.

She was too weak to do anything impressive in return. She simply wrapped her arms and legs around him. Good heavens, her mind might be fuzzy and light-headed, but her body was still wonderfully sensitive. He gently rocked her till every nerve ending shuddered with pleasure.

Then, all of a sudden, it wasn't enough. For either of them. Her body screamed for more, and she dug her nails into his back. He responded, his eyes blazing red. His thrusts became strong and forceful.

You're mine, Emma, mine. He rose onto his knees and seized her by the hips. He ground against her. She cried out. He drove in hard, then tilted his head back and groaned. His climax merged with hers mentally, and they both throbbed in unison before collapsing onto the mattress.

Incredible. Emma smiled as her eyes flickered shut.

He smoothed her hair back from her brow. "I'm afraid I fed too much. I made ye weak."

"You made me happy." She drifted off to sleep.

Angus paced around their cell. He had to find a way out. Last night he'd been useless, overcome with hunger. But tonight he was strong, vibrant, and ready to take on the enemy.

He stopped next to Emma. She was still asleep and still pale. He adjusted her blanket and listened to her heartbeat. Steady, but weak. The devil take it. He'd taken too much blood. How could she fight in this condition?

And it would only get worse. He resumed his pacing. Tomorrow night, his hunger would return, and if he fed off Emma, she would become even weaker. Eventually he would kill her. No doubt that was exactly what Katya hoped would happen. She wanted the slayer dead, and she wanted to force him to be the executioner of the woman he loved. If he and Emma didn't escape soon, Katya's evil plan would come to pass.

He eyed the window. It was crisscrossed with silver chains, but if he managed to rip them off, could he teleport through such a small opening? Past experience warned him that the silver-covered walls would block him. The door would be a safer bet. If anyone opened it, he could teleport out, taking Emma with him. No doubt that was why no one ever came at night.

The last time he'd seen Katya and her Russian vampires had been the night he'd been paralyzed with nightshade. They knew better than to open the door if he was mobile. The mortal guards came inside during the day while he was incapacitated. And they probably reported to their masters that Emma was still alive.

The door was still his best bet. If he could cause enough ruckus, maybe someone would come to check on them. Once he teleported out, he wouldn't be able to go far. The sun had only set about an hour earlier, so the locations embedded in his psychic memory—Western Europe and North America—would still be in daylight and off limits. The best course of action was to teleport with Emma a short distance, then join his friends who were looking for them.

He grabbed Emma's underwear from the top of the screen, then knelt beside her. "Sweetheart, I need ye to get dressed. I have a plan."

She moaned and turned her head away. The sight of his fang marks on her neck made him wince.

"Come, I'll help you." He pulled the blanket off her legs and slipped her underwear over her feet.

Her eyes opened. "Yuck, they're still damp."

"I know, but we need to be ready."

"Ready for what?" She sat up, then touched her forehead and closed her eyes.

"Are ye all right?"

"Black dots." She rose onto her knees so he could slip the underwear over her hips. She grabbed his shoulders to steady herself.

He cursed himself silently. "I fed too much."

"I'll be all right." She put her bra on.

He found her pants and handed them to her. "My plan is to lure someone into opening the door, then teleport us out."

She stuffed her legs into the pants. "Sounds good to me. And as soon as you get out of this room, you can call your Vamp buddies." She shrugged on her shirt and buttoned it. "They should be close by now. The last time I talked to Austin, he was zeroing in on us."

"Great. We just need to lure them here—" He stopped when the bolt scraped. "Och, that was easy."

Emma grabbed the stake off the floor, stuffed it into the waistband of her pants, and covered it with her shirttail. She scrambled to her feet. She swayed, and Angus steadied her.

"As soon as the door opens, we leave." He led her around the screen.

The door cracked.

Movement by the window snagged his attention. Moonlight gleamed off the barrels of two hunting rifles. The mortal men were reclining on the ground, their rifles poking through the window, aimed at Emma and him.

"Silver bullets," Katya's voice announced through the cracked door. "Back away from the girl, Angus, or we'll shoot her."

He realized she had the mortals under such deep mind control, she could see what they saw through the window. There was no way to fool her. He released Emma and stepped back.

"Give me any trouble, Angus, and we're shooting you with so much nightshade, it'll be a week before you can move. Of course, by then you'll have starved to death." Katya opened the door just wide enough to slip inside. She had her blowpipe ready. Angus considered zipping toward her at vampire speed and breaking her foul neck, but she was as fast as him. She'd drug him for sure, and then how would he protect Emma?

Alek came in, followed by two more Russian vampires with revolvers.

"Burien and Miroslav have an endless supply of silver bullets," Katya boasted. "You will accompany them up the stairs."

Alek grabbed Emma and pressed a knife to her neck. "And if you teleport away, I'll slit her throat."

"I'll behave." Angus gave Emma what he hoped was a reassuring look. "So have ye decided to let us go?"

Katya snorted. "Casimir is coming to take you and your mortal whore. I'm sure he has lovely plans for the two of you."

Alek dragged Emma toward the door. When he had her halfway up the stone steps, Burien motioned for Angus to follow.

"Slowly," Katya reminded him. "Or I'll shoot you with nightshade."

Angus went up the stairs. The two mortals had hunting rifles aimed at Emma. Alek had released Emma, but stood on one side of her with his sword drawn. Galina was on the other side, also with a sword. That made a total of seven bad guys, Angus counted, including the two mortals. And they were all armed. Still, if he could get close enough to Emma, he could teleport her away. He sauntered across the grassy courtyard, hoping they wouldn't notice.

"Stop, or she dies," Katya warned him.

He halted. Emma looked far too pale in the moonlight. He'd left her too damned weak.

And if things weren't bad enough, three figures

shimmered in front of the stone manor house, then solidified. Angus's breath hitched. He hadn't seen Casimir since the Great Vampire War of 1710, but there was no mistaking that harsh face and those cruel eyes. The war might have left him weak and injured, but he appeared fully recovered. Or was he? His left arm seemed bent at an odd angle, and he was wearing one glove. His dark eyes scanned everyone, his face blank until he spotted Angus.

He lifted his chin and narrowed his eyes. "General MacKay."

Angus nodded once. His old enemy had two bodyguards. He recognized Jedrek Janow on Casimir's left, perhaps to protect Casimir's weak spot. That was how Casimir worked. He sacrificed others to keep himself alive. With a pang, Angus realized he might have done the same thing with Emma.

Katya stepped forward and bowed from the waist. "We are honored by your presence, my lord."

Casimir's cold gaze wandered to Katya. "You kept calling and pestering me until I agreed to come."

"I meant no disrespect." Katya bowed again. "I merely wished to give you these gifts as a token of my gratitude and allegiance."

"You were told to deliver the slayer to Jedrek, and yet you did not. Is that how you display your allegiance?"

Katya gripped her hands together. "I wanted to deliver her personally, so I could assure you of my loyalty. And I have a special gift for you—General MacKay. I also saved your servant Jedrek a trip to New York."

"Your kindness is overwhelming," Casimir muttered.

"Tell me, how did you display your allegiance to Ivan Petrovsky?"

Katya stiffened.

Angus knew she was in big trouble. If he could get these vampires busy killing each other, he might have a chance to get close to Emma and teleport her to safety. "Katya murdered Petrovsky," he yelled. "I saw it myself. She and Galina staked him through the heart when he was unarmed."

Katya shot him a venomous look, then turned to Casimir. "MacKay is a traitor to our kind. He was helping the mortal woman slay my men."

Casimir glanced at Emma with a dismissive look. "A mere cockroach, easily disposed." His gaze returned to Angus. "But to have the general who defeated my last army—I shall savor his death."

"Then remember that I am the one who delivered him to you," Katya insisted. "I *am* your faithful servant."

Angus tilted his head. Was that an owl hooting in the woods? It sounded like the signal Ian and Robby liked to employ. "Ye canna trust her, Casimir. She betrayed ye once. She'll do it again."

Katya turned to Alek. "Kill him!"

Casimir lifted a hand, and Alek froze. "Are you giving orders, Katya, without my permission?"

She winced. "Forgive me. MacKay's lies make me forget myself."

"Lies?" Casimir's dark eyes shifted to Angus. "As much as I detest his kind, I have to admit they are disgustingly honest."

A blur of motion caught Angus's eye. A dozen people were standing on the three-foot-high stone wall that encircled the courtyard. Relief swept through him as he recognized his friends and employees—Ian, Robby, Jack from Venice, Mikhail from Moscow, Austin and Darcy Erickson, Jean-Luc Echarpe from Paris with two from his coven, and Zoltan Czakvar, the coven master of Eastern Europe, with two from his coven. Austin and Darcy had revolvers. The ten Vamps drew their swords.

Jean-Luc swished his foil through the air. "Let us settle this now, Casimir."

Casimir paled. He glared at Katya. "You traitor! You led me into a trap."

"No!" Katya shouted.

Casimir zoomed toward her and grasped her by the throat. "I will remember this betrayal."

Jedrek dashed forward and whispered in Casimir's ear. Casimir released Katya and stepped back.

She fell to the ground. "I didn't betray you. I swear I didn't."

Angus's friends jumped from the stone wall and slowly advanced.

Casimir eased behind his bodyguards and glared at the Russian vampires. "You will die tonight. You deserve to die." He and his bodyguards shimmered.

"Nay!" Angus ran toward Casimir just as the evil vampire vanished. "Damn!" He'd wanted to kill Casimir tonight. A sword swiped close to Angus's ear, and he jumped back. Alek was trying to kill him. "A sword!"

Alek lunged, aiming his sword at Angus's heart.

Angus leaped to the side and caught the sword Ian tossed him. Ian whipped his dagger from his sock and ducked when Burien took a swing at him. Robby jumped in to engage Burien and protect Ian.

Angus parried with Alek, drove him back, then skewered him through the heart. He watched with satisfaction as Alek turned to dust. No longer would the bastard stick a knife to Emma's throat.

Angus swiveled, looking for Emma. Jean-Luc was fighting Miroslav. Jack was taking his time with Galina, no doubt uncomfortable with the thought of killing a woman. But where the hell was Emma? Burien cried out as Robby stabbed him through the heart. The two mortals dropped their rifles and ran for the woods. Zoltan and his men chased after them. Galina screamed. Jack must have gotten over his hesitation.

Angus froze when he spotted Emma. Katya was dragging her toward the barn. Emma struggled, but was too weak to escape. He zoomed toward them, but Katya saw him coming and vanished, taking Emma with her.

"Nay!" Angus halted where they'd disappeared. There was no telling where they'd teleported to. And Emma was too damned weak to fight. It was all his fault. Guilt slammed into him, doubling him over.

Robby lay a hand on his shoulder. "We'll find them."

Angus nodded, unable to speak.

"Spread out and search!" Robby yelled.

The Vamps blurred as they all zoomed around the property and into the woods, hunting for Emma. Minutes ticked by but felt like hours. Robby and Ian ran from the barn, declaring it clear. Seconds later, Jean-Luc and his two coven members emerged from the manor house, yelling that it was clear. The others had fanned out into the woods.

Angus jumped onto the stone wall and listened carefully. He turned north. Was that a scream? A woman's scream.

"This way!" He dashed into the woods. His companions spread out behind him.

"Emma!" Angus heard no response. God, he hoped he wasn't too late. If Katya kept teleporting, she could be far away.

He charged into a small clearing and skidded to a halt. His heart stuttered.

Ian stopped behind him. "She's still alive."

Barely. Angus knelt beside Emma. His heart twisted at the sight of her torn neck. Damn that Katya. She'd almost drained Emma dry.

A large amount of dust covered Emma. Her stake lay in her limp hand. She'd managed to use it while Katya was feeding. The slayer had killed one last vampire. Angus thanked God he had made her a stake. But he'd also made her weak.

"Oh, Emma." He pulled off his T-shirt and pressed it against her bleeding neck. His eyes welled with tears.

Tree branches and bushes rustled as more people rushed into the clearing.

"How is she?" Austin demanded.

Darcy gasped. "Oh my God. Are we too late?"

Robby squatted beside Angus. "I'm so sorry."

Angus gritted his teeth. "She's no' dead yet. We can give her a transfusion." He looked at Ian and Robby. "Doona ye have some bottles of blood in yer sporrans?"

Robby looked at him sadly. "We doona have the equipment for a transfusion."

"Then we'll teleport her," Angus said. "Roman can fix her."

Jean-Luc knelt on the other side of Emma. "It's still daylight in New York. There's only one way to save her, Angus, and you know what that is."

"Nay!" Angus blinked back tears. "I canna transform her. She couldna stomach being a vampire. They killed her parents."

"But she can be changed back," Darcy suggested. "I'm living proof of that."

Angus blinked. Of course! He'd been too panicked to realize there was another option. Did Emma still have the scrap of stained cloth? If not, he could leave her his T-shirt. It was soaked with her mortal blood.

"She's going fast," Jean-Luc warned him. "If she bleeds out, it will be too late to transform her."

Angus rubbed his brow. What choice did he have? And Roman could change her back. "This is all my fault. She's going to hate me."

"She'll understand." Ian touched his shoulder. "I always understood."

Angus looked up. "I trapped ye in the body of a fifteen-year-old for all eternity."

Ian smiled. "Ye saved my life."

Angus took a deep breath, then unwrapped the shirt from Emma's neck. He'd have to drain the last drop of blood from her. It had to be done by a vampire in order for her to slip into a vampire coma. Then he'd have to feed her his own blood. If she accepted it and drank, she'd become one of the Undead. If she rejected his blood, she would die.

"Can I borrow a *sgian dubh*?" He'd have to slice his arm to feed her.

Ian handed him a knife.

Angus glanced at all his friends. "Could ye leave us alone?"

Chapter 23

Emma remembered pain and darkness. Fear and terror. Katya's fangs ripping into her neck. A last cry for survival and the desperate use of her stake. More darkness. Murmuring voices. More fangs. How could Katya be back? Hadn't she killed that bitch? More darkness as Emma slipped deeper into a black pit.

Then a strange dream. Her mouth tasted of blood. She choked on the metallic bitterness.

"Swallow," a voice urged her. "Ye must swallow."

More blood drizzled into her mouth. She was drowning in blood. Katya was killing her. She turned her head and coughed.

"Emma," the voice pleaded. "Drink it, please."

Angus? She opened her mouth to speak, but the words wouldn't come. She couldn't even open her eyes.

More blood poured into her mouth. She swallowed, and a comforting warmth spread through her body. She swallowed again, and it tasted sweet. What a silly dream. This couldn't be blood. It tasted too good. She drank and drank.

"That's it, sweetheart. Ye're doing fine."

Angus was happy with her. Angus loved her. Emma smiled. Angus was with her, and Katya was gone. This time when the darkness descended, she wasn't afraid.

With a jolt, Emma woke up. Her heart pounded in her chest so loud, she could hear it. A moment of panic seized her. She must be having a heart attack. She felt so strange, and she didn't know where she was.

"She's awake, Darcy! Get a bottle ready."

Emma saw Austin standing by an open door. He had found her? Then she and Angus must have been rescued.

"I just popped it into the microwave," a woman's voice yelled from a distance.

Emma sat up. Black dots swirled around her head.

"Easy." Austin stepped toward her with a worried expression.

"I—I guess I'm still weak." Emma blinked and focused on Austin. He seemed sharper than usual. She could see the stubble on his chin and every individual strand of hair on his head. And his heart was beating so loud. How could she hear that? How could she hear her own heart? She pressed a hand to her chest and noticed she was wearing flannel pajamas. "How did I get these?"

"Those are Darcy's," Austin answered. "She tried to clean you up a bit."

Right. Katya had attacked her. Emma suspected her

old clothes were covered with blood. Her stomach rumbled. "I feel so hungry."

"I'm sure you are." Austin eyed her warily.

She looked around the room. It was a nice bedroom. Blue comforter. Full-sized bed. No windows. Only a night light in a wall socket. How could she see so well? Her stomach rumbled louder, then cramped. She pressed a hand to her belly. "Ouch!"

Austin strode toward the door. "Hurry, Darcy!"

Emma inhaled deeply and let it out slowly. "Where am I?"

"Zoltan Czakvar's house in Budapest."

"Who?" Another hunger pang rocked Emma. She grimaced. Austin's heart seemed to pound in her ears. She could hardly hear. Hardly think.

"Zoltan Czakvar. He's the coven master of Eastern Europe."

"I'm in a vampire's house?" Emma noticed the vein in Austin's neck. It was pulsing. And it smelled so good. Like food. "What's happening to me?" A hunger pain struck her hard. With a cry, she fell back on the bed and curled into a ball.

"Is she all right?" Darcy rushed into the room with a tray and set it down on the bedside table.

Darcy was so close, and she smelled so good, Emma fought an urge to grab her.

"I have your breakfast." Darcy offered her a glass. "Type O. A little bland, but you should start off with a simple diet."

Emma's eyes widened. The glass was filled with blood. "No!" A sudden jab of pain pierced her mouth. She cried out.

Darcy set the glass down. "You poor thing. The same thing happened to me. They always come out the first night."

Emma covered her mouth and whimpered. Her gums were ripping in two. With a scream, she felt them rip. She lowered her hand and saw blood splattered on her palm. It was horrible! And it smelled delicious. The pain in her mouth subsided as another hunger pang struck her.

Darcy plopped a straw into the glass and handed it to Emma. "Here. It's hard to use a glass when the fangs are out."

Fangs? Emma touched her mouth. Her canine teeth were long, pointed, and sharp. "No!" She shook her head. This was another bad dream. It couldn't be true.

"I know it's upsetting." Darcy perched on the bed beside her and pressed the glass into her hand. "You'll feel better once you eat."

Emma's hand shook as she took the glass. She had a terrible desire to throw it away and sink her teeth into Darcy. Oh God, it was true. She was a vampire.

She stared at the glass, stunned. The blood actually smelled good. Was this the sort of agony Angus had endured all night when he'd refused to bite her? She closed her mouth around the straw and sucked. The blood was sweet and warm. It flowed into her, filling her with an energizing sense of strength and power. Too soon, she reached the bottom of the glass.

"I need more." Her gums tingled, and she realized her fangs were retracting.

"I'll be right back." Darcy stood, taking the glass. "It's normal to be very hungry the first night."

"You were a vampire," Emma whispered.

"Yes, for four years. But you needn't stay this way for long. Roman can change you back. You'll be all right."

Emma nodded. She watched Darcy leave the room. Austin smiled at his wife as she passed by. A gentle, loving smile. And Emma knew exactly what she needed. "Where is Angus?"

Austin's smile faded. "He's, uh, not here right now."

Emma looked around the room. She still felt strange. Sort of numb. Maybe this was all a dream. She'd had a lot of them lately. Or were they memories? She'd made love with Angus. Katya had dragged her away and attacked her. Good heavens, Katya had killed her.

She lifted a hand to her neck. The skin was smooth and unbroken.

Austin walked toward her. "You healed during your death-sleep. One of the advantages of being undead." He smiled. "You look great, but you'll have to take my word for it. You can't see yourself in a mirror. One of the disadvantages of being undead."

"There are no disadvantages." Giacomo strolled into the room, sipping blood from a wineglass. "*Buona sera, signorina.* I came to see how you are faring." His brown eyes twinkled. "And to welcome you to the club."

The full extent of her circumstances sank in. She was dead. She pulled the blue comforter up to her chin. Where was Angus? She wanted to see him. She wanted his strong arms around her. She felt her neck where he'd fed from her while making love. The puncture wounds were gone. As if it had never happened.

Robby sauntered into the room. "How are ye, Miss Wallace?"

I'm dead. Emma wrapped her arms around herself underneath the comforter.

"I think she's in shock," Austin whispered, but Emma could hear it.

She could hear everything, even the whir of a microwave across the house. "I want to talk to Angus."

Robby exchanged a worried look with Giacomo. "He's no' here. He went to Paris with Jean-Luc and Ian."

"Then call Paris and ask him to teleport here. Please." Emma shuddered under the blanket. She hated being this needy. She'd always been strong and decisive before. But then, she'd never had to handle being *dead* before.

"He was going on to New York," Robby continued. "He willna be awake now."

New York? She was going through a crisis, and he was in New York? She gritted her teeth. He needed to be with her. She was dead, dammit. He needed to show respect for the dead. And for the woman he loved. "I need to talk to him."

"I'll send an e-mail," Robby offered. "He'll see it when he wakes."

"I bet you'll see him soon," Austin added. "As soon as you're strong enough, you can go to New York and have Roman change you back."

"Aye." Robby nodded. "Angus left me his T-shirt coated with yer blood."

"Your ticket back to mortality." Giacomo sipped from his wineglass. "Although I cannot imagine why anyone would want to be mortal again."

"Then you have a lousy imagination, Jack." Darcy

strode into the room, holding a glass filled with blood. "Here you go." She handed it to Emma.

How could blood taste so good? Emma could drink easily now that her teeth were normal. It was like drinking raw power.

Another man entered the room. He was shorter than Angus, of medium height with dark brown hair and almond-shaped, amber eyes. "How are you, my dear?" He had a slight accent.

"Okay." How come her bedroom was Grand Central Station? Everybody wanted to come and gawk at the brand-new vampire. "I'm not performing any tricks today."

The man chuckled. "I'm glad you're all right. We were worried about you."

Obviously Angus wasn't too worried. He'd gone off to New York and left her alone to adjust to her new undeadness.

"I am Zoltan Czakvar." The man bowed slightly. "You are welcome here as long as you like."

"Thank you." Emma's gaze wandered over Zoltan, Robby, and Giacomo. "You're nice guys. It makes it easier to be . . . like this when I know how nice some of you are."

Darcy perched on the foot of the bed. "You don't have to stay like this, Emma. You can be mortal again."

But Angus was a vampire. If she stayed a vampire, she could be like him. She could zip around at incredible speed, levitate, and teleport. She'd be stronger than ever. She'd been a good slayer as a mortal, but as a vampire, she'd be a super slayer.

But if she stayed undead, it could be centuries before she saw her parents, or her brother, or Aunt Effie. That was bad.

But then again, that was centuries that she could love Angus. And he could love her. Her reservations about their relationship would be gone, now that they were the same.

"I need to talk to Angus," she repeated. Why couldn't these people understand? Why didn't Angus understand? Why did her leave her? She noticed the worried looks everyone was exchanging. Something was going on.

A sudden thought occurred to her. "Oh no! Was he injured?" She scrambled to her feet. Black dots circled her head.

Darcy reached out to her. "You should stay in bed tonight. It takes time for your body to adjust."

"No! I want the truth. Was Angus injured? Is that why he rushed off to see Roman?"

Robby shifted his weight. "He's fine. I'll send him that e-mail now." He rushed from the room.

"I'll show you the computer." Zoltan hurried after him.

Giacomo shook his head. "He should have stayed. I told him that, but . . ."

"But what?" Emma asked. "Why did he leave?"

Giacomo looked at her sadly. "He feels guilty."

"He left you a note." Darcy pulled a piece of paper from her pants pocket and set it on the bed.

A note? Emma frowned at it. After all they'd been through, he'd left a note? She gave Giacomo a confused look. "Why would Angus feel guilty?" It suddenly dawned on her. "Oh, he feels bad about Katya attacking me? But we were all under attack. I understand he had to protect himself."

Giacomo sighed. "He feels bad about making you weak."

"It's not his fault Katya killed me."

Giacomo winced. "You actually killed Katya."

Emma stared at him. She must have been alive to kill Katya. Then how did she end up a vampire?

"I should go now." Giacomo hurried out the door.

"He had no choice, Emma." Austin left the room, too.

He? There was something terrible the men didn't want to say. She turned to Darcy. "Katya didn't do this to me?"

"No." Darcy's eyes were full of sympathy. "You would have died if he hadn't done it. He really had no choice."

He? God, no. Emma's knees collapsed, and she sat on the bed. Her eyes welled with tears. That was why he'd run away, plagued with guilt.

"I'm so sorry." Darcy touched Emma on the shoulder. "He insisted on doing it himself. He felt . . . responsible. And he knew you could be changed back."

A tear rolled down Emma's face. She caught it on her finger and saw the pinkish tint. Bloody tears, just like a vampire.

Darcy patted her on the back. "He gave you a second chance at life."

Emma swallowed hard. She'd become the kind of creature that had murdered her parents. To be transformed into a vampire, she'd had to die first. Her stomach cramped. "Angus killed me."

Her stomach heaved, and Emma lost her first meal as a vampire.

"*En garde*." Giacomo saluted Emma with his foil, then pointed it at her.

She attacked with a flourish of thrusts and lunges. Giacomo defended himself easily enough, but Emma knew she was making progress. Three days ago, during her first fencing lesson, he could have defeated her blindfolded. Now he was fully engaged.

"Remember, the Malcontents do not fight fairly." With a flick of his wrist, Giacomo sent her foil flying through the air. It landed with a clatter across the exercise room.

"How will you handle this?" He charged at her, his sword pointed straight at her heart.

She pushed off the ground as hard as she could, thinking *levitate*. She soared up so fast, she clonked her head on the ceiling. "Ouch." She hovered, rubbing the crown of her head.

Giacomo grinned up at her. "You're a natural."

Austin stood by the door, chuckling. "I think she's underestimating her strength."

She glared at him. "I pinned you yesterday in forty-five seconds."

He shrugged. "Yeah, but you could whip me when you were a mortal, too."

Giacomo laughed. "*La signorina* is a fierce one."

"And don't you forget it." Emma whipped the dagger from her belt, teleported behind Giacomo, and poked him in the rear.

"Ouch!" He jumped forward, spinning to face her.

She smiled sweetly. "How am I doing, teacher?"

He narrowed his eyes. "Do I detect some latent anger, *bellissima*?"

Emma sighed as she stuffed her dagger back under her belt. Maybe she was angry. She was certainly frustrated. She'd been at Zoltan's house for one week, and Angus hadn't returned any of her e-mails or phone messages. She'd read his note so many times, she had it memorized.

Dearest Emma,

I do not expect forgiveness for the terrible thing I've done to you. I only hope you can be changed back as soon as possible, so you can reclaim your life. You deserve a happy life, filled with light and peace.

Peace? Did he really think she wanted peace when bad vampires like Casimir roamed the earth? She was a warrior like him. And now she was a vampire like him. Sure it had sickened her at first to think of him draining her dry and transforming her, but after a few nights of serious contemplation, she'd decided she was glad he was the one to induct her into this new life. She was undead because someone she loved had performed an act of mercy. That was so much better than dying the victim of an enemy's act of violence. And it was fitting that Angus had been the one. He'd been the one all along.

He'd taught her the difference between wreaking revenge and seeking justice. She no longer wanted to kill every vampire in her path to relieve the pain of her parents' murder. She wanted to put that pain behind her and move on. She wanted to use her new power to protect the innocent, so others wouldn't suffer as her parents had.

Angus had taught her that love was so powerful, it survived death. She still loved him with all her heart. And she understood now that death couldn't disfigure or corrupt a person's soul. She was surrounded by loving, honorable Vamps.

So why was Angus ignoring her? Was he averse to a commitment that might last for centuries?

Darcy joined her husband at the doorway. "We just received an e-mail—"

"From Angus?" Emma interrupted.

Darcy gave her a sympathetic look. "From Roman. He reports that baby Constantine is healthy, happy, and normal."

"That's good," Austin murmured.

Darcy offered Emma a sheet of paper. "Some of his message was for you, so I printed it out."

Emma took the note and wandered across the large exercise room to read it.

Dear Miss Wallace,

I couldn't help but notice the e-mails and phone messages directed here for Angus. I thought you should know that he left here two nights ago for England. He's expecting you to come to New York to be changed back, and I don't believe he wants

*to be here for the event. This is not because he
doesn't care. He cares very much. He's suffering
greatly for what he did to you. Perhaps, in time,
he'll be able to forgive himself. I think he'll begin
healing once he knows you have safely returned
to your mortal life. I am at your disposal, as soon
as you are ready.*

Sincerely,
Roman Draganesti

Emma folded the note. "Why does everyone want
me to be mortal again?"

Darcy gaped. "You'd rather be undead?"

"Of course she does," Giacomo said. "It's a superior
life."

Darcy snorted. "I didn't care for the diet."

"The blood tastes good to me." Emma crossed her
arms, frowning. "Why shouldn't I remain this way?
The man I love is a vampire." She grimaced. "Unfortunately, he won't speak to me."

"*Amore.*" Giacomo pressed a hand against his heart.
"How we suffer for it."

Darcy snorted. "Especially you, Jack, since you're
so in love with yourself."

He stumbled back as if he'd been wounded.

"I'm not taking it anymore." Emma turned to Giacomo. "Will you help me teleport to England? Tonight?"

"Anything for *amore.*" Giacomo grinned. "There are
two places he could be—either his office in Edinburgh
or in London."

"You'd better go to London," Darcy warned.

"Of course." Giacomo's dark eyes twinkled. "Edinburgh would be . . . awkward."

"Why?" Emma stepped toward him.

Giacomo shrugged. "That is where Angus has stashed his harem, and I doubt—"

"His *what*?" Emma shrieked.

Giacomo winced. "Oops."

Darcy groaned. "Way to go, Jack. Emma, it's not as bad as it looks."

"You think not? The bloody man has a *harem*!" Emma's heart thundered loud in her ears. Was this why he was refusing to see her? Why would he want one vampire girlfriend when he already had a freaking harem?

She crumpled the note in her fist and tossed it across the room. "Take me to London now, Giacomo. Angus is going to talk to me whether he likes it or not."

Chapter 24

Angus wandered quietly into the nursery at Roma-
tech. Shanna had wanted a nursery next to her dental
office, so she could tend the baby and the occasional
patient, and Roman had readily agreed, for he liked having his family close by. She was busy changing the baby's diaper, and the mirror over the table reflected both
her and the bairn. Of course Angus didn't show up, so he
cleared his throat to let Shanna know he was there.

She turned her head. "Angus!" Her smile started off
joyful, but quickly faded to a look of concern.

He was used to that now. People looked at him like
he was some sort of ghost. He felt like one, a shadow
without a soul.

Shanna's gaze shifted back to the baby. "I didn't
know you were in town."

"I just arrived."

She snapped the baby's outfit around his chubby
legs. "Are you staying at the townhouse?"

"Aye." He could see her frowning in the mirror.

"That's good. Stay as long as you like. You . . . probably shouldn't be alone right now."

Did she think he was suicidal? Why kill something that was already dead? His body still functioned, but his heart had shriveled from constant aching, and his mind was worthless. He'd tried to get some work done at his London office, but he couldn't concentrate. It was so bad, he was considering passing the business on to Robby. Every time Angus tried to look at a report, it blurred before his eyes. All he ever saw was a mental picture of Emma releasing her last breath of life. The image haunted him. It was the last thing he saw before slipping into death-sleep, and it greeted him each time he awakened.

He choked on his meals and could barely swallow. It always tasted like the last drop of blood he'd taken from Emma. He roamed from one place to another—Paris, London, New York—but there was no escape from what he'd done.

He handed Shanna a package wrapped in brown paper. "I brought this for the bairn."

"Oh, how sweet!" Shanna showed the package to Constantine. "Look! Uncle Angus brought you a present!"

The baby waved his arms and legs.

Shanna ripped off the paper, opened the box, and dug through the tissue. Her eyes widened as she pulled out a small pouch of black moleskin. "Oh, it's . . . lovely. Thank you."

"Ye're welcome."

Her blue eyes twinkled as she gave him a devious look. "So, you gave him a . . . purse?"

Even that didn't get a rise out of him. " 'Tis a sporran for a young lad."

"Ah." Shanna opened it and removed the tissue paper from inside. "This will actually come in very handy. He can use it to carry around little toys or . . . a small chemistry set." She made a face. "Roman's already bought him one."

"I would suggest duct tape."

Shanna laughed and gave him a hug. "Thank you. It was a very thoughtful gift."

He nodded. Now that he'd delivered the present, he didn't know what to do with himself.

Shanna picked up Constantine and swayed gently from side to side. "Does Roman know you're here?"

He shrugged. "I doona think so."

"I'll get him. And don't make fun of his hair."

"What?" Angus stiffened when she shoved the baby into his arms.

"Watch the baby till I get back." She rushed from the room.

"But—wait!" Angus experienced a moment of sheer panic. What was she thinking, handing him a wee baby? He hadn't held one in five hundred years. His heart raced, pounding in his ears. What if he dropped the wee thing?

He squeezed it against his chest and felt the wee legs kicking him. Bugger, he was probably crushing the poor babe. He relaxed his grip and swiveled, looking frantically for a safe place to put the wee beastie down. The changing table? Nay, he might roll off there.

Angus spotted the crib and walked toward it. He passed by walls painted like a pastoral scene—blue sky, green fields, fat cows, and fluffy sheep. "Are they expecting ye to be a farmer?"

The baby thumped him in the chest with a closed fist.

"Och, a warrior then?" Angus glanced down at the baby and halted mid-stride.

Constantine was studying Angus with the brightest blue eyes Angus had ever seen. More than that, there was an intensity to the baby's eyes that seemed to hold Angus captive. Instantly Angus's heart calmed to a steady beat. The pain that had muddled his brain for the past eight days slowly melted away. He took a deep breath as a sensation of peace flowed through him.

The baby gurgled.

"Did ye do that?" Angus whispered.

The baby stared back, and Angus sensed an intelligence that was far from infantile.

"Angus!" Roman called as he entered the nursery.

"Roman, yer bairn—" Angus looked up and forgot all about the baby. "What happened to you?"

Roman shrugged. "I didn't even know about it till Shanna noticed it." He ran a hand through his dark hair, now shaded silver at the temples. "Fortunately, she likes it."

"Yes, I do." Shanna followed him into the nursery with Connor. She smiled at Roman. "He looks very distinguished."

He smiled back and wrapped an arm around her shoulders.

"How did it happen?" Angus asked.

"Remember the drug I invented that enables us to stay awake during the day? Well, after a few days of trying to take care of Constantine 24/7, Shanna looked really exhausted."

"And being the noble guy that he is," Shanna added, "Roman took the drug every day for five days to help me out."

"And it turned yer hair gray?" Angus asked.

"Silver," Shanna corrected him. "And only at the temples. I think it's gorgeous."

Roman snorted. "But you forbid me to take the drug again."

"Because it's aging you." Shanna turned to Angus. "Laszlo did some blood work on him and discovered that he aged a year for every day he stayed awake."

"Bugger," Angus grumbled.

"It *is* bad," Connor added. "I had hoped we could use the drug in the war against Casimir, but we're no' likely to get Vamps to volunteer for it if they know it's going to make them older for the rest of eternity."

That was bad news. Angus looked at Roman. "So ye're five years older now?"

"Six, actually. I used it once before to rescue Laszlo. But I doubt we'll ever get anyone else to use the drug."

An idea sprung to Angus's mind. He glanced down at the baby in his arms. His mind seemed to be working clearly again. "I think I know someone who wouldna mind aging about ten years."

"Not the baby," Shanna muttered.

"Nay." Angus looked up. "Ian MacPhie."

"Oh, aye," Connor whispered. "Ian would take it."

"Good." Roman nodded. "You're looking a little better, Angus."

Only because of the bairn. "Yer baby is . . . special."

"Of course he is." Shanna took Constantine from him. "How did you two get along?"

"Verra well." Angus followed her to the crib. "He has . . . bonny eyes."

"Yes." Shanna smiled as she placed Constantine in the crib.

"What is this?" Angus touched the unusual mobile hanging over the baby's head. "Bats?"

Roman chuckled. "A gift from Gregori. His idea of a joke."

"Aye." Connor wound up the contraption. "It plays the theme song from the *X-Files*."

The tinkling music started, and the blue plastic bats flew around in a circle. Constantine's eyes widened, and he flailed his arms and legs.

"I heard you gave the baby a sporran," Roman said. "Thank you."

Connor chuckled. "Just doona give him any Scotch whisky till he's—oh, about eight."

"Eight?" Shanna gaped in horror.

Connor grinned. "He'll need a claymore by the age of ten."

Shanna shook her head. "Men. Always planning ahead for a violent world."

Roman frowned. "As long as evil abounds, we have no choice." He put a hand on Angus's shoulder. "How are you, old friend? Are you ready to talk?"

Angus wandered back to the crib and stared at the mobile. The bats were circling now at a slower pace. "There's nothing to say."

Shanna huffed. "Emma obviously disagrees. She's been trying to contact you for a week."

Angus closed his eyes briefly. He knew he was being a coward.

"I e-mailed her," Roman said. "I told her to come and be changed back whenever she was up to it."

"Did she say when she was coming?" Angus asked. The bats were slowing to a stop.

"She didn't answer," Roman said. He joined Angus at the crib. "She may want to discuss the matter with you first."

Angus gripped the crib railing. "She wants to rant at me for killing her. I know she hates me."

"Are you sure about that?" Shanna asked softly.

"Of course she hates me!" Angus paced across the nursery. "I turned her into the verra creature she hates the most."

"Then why hasn't she come here to get changed back?" Shanna asked.

"I think you should see her," Roman said. "What if she wants to forgive you?"

Angus snorted. "How could she?" He couldn't forgive himself.

"All things are possible through love," Roman whispered.

Angus closed his eyes as he felt tears gathering. He swayed and placed a palm on the wall to steady himself. He couldn't go on like this, overwhelmed with such guilt and failure. He'd sworn to protect her, but he had killed her.

A knock sounded on the door. "I'm looking for Angus MacKay," a strange voice announced.

Angus turned to see a young man in a suit, hovering by the door. "I am the MacKay."

The young man entered the nursery, smiling. "You're a hard man to find, Mr. MacKay." He handed Angus an envelope. "You've been served." He strolled from the room.

Angus ripped open the envelope and scanned the papers. "The devil take it." The papers slipped from his hands and fluttered to the floor.

"What is it?" Roman asked.

Angus leaned against the wall, stunned.

"I have to return to London. Emma is suing me for pain and damages."

"I have good news and bad news," Richard Beckworth announced when Angus strode into the solicitor's London office.

"Is she here?" Angus's heart thundered in his chest. A part of him dreaded seeing Emma again. He recalled her beautiful face that had once gazed upon him with so much love. Now he imagined it full of hatred and recrimination. How much more pain could his heart endure?

But another part of him longed to see her. She had every right to be angry. He'd transformed her against her will. If she needed money so she could take time off to recover from the trauma he'd caused, he could understand that. In fact, he'd give her enough to make sure she never wanted for anything. He just wanted her to return to a normal, happy, mortal life.

"Miss Wallace and her solicitor are in the conference room." Beckworth relaxed in the chair behind his desk. "First, I wanted to catch you up to speed, old chap. The good news is they want to settle out of court."

"Of course they do." Angus sat in a wingback chair facing Beckworth. Richard had been his solicitor for the past hundred and seventy-five years. "She can hardly walk into a mortal courtroom and claim that I killed her. Even though I did."

Beckworth winced. "Don't admit to any wrongdoing in their presence. It was also a brilliant move on your part to get rid of your harem last week."

"What was brilliant about it? It cost me a bloody fortune." Angus had inherited five Vamp women when he became the British coven master in 1950. He'd ignored them for years. They were stashed away in his castle in Scotland, and Beckworth handled their monthly allowance.

After this ordeal with Emma, Angus had wanted to return to his castle, but he didn't want the harem there. Beckworth had drawn up the necessary papers to set them free. Unfortunately, the price of their freedom had been high. Angus had agreed to buy them a townhouse in London and pay support for ten years.

Beckworth shook his head. "Imagine how upset Miss Wallace would be if your harem was still intact."

Angus swallowed hard. "Does she know about them?"

Beckworth snorted. "Of course. Her solicitor was eager to add the harem to her list of grievances, accusing you of polygamy."

"Bloody hell. I was never married to them."

Beckworth shrugged. "Common-law marriage. The point is moot, though, since you've already legally separated from them. Her solicitor will make a stink of it, but don't worry, their case is weak."

"Richard, I doona mind paying damages. How much has she asked for?"

Beckworth winced. "That's the bad news, old chap. She doesn't want money. She—she's asking for controlling interest in MacKay Security and Investigation."

"*What?*" Angus leaped to his feet. "She wants my business?"

"Not entirely. Just fifty-one percent."

"She canna have it!" Angus paced across the office. "Why would she ask such a thing?" The answer dawned on him immediately. That clever vixen. She knew exactly how to inflict the sharpest wound. His business was the closest thing to his heart, other than her.

"The obvious reason is revenge, but there could be more to this request." Beckworth steepled his fingertips as he considered. "Perhaps she feels insecure about making a living for the rest of eternity. This move would certainly give her long-term job security."

Angus snorted. "I would have gladly given her a job. And a damned good salary."

Beckworth frowned. "If this goes through, she'll be giving *you* a job."

Angus scowled at the carpet as he paced. "I'll offer thirty percent." That might be a good idea, actually. If he could keep her working alongside him, perhaps her anger would dissipate in time, and she would learn to love him again. "She can have up to forty-nine percent, but no more."

Beckworth's eyes widened. "Are you serious? Your company's worth a fortune."

Angus shrugged. His mission of protecting the innocent and tracking down murderous vampires had always been more important than the money. He had very few needs, other than bottled blood and a safe place to sleep. "I need to take care of her."

"You're in love with her, aren't you?"

Angus slowed to a stop. "Aye, I am."

There was a hint of a smile before Beckworth schooled his features. "Go on to the conference room. I'll be there as soon as I get some papers together."

Angus took a deep breath. It was time to see Emma.

Emma fidgeted in her chair. What was taking so long? Her stomach was in knots and her heart was pounding. What if Angus was furious? What if he thought she was attacking him? Shame on him for driving her to such drastic measures. She jumped at the sound of footsteps outside the door. Angus was coming. She stood.

The door opened. Her breath hitched when he entered. His face was slanted downward, so she couldn't see his expression. He turned to shut the door.

He was wearing the familiar blue and green plaid kilt. Her heart ached with longing. He turned to face her. His green eyes widened.

Oh God, he looked pale and thin. Wasn't he eating right?

He gazed around the room. "Where's yer solicitor?"

"I asked him to leave for a moment." For the whole night, actually.

Angus stepped toward her. "Ye're looking well."

"Thank you." He didn't seem very angry. "I thought we should talk."

He frowned. "I doona think that is wise without our solicitors present."

"I really don't want to involve them."

Angus snorted. "Then ye shouldna have sued me. Do ye hate me so much?"

She folded her arms across her chest. "Why didn't you tell me about your harem? You told me all kinds of stories about your past, but you conveniently left them out."

"There was nothing to tell. I inherited them like ye would an automobile."

"And you never took them for a test drive?"

"Nay, I did no'."

Emma's mouth fell open. "You didn't? Not even . . . around the block?"

"Nay." He glowered at her. "I wasna interested in them. I wanted the job of British coven master. 'Tis an honor, and I was proud to be the first Scotsman to hold the position."

"Oh. Congratulations."

He grunted a response.

"And they never tried to seduce you? Are those women crazy?"

"Enough with the harem," he growled. "They're gone."

"I know, but surely they were . . . attracted to you."

He arched a brow. "Ye think I'm a fine catch?"

"Of course."

His mouth twitched. "They thought I was a barbarian."

"What silly women." Emma stepped toward him.

"Aye." He gave her a wary look. "I suppose ye want to rant at me now."

"A little. I suffered through the most traumatic event

of my life, and you didn't stay with me. You left me in a stranger's house, and you wouldn't answer any of my calls."

He grimaced. "I know ye hate me. I know what I did was unforgivable." He squared his shoulders. "So I'm willing to give ye forty-nine percent of MacKay Security and Investigation."

Her mouth fell open. "Forty-nine percent?"

He gritted his teeth. "I know ye want fifty-one, but that's no' reasonable. That's revenge."

"I don't want revenge. I don't want you to suffer at all."

He gave her an incredulous look. "Then why are ye doing this?"

Idiot! She wanted to strangle him. "Did you give me any choice, Angus? I tried and tried to talk to you, but this was the only way I could get your attention!"

"Fine, ye have my undivided attention. Feel free to rail at me for destroying yer life and causing ye so much pain and misery."

"The only pain you caused me was your neglect."

He snorted. "I overfed on you and left ye too weak to defend yerself. And then, when ye were injured and dying because of me, I killed you."

Her breath hitched. Now she understood. He'd left not because he was rejecting her, but because he was overwhelmed with guilt and shame. And that could only mean that he still loved her. There was still hope.

She took a deep breath. All the things she had planned to say flew from her mind. "I . . . missed you."

"I missed ye, too." He watched her warily. "Why did ye no' go to Roman to be changed back?"

She wandered down the table to the window. "I decided I liked being . . . undead. I can kick major ass now." *And I could be with you.*

"Ye would give up being mortal to become a creature ye hate?"

"I don't hate all vampires." She gazed out the window at the lights of the city. "And all the people I love are already dead." *Including you.*

"Then why are ye suing me?"

She turned to face him. "I never wanted to sue you. This was all just a ploy to force you to talk to me."

His mouth dropped open. "Then . . . ye want nothing from me?"

She walked down the length of the table, skimming her hand along the tops of the chairs. "Actually, I do want a few things."

"I'll give ye whatever I can."

"I want the harem completely out of your life."

He shrugged. "They were never in it. Ye shouldna let them concern you."

"Well, they do." She reached the end of the table. "You see, I want you legally free in case you decide to marry." She slanted him a nervous glance. "That was what you call a strong hint."

His mouth dropped open.

She winced. "Okay. Not a very well-received hint."

"I—I thought ye hated me."

"No, Angus. I want you. I love you. Even when I was throwing up, I loved you." She winced inwardly. That was not the romantic confession she had practiced the night before. Fortunately, he appeared too dumbfounded to notice.

She stepped toward him. "I'm glad you're the one who changed me. Do you know why?"

He shook his head.

Her eyes welled with tears. "Because you had already changed me on the inside. You taught me the true meaning of love. Love doesn't please itself by seeking revenge. Love sacrifices itself for the good of others." A tear rolled down her cheek as she drew closer. "That's what you did, Angus. You gave up all hope for peace and happiness in order to save me."

His eyes glimmered with moisture. "I love you, Emma. I feared ye could never forgive me."

"Forgive what?" Another tear slipped down her cheek. "You did me no wrong."

"I fed from you to save myself. And it left ye too weak to defend yerself."

"I gave myself willingly. I couldn't bear the thought of living without you."

"Oh, Emma." He wiped a tear from her face and looked at the pink stain on his finger. "Look what I've done to you."

"I know." She grabbed his hand and kissed it. "Look at me. I'm stronger and wiser because of you. I used to live for revenge and hate, but now I want to live for love."

His breath caught as a tear tumbled down his face. "I should have listened to Roman. He was right."

"What did he say?"

Angus cradled her face in his hands. "He said all things are possible with love." He kissed her brow. "I'm still having trouble forgiving myself."

"Don't worry." She skimmed her hand down his kilt. "I think I can help you feel much better."

He smiled. "In that case . . ." He lowered himself onto one knee. "I should ask ye to marry me."

She fell to her knees in front of him. "Yes, you should."

"Then ye agree?"

"Yes." She wrapped her arms around his neck. "And we have to live happily ever after. That's part of the contract."

His smile widened. "I just happen to have a solicitor nearby. We could have it put into writing."

"Your word is good enough for me." Emma glanced to the side. "Right now, I can think of a better use for that conference table."

Angus's eyebrows rose. "Och, ye're a clever lass." He scrambled to his feet. "I'll lock the door."

Emma wandered to the window and smiled at the city lights and starry sky. The night was her life now. And she had an eternity of nights to spend with the man she loved. She closed the blinds as she felt his arms circle her waist.

He nuzzled her neck. "I love ye, Emma Wallace."

She leaned back against his sturdy chest. "Forever and a night."

Epilogue

Three months later . . .

"Thank you for coming." Shanna gave Emma a hug.

"No problem." Emma smiled. "You know we would do anything for our godson." She and Angus had been thrilled when they were asked to be godparents. It was the closest they could ever come to being real parents.

Angus stood by the crib in the nursery at Romatech, studying the sleeping child. "He's verra special."

"Of course he is." Shanna's glowing smile faded a bit. "I just hope my dad agrees."

"I'm sure he will." Emma tried to be encouraging, but she had her doubts. Sean Whelan was supposed to arrive any minute now to meet his grandson for the first time.

Shanna had made the arrangements a week ago and was so nervous that Emma had agreed to come for moral support. She knew how volatile Sean could be.

He'd cursed and ranted when she'd turned in her resignation. He'd demanded to know why. She'd told him that she was homesick and moving back to Scotland. As furious as he was, she hadn't dared tell him she was marrying the coven master of British vampires. Or that she had become a vampire herself.

"He's awake." Angus grinned as he playfully tugged on the baby's toes.

Constantine gurgled with laughter.

"He adores you, Angus." Shanna approached the crib.

"Aye." Angus picked up the chubby baby. "How are ye, lad?"

Emma's heart filled, watching Angus hold the baby.

The door swung open, and Connor escorted Shanna's father into the room.

Sean quickly scanned the nursery.

"Thank you for coming," Shanna said quietly.

Sean glanced at her, frowning. "I'm glad to see you're still alive. Have they been hurting you?"

Her jaw tensed. "I'm perfectly fine. And very happy."

He frowned at his grandson. "You let bloodsuckers handle your baby?"

Angus snorted. "I am Constantine's godfather."

Sean looked at Emma. "What are you doing here? I thought you were in a hurry to get back to Scotland."

"I'm visiting." She folded her arms across her chest. "I like to visit Constantine often. He's an adorable child."

As if on cue, Constantine squealed happily. He kicked and wiggled.

Angus chuckled. "He's a lively one."

"Is he?" Sean looked askance at the baby. "Is he . . . alive?"

Shanna scoffed. "I have gone whole weeks without sleep. I could actually do with a little less liveliness from him."

"He's a happy lad." Angus swung the baby around in a circle. Constantine chortled.

Sean shifted his weight. "Is he . . . normal?"

Emma was ready to kick his teeth in. "Of course he's normal."

"Which is amazing, considering *my* gene pool," Shanna muttered.

Connor chuckled.

Sean glared at him.

Angus walked toward them. "Do ye no' want to hold yer grandson?"

Sean looked worried as Angus came closer. "What does he eat?"

Connor arched a brow. "He takes three pints a night. Be careful, or he'll go for yer neck."

Sean jumped back.

Connor laughed.

Shanna gave him an annoyed look. "Behave yourself." She switched her glare to her father. "Constantine is a normal baby. He can't bite you. He has no teeth."

The door to the hallway opened and a woman peeked inside. "I'm so sorry to interrupt."

Emma recognized her as Radinka, Gregori's mortal mother, who was now managing Shanna's dental office.

"Shanna, dear," Radkina continued, "we have a bit of an emergency. Laszlo has chipped a tooth."

"Oh my. I hope it isn't a fang." Shanna strode toward the door. She glanced back at her friends. "I'll be back as soon as possible."

"Doona worry," Connor reassured her. When the door clicked shut, he continued, "We willna let this fool hurt his grandson."

"What?" Sean walked toward Connor. "You think I would hurt him?"

"I think ye would if he suddenly grew some fangs," Connor replied.

Angus set Constantine down in the crib, then joined the other men by the door. "Connor has a point. Ye shouldna be asking if yer grandson is normal. Ye should be ready to love him no matter what."

Sean snorted. "You have some nerve, lecturing me. How many people have you attacked over the centuries?"

Emma sighed. So much for the happy family reunion. She wandered toward the crib to see how Constantine was faring. Suddenly his head appeared above the crib railing. Then his chest and chubby belly.

Emma's mouth fell open. Good heavens, Constantine was levitating! He kept going up and up. She glanced back at the men. Sean's back was turned, and Angus and Connor were so busy defending their honor, they hadn't noticed the baby floating up to the ceiling.

Constantine chortled, clearly pleased with himself. Sean started to turn.

Emma leaped and levitated fast to the ceiling where she caught the baby in her arms.

"What the hell?" Sean stared at her, aghast. His eyes widened. "Shit! You're a vampire!"

Emma smiled faintly. "I've been meaning to tell you."

Sean turned to Angus. "You bastard! You did this to her. You killed her."

Angus stepped forward, his fists clenched.

Connor grabbed Sean from behind. "Ye will calm yerself, Whelan."

Sean's eyes blazed with anger. "I should kill you, MacKay." He glanced back at Connor. "And you, too, you bastard. Let go of me."

"Stop it," Emma shouted, cradling the baby against her chest. "You will not fight in front of the baby."

Connor released Sean, and the men spread out, eyeing each other suspiciously.

"Sean, I was mortally wounded, and Angus saved my life."

He gave her an annoyed look. "You're not alive."

Emma descended slowly, taking the baby with her. "I *am* alive, just . . . different. I wanted to tell you earlier when I turned in my resignation, but you were too upset to listen to reason."

Angus folded his arms. "He is always too upset to listen to reason."

Sean frowned.

Emma landed in front of the crib. "I want you to listen now, Sean. I am the same person you knew before. Death did not change me." She set Constantine down in his crib. "I am more determined than ever to defeat the evil vampires."

Sean remained silent.

She hoped she was getting through. Constantine giggled. She looked at him and he smiled back. A warmth seeped into her, and a sense of peace. The baby's eyes glimmered with a surprising intelligence.

He started to rise again. Emma placed her hand on his head and pushed him down.

"I am . . . disappointed in you," Sean murmured. "But I can concede that you are not evil."

"None of the Vamps here are evil. We—" She noticed Constantine rising once again and pushed him down. "We want to make the world safe, not only for us, but for all mankind."

"Ye should let us do our job," Angus added. "Stop interfering with us when we're trying to protect you."

Sean sighed. "I'll think about it." He turned to Connor. "I'd like to talk to my daughter."

Connor nodded. "This way." He led Sean out the door.

Emma sighed with relief.

Angus smiled. "That was a good speech, though I was surprised to see ye floating about with the bairn."

"I wasn't taking him up. I was bringing him down." Emma let go of Constantine. He squealed and started to levitate.

"Good God." Angus strode forward.

"I know." Emma watched as the baby rose to the ceiling. "I let Sean think it was me. I didn't think he could handle this."

Angus wrapped an arm around her shoulder. "We're making progress with him."

"I hope so." Emma linked her hands around Angus's neck. "Have I told you recently that you're the most amazing man in the world, and I love you to distraction?"

He grinned. "The only amazing thing about me is that I found the most amazing woman to love."

Emma touched his cheek. "And it only took about five hundred years."

As they kissed, Constantine lowered gently into his crib, an angelic smile on his face.

STEAMY AND SENSATIONAL
VAMPIRE LOVE
FROM THE REMARKABLE

Kerrelyn Sparks

"An absolute delight!"
USA Today bestselling author
LYNSAY SANDS

NOW AVAILABLE

How to Marry A Millionaire Vampire
0-06-075196-7/$5.99 US/$7.99 CAN

Roman Draganesti is charming, handsome, rich...and a vampire. But he just lost one of his fangs sinking his teeth into something he shouldn't have. Now he has one night to get sexy dentist Shanna Whelan to repair his teeth before his natural healing abilities close the wound, leaving him a lop-sided eater for all eternity.

Vamps And the City
0-06-075201-7/$5.99 US/$7.99 CAN

TV director and vampire Darcy Newhart thought it was a stroke of genius—the first-ever reality TV show where mortals vie with vampires for the title of The Sexiest Man on Earth. The only problem is sexy contestant Austin Erickson is actually a vampire slayer...and he's got his eye on the show's leggy blond director.

Visit www.AuthorTracker.com for exclusive information on your favorite HarperCollins authors.

Available wherever books are sold or please call 1-800-331-3761 to order.
KSP 0506

Sink Your Teeth Into More
Delectable Vampire Romance From
New York Times Bestselling Author

LYNSAY SANDS

A QUICK BITE

978-0-06-077375-5

Lissianna has been spending her centuries pining for Mr.
Right, not just a quick snack, and this sexy guy she finds in
her bed looks like he might be a candidate. But there's
another, more pressing issue: her tendency to faint at the
sight of blood…an especially annoying quirk for a vampire.

A BITE TO REMEMBER

978-0-06-077407-3

Vincent Argeneau may be the hottest guy PI Jackie
Morrisey's ever met, living or dead, but she's out to stop a
killer from turning this vampire into dust, not to jump into
bed with him.

BITE ME IF YOU CAN

978-0-06-077412-7

Lucian Argeneau, hunter of rogue vampires, has been alive
for over two thousand years, and there's very little to excite
him anymore. Then Leigh drops into his life. Suddenly he
finds himself imagining the sassy brunette atop the black
satin sheets on his nice big bed.

Visit www.AuthorTracker.com for exclusive
information on your favorite HarperCollins authors.

Available wherever books are sold or please call 1-800-331-3761 to order.
LYS 1207

PROWL THE NIGHT WITH
NEW YORK TIMES BESTSELLING AUTHOR
KIM HARRISON

DEAD WITCH WALKING
978-0-06-057296-9 • $7.99 US/$10.99 Can
When the creatures of the night gather, whether to hide, to hunt, or to feed, it's Rachel Morgan's job to keep things civilized. A bounty hunter and witch with serious sex appeal and attitude, she'll bring them back alive, dead . . . or undead.

THE GOOD, THE BAD, AND THE UNDEAD
978-0-06-057297-6 • $7.99 US/$10.99 Can
Rachel Morgan can handle the leather-clad vamps and even tangle with a cunning demon or two. But a serial killer who feeds on the experts in the most dangerous kind of black magic is definitely pressing the limits.

EVERY WHICH WAY BUT DEAD
978-0-06-057299-0 • $7.99 US/$10.99 Can
Rachel must take a stand in the raging war to control Cincinnati's underworld because the demon who helped her put away its former vampire kingpin is coming to collect his due.

A FISTFUL OF CHARMS
978-0-06-078819-3 • $7.99 US/$10.99 Can
A mortal lover who abandoned Rachel has returned, haunted by his secret past. And there are those willing to destroy the Hollows to get what Nick possesses.

FOR A FEW DEMONS MORE
978-0-06-114981-8 • $7.99 US/$10.99 Can
An ancient artifact may be the key to stopping a fiendish killer.

Visit www.AuthorTracker.com for exclusive information on your favorite HarperCollins authors.

HAR 0907

Available wherever books are sold or please call 1-800-331-3761 to order.

*At Avon Books, we know your passion
for romance—once you finish one of our
novels, you find yourself wanting more.*

May we tempt you with . . .

- **Excerpts** from our upcoming releases.

- Entertaining **extras**, including authors'
  personal photo albums and book lists.

- Behind-the-scenes **scoop** on your favorite
  characters and series.

- **Sweepstakes** for the chance to win free books,
  romantic getaways, and other fun prizes.

- Writing **tips** from our authors and editors.

- **Blog** with our authors and find out why they
  love to write romance.

- **Exclusive content** that's not contained
  within the pages of our novels.

Join us at
www.avonbooks.com

AVON

An Imprint of HarperCollinsPublishers
www.avonromance.com

Available wherever books are sold or please call 1-800-331-3761 to order.

She scoffed. "That's quite beyond the point. I know you're a vampire."

"I know ye're the slayer. 'Tis time for you to stop."

She widened her stance and prepared for an attack. "Tonight, you die by your own sword."

He shrugged. "I died once. Dinna care for it much." He stepped toward her.

She raised the sword so the blade was even with his neck.

He gave her a sympathetic look. "Och, lass, ye can hardly lift it, much less wield it."

"Just come a bit closer and find out."

"Verra well."

She blinked as his body zoomed past her on the right.

He halted on the other side of the clearing. "Ye missed."

Vampires were such an arrogant bunch. "I didn't think you'd run like a coward."

His brows shot up. "Ye expect me to stand still while ye run me through?"

"I expect you to face me like a man."

He chuckled. "Ye slay me."

Avon Books by
Kerrelyn Sparks

THE UNDEAD NEXT DOOR
VAMPS AND THE CITY
HOW TO MARRY A MILLIONAIRE VAMPIRE

ATTENTION: ORGANIZATIONS AND CORPORATIONS
Most Avon Books paperbacks are available at special quantity discounts for bulk purchases for sales promotions, premiums, or fund-raising. For information, please call or write:

**Special Markets Department, HarperCollins Publishers, 10 East 53rd Street, New York, New York 10022-5299.
Telephone: (212) 207-7528.   Fax: (212) 207-7222.**